CONDUCT IN QUESTION

CONDUCT IN QUESTION

THE FIRST IN A TRILOGY

Mary E. Martin

Mary E. Martin
November 27, 2005

iUniverse, Inc.
New York Lincoln Shanghai

CONDUCT IN QUESTION
THE FIRST IN A TRILOGY

iUniverse books may be ordered through booksellers or by contacting:

iUniverse
2021 Pine Lake Road, Suite 100
Lincoln, NE 68512
www.iuniverse.com
1-800-Authors (1-800-288-4677)

ISBN-13: 978-0-595-35820-5 (pbk)
ISBN-13: 978-0-595-81201-1 (cloth)
ISBN-13: 978-0-595-80285-2 (ebk)
ISBN-10: 0-595-35820-9 (pbk)
ISBN-10: 0-595-81201-5 (cloth)
ISBN-10: 0-595-80285-0 (ebk)

Printed in the United States of America

To my family, David, Stephen, Timothy and Susan.
And to my muse.

PROLOGUE

▼

Was it wrong to take a life so young?

Such beautiful skin was soft, smooth, and white as cream. He stroked her lustrous brown hair. A nervous smile flitted across her face.

He stared into her eyes. She was a university student, filled with the idealism of youth, but her lips and nails were painted red.

The ceaseless debate pounded in his head. A painter should not discard a sketch for its lack of finish. With time, a musician could weave a simple tune into a great symphony. A true artist never rushed to judgment. He shuddered at the prospect of mistakenly snuffing out a life of promise. He had to contemplate her value before the final moment.

In time, she might become a doctor, a judge, or a professor. But how could that be? Her dress was tight and low-cut. She would create a scandal wherever she went. He could resist no longer.

He caressed her long, slim neck. Fear flickered through her body.

His fingers dug deeper. She gasped. Like tiny birds, her hands fluttered upward to pry away his fingers.

Passion overcame his reason. The desperate pleading in her eyes drove him to heights of ecstasy. Her arms and legs thrashed pitifully. Her fear thrust him into his dark world of freedom, where only he could redeem her soul. It was an act of compassion.

Lacing his fingers around her throat, he twisted his hands hard and fast.

"Just a common harlot, begging for it," he panted.

At last, she was quiet.

He stroked her long neck and hummed a lullaby. An exquisite subject, he thought. He withdrew a silver knife from his pocket. An artist, who sought new challenges, deserved the finest tools.

Carefully, he drew back her long black hair and exposed her face. On her cheek he carved a tiny petal. Pausing to admire his work, he drew another petal close to her chin and then scrolled a graceful stem down her neck.

Disappointed, he sat back. He had not yet perfected his artistry. The line lacked the easy flow of a master. But with his mark, now she was truly beautiful.

The next morning, he sat at a café on the mews, which was suffused with a calm, ethereal light. He sipped his coffee and scanned the front page of the news-paper. He wanted to savor the latest review of his artistic work. The media called him "The Florist." He would send the editor a sketch of his next carving. Soon he would be known as an artist with daring in his soul.

CHAPTER 1

▼

Trapped next to the open casket, Harry Jenkins glanced at the deceased woman, an elderly client whose face was rouged into a grotesque parody of life. Poor Miss Richardson. Only at her death did her relatives come out of the woodwork. He brushed back his thinning hair and swallowed hard. His senior law partner, Richard Crawford, stood close by. His fine features and elegant attire made Harry feel clumsy and overblown.

Crawford always found just the right inflection for his softly spoken words of condolence. Even after countless funerals, Harry's own phrases seemed stilted and woefully inadequate. Crawford moved gracefully amongst the damp-eyed mourners, greeting each one with a grave but gracious air. Taking the hand of one, giving a dry kiss to another, Crawford worked the room for new clients. Harry's teacup rattled in his hand as he sought a place to set it down.

Natasha Boretsky, a realtor for Crawford, gently touched Harry's arm and drew him closer. "Harry, good to see you. I called you the other day."

Her hair was dark and lustrous. He caught a hint of her perfume. Smiling, he awkwardly took her hand and managed to say, "Really? I'm sorry I missed your call."

Her dark brown eyes widened with pleasure. His cup threatened to tip, but still he held her hand for just a moment longer, until they were parted in the crush of the crowd.

His back turned, Crawford stood in front of him. Trapped, Harry gazed over the sea of mourners and out the window. Caught in the afternoon light, dust motes hung motionless in the funeral-parlor air. A promising spring day lay beyond the curtain. Outside, a man and a woman were kissing. She laughed and broke away. A gentle breeze lifted her broad-brimmed hat and sent it soaring upward to the sky. Enchanted, Harry watched the man rush to catch the hat and place it on her head. Arm in arm, they disappeared down the block.

Suddenly, he had to escape. He touched Crawford on the arm in order to pass by, and the old man jerked backward. Harry's cup was knocked to the floor. The clatter silenced the mourners only for a moment. Harry swept the shards of china to one side and strode from the room. Crawford shook his head and smoothly returned to his conversation.

Harry heaved open the heavy brass doors of the funeral parlor to find a congregation of smokers huddled under the canopy. As he shouldered by, conversation rippled about him.

"The police are calling the killer 'The Florist.'"

"Because of his handiwork?"

"Yes. Apparently, he carves naked flesh in absolutely beautiful designs."

"Must be a real fruitcake on the loose."

Harry hurried past. He could not conceive of a being who could ravage and create in one instant.

In his car, he stared blankly at a beer advertisement on a billboard. Funerals always made him restless with questions. At forty-two, the great divide of half a century loomed in his path like a foreboding angel. Time had been steadily measured out to him in hours and days, to the point of tedium. Yet, twenty years had passed in just a moment. What did that mean for the future? Despite his years of faithful tutelage under Crawford, Harry was still trapped under the old man's thumb. All his offers to purchase the practice had been adamantly refused.

Backing up, he slammed on the brakes. *Good God!* He had almost smashed the side panel of a Jaguar parked way over the line. Carefully, he exited the lot and headed for home. He and his wife, Laura, could have a relaxed dinner together. Lately a silence had grown between them, and the house had acquired a hollow sound. It wasn't too late to mend the rift, he hoped.

When he opened the front door, he saw the note, which read: *Out for dinner with Martha. Laura.* Slowly, Harry set his briefcase down. In the kitchen, he opened the refrigerator and found some cold meat for a sandwich.

As Harry entered his office next morning, Miss Giveny (the secretary for the firm Crane, Crawford, and Jenkins) announced, "Mr. Crawford needs a trust prepared by noon for Marjorie Deighton."

That's it! No more last-minute demands. "I have a client at ten, Miss Giveny," Harry said.

Miss Giveny bristled in the doorway. "Mr. Crawford said that it's urgent."

"I have to close the Robertson purchase today." Harry sat behind his desk and peered at the large spectacles perched on Miss Giveny's narrow nose. "Are all the documents ready for signature?"

"Of course they are," she sniffed, as if greatly offended. "The bank called. The funds are ready for closing." She turned abruptly and walked away.

"All right," he called after her. "Bring me the file, and I'll look at it."

When she returned with the file, Harry rifled through it, searching for instructions. Nothing made sense. Turning the page, he caught his breath. The entire sheet was scrawled with intricate and detailed pen sketches of female genitalia, viewed from the most surprising angles. A neat border of rose petals edged the drawing.

Harry gasped, then choked with laughter. At the foot of the page was written: *R. A. Crawford…secret trust/will instructions from Miss M. Deighton.* Holding the page at arm's length, Harry squinted, then turned it upside down.

There was absolutely no doubt about the subject matter. Harry was quite impressed with his partner's skill. The prim Mr. Crawford must have hidden his lustful artistry as he diligently recorded Miss Deighton's will instructions.

Richard Crawford always presented an image of elegance and refinement to the world, but his file revealed the dark cracks of derangement in the old man's polished surface. Adjusting his reading glasses, Harry stole another look at the drawing.

Crawford strolled into the waiting room with a newspaper neatly tucked under his arm. He softly whistled to himself. Instead of going directly into his own office, he knocked and entered Harry's office.

Harry hastily closed the file.

"My good man," Crawford beamed, "I see you have the Deighton file. Be sure you get Marjorie's secret trusts right. If you've any questions about technical aspects, just ask me."

Harry was speechless. His face burned with embarrassment for the old man. Finally he asked, "But where are the written instructions?"

Crawford waved impatiently and spoke as if to a lowly student. "Everything you could possibly want is in the file, Harry. Study it carefully." Crawford paused. His eyes glazed over. Apparently lost in pleasant recollection, he sighed, "Marjorie." Suddenly, he turned on Harry, eyes hardened with the memory of lust.

Harry hastened to stand.

"That delectable woman!" Crawford seemed to be addressing someone over Harry's shoulder, just outside the window. "She has the spirit of a saint, but, as

God is my witness, the body of a…" A nasty purple flush rose from Crawford's collar. "Do you understand how a woman can possess a man?" he demanded, teetering heel to toe. He whispered hoarsely, "Jenkins! Have you ever experienced the passion, the thrall?"

For an instant, Crawford's left side sagged with the ravages of stroke. He sought to right himself. "If you have not, my good man, then you have not lived." The old man's eyes momentarily turned upward. Only the whites could be seen.

Harry panicked. "Richard, are you ill?" He rushed to his partner's side, but Crawford did not answer. His face engorged with dark pleasure, he gave a lurid and distorted wink. The effect was horrific. Harry's stomach heaved.

Crawford lurched forward. His chin struck the desk with such a crack that Miss Giveny came running.

Harry shouted, "Richard! Are you all right? Can you hear me?"

Dropping to all fours, Harry pressed his ear to Crawford's chest and listened intently. He shook his shoulder, making Crawford's head loll to one side. One glassy eye stared up at him. The ghastly wink had frozen the other eye shut. Ravenous demands of the flesh had consumed his body and soul. As the paramedics crowded in with the stretcher minutes later, Harry tore up the artwork.

CHAPTER 2

▼

Several days after Crawford's funeral, Harry strolled down the corridor to his office, lost in his study of the newspaper. The Florist had carved again. This time he had left an intricate scroll of stems and thorns on his victim. For Harry, the artistry only highlighted the grotesqueness of the act.

He opened the door. *Good Lord!* Frank Sasso, a friend of Suzannah Deighton, Marjorie Deighton's niece, was sprawled in a chair.

Heaving himself to his feet, Frank Sasso demanded, "Where's the check from Suzannah's trust, Jenkins?"

Frank was back at the trough. He was a lout and a bully, intent on stripping Deighton funds.

Another man rose silently behind Frank. He was at least a head taller than Harry. Muscles rippled everywhere.

Harry swallowed hard. "What are you talking about, Frank? You know any application for money has to go through Gideon Trust."

"Listen, Jenkins. That partner of yours said the check was gonna be ready this morning."

"Mr. Crawford's dead, Frank. You'll have to go back to Gideon Trust Company. It makes the decisions." He tried to shoulder past the men.

"Now, let's sit down and talk this over," said the other man, adjusting his sunglasses. He touched Harry's arm. Every gesture contained an unspoken threat.

Harry led them into his office and reached for the Deighton file. He saw the trickles of sweat on Frank's cheek and the sickening fear and pleading in his eyes.

Harry's gut contracted and bile rose to his throat. Hurriedly, he began shuffling papers.

"Everyone, just be reasonable," the man said quietly.

"I'll call the trust company today," Harry replied.

"Do it now," the man said. "We'll wait."

Harry called the trust officer, Cameron McCrea, only to encounter the maze of an automated telephone system . He left a message.

The man nodded and rose. "We'll be back, Mr. Jenkins." Grasping Frank's elbow, he propelled him out the door, saying, "You better pray you get that money back, Frank. They don't like it when money goes missing."

Harry exhaled. He would have promised them anything just to get them out. Thank God Frank Sasso was no client of his. He closed his eyes against visions of Frank being led to some deserted spot and then…what? He waited until the churning in his stomach died down.

The firm prided itself on attending to the legal affairs of Toronto's well-off families. Frank's very presence grated. What a great beginning to Harry's solo practice of law!

He called Miss Giveny into his office.

"Yes, Mr. Jenkins?" she said, grimacing.

Harry strove to catch a suitable note of regret. "Even though Richard's passed away, we still have to carry on."

She stared back at him. At last, she spoke. "That's what Mr. Crawford would want." She snapped open her steno pad. "Do you have some dictation for me?"

Briefly, he contemplated life with a new secretary. A pleasant and attractive helper, or at least one who would not bristle when spoken to. But Miss Giveny was, at least for now, indispensable. She knew the ship would founder without her.

He stretched back in his chair. "Not at the moment. But I'd like to talk to you about the future of the firm." With one glance at her narrow face, he saw a thousand doors closing. She did not and could not understand the new Toronto. The old, established families were dying out and in their place was a younger breed of new-moneyed clients less attuned to courtly ways and much more demanding. For her, Harry would always be Crawford's junior.

"Bring me all the Deighton files, please," said Harry. She nodded and left the office without further comment. Annoyed, he tossed down his pen. Although Miss Giveny brought continuity, her loyalty to Richard's ghost could cause untold problems.

For years, Crawford had played front man and rainmaker. Kept in the back room, Harry had prepared the legal work. No one would believe that such a miserly soul existed within the warm, magnanimous personage of Richard Crawford. The clients loved and trusted him; the profession revered him. Harry knew that the man's gracious and regal exterior hid a shameless, pinched soul. Although many clients had never met Harry, Marjorie was an exception, fortunately.

His secretary returned with a stack of Deighton files.

"Thank you, Miss Giveny." Harry extracted the will file and spread it on the desk. To banish the image of Richard sprawled at his feet, he determined to sort out the business of the will and the secret trust.

According to Crawford's disjointed memos, Marjorie Deighton had changed her will again. In the prior one, Suzannah, her niece, received the valuable Deighton residence. At the epicenter of Toronto's real-estate boom, the property would be held in trust for her until she was thirty, and then it would be hers outright. But she had to be well over thirty by now. Along with Katharine, the other niece, and Gerry, the nephew, she had a one-third interest in the cash and other assets, estimated at about three million dollars.

Under the newly executed will, Suzannah lost sole entitlement to the house. Everything would be sold and the proceeds divided equally among the three of them.

But the memo had called for a secret trust for Suzannah to be attached to the will. Crawford had scrawled at the foot of the memo: *Be sure to get the secret trust right!* So where were the damned notes? Harry drummed his fingers on the desk. He would have to call Marjorie as soon as possible.

In his will, Sir William Mortimer Deighton, father of Marjorie, had set up trusts for each of his three grandchildren. Regular monthly income and generous access to capital had always cushioned the lives of Suzannah, Gerry, and Katharine. Fortunately, neither Harry nor Crawford was the sole arbiter of the trust: Toronto's Gideon Trust Company had the final say most of the time. They also had the pleasure of dealing directly with Frank Sasso in his efforts to deplete Suzannah's trust.

Miss Giveny bellowed from the outer office, "Marjorie Deighton on line two!"

Harry winced. Despite his frequent attempts to educate her on the new phone system, she studiously refused to master the intricacies of the hold and intercom buttons.

He strove to hit the right note of graciousness and formality. "Miss Deighton, how are you today? It was good to see you at Richard's funeral. Such a shock for us all," he murmured.

"It's so terribly sad." Harry heard sniffles. Once she had collected herself, her voice became soft, sibilant, and rapid, with an underlying note of distraction.

"Now that Richard's gone, you're the only one I can turn to for advice. I do have a problem." She paused ominously. "I want to make some changes to my will. Could you come to the house this afternoon?"

"Would four o'clock be all right?"

"Yes, and thank you, Harry, for coming on such short notice. I'm seeing someone at two and will need your advice afterwards about certain matters." Miss Deighton paused as if debating whether to explain further. "Also, I'm terribly worried about two people who mean a great deal to me."

"Yes?" Harry picked up his pen.

"My niece, Suzannah, with that man Sasso…" She paused. "And, of course, Donald, my great nephew. He's a fine youngster, you know, but his parents seem determined to misunderstand him." Marjorie sighed deeply. "There's simply too much pressure on the child."

"How old is he?"

"Donnie's only fifteen—just at the very beginning of his life. I'm letting Rosie go early today. I'll leave the door unlocked, so just let yourself in. I'll be in the front parlor."

"Should I bring Miss Giveny with me?"

"Yes, please. I'm afraid I may have rather lengthy instructions. But perhaps we'll still have time for a sherry."

Harry leaned back in his chair and stretched. He hoped to get the business of the secret trust straightened out at last. She had mentioned Donnie only once or twice before. Gerry's son, he recalled. He smiled to himself. Many times he had seen love and concern uniting the eldest and the youngest generations. As far as he knew, Suzannah and Katharine had no children.

"Mr. Jenkins!" Miss Giveny called out. "Someone on the line. Won't say what he wants. Calls himself…*Chin*." Upon hearing a different accent, Miss Giveny's drawbridge slammed shut and her suspicious tone reflected her narrow world.

Harry reached for the phone. "Jenkins here."

"Mr. Jenkins, my name is Albert Chin. I require the services of a lawyer to transact certain land purchases. There may be some rezoning applications and offshore interests to consider as well. You have been highly recommended to me."

"Certainly, Mr. Chin." Harry sat up straighter in his chair and glanced at his appointment book. He could not miss the urgency in his caller's voice. Obviously, it was very lucrative work.

"Would it be possible to come to your office at two o'clock today? These matters are most pressing."

"Yes. That would be fine," Harry said slowly, wondering about the traffic on the way to Marjorie's house.

Albert Chin murmured his gratitude.

"May I ask who recommended me?" asked Harry. But Mr. Chin had hung up.

Although cautious, Harry was elated. Hong Kong money had been swamping Toronto for years and had funded a massive construction boom. Sadly, none of it had drifted his way. With his elderly client base dying off, it was only good business sense to crack new markets.

Since Harry's childhood, the city had changed beyond recognition. He had grown up on the southerly face of Hoggs Hollow, at the city limits. Near his house, the streetcar line ended. Looking north, he could see Yonge Street, just a strip of pavement, cutting a narrow swath through the waving treetops, underbrush, and river lands until it reached the far side of the valley. Today, he faced a brand-new city of gleaming office towers and condominiums on the far hill.

When he came home from school, the streetcar would let Harry off at the loop under a red-tiled shelter, reminiscent of rooftops in exotic lands. The afternoon sun slanted sharply, illuminating the row of houses. His home was there: neat, square, and ordinary.

Most of all, he remembered Sunday afternoons when his father would take the family for drives around the city. Dad would go to any part of town, and there seemed to be a message in every trip. Often, they would start down Mount Pleasant Road, which wound its way through the ravines. Queasy with the smell of sun on the fabric-covered seats, Harry would try to hold his breath. His sister Anna, always with a book, sat beside him. He would keep the window rolled down until the green of the ravines gave way to the shops on Bloor Street. Sometimes he would grab her book and tussle in the back seat, until they started down Jarvis Street. Then they rolled up the windows and stared out.

In front of the old sunlit housing and the vast shadowy churches and parks lay a world unknown to them. Men, the kind they never saw uptown, stumbled drunkenly along the sidewalks. Noisy scuffles broke out, and lonely cries echoed up and down the empty street.

In Sunday school, the virtue of hard work—mingled with compassion for those less fortunate—had been drilled into them. Girls in prettily smocked dresses and boys in starched white shirts and gray flannels learned to count their blessings. "Be honest, truthful, and kind. Work hard, and you will be rewarded," the teachers would always say, and then they'd warn, "Jesus is watching you."

Harry had learned his lessons well. He had kept his part of the bargain. But where was his reward? Flashy cars and grandiose houses were the supposed perks of his profession. His Ford was surrounded by Audis. Playing by the rules had not gotten him far. Of course, he wasn't poor. Laura and he were comfortable. Yet, there was a yearning, a sense that the time for making real money was passing. But it wasn't just the money. A dull emptiness nagged at his spirit.

Reaching to the back of his desk drawer, he fumbled for a pack of cigarettes. He took one and opened the window to the fire escape. With any luck, the breeze would dissipate the evidence. Closing his eyes, he drew deeply on the cigarette.

If you played by the rules and did not stray, your reward would come. It was ridiculous to be still burdened by Sunday school lessons at the age of forty-two! By now, he should have developed some personal moral code, suitable for most occasions. Spots of sunlight permeated the gloom of the alleyway. He watched as a few people walked between the buildings far below.

Laura and he had argued a few weeks ago about money—a topic fraught with land mines. Her hardened face floated up in his mind.

"Law practice is more than just making money," Harry had insisted.

"Of course!" she said in wearily impatient tones. "But it certainly doesn't hurt to set the right value on your services."

"So I'm not making enough. Is that it?"

"No. But if you didn't get so personally involved with your clients, maybe you'd do better."

Harry was astonished. "So I care too much about them? I care about what I'm doing?"

She glared at him. "Why do you practice law, Harry?"

"What?"

"Maybe you should have been a social worker." She was goading him. She knew he hated that mentality. "Always holding the client's hand."

"Clients trust me! I've earned that. I can't turn around and fleece them."

She smiled up at him. "Harry, you're a true knight in shining armor."

She was laughing at him. Locked in a futile dance, neither of them had heard nor understood the other.

Harry realized he had been gripping the window ledge. Maybe more money would help, but he yearned for something more. He flicked his cigarette out the window and watched it twirl into the abyss.

CHAPTER 3

▼

Mr. Chin was the smallest man Harry had ever seen. The phrase "*the elegant Mr. Chin*" formed in his mind as he half-bowed to welcome his new client. The finely cut, light silk suit hung from Mr. Chin's delicate frame in exactly the correct fashion. Harry ushered him to his office.

At the door, Harry surveyed the scene. For years, he had regarded the décor as warm and inviting. Now he saw it through Chin's eyes. It was tacky.

"Please have a seat, sir," Harry began heartily.

Mr. Chin never stopped smiling as he neatly arranged himself in the chair across from Harry's desk. Glancing briefly about, he betrayed no reaction to his surroundings.

"Mr. Jenkins, I am grateful you have been able to see me on such short notice. If my business is to be transacted, it must be done speedily."

Harry nodded. "You said you were referred to me?"

"Indeed, Mr. Jenkins. Mr. Niels at Cheney, Arpin recommended you."

Surprised, Harry could not imagine why such a major Toronto law firm would direct any business his way. Yet, he had worked briefly with Peter Niels on a bar association matter. Perhaps there was a conflict of interest which could only be solved by completely independent representation.

"What would you like me to do?" he asked.

"There are several parcels of land that I wish to purchase near Highland Avenue, at the intersection of Mount Rose."

Harry stiffened. Marjorie Deighton's house was right near that corner. The coincidence was worrisome.

"Are you familiar with that area, Mr. Jenkins?"

Harry nodded.

Albert Chin placed a slim leather case on the desk and extracted a sheaf of papers. Carefully, he unfolded a survey. Harry stood to remove files from his desk. He had seen the survey many times before.

"I am wishing to purchase the three lots fronting on Mount Rose." Chin outlined them on the plan with his gold Cross pen. "And also the three immediately behind them." Chin's smile never faltered.

Harry considered the situation. None of the lots belonged to Marjorie, but with Chin's purchases, she would certainly be surrounded. So would St. Timothy's Church. He had to tell his new client that he acted for an adjoining landowner, but he decided to wait for more information.

"Are these offers to be conditional?"

Mr. Chin smiled broadly. "No, that will not be necessary. We will pay for the properties from our cash resources. Also, Mr. Jenkins, we will seek an option to purchase from the owner of 42 Highland Avenue and the church at some future date." Setting down his pen, he smiled at Harry. "I trust you will be able to act for our conglomerate."

Harry knew Marjorie would never sell to a developer. A conflict was looming. But his new client breathed money, body and soul. His work could be the start of new lifeblood for Harry's teetering firm. He couldn't afford to lose either client.

"I gather this is some sort of land assembly. Are you planning to rezone?"

Mr. Chin became all business. "That, sir, remains undecided. If we do, we trust you will act on our behalf in such applications."

Holy God! The value of Chin's work was escalating by the minute.

Harry said, "There are other interests I must consider, Mr. Chin."

Harry could act for Chin in the purchase of the lots, but any option to purchase on Marjorie's house or rezoning of adjacent lands would pose a direct conflict. Of course, he could send both clients to other lawyers, but Marjorie would feel abandoned.

His discomfort grew. "I have to tell you, Mr. Chin, that I act for the owner of 42 Highland." He pointed to Marjorie's lot on the survey. "Of course, you would require separate representation for any option to purchase on her land."

Nodding slightly, Chin slid two checks across the desk. "I have a retainer payable to your firm in the amount of two hundred thousand dollars, and another check, for one million dollars, to be used as a deposit of ten percent on each of the six lots."

Harry's mouth went dry.

"I trust the amount is sufficient. If not, more will be forthcoming," murmured Chin.

Harry held the checks, but did not speak. He feared that if he moved, the dream would be dispelled. He stared at the survey still spread on his desk. Large sums of money were at stake, but he could not dismiss the looming conflict. Marjorie had a major development on her doorstep, but if he warned her, he would be in immediate conflict with Chin. Something had to be worked out.

Chin lowered his eyes. "I find, sir, that many problems disappear, provided there are sufficient funds. If you require more, please let me know, and you will have it immediately." Chin handed him his card.

As if suddenly awakening, Harry said, "Mr. Chin, would you care for some coffee?"

Chin nodded, and Harry lifted the receiver to buzz Miss Giveny.

"When do you need these offers?" he asked.

"At your very earliest convenience. Say tomorrow at noon?"

Tight, but not impossible, thought Harry. With any luck, Marjorie's business would be fairly simple. "Certainly," he assured his new client. "But I'll need some more details from you, of course."

Oh God, thought Harry. *Does Miss Giveny have the sense to get out the decent cups? She'd better not be using those ridiculous Styrofoam things.*

"Could you excuse me a moment, while I check on something with my secretary?"

"Of course, Mr. Jenkins, please take your time." As soon as the door closed, Albert Chin rifled through a stack of files on the credenza behind Harry's desk and found the file marked *Deighton. M.\will.* In moments, he had scanned the most recent copy of Marjorie's will.

Harry found Miss Giveny in the kitchen unplugging the kettle. There they were: two Styrofoam cups on the counter, with those dreadful plastic stirrers sticking out of them.

"Really, Miss Giveny. Get the proper cups out, please! Make some real coffee, if you don't mind."

The cups and saucers rattled in her hands when she took them from the cupboard. Glaring at her employer, she sniffed and said, "As you wish, *sir*."

"And by the way," Harry continued to grumble, "we have some excellent work, courtesy of Mr. Chin. And, I'll need you at Miss Deighton's at four today for will instructions. Mr. Chin's offers are for noon tomorrow." Abruptly, he turned from his secretary's glare and headed back to his office.

Opening the door, Harry saw his new client examining the prints on the far wall. Swiftly, Chin seated himself. "I was admiring the framed sketches. Are they the law courts?"

"Yes, and they're of some historical significance. Are you interested in art?"

Chin nodded. "Indeed, Mr. Jenkins, I am fascinated with the history of this beautiful city. In developing lands, we must always be sensitive to the history and architecture."

A sharp rap came at the door. There stood Miss Giveny, tray in hand, laden with coffee cups, silver spoons, and even some biscuits.

"Thank you, Miss Giveny. Now, would you please ask our conveyancer to check the ownership of these lots at the registry office?" Harry handed her the list of properties.

He tried to glean information about his client's background and the land assembly scheme as they sipped their coffee. While Chin answered all questions carefully and with the utmost politeness, Harry felt just as much in the dark as before.

"Have you many real estate investments in Toronto, Mr. Chin?" he asked.

His new client spoke softly. "A few."

"Why Toronto?"

Mr. Chin flashed a broad smile. One incisor was neatly capped in gold. All the other teeth gleamed with impeccable whiteness. "As I said, it is beautiful and one of the safest and cleanest cities in the world."

"We have our share of crime too," said Harry. Briefly, he wondered at his comment.

Mr. Chin nodded. "Naturally, Mr. Jenkins. Every country does. It is part of human nature." He rose to go.

Harry sensed that his new client was not forthcoming. Something lay in the background. He remembered his own angry words when he had argued in endless circles with Laura: *"You have to watch some clients. Their moral landscape is as surreal as the face of the moon. But there is a line, which most people can see. Some traipse back and forth across it, calculating all the risks of getting caught. Others don't even know or care the line exists. Sure, they pay big money to lawyers, who get them out of scrapes, but I'm not one of them."*

Glancing at the two checks on his desk, he decided to withdraw from the deals if Marjorie's interests were compromised.

Within half an hour, Miss Giveny entered his office, struggling with reams of curled-up fax paper containing the conveyancer's search of title. Harry smiled. The fax machine was almost the last straw for the poor woman.

After he had spread the search results on the library table, his smile faded. The chain of ownership for all six lots was an ugly tangle. Over the past few years, the lots had been transferred back and forth among at least six or seven companies at ever-escalating prices. No names were assigned to such companies, only numbers. It was a strange pattern for residential and small commercial lots. But at the bottom, in a footnote, was penciled one corporate name: *Zaimir.*

Usually the search revealed the titles as they passed down the generations from one individual to another. Harry loved to trace a whole family tree through three or four generations. It would be tough to figure out the real owners in this swamp of faceless companies, identified only with numbers. Some help could be found at the corporations branch, but only the names of appointed directors were recorded, not the names of the shareholders, who were the real corporate owners. Ownership was often disguised in this fashion. Picking up his pen, he sought the root of the title—the starting point, required by law to be at least forty years back from the present.

He found simple beginnings in 1955, when the lots had been owned by the Deighton and Garvey families. Starting with the root, Harry's drawing of the chain of ownership rapidly began to take on the appearance of an ancient and gnarled tree, with branches twisting out in all directions. *A black snarl of confusion,* he thought.

Staring out the library window, he contemplated the maze of rusted-iron fire escapes and rows of paint-chipped windows. He shook his head. There was no reason to stay in such abysmal quarters. Surely he could afford much better than this. Tomorrow, he would check the papers for new office space—something light and airy.

CHAPTER 4

▼

Frustration with his lack of artistic skill flooded the Florist as he walked swiftly up Yonge Street. He glanced at the rows of dingy porn shops. Through grimy windows, he saw magazines with pictures of women, twisted and bent. There were photographs of men posing naked together. How sick, disgusting, and depressing, he thought. Sometimes he yearned for the cleansing power of fire to destroy such depravity.

He shook his head. No one appreciated fine art anymore. At last he reached Bloor Street, where the shops were more suited to his taste. In one small bookstore he examined the art section, finding what he was looking for deep within the racks of books: a selection of line drawings by the masterful French painter, Matisse.

Sinking into a comfortable chair, he was transported by the beauty and expression in the effortless flow of line. Matisse had captured his imagination. How could an artist achieve such life and magnificent truth with just one or two lines?

Setting down the book, he gazed out the window. His carvings were much too fussy. On his last one, he had striven for greater artistic style and flair. The scrolling stem along her neck was a good beginning. How splendid it was to create a masterful mark with just a few lines.

Quickly, he paid for the book and checked his watch. It was getting late. He hailed a cab and resolved to practise his drawing tonight. He would learn from Matisse. An artist must rise to the challenge. This time, he would seek the finest canvas to satisfy his requirements.

CHAPTER 5

▼

Better get Chin's money into the trust account, thought Harry. *One million for the deposits and two hundred thousand for legal costs.* Surely the huge retainer must include work on the rezoning applications.

Harry nursed a deep-seated grudge against banks. Usually his stomach rebelled as he approached them. *Banks are not your friends,* he reminded himself while riding down in the elevator. In good times, bank managers—beaming like carnival hucksters—lured solvent citizens into the valley of debt. Scowling in the bad times, they tallied up arrears and heartlessly called in loans. This particular bank, the Toronto-Royal, had refused to finance his attempts to buy Crawford out.

Memories of his father's own battles with banking institutions leapt to mind. Vividly, he recalled one night at dinner, when he was eight. The banging at the door had made him drip spaghetti sauce over the stove-top.

There, in the porch light, had stood a tall, burly man.

"You Stanley Jenkins?" the man demanded, thrusting a sheaf of papers into his father's hand. The top page was decorated with a bright red seal. *"Greetings!"* it began.

Dad's shoulders sagged and his chest caved in. Shaking his head, he sighed and turned the pages as Mother hovered in the doorway.

"What is it, Stan?"

The house was entirely silent, except for the ticking of the kitchen clock. Finally, well-educated, hardworking Stanley Jenkins looked up at his wife and said, "They're going to sell the place, Alice."

"Who?"

"The bank," he said quietly. Then anger flared. "Who else, God damn it?"

Harry and Anna were shocked, less by the swearing, than by the lonely frustration in their father's voice.

Harry wasn't old enough to be really worried, even when he and his sister, were sent to bed early. Lying in the darkness, he listened to the rise and fall of his parents' voices. He was puzzled by a phrase his father used over and over again.

"In arrears, in arrears." His father's voice peaked in frustration. "We're three months in arrears." To Harry, it sounded like a jail sentence.

Harry knew about money. Sometimes, he could almost hear it sloshing up and down the financial canyons of the city. But not enough of it was his.

Money…always the money! He sighed. He knew his wife had other standards, but her family's wealth spun a soft cocoon that protected them from the rest of the world. From within their silken web, her parents peered out at the populace in general and at Harry in particular. Their intense scrutiny was more than disconcerting. A tilt of the jaw or the pursing of lips spoke volumes. He could seldom measure up against their silently shifting boundaries. Money was the only true and absolute indicator of success. It poisoned their love.

Awed by her beauty, he used to love stroking her soft blonde hair. Once, her green eyes had been filled with love for him. Now they appraised him with brisk efficiency.

As an art dealer for Sotheby's, she had recently invited Harry to an auction. "Harry, come with me. It'll be fun." He had not realized it was a last attempt to draw him into her world.

"Oh, I don't know," he hesitated, but could find no excuse. It was foreign territory to him, and he railed at any form of profligacy or flamboyance.

The auction was held in the ballroom of the Royal York Hotel. Immense crystal chandeliers and heavy brocade drapes graced the room. Silent tension hung in the air. The auctioneer, handsome in his pin-striped suit, rapped sharply with his tiny gavel, driving the bidding even higher.

"Eight hundred and fifty thousand." Looking expectantly over the sea of impassive faces, he called out, "Do I hear nine hundred thousand?" At the back of the room, a small yellow paddle shot up. "Sold…going…going…gone."

Harry's stomach had sunk as the figures danced ever higher. Shocked by Laura's intense excitement, loneliness crept over him. She gloried in this recklessness so foreign to him. She was betrothed to her career and a family would only interfere.

"Why not a child?" Harry used to ask, years back.

"Not yet, darling. Perhaps next year, when the projects at the museum are done." But there was always another project.

After the auction, they had driven in silence past dark mansions on Sherbourne Street, now a jumble of converted rooming houses. At Gerrard Street lay the Allan Gardens, where men drifted about and fought for park benches. At the end of Sherbourne Street they turned into the tree-lined crescents of Rosedale. Before he knew it, the house in which Laura had grown up, loomed ahead. He gazed at the portico and the stately, broad oak door.

"Home sweet home," said Harry. He thought the remark was innocent.

"Why did you come this way?" Laura's voice was flat and hollow. Surprised, Harry glanced at her. Lights of an oncoming car illuminated her thin, drawn face.

"Just trying to get to the parkway." He hesitated, "Something wrong?"

Angrily, she twisted around in her seat. "You hated the auction, didn't you? You couldn't stomach watching people spend money."

"What?" Harry was alarmed.

"You don't need to spell it out." She waved at her old house, grand with its columns and porticos. "Just because I grew up here doesn't mean I measure everything in money. Am I supposed to apologize for our money?"

Harry was silent. There was no stopping a bursting dam.

"You're so superior about your ethical values, Harry. As if having money were a crime."

"Laura, I didn't say a word."

"You didn't need to. It's written all over your face."

After several moments of silence, Harry spoke evenly. "Actually, Laura, I was just thinking how well the auction went. You and Dr. Stover must have worked very hard."

Laura glared at him. "What has *he* got to do with this?"

He tried to placate her. "Nothing at all. Can't I give a compliment without getting into trouble?"

Laura stared out the window in silence. At last she spoke as if setting down a heavy burden. "Harry, I think we need time to think things through."

"What things?"

They were on Bayview Avenue sweeping northward along the Don River. Red taillights crept up the parkway on the other side of the river. The city, always so familiar, seemed hostile and foreign to Harry, as if he had lost his bearings in the dark.

"Us," she said.

"Yes?" He tried to maintain an even tone.

Her voice was weary. "We're in completely different worlds, Harry. Your old clients, with their Depression-era thinking, hoard their fistfuls of money, never taking a moment of pleasure in life."

"And that's what Dr. Stover gives you? A sense of pleasure in life?" Instantly, he regretted his words. Now they were hurling stones at each other.

As Harry mounted the stone steps to the bank, he vividly recalled Laura's ashen face as they had argued back and forth in the car. Then he remembered Natasha Boretsky's eyes widening with pleasure as he took her hand at the funeral parlor. The bank's vaulted ceilings rose up from the hushed main concourse. Despite any bureaucratic trial visited upon him, no customer would dare to vent his rage in this sepulchre. Crawford had chosen this branch, considering it a suitable extension of his old Toronto practice. Security and gentility were to be found within, or so he had thought.

On several occasions, Harry had accompanied Marjorie Deighton for tea after a bond coupon-clipping expedition, in which interest from solid investments was safely tucked away in an account. Laura was right. Money, according to his clients, was for careful investing, not lavish or frivolous spending. Tables of white linen laden with crystal and delicate teacups dotted Eaton's Round Room near the bank. In these elegant surroundings, between the business of pouring tea and passing plates of tiny sandwiches, Marjorie had first discussed her personal affairs.

"The secret trust? Yes, Mr. Jenkins, I've taken care of that. It is quite safe." Marjorie dabbed the corners of her lips with her napkin.

"Should I have a copy of it, Miss Deighton?" He hated being in the dark.

"No, not yet. Someday, perhaps," she said wistfully. "I'd like your advice about Suzannah, and about another matter."

"Certainly." Harry was delighted by her confidence.

"She's very much influenced by her friend Mr. Sasso. I believe he has a *reputation*." Although Harry knew Frank Sasso only slightly, the word 'lout' readily came to mind.

"I want to ensure that none of my estate comes into his hands. I am sure he has unsavory connections."

Harry spoke reassuringly. "That can be arranged. Certain legal stratagems…"

Marjorie smiled sadly at him and said, "I have a very special tie with Suzannah. One day, I'll come to your office and change my will."

"And the other matter?" Harry asked.

Marjorie averted her eyes. "I'm very worried about my great-nephew, Donald, Gerry's son. They call him Donnie. He's getting in some trouble at school, and he's had a few minor brushes with the law. His parents throw up their hands and march him off to a psychiatrist." She examined her hands neatly folded in her lap. "They should be talking with him, not abandoning him. He has so many good qualities, but I'm afraid his parents are too busy with their own lives to notice."

"Perhaps he needs their understanding. It's hard for young people, these days," he murmured. "Is there something you'd like me to do?" Harry spoke carefully. He remembered Laura's accusations of social work.

Marjorie smiled sadly. "There's not much you can do. But it helps to be able to talk. You give good advice—not just on legal matters."

Harry smiled. His client's trust meant a great deal to him. "You can talk to me anytime, Miss Deighton."

Inside the Toronto-Royal, Harry took his place in the single line before the wickets. Miss Priverts the head teller, pursed her lips when she spotted Harry.

Stepping up to the counter, Harry slid the deposit books across the cool marble countertop and under the brass rail.

In his most soothing tone, he began, "Good afternoon, Miss Privets." He could not prevent a smile. She really did look like a colorless prune.

"The assistant manager wants to speak with you, Mr. Jenkins." When she deigned to open the deposit books, her voice trailed off. First she squinted and held the checks at arm's length, then she adjusted her lamp for closer examination.

"I have to speak to Mr. Mudhali," she began faintly. Snapping shut her cash drawer, she scurried off in search of help. Clearing his throat, Harry assumed a posture of impatience. He became aware of shifting feet and rustling papers in the line behind him. Lost in a study of the checks, Mr. Mudhali emerged from his office.

"Mr. Jenkins, could I see you, please? In my office." Harry summoned his slightly frayed dignity and followed the man to the inner recesses of his office.

"Mr. Jenkins." Mudhali's tone was formal. "I attempted to reach your partner this week, regarding the firm's line of credit."

"Mr. Crawford is dead. He had a stroke on Tuesday."

The man's eyes widened. "I'm terribly sorry," mumbled Mudhali. "This does cause a problem. The firm's line of credit is fifty thousand dollars in arrears. If immediate arrangements are not made…"

In arrears…in arrears. Three months in jail. The words rang out in Harry's mind.

"What in the hell are you talking about?" he demanded.

Mudhali consulted his file. "Mr. Crawford pledged the firm account as security for a personal line of credit."

"He can't do that!"

"Do you want to see the accounting?"

"No. I want to see his signature."

"Certainly, Mr. Jenkins." He passed a sheet of paper across the desk.

Harry searched, but could not find his reading glasses. He squinted at the document. It sure as hell looked like Richard's signature. "The bank can't secure a personal loan against partnership funds," said Harry, tossing the sheet back at the assistant manager.

Mudhali paled only slightly. His voice remained stubbornly calm. "Our lawyers will have to deal with the issue."

Harry was on his feet. His hands pressed on the table so hard that his knuckles were white. "This banking relationship is in trouble, Mr. Mudhali."

"If suitable arrangements are not made," Mudhali said, lowering his eyes to the checks on the desk, "we will have to freeze the account and refer the matter to the head office."

"You do that, sir, and I will have you in court faster than—"

Mudhali fingered Harry's retainer check. "A substantial immediate payment on account would permit me to deposit these checks and avoid such unpleasantness."

If he hadn't been so angry, Harry would have laughed. "A bank hold-up? Listen, Mr. Mudhali, my firm has been a customer for more than fifty years."

Mudhali held up his hand. "As for any balance remaining, the bank would accept other collateral. Do you own a house?" The assistant manager reached for his loan manual.

"Listen, you are dead wrong on the law. That security is useless."

"I am not a lawyer, sir, but I understand such legal points take months, if not years to determine in court."

Considering the complexities of legal partnerships, Harry seethed. Either he went along with the bureaucratic twit (for the moment), or he would be tied up in red tape for months. The Chin retainer would be either uncashed or frozen.

Harry stood up. His chair screeched backward, smashing against a filing cabinet. Only a tiny amount of the trust money had been earned with the interview of Chin, the instructions, and the title searches. If the deals did not go through, he would have to return most of Mr. Chin's money.

Harry was scrupulous about client funds, and would fret if the bookkeeper missed a penny. Snatching up his checkbook, he saw in his mind the bright and trusting faces of a hundred clients. He saw those faces turn gray in disbelief when he uncapped his pen.

Petty triumph gleamed in Mudhali's eyes.

Despite years of circumspection and care, Harry was driven by a new and reckless fury. Either he made a payment, or the bank would freeze his accounts. Mudhali had nailed him to the wall.

He exploded. "You'll have payment of half the damned arrears right now!" He scrawled a trust account check for twenty-five thousand dollars to the bank, from Albert Chin's money.

"Thank you, Mr. Jenkins. However, you do realize that this takes care of only part of the arrears of interest on the loan."

Harry grew cold. "How much is the loan?" He held his breath.

"Five hundred thousand dollars."

"Jesus Christ," Harry breathed. "That loan can't legally be secured on the firm's account." He prayed he was right. Time to read up on partnership law. Otherwise, Crane, Crawford and Jenkins would be dead.

Mr. Mudhali closed the firm's file. "As I have said, that's for our legal department to consider, sir." His expressionless brown eyes disclosed nothing.

White anger and fear propelled Harry along King Street in record time. That pompous paper-pusher had goaded him into taking twenty-five thousand dollars of the Chin money before he'd earned it. If he couldn't straighten out Crawford's mess, he'd be sunk. Damn that womanizer! Suddenly, he stopped and grinned. Even if the old bastard could secure a personal line of credit on partnership funds, his estate would be liable to repay the debt. Dorothy, Crawford's long-suffering wife, would not be pleased. For a moment, he breathed more easily.

As to his rashness, Laura's voice rang in his ears. *"You're so tied to your outdated morality, Harry. Everybody else takes risks. But not you. Are you that much better than everyone else?"* Jesus! Laura would be proud, he thought bitterly. In anger, he had put one foot on the wrong side.

Albert Chin had said that money was no problem, and after all, there was lots of work in preparing those offers. He would search the titles to the properties, do the corporate searches, and prepare six offers and submit them. Surely that would add up to twenty-five grand. Besides, Chin would not have given him such a munificent retainer had he not expected a sizable bill. And Harry knew that he was not the only lawyer guilty of such an infraction.

But the dreaded Section Four of the Code of Conduct refused to let go of his thoughts. *Thou shalt not withdraw monies from trust without an accounting delivered within four days of any such transaction.* The deed was done. Mudhali would have transferred the funds immediately.

Suddenly, Harry brightened. When Chin came in to sign the offers tomorrow, he would give him a letter setting out the withdrawal on account of services to be rendered. It was likely that this maneuver would ensure compliance at least with the letter of the law, if not the spirit. Despite his rationale, Harry knew that his pride had driven him to rashness.

Miss Giveny was waiting by the car, exuding a steam of impatience. He forced the Mudhali encounter to back of his mind.

"Things are beginning to hum," he said, with forced cheeriness. "The Chin money is safely tucked in the bank. Now, let's see what Miss Deighton wants. Oh, by the way, did you bring Marjorie's existing will?"

She sniffed, offended that her competence might be in question. "Of course. I brought two copies of it and put the original back in the vault."

"Good. I wonder what changes she'll want to make."

Harry climbed in next to his secretary. "She'll only cause trouble," muttered Miss Giveny sullenly.

Astonished at the unmitigated bleakness of her tone, Harry stared across at her. "Why would you say that?"

Miss Giveny shrugged. Staring straight ahead, she said, "Because it's true. She was a great worry to Mr. Crawford. Always demanding his time over the silliest things."

"Really? She always struck me as a very pleasant, reasonable sort." In the slanting sun, Harry could see the tightening at the corners of her mouth. "What sorts of things?"

"Oh, I don't know. She was always fussing about her nieces and nephew, and how they treated her." Miss Giveny paused, as if debating whether to continue. "She was always talking about how to end it all, if she got really sick. Almost an obsession, if you ask me."

"You mean you think she'd try to kill herself?"

Miss Giveny gazed at Harry as if he were a lowly student. "Hardly! She's far too vain and selfish for that. All she wanted was to worry Mr. Crawford, just to get his attention. She never gave Mr. Crawford a moment's peace. Always having to protect her."

"Protect her? From what?" asked Harry.

Miss Giveny sniffed and crumpled up her Kleenex. "Mostly from her relatives."

Such fears often preoccupied lonely old aunts, thought Harry. Particularly the wealthy ones, and with good reason. Was a niece or nephew visiting this afternoon? He'd need to watch out for telltale signs of duress. Lots of clients had to be protected from their nearest and dearest.

"If there's anything more...?"

"No, nothing," she said, snapping her purse shut. "It was all before your time, anyway."

The conversation ended. Miss Giveny could speak volumes with her silence. They turned north onto Spadina Avenue, which, at the southerly end, was one of the broadest and most desolate streets in the city.

Chinatown was further north. New buildings, oriental in shape and design, had appeared overnight. With waves of Hong Kong money swamping the city, the Seniors' Home and the Chinese Emporium had replaced the older, worn structures. Beyond Chinatown, Spadina Crescent wound around the massive, turreted Connaught Laboratory, which was ensconced like a Victorian dowager protecting the leafy residential district of the Deightons further north.

Time and again, he was reminded that Toronto was no longer the staid city of his childhood. Sometimes it resembled an ancient heap of unrelated jigsaw-puzzle pieces; at other times, the city seemed unified by a raw, surging energy, teeming with life.

They arrived ten minutes early. Harry parked in front of St. Timothy's Church, which stood next to the Deighton mansion. He decided to take a walk. Miss Giveny remained in the car.

On the south side of Mount Rose was a small sporting-goods store, which resembled a concrete bunker. On the other side, shabby stores crowded in along the sidewalk. Three of Chin's lots fronted on the north side of the street, just west of the church. Tenanted housing occupied the other three lots directly behind them.

Harry turned back to the car. Without a word, Miss Giveny climbed out and followed him up the walk.

The Deighton residence was a handsome example of mid-Victorian architecture. Like a fortress against the world, the house had two turrets rising up the three stories. A chill wind swept them up the steps to the broad veranda, which ran the along the front and down one side of the house. The sun was fading fast, leaving behind the bitter chill of an early spring.

As promised, the front door was unlocked. Although he loved the oval expanse of beveled glass set in the door, Harry shook his head at the lack of security. Some of his elderly clients were terrorized by reports of rising crime. Undoubtedly, they would be hiding behind locks and latches, fearful that the Florist would break in. Others, such as the Deightons, were so insulated by their attitudes of class and status that they felt safe. An attack on their property or person would signal the total disintegration of society.

Harry pushed Marjorie's front door open.

"Miss Deighton," he called, as they stepped inside.

The interior was dim and cold. The twilight flickered momentarily, illuminating the broad staircase, which led off the foyer. Harry rubbed his hands together for warmth, then took off his coat. The brass rings screeched along the rod as he drew back the heavy brocade curtains of the cloakroom.

"Good afternoon, Miss Deighton," he said more loudly, opening the parlor door. Her chair by the fireplace was empty, and the grate was cold. Miss Giveny shivered at his side.

A strong draft caught his ankles from somewhere at the back. Moving through the shadowy parlor and dining room, he entered the kitchen. A naked ceiling bulb swayed slightly in the pantry off the kitchen, casting a stark and ugly light. The draft came from the back door, which was not properly closed. Shoving his weight against it, Harry slammed it shut.

The telephone rang in the still house: once, then twice. Harry waited for it to be answered. The phone continued its ringing.

On the main staircase, he called out, "Miss Deighton, it's Harold Jenkins. Are you all right?"

He held his breath to listen. Was that movement upstairs?

Harry peered upward in the gray light. A shadow seemed to pass on the wall of the upstairs landing. The cursed phone continued to ring.

On the stairs, Miss Giveny held him back. "I'll go. She wouldn't want a man coming up."

Abruptly, the telephone stopped. Miss Giveny rushed up the stairs. She rapped on the door and then twisted the knob.

The staccato bursts from the telephone were the only sound throughout the house.

White-faced, Miss Giveny stood at the head of the stairs. "The door won't budge."

Harry mounted the stairs, two at a time. His sleeve brushed a potted plant, pitching it to the floor. He knocked again. "Miss Deighton, are you in there?"

The knob was so loose that it might easily snap off. At last the catch turned, but the door still would not budge. He threw his weight against the door and it gave way.

Marjorie lay peacefully on the bed, dressed in a deep-blue silk dress, as if ready to go out for afternoon tea. Her ankles were crossed rather primly and her arms lay in repose at her sides.

Two straight-backed chairs were pulled up beside the bed. A broken teacup lay on the floor, its contents forming a dark stain on the carpet.

A bedside lamp bathed her face in a soft rose light. He was moved by the utter peace in her expression. How clear her skin was—almost translucent. Care seemed washed away. Lowering his head to her chest, he listened for breathing. Gently, he took her wrist, but could find no pulse. He winced at the cold and stiffness of her fingers.

No long suffering, no clinging to respirators, no indignities inflicted upon body and soul by modern medicine. A neat and peaceful passing, thought Harry. Just what Marjorie had wanted.

The telephone broke the silence of the house again. Harry picked up the receiver.

"Hello?"

He heard an indistinct sound. Was it breathing? Throat-clearing?

"Yes? Who is it?" he asked.

The line went dead. Harry shook his head and hung up.

Briskly, Miss Giveny drew back the curtains. The orange twilight flooded the room. She straightened the upended pot in the hall. Watching her, Harry reflected that death seemed to compel the living into a frenzy of activity.

He sat down and gazed at his client, then he dialed emergency services. He spoke quietly on the phone.

At the death of an old client, Harry often felt a chapter in his own life had closed. A woman with eighty-five years of experience had valued his advice—and not just as a lawyer. Surprised at the keenness of his sense of loss, he took her hand once more. Here lay Richard Crawford's lover. Such a union he could scarcely imagine. But then, their love needn't make sense to him. With her passing, perhaps Crawford's critical ghost would fade from his mind.

Again the phone rang. Harry stared at it, then picked it up. "Yes?"

This time the phone was slammed down. *What in hell?* he thought.

Loud banging at the front door shattered the silence.

Miss Giveny answered. Four men crowded into Marjorie's bedroom. After a brief examination, the coroner pronounced her dead. A weary-looking sergeant named Welkom took perfunctory notes.

"So, you related to the deceased?" Welkom asked.

"No, I'm Harry Jenkins, her solicitor."

The sergeant sighed as if this fact were a troublesome complication. "When did you find her?"

"Ten minutes ago. We called right away."

"Touch anything?" he asked, glancing about.

"Just her. To see if there were a pulse."

"What were you doing here?"

"I had a four o'clock appointment with her, but she had a visitor at two." Harry pointed out the two chairs drawn up to the bed, and the tea tray. "Certainly looks as if she had some visitors," he said.

The sergeant closed his notebook. "Well, we can send forensics around to check the place out."

"She was quite elderly, and she may have just passed away in her sleep." Harry hesitated. "But she really was concerned about the appointment. Said she'd need my advice. Also, when we got here, the phone started ringing on and off. I picked it up twice and the line went dead both times."

Welkom shrugged and said to the coroner, "What do you think, Mel?" His eyes briefly lowered to the floor. "No signs of violence? No petal designs anywhere?"

"You mean like the Florist's handiwork?" said the coroner, examining the body. "No, none. But those were all young girls." Mel shook his head. "Given her age, I think she just died of natural causes."

The paramedics moved the body onto the stretcher and headed downstairs.

Welkom shouldered past the coroner out into the hallway. "Next of kin, Mr. Jenkins?"

"Yes, two nieces: Katharine Rowe and Suzannah Deighton. And a nephew, Gerald."

"We'll have to contact them," the sergeant said, jotting down the names.

Harry started down the stairs, only to stop on the landing. He tried the door to the back stairs, but it was jammed. He'd get someone in to make the minor repairs. Buyers with lots of money loved features such as back stairs and French doors. He smiled. Natasha would be the perfect appraiser of the property. As Marjorie's executor, along with Gideon Trust, he would net substantial compensation. With a lighter step, he descended the staircase.

At the foot of the stairs, he stopped again. Something was not right.

"Shouldn't there be an autopsy, sergeant?" he asked.

Welkom shrugged. "That's up to the coroner. There was no violence. Probably she just died of natural causes."

Harry began, "Yes, but—"

"Listen, Mr. Jenkins, Leave it to us. We'll let you know." The sergeant snapped his pad shut and left.

Once the body had been removed, Harry left a note for Rosie, Marjorie's housekeeper, to call him when she came back from her afternoon off. Then he tried to reach the next of kin.

Katharine Rowe, Marjorie's eldest niece, was still in meetings. There was no answer at Suzannah's. Gerry Deighton had left his dental clinic at noon and had not returned. Harry left his home and office numbers. He knew almost nothing of Marjorie's relatives. Except for Suzannah and her problems with Frank, Marjorie had rarely spoken of them. Harry knew a client's death could prove interesting. Next of kin frequently shed new light on clients he thought he knew well. It worked both ways. Relatives, formerly only names typed in wills, often came to life in the most surprising fashion. The maze of human relationships fascinated him. Together, Miss Giveny and Harry closed up the empty house.

"I'll take you right home, Miss Giveny," he said as he opened the car door for her.

"Thank you. I usually take the bus, but tonight…"

"I know. After all of this, we ought to get home as quickly as possible."

"All these reports of the Florist are so troubling," she sighed.

CHAPTER 6

▼

The Florist was pleased with his name. It suggested an appreciation of his artistic talent and sensibility. That other name, "the Mad Artist," that had been originally splattered all over the press, had infuriated him. Sipping his coffee, he glanced at the newspaper. Good! His letter to the editor was on the front page. It read:

This world is filled with dreary, lackluster souls plodding through their lives. Those who criticize me for destroying and creating are philistines. Those who call me mad shall fear my judgment, which has the cleansing power of fire.

His smile was thin as he lit his cigar. A photograph caught his eye. The woman's head was tipped at lovely angle, exposing her long, slender neck. The line conveyed perfect elegance and grace, just like a Matisse drawing. He rose from his breakfast table to go to the window.

In the bright morning sun, he examined her features. Such startling beauty. But then again, she had the haughty look of one spoiled by class and status. He despised that kind of woman: a socialite engaged in useless charitable work to salve her conscience. Her cheekbones were high and fine; her mouth was only slightly too wide, suggesting an untamed sensuality beneath a painted exterior. The short blurb read:

Katharine Rowe (pictured above) accepting an award for her charitable works at Emma's Hostel for abused women.

In his office, next to the bedroom, he made ten enlarged copies of her photograph. Tonight, he would get out his book on Matisse and practice his drawing on the copies of her photograph.

"Mother?" the Florist said softly. "At last I have found the perfect one." He cocked his head, as if straining for a response.

His eyes flashed with anger. "I do not understand you, Mother! Just what do you mean by 'compassion'?"

CHAPTER 7

▼

Harry found every possible traffic jam between Marjorie's and Miss Giveny's streets. Mercifully, his secretary remained encased in silence throughout the long ride. She lived on Mortimer Avenue, a broad and desolate thoroughfare cutting across the east end of the city. One dwarf maple per lot dotted the roadway, and each tiny bungalow had a huge carport attached, creating an unsettling, lopsided effect. Despite the early spring, not a soul walked along the dreary roadway. Perhaps the Florist had frightened people inside.

As he pulled into the driveway, his secretary sat in tense silence.

"Good night, Miss Giveny," said Harry, opening the car door for her.

"Thank you for the ride," she said stiffly. "Everyone's worried sick about that dreadful Florist. I hope they catch him soon. People should be able to go about without worry." Pursing her lips, she stared straight ahead in the gloom. Harry only nodded.

Suddenly, the front door of the house flew open. A woman, about Miss Giveny's age, stepped out, wearing a pink nightie. Framed in the light of the doorway, Harry saw her sagging body. With the eagerness of a small child, the woman waved and called out,

"Hiya Gladdie! Where ya been?" Then she crouched down on the top step and giggled, clasping her hands around her knees. "Gladdie's got a gentleman friend, I see."

Miss Giveny almost stumbled in her haste to get out of the car. Turning back, she peered in the dark at Harry. "It's my sister, Merle, Mr. Jenkins." She spoke with somber dignity. "She's my responsibility. She's not right in the head." She shut the car door and took Merle inside.

Heading home, Harry reflected on Miss Giveny's world. Never once had she spoken of her burdens. Her truculence was much more understandable now.

Squinting in the lights of oncoming traffic, his mind wandered to the worlds of Marjorie's relatives. Although his client had rarely spoken of her niece, Katharine Rowe, he thought she worked in architectural design. The nephew, Gerry, was a dentist. Only her concerns for Suzannah had been voiced. And Donnie sounded like plenty of trouble. But for Harry, raising kids was unknown territory.

Switching on the radio, he caught a tune from his early undergraduate years in the seventies. The face of Dean Faulkner, a friend from back then, floated in front of him. Only a few days ago, he had met him for a drink. Dean had done a better job of keeping his hair than Harry had.

Dark figures had crowded around the bar. Even with the noise, Dean's bitterness had come through loud and clear.

"Orion's been in the forefront of architectural planning for decades. But it's running out of steam." Dean stared into his glass, then looked up into Harry's eyes. "I'm an 'old-school' planner accused of creating idyllic pastures for sheep." He snorted. "Higgledy-piggledy neighborhoods are in fashion. Like untended gardens of weeds. Soon there'll be no work for planners."

"They're firing you?"

"Hardly! They're smarter than that. One woman, Katharine Rowe, along with two guys, Taylor and Metzler, have orchestrated my departure."

"Are they offering a package?" asked Harry. Having represented a few disgruntled employees, he was well aware of the Machiavellian strategies of employers.

"A pittance!" Dean's face was an ugly knot of fury. Harry's concern mounted. Dean was on his third scotch.

"See...these two young guys, Taylor and Meltzer, have this project." He sneered. "It's supposed to revitalize the firm. St. Timothy's Church on Highland Avenue wants to sell to a shopping-mall developer, but they have to get it zoned commercial before closing. These guys are a couple of interior decorators, with all their artsy-fartsy stuff." Dean waved his hand in the air, then poked his finger at Harry. "But underneath, they're still a couple of fucking cutthroats," he muttered.

Dean lapsed into black silence. Harry prodded gently. "Have you gotten legal advice?"

Dean shook his head. "Not yet." He stared into his drink. Fury rose in his voice. "But you know what really kills? No loyalty from Katharine. Another outmoded concept of mine. Jesus, I mentored the woman. Without me to protect her, her career would have been in the toilet. How's that for gratitude?"

Harry shook his head in sympathy. Everyday he was thankful to be spared the bloodiness of corporate warfare.

"That bitch! Did plenty to advance her career."

"What does she do at Orion?"

"She used to be my assistant." Dean's lip curled. "I should've seen it coming. She's gunning for my job. Thinks she can bring new life to a worn-out firm."

"Yes, I've heard of her," Harry said carefully. Marjorie had said little about her niece Katharine. It was just as he always thought. Names mentioned in wills often took on surprising life on the death of the testator.

"Tough lady. Lots of times, when she was my assistant, I could have taken advantage." Dean held up his hands in innocence. "Never touched her once…a real ball-buster, though."

The two men sat in silence. The bar was getting hot. Suddenly, Dean said, "Ever hear of a lawyer, Tony McKeown?"

Harry had read a few articles by McKeown in the *Law Times* about a new master plan for the city. He had been alarmed at his zeal for a vision of cool, sleek lines, uncluttered by any trace of humanity. Harry shrugged. "Just heard of him. He's an urban planning lawyer. Why?"

Dean chuckled." "He's the shark who gulps up all the little fish. Just like that." He snapped his fingers almost under Harry's nose. His friend was getting pretty drunk.

Dean leaned across the table and said, "Some of his buddies are planning a takeover of Orion. Nobody's safe there." He smiled bitterly, "Not even Taylor and Meltzer. They don't know McKeown hates their planning concepts."

Harry patted Dean's arm. "Listen, if you need help, call me. You're entitled to a good severance."

"You're goddamned right, Harry. I will." His voice was fierce, but Harry saw his eyes were damp.

As Harry pulled into his driveway, thoughts of Katharine and Dean faded and his mind returned to Marjorie. Someone else had been in the house at two o'clock. The evidence had been there: spilled teacups, and chairs pulled up around the bed. The cop had seemed out-and-out lazy, and too quick to decide that her death was from natural causes. In order to make the funeral arrangements, he needed to know whether there would be an autopsy, as he had suggested.

As he opened his front door, he heard the telephone ring. Katharine Rowe was on the other end.

"She was an amazingly strong woman," Katharine sighed after he told her of Marjorie's death. "At least she's at peace, now." There was a pause. Harry wondered if she were overcome with grief. "I haven't seen her for almost two weeks. Was anyone with her when she died?"

"Not that I know of. But someone was there earlier."

"Who?" Katharine's voice was sharp.

"I don't know." Harry hesitated. "Of course, I called the police, and they came with the coroner."

"The police?"

"Yes. It's customary when someone dies alone at home."

"Where was Rosie?"

"Marjorie said she was letting her go for the afternoon."

"Strange," Katharine said. "I was in meetings all day, and I called you back as soon as I could. I didn't know she was unwell."

"I didn't either, but of course, people *do* die suddenly, without warning."

"I suppose." Katharine sounded unconvinced.

Harry hesitated and then said, "I did ask the police about an autopsy."

"What on earth for? Do you suspect something?"

Harry hesitated. "No. I just wanted to be sure I could go ahead with the funeral arrangements." He hoped he sounded convincing. Briefly, he closed his eyes.

A certain serenity had filled Marjorie's bedroom. As she lay in repose, his first thought had been: *She got what she wanted...a neat and peaceful passing.* He frowned. On the stairs, it had seemed as though something was wrong, like reverberations after a violent clap of thunder. He had asked the officer about an autopsy. Now he *had* to know what happened.

He heard Katharine sigh. "Listen, Mr. Jenkins, I've had an absolutely exhausting day. Meetings nonstop all day, and more tomorrow. What happens next? Are you her executor?"

"Yes. I'll be in touch the next day or so."

"Good. Well, thank you. Goodbye." Katharine hung up.

She's all business, he reflected.

Looking about his empty kitchen, he sought refuge from his circuitous thoughts. Leafing through yesterday's paper, he was surprised to find Katharine's photograph. He read the article about her award for tireless efforts in support of Emma's Hostel for Women.

Perhaps Dean did not have the whole picture of Katharine. Harry was sympathetic to the plight of women in the so-called man's world. The survivors almost became a parody of the men with whom they competed.

Where the hell is Laura? he wondered. *Hardly ever here!* Sadly, he remembered a time when she would turn to him for comfort. Her climb on the corporate ladder had been perilous. Sometimes all he could do back then was to hold her close in bed at night, until she drifted off. Now, at the top of her profession, maybe she did not need him anymore.

He checked his watch. Strange: no word from Rosie yet. He called Marjorie's house, but there was no answer. Without even knowing her last name, he could not reach her. Slowly, he started upstairs for bed.

CHAPTER 8

▼

On the day that Marjorie died, Katharine had been in the midst of appointments, struggling to maintain control of Orion's newest client, the archbishop of the Anglican Church. Inexplicably, Archbishop Staunton had decided to personally promote the plans of St. Timothy's Church to sell out to a shopping-mall developer.

Katharine's male partners had voted unanimously to assign personal charge of the client to her. The senior partners would control the important matters of design and structure. Surely, a man of the cloth required special tact and sensitivity to guide him through the shoals of planning departments, city council meetings, and legal briefs. A woman's gentle touch was needed; no male was suited for the role of handmaiden.

They did not know Archbishop Staunton. In their ignorance, they expected a kindly, older gentleman, ready to bless their every thought and deed. Shielded by their preconceptions, they saw what they expected. For Katharine, this new client was surprisingly difficult, exhibiting keen intelligence, sophisticated worldliness, and outright pigheadedness. A clerical collar was no guarantee of benevolence. No robe could disguise his cool and calculating manner. His interest in the project was intense. *Just like a domineering white male,* she thought.

Katharine had revised plans to present to the archbishop at his legal counsel's office. The head of the church knew the wisdom of retaining the law firm of Cheney, Arpin. The expertise and connections of their most senior urban development lawyer, Tony McKeown, were at their disposal. McKeown was at the pinnacle of the urban-planning law world.

According to Katharine, a woman needed the right combination to succeed in a man's world: hard-nosed business acumen, tempered with just enough femininity; competence mellowed with just the right degree of vulnerability.

Last night she had sensed that McKeown was buying into the package. She could guess at his assessment of her: competence, yes; smarts, yes; killer instinct, undoubtedly; easy lay, maybe. But for her, McKeown was hard to read.

"We advise. The client instructs," McKeown had said last evening. Then, with eyes lowered, he added, "Tomorrow, Mrs. Rowe, you and I will woodshed a priest. By the time I am finished, he will have become an effective witness." The wry smile and the depth of pleasure in his eyes were more than disconcerting.

Although she sensed danger, she could not place its source. He was very attractive, in a rough and threatening way.

For Katharine, sex was an indispensable weapon in any woman's arsenal. As a rule, men were weak and vulnerable pawns. But McKeown was different. He was polished like an elegant stone, but there was a sharp and dangerous edge to his charm—a challenge she could not resist.

The next morning, as the elevator to McKeown's office slowed, Katharine glanced into the mirror. The woman who stared back seemed remote and disconnected from her. She could not deny the desperate hunger in her eyes. Although she had everything in life, no man had ever satisfied her, at least not in bed. And then there was the business of love, she thought bitterly. Her husband, Bob, claimed he loved her, but it was a suffocating, deadening kind of love. Stepping from the elevator, she caught the reflection of her bright and brittle smile.

First Katharine visited the washroom. As she checked her makeup, she heard sobbing from the lounge. Two women were seated on a low cushioned bench. The soft cries threatened to rise, but then subsided.

"He really was a bastard. No, a monster!" choked the younger woman.

She's only a child, thought Katharine.

"All through dinner, he was wonderful. So I thought it'd be okay to go back to his place." The older woman put her arm around the girl.

Heard this one a million times before, Katharine thought. Women could be so stupid and trusting. At the shelter, they tried to teach women—girls, really—how to protect themselves. Usually, it was a hopeless task. To Katharine, such naïveté was a cardinal sin.

"He said that some women were meant to be hurt. Then he dragged me into the bedroom and told me to take off all my clothes." The girl's face streamed with tears. "He said that before he touched me, he had to examine me. He was holding a tiny silver knife in his hand."

The girl's shoulders shook. She could not continue for some moments. "And when I said no, I didn't want to do that, he hit me right across the mouth, real hard. Then he just dragged me to the door and shoved me out." The girl flung herself into the woman's arms. "He called me 'filthy trash' and slammed the door."

Oh God, thought Katharine, *the child doesn't stand a chance.* But even so, she had to concede that it was nearly impossible to protect yourself from a charming madman. Katharine could do nothing. While she pitied the girl, she was contemptuous of such naïveté.

After pausing to collect herself, Katharine proceeded to the reception desk of Cheney, Arpin. She was right on time for her meeting with the archbishop and Tony McKeown. Moments later, she was ushered past the circular staircase and down the paneled hallway to the boardroom. The rosewood conference table was twenty-five feet long. Richly upholstered armchairs lined both sides of it. The dark wainscoting gleamed in the sunlight. In the shadows at the far end of the table sat the archbishop who was talking to a woman who was filling his coffee cup from a silver carafe.

"Good afternoon, Archbishop Staunton." Katharine quickly covered the length of the boardroom and extended her hand. The archbishop began to rise.

"Please don't get up," she said.

The sunlight caught the unyielding angle of the cleric's jaw. A wintry smile graced his lips as he replied, "It's good of you to come on short notice, Mrs. Rowe. I see you have the revised plans."

Straight to business, thought Katharine, placing the roll of plans on the table and sitting down.

The archbishop glanced at his watch and frowned. "Mr. McKeown is on the phone with the planning department." His words were clipped and his manner brusque. "The whole diocese is very much concerned about the opposition to the church application. Tell me, Mrs. Rowe, what are our chances?"

A clear, honest answer was demanded by this intelligent and perceptive client; no glossing over or false promises for him. Katharine took a deep breath and proceeded. "Mr. McKeown is really the one to answer your question, sir. But the city councilors I've talked to consider the proposal somewhat unusual."

"Really? Why?" The archbishop's heavy eyebrows shot up, animating his face.

Katharine met his eyes, then opened her maroon leather binder, which contained notes of conversations with various aldermen. With her best level gaze, she began. "Bottom line, sir, they don't want increased commercial development in the neighborhood. Somehow, the idea of a church property being used for commercial retail space is a problem for them."

The archbishop turned angrily and said, "But we have the evidence! What about all those planning reports the church has paid for? They recommend the project because the tax base will increase." Staunton waved his hand in disgust and sat back in his chair. "I thought aldermen always liked that sort of thing."

Katharine waited until he had finished, and then began quietly, "Unfortunately, the element of resentment is strong. The council sees the church as a wealthy institution owning valuable property and not fairly bearing the tax burden. Other businesses see it as a threat, while the residents regard it as an intrusion." Katharine did not speak of the alderman who joked about driving the moneychangers out of the temple.

She was surprised at the archbishop's low chuckle. "Mrs. Rowe, don't they realize that the church is building up a colossal debt just to pay its heat and light bills? No one tithes anymore. We can't count on donations. If people want churches for their weddings and funerals, they'll either have to become reliably generous, or else let us raise it in our own way. What business ever survived on charity?" Spent with frustration, Archbishop Staunton sank back in his chair and glared at Katharine.

A clerical collar was no guarantee of immunity from secular concerns. The aggressiveness of the archbishop was disconcerting, and the idea of a church dirtying its hands in a commercial complex did seem undignified. She spread the plans on the table.

Memories flooded through her. St. Timothy's was an immense limestone structure built on a triple lot, right next to the house in which she had grown up. Katharine's grandfather, Colonel William Mortimer Deighton, was a decorated war hero. Wishing to dominate the congregation of St. Timothy's, the colonel had built immediately to the north, preventing the construction of the manse nearby. This act ushered in several decades of an uneasy balance of power between the church and the Deighton family.

Katharine had lived there for eighteen years with her parents, George and Mildred Deighton, and her Aunt Marjorie. Katharine was the eldest, then came Gerry, and last, Suzannah.

Until she was eleven, Katharine had attended Sunday school at St. Timothy's. Shortly after her confirmation, she had simply refused to go back. She despised the sanctimonious vicar and his church. Hadn't Jesus said, *"Come, little children, unto me"*? she thought bitterly. Without her, Gerry would not go. Despite threats, cajoling, and even bribery by her parents and Aunt Marjorie, she had sullenly resisted. None of them had thought to ask why, and Katharine preferred to keep secrets. Secrets gave her power.

One Sunday in early April, a week before her eleventh birthday, Katharine had been waiting for Gerry to come out of the junior class. She and her friend Betty had been talking about birthday-party plans outside on the lawn, and had almost forgotten him.

Pulling the heavy side door open, she walked down the darkened and silent hall to his classroom. Everyone was gone. A gentle breeze filtered through the windows stirring the Lent calendar on the notice board. The secretary in the office directed her to the vicar's study.

Standing silently in the hallway of vaulted ceilings, she heard muffled sobs and pleading. Cupping her ear to the vicar's door, she held her breath. Gerry's voice! She was able to hear it plainly. She turned the knob slowly and silently the door swung open.

Reverend Purvis, in his surplice, stood motionless. A belt dangled from his hand.

Gerry, a slight and submissive figure, was bent over the arm of the sofa, his buttocks bared and his legs splayed. Slowly and confidently, Purvis strode about the room, as if delay might heighten his pleasure. Katharine was transfixed as the man unbuttoned his gown. He did not see her. Suddenly, the Reverend's face became florid. He approached her brother with a brutal rush of energy.

Katharine screamed. The Reverend turned. Only two Sundays before, he had smiled down on her at her confirmation. Now he scowled. Disgust rose in her. *Confirmation of dedication to Jesus and the Church.* For an eternity, she and the Reverend stood motionless, staring at each other. Horrified, she could see the blood vessels engorged at his temples. At last, the man drew his robe about him.

Her screams rebounded on the vaulted ceilings. The Reverend slapped his hand across her mouth, but she broke free. Dragging Gerry by the hand, she raced from the study, down the hallway and past the locked office. He did not follow them. At the outer door, she turned back to see Purvis silhouetted against the stained glass window.

Frightened senseless, Gerry begged her not to tell.

After that, Purvis looked pale and sick, in her presence. Drawn by the power of the Reverend's dark secrets, a thrill coursed through her body. A sense of control over both her brother and men grew swiftly within her. The keeper of secrets was the master of the game. So thought Katharine at eleven, as her burgeoning sense of power became inextricably linked with dark sexual stirrings.

To banish the recollection, Katharine smiled warmly at the archbishop, who rose from his chair and rested his hand on her shoulder as he looked at the plans. With his gold pen in hand, he traced the perimeter of the church lands and the property to the north. "Any word, Mrs. Rowe, whether we can get the Deighton lands incorporated into our plan for the shopping mall?"

Shocked, Katharine stared at him. "I didn't know they were part of the development." She withdrew slightly from his touch.

He jerked his hand away. "They're an integral part. Didn't Mr. McKeown explain that to your *senior* partners?"

Momentarily, Katharine appeared confused. "It's the first I've heard of it," she managed to say. Her office was full of cutthroats. Intentional neglect to pass on key information was a common form of sabotage. "How does the property fit into the plan?" she asked.

"We need parking."

"But isn't it underground?" Katharine consulted the plan.

"Some is. But we need more."

Katharine found nothing in her file. "I'll speak to the senior partners, sir. I'm sure it's an oversight."

The Archbishop asked, "Don't you report to Donald Coventry?"

Katharine nodded, furious that the vice-president of planning had succeeded in such a simple game of corporate subterfuge. Wearily, she exhaled.

"Then he should be here, I think," Staunton grumbled.

The boardroom door flew open. Tony McKeown strode past, closely followed by two young men laden with stacks of legal texts. The lawyer was in his shirtsleeves, collar open and tie loosened. He acknowledged no one's presence. Throwing himself into the chair next to Staunton, he motioned the junior lawyers to set out the books. Only then did he look at the archbishop.

"Now, Mr. Staunton," Tony began, "we've got problems, and they have to be sorted out before tomorrow. One of them is you, sir."

The archbishop remained in shocked silence. His eyebrows shot up and his mouth dropped open. Finally he said, "Me? And why am I a problem?"

Chewing on his cigar, Tony rose and began to pace. "All our work goes down the drain unless you can sell the plan to our esteemed council members. So let's get to it. We've got to get you prepared for your examination tomorrow."

With that, he turned a brilliant smile on the archbishop. "You'll be on the hot seat, sir. Don't worry about all the detail stuff. We've got experts like Mrs. Rowe to do that. Are you ready, sir?"

The archbishop nodded curtly. Never had he been addressed in such a discourteous manner. This lawyer would have to learn respect for the office.

"Good. Now remember, the aldermen will be throwing all kinds of questions at you. They're not all that smart, but those questions have been fed to them by the ratepayers, who pay their exorbitant taxes to the city." McKeown waved his cigar dismissively. "And those aldermen and ratepayers are a bunch of holier-than-thou armchair socialists with the brains of sheep."

Katharine caught her breath. She had entered a world of domination by a master. Last night's smoothly polished lawyer had turned into a barroom brawler and bully. A courtroom lawyer, a consummate actor...undoubtedly there were other personae in his repertoire. McKeown lurched forward in his chair and touched the archbishop's arm.

"Think of it this way, sir." His tone was deferential at first. "You must surrender yourself into my hands. I am about to create an appropriate personage in you to address these aldermen."

Smiling, Tony paused to tap his cigar. "It's something like trusting in God," he concluded softly.

The archbishop gave an almost imperceptible nod.

McKeown grinned and sprang from his chair. "Let's get to work, sir!"

With a small smile, the lawyer began strolling the length of the conference table. "Archbishop Staunton," he began in a respectful tone. "You preside over the diocese of this city?"

The Archbishop was quick to reply, in clipped tones. "I do, and, I might add, my authority and responsibility cover the extended metropolitan area."

"And in your position, sir, you are primarily concerned with matters of the spirit, church doctrine, and the like?" The lawyer's tone was casual, even friendly.

"Yes, I am." The archbishop spoke authoritatively.

"You must be extremely busy, then. How is it that you have time to take such a personal interest in the application of one parish church, out of perhaps two hundred, to sell out to a shopping-mall developer?"

Momentarily, Staunton flushed in confusion, "Why, the church always takes a special interest in the neighborhoods where its parishes are located."

Tony gazed intently at the archbishop. Delving his hands in his pockets, he nodded thoughtfully and said, "Not bad, sir. Not bad at all."

Staunton looked vaguely pleased with himself.

"With respect, then, sir, why would you persist in supporting an application that is obviously unpopular with the ratepayers?"

Momentarily, the archbishop looked puzzled, but gaining his composure, he replied smoothly, "Obviously, they don't see, at least not yet, that the increased revenues will help not only the church, but the neighborhood as well."

McKeown was at the far end of the boardroom. Wheeling around, he jabbed his finger at Staunton. "Wrong, Reverend. Wrong!" he shouted.

With his voice beginning in a low growl, but quickly rising in strength and resonance, he strolled the length of the room, as if addressing a jury. "You're not in your pulpit now, Rev. You're talking to real people like they're out on the street and you're one of them. You can't say 'obviously.' That makes them feel stupid. You can't say 'yet.' That's telling them they're going to see it your way, once they've stopped being so stupid. And, Reverend, you can't use that god-damned sanctimonious tone of yours, because it makes them real mad."

Tony dropped into the seat beside the Archbishop Staunton and grinned at his frozen countenance. "Now sir, please," he said with weary patience "I'm going to tell you what to say and how to say it."

God, thought Katharine, *this is more than woodshedding.* She permitted herself a small smile. *Staunton deserves it, and McKeown is enjoying humiliating the man.* But as the afternoon of grilling and rehearsing wore on, she was surprised to see a more convincing and likeable witness emerge from the austere personage of the archbishop.

Signaling the end of the session, McKeown reached across the table and covered Katharine's hand. Startled, she drew back. McKeown held her wrist tightly and winked. "Tonight, Mrs. Rowe, we'll work on you." With that, he strode from the room, leaving his two silent assistants to clear the materials from the table.

CHAPTER 9

▼

After speaking with Katharine, Harry looked about his empty kitchen. From the hollow sounds of the house, he knew Laura had not yet been home. Her absence disoriented him.

Later that evening, with sleep eluding him, he lay still in the darkness of his empty bed. He saw the placid face of Mudhali regarding him as a deadbeat. *Jesus!* As if refusing to shoulder his deceased partner's personal debts were a serious crime. Turning onto his back, he stared at the ceiling. He saw his hand scrawl the check in anger. Never mind; he could fix it in the morning. He just needed to give the client the accounting, and all would be well. Dorothy Crawford would just have to pay Richard's debt to the bank.

Then Laura's face floated up. Beset with different worries, he tortured himself with visions of the charming Dr. Stover. Harry had never met the man, but now Stover leered at him and stroked a pretentious beard. In his thrall, he thought.

No longer could he drive out recollections of his Sunday afternoon walk in the ravine with Laura. Together, they had strolled down the dirt road past the formal gardens of Alexander Muir Park. Holding hands was the public pretence of intimacy. Up ahead lay the sun-filled tennis courts and the neat white-and-green clubhouse.

"What do you want to do this summer?" asked Harry, testing the waters.

"I'm not sure I can get away."

"You always have."

She shrugged and poked a stick at a muddy patch of dead leaves. "Work schedules."

In the distance, a small boy was reeling after flocks of birds.

Harry's shoulders slumped.

"You're thinking we should have had children."

"No. Why?"

"You'd make a lousy poker player, Harry."

Saddened at being so intimately known by someone drifting out of reach, he admitted, "Yes, actually, I was."

"You know it wouldn't have worked."

"I would have helped." Harry heard his own wistfulness.

"Sure, Harry. But that would have made it my responsibility."

They walked on underneath the ancient, gnarled trees. "Let's talk about it next month," she said.

Nothing resolved. Everything postponed.

At last, exhaustion swept over him, and he slept straight through the night.

To his surprise, he woke almost an hour early. Laura lay beside him. He drew her close and gazed at the line of her shoulder, smooth and still in the early rays of sun.

"What is it?" she mumbled into the pillow.

He dismissed her grumpy tone, and contemplated the pleasures of their early morning lovemaking—years ago. He slid his hand under the covers, reaching down until it rested on her thigh.

"What are you doing, Harry?" She clutched the blankets around her. "It's not seven, is it? I've got a meeting at the museum at eight-thirty." Pulling her robe on, she headed for her bathroom.

Harry sighed. Reality clashed with fantasy. But good Lord…what about the Chin offers and the Deighton funeral arrangements? In the bathroom, he began shaving. With determination, he looked beyond his puffy eyelids to concentrate on the intense blue eyes. He rinsed and patted his face dry.

He took stock. Time to cultivate a new image: shed a few pounds and cut down on the smoking. With the new business, he could afford a squash-club membership.

In the bedroom, Laura was almost dressed. He sat on the bed. Her gaze in the mirror told him she was already miles away.

"Harry, I'll be late tonight. The meetings will go straight through dinner."

"You were late last night too," he said mildly. Her glance was wary. "I do worry about you, what with this murderer about."

"Don't worry. I'm with a group, never alone."

"Maybe we could go out for dinner Friday night. Have some time together."

She nodded. "I think that could work. I'll check my agenda and leave you a message."

"Friday night? Surely you can't be booked with work then!"

She shrugged and gathered up her purse.

When she was gone, he chose his suit and squinted in the sunlight to coordinate his shirt and tie. Maybe, if he got into the real money, they could retire somewhere really nice. Fishing boats and brilliant blue waters flashed into his mind. But then, would she ever retire? He had to admit that it seemed doubtful. She was wedded to her career more than to him. But how could she leave him after twenty years? Had passion for Stover entirely blotted out her reason? It wasn't unlike Richard Crawford and his thraldom. He chose the cufflinks she had given him last Christmas.

When he entered his office, Miss Giveny was hunched over her typewriter, fuming as she tried to replace the ribbon. "The Chin offers are on your desk," she said flatly.

Harry examined all the offers. Not a single error—that was why he put up with her crankiness. He sighed, as the image of her poor sister, Merle, in her nightie, floated into his mind.

She had already opened a new file for the Deighton estate. Marjorie had executed the will last year, appointing Gideon Trust and Crawford as her executors. With the old man gone, Harry stepped into his place. The house was to be sold and the whole estate divided equally among Katharine, Gerry, and Suzannah. But Suzannah's share was subject to a secret trust, which he had not yet found.

Staring out the window, he remembered. At tea, Marjorie had said the trust was safe with her. He made a note to hunt through her papers at the house. Usually, a secret trust was in the form of a letter addressed to the executors. Unlike a will, a secret trust did not have to be submitted to the Probate Court, and consequently it did not become part of the public record, available for all to see.

Harry liked to think such documents contained clues to the dark side of the testator's personality. After all, only the dullest person would have no secrets best kept from prying eyes.

After instructing Miss Giveny to photocopy the will and return the original to the vault, he tried to reach Gerry and Suzannah, without success.

"By the way, Miss Giveny," he called from his office. "Have we heard from anyone named Rosie this morning?"

His secretary appeared in his doorway and shook her head. "What's her last name?

Harry shrugged and reached for the phone. Minutes later, he had Sergeant Welkom on the line. "I've heard nothing from Miss Deighton's housekeeper, Rosie. She was supposed to be coming back last night."

Welkom grunted. "We're on it, counselor."

"What about an autopsy?"

"We'll let you know when we hear from the coroner."

Damn lazy cop, Harry thought as he made a note.

Expecting Chin at one o'clock, Harry went out for an early lunch. He needed time to think. Miss Giveny had given him a message from Frank earlier that morning, inquiring about Marjorie's death and her will. Pulling open the door of Moffat's restaurant, he stopped. He hadn't even reached Suzannah. How in hell did Frank already know? Maybe Katharine had spoken to him.

He entered the restaurant. The wide expanse of windows gave an excellent view of Richmond Street, which ran through the old business district. Sunlight flooded in. The long butcher-block countertops gave the restaurant an appearance of fastidious cleanliness and an airy lightness. Sam was at the back, polishing the salt and pepper shakers. Everything gleamed in the sunlight.

"Harry, how are you?" he called out. "You're early today." Only a few customers sat at the counter. "What can I get you?"

Harry scanned the menu. Realizing he'd only had coffee this morning, he decided on an omelet and a salad. Sam nodded and headed for the kitchen.

Thinking of Marjorie, Harry stared out the window. Someone had been in her house before him. No Rosie, and no word on an autopsy. And then there were those damned telephone calls at Marjorie's house when he had found her.

He opened the newspaper to the Osgoode Law Reports, which listed decisions made the previous day by the learned Supreme Court Justices.

A name caught his eye as he scanned the law reports: *995607 Ontario Ltd. [Zaimir Heights Ltd.]*

Where had he seen that name before?

The lawyer for Zaimir was Tony McKeown. *Jesus,* Harry thought. *Tony McKeown has a finger in every development project in the city.*

The report stated that the city fathers from years ago had declared that no construction permit would be issued for a building taller than forty-five feet. While the planning board granted exceptions, such decisions were rare. Another edict from City Hall required low-density structures to create open space to prevent overcrowding. Unfortunately, these policies caused the weedy proliferation of squat, ugly structures sprawling across the cityscape.

McKeown, a smooth and polished Bay Street lawyer, was a creative genius at circumventing arcane building by-laws. Harry still could not figure out Zaimir. Folding his paper, he paid the bill and headed back for his office.

Opening his office door, he found Dean Faulkner pacing the foyer.

"Harry! I need you. They're screwing me around with my package."

Harry sat him down on the sofa. "What are they doing?" Dean's bloodshot eyes looked even worse than they had last week.

"No vacation pay! No sick pay!" He almost sobbed. "If I don't take their offer, they're going to cook up some case for termination for cause."

"But they have to have documented grounds for that, Dean."

"Fuck! I can't sleep or eat! I'm just walking all over the place, not knowing what I'm doing."

"Look, Dean." Harry grasped his shoulder. "I've got a client in a few minutes. Can you come in first thing tomorrow morning?"

Reluctantly, Dean stood up. "It's that bitch, Katharine Rowe."

Harry patted him on the shoulder. "Listen, Dean, come in at nine. Okay?"

Dean backed out the door. "Thanks, Harry."

When he was gone, Harry shook his head sadly. Dean was on the bottle pretty heavily.

At one o'clock on the dot, Mr. Chin glided through the front door.

Seated in his office, Harry said, "You mentioned a conglomerate the other day. Who are the members?"

"Four Hong Kong businessmen, including me. They are from the finest families, Mr. Jenkins." Chin smiled broadly, revealing his gold incisor.

"Really? What sorts of businesses?"

Waving expansively, his client said, "Mainly computer software; some investment bankers."

As much as Harry tried to get further background information about his new client and the conglomerate, Chin would give up nothing.

The man read carefully through the paperwork and then, without comment, signed each document.

"Mr. Chin?" Harry coughed gently. "I have prepared an invoice, sir."

Chin's eyelids flickered and he nodded slightly.

"I have transferred a relatively small portion of the retainer into my own account, for services rendered in preparing the offers, and services to be performed." He handed Chin the envelope.

Chin slit it open and glanced briefly at the statement.

"Very good, Mr. Jenkins," Chin murmured. Then, looking up, he smiled at Harry. "Please let me know when you require more funds. The conglomerate has much work to do in the city."

Harry breathed more easily.

Chin withdrew an envelope from his breast pocket. "I have a small gift for you, Mr. Jenkins."

Harry frowned, only for a moment. "Really? What is it?"

"Please open it and see." Chin lowered his eyes as he slid the envelope across the desk.

Harry withdrew two first-class tickets for flights and a voucher for a three-night stay in a luxury suite in Nassau. "The Atlantis Resort," he whispered. Shimmering blue waters danced before his mind's eye.

After a moment, he said, "This is more than kind of you, sir, but—"

Mr. Chin held up his hand. "Please. The conglomerate wishes to express its gratitude for your most timely service. We know you have made room for us in your busy schedule."

"But surely not. The retainer is very substantial, and..." He fingered the brochure, which featured a photograph of sunny beaches and gently lapping water.

"As I have said, the conglomerate has very substantial resources and plenty of work for you. We can only hope that you will be able to provide such timely service on future matters."

Harry picked up the tickets and gazed at them.

Chin rose to go. "Husbands and wives in such a busy world can drift apart, Mr. Jenkins. I am sure you and your wife, Laura, could use a vacation."

Then Chin gave instructions to deliver the offers to Jonathan Conroy at Cheney, Arpin and left.

Good grief! Never had Harry received such a gift. He sank into his chair and stared at the offers. But how did they know he had a wife and her name?

It had to be all right. Peter Niels at Cheney, Arpin—a Bencher of the Law Society—had referred Chin to him. Conroy must know something about the conglomerate. Not only was he the Treasurer of the Law Society and Head of the Ethics Committee, he was also Chair of the Real Estate Section of the Bar Association. He tucked the envelope into his desk drawer.

"Mr. Jenkins?" Miss Giveny called from the outer office. "There's a Mr. Mudhali on line one."

Bracing himself, Harry snatched up the phone. "Yes?"

"Mr. Jenkins? Head office would like to meet with you in the morning to discuss payment arrangements."

"You tell head office that I am busy the next few days and will call to arrange a mutually convenient time next week. In the meantime, I expect full access to any and all accounts." Harry hung up.

He placed a call to Jonathan Conroy to arrange for the delivery of the Chin offers. He was surprised when Conroy answered on the first ring.

"I must thank you for the referral of Mr. Albert Chin." Harry had opened the desk drawer and was fingering Chin's envelope. "He's instructed me to deliver some offers to you."

"Wonderful, Harry. Send them over, and I'll get them to the clients right away," Jonathan said heartily.

Harry agreed. "Albert Chin seems very interesting. Do you know him well?"

"Fine fellow!" Conroy boomed. "He's been a client of Peter Niels for a number of years. We had to refer him on these transactions. Can't be too careful these days about conflicts."

"No, of course not. Well, thanks again. I'll await your client's response."

Jonathan stretched back in his chair. He was surprised that Chin had been referred to Crane, Crawford and Jenkins. He chuckled at the thought of Richard Crawford: an old dog, if ever there was one. He knew little about Harry, except that he belonged to the Alton Club, where only the most reputable lawyers and businessmen were permitted membership. If Crawford's firm were worth something, perhaps he should invite Harry for drinks at the club.

He gazed at the spectacular view of Lake Ontario. In the late afternoon sun, the ferryboats looked like silver darts on the glistening water. Seagulls swooped about the little boats. From time to time, such a view inspired him to write poetry.

Cheney, Arpin, founded by his maternal grandfather, was the most prestigious law firm in the city. Throughout its corridors, its illustrious history was displayed in photographs, paintings, and print. The Grand Corridor (as it was called) was graced with original portraits of the many senior partners who had been elevated to the bench. Any bright young lawyer graduating from Upper Canada College and Osgoode Hall coveted a position with Jonathan's firm, where every member was, first and foremost, a gentleman.

C H A P T E R 10

▼

In the darkened room, the Florist watched the flickering images on the silent television. When the smiling face of Karla Jones appeared, he turned up the volume. She had been a university student majoring in economics, with aspirations to work with the United Nations. He gnawed reflectively on his drawing pen.

The old debate consumed him. Had she been worthy to live, she might have made a contribution. Perhaps his judgment had been clouded. Too swift? Ungovernable passion? No, of course not.

He tossed down his pen. Her lips had been painted bright carmine and her eyes made up with luminescent, garish blue. She had been begging for it. Permitted to live, she only would have tortured men with her grossly seductive charm.

A true artist must prevail over any adversity. Fire set substance free. His work set souls free. If he were to fail in his artistry, then—and only then—would he destroy with fire.

CHAPTER 11

▼

In the late afternoon, several floors down from Conroy, Archbishop Staunton was shown into McKeown's outer office. Sitting in a straight-backed chair, he glanced about him. Photographs of African masks lined the far wall. He frowned and picked up a magazine. Five minutes later, he was ushered into the lawyer's office.

"Yes?" said McKeown coldly.

The archbishop took a seat. "Mr. McKeown, what are our chances with this rezoning application?"

McKeown gave a brief smile and said, "As I have said, sir, if you find the ability within yourself to leave your clerical collar at the courtroom door, the church has a reasonably good chance."

The archbishop pursed his lips and then replied, "So if we do not win, it will be my fault?"

The lawyer sprang from his chair. "Not entirely, sir. But you must understand that these aldermen fancy themselves to be representatives of the people. They will resent your talking down to them."

Staunton grasped the arms of his chair. "We *must* win."

A smile spread across the lawyer's face. "And why is it so imperative?"

Twisting around, the archbishop glared at him. "If we are unable to rezone and complete the sale, the church will have no resources to pay it debts."

"Really? What debts are so pressing?"

Staunton waved him off. "It's been in all the papers. The lawsuits."

McKeown perched on the corner of his desk. "Ah, yes, I see. You mean those suits brought on behalf of the abused youngsters against some of your clergy."

"Yes," Staunton whispered.

McKeown's face darkened. He folded his arms across his chest. "I cannot imagine a fouler deed than the abuse of such innocents, particularly in the name of the Lord."

The archbishop threw his hands out in a gesture of futility. "What can I say? The church has been put in this position by a few—"

"Who remain protected by your church." The lawyer turned away in disgust.

"Nevertheless, we must win."

McKeown smiled broadly. "Do not worry, Archbishop Staunton. If that is your concern, I can provide a solution. I am sure I can bring the church a very favorable offer, should the application to rezone fail."

"Really? From whom?"

"I can't say at the moment. But be assured, I'll not let the church founder. The institution is far too important, despite its long-standing record of abuse."

Sighing audibly, the archbishop rose. "Thank you, Mr. McKeown. I hope that won't be necessary." Nodding curtly, he opened the door and left.

Although the light was fading, Tony did not turn on the lights. Instead, he stood at the window. A dirty rain spat against the glass. His headache began to clear.

He chuckled softly. It was child's play preparing the archbishop—so easy to mold him into the witness he wanted. Given the right circumstances and guidance, a person could be persuaded to say almost anything in the right fashion. But the deck was stacked against the church. Local opposition was fierce. If the application were to be dismissed, then he would have the right purchaser for the church, who would make an offer unconditional upon rezoning.

He checked his watch. It was time to prepare for Mrs. Rowe tonight. He checked her file and made several notes.

In a charitable mood, he regarded her as a victim of her breeding and class, just like the Archbishop. If he didn't prepare her properly, she could blow the whole application with the wrong inflection, by talking down to the representatives of the people. But, unlike the archbishop, it would be a pleasure to work with her.

At the Vivaldi Salon, in the underground mall of Tony's building, Katharine lay back in her chair for the shampoo and a hot oil treatment.

Her mind wandered to Tony. Who else but McKeown could have molded Staunton from a cold fish into a personable and effective witness, within the space of a few hours? What power did he possess?

Closing her eyes, she sighed with pleasure. Tony's image—his eyes, especially his eyes—floated up before her. She imagined his touch, perhaps rough at first. Her breathing slowed and deepened as the hairdresser began the rinse.

Her husband, Bob, brought stability to her life, but little else. In exchange, she tolerated his timid attempts at lovemaking. It was a bitter bargain, struck years ago. She visualized Tony striding about the boardroom, powerful and masterful. As the hairdresser towel-dried her hair, she tried to imagine Tony's hands. How would they feel to the touch? Perhaps he could melt the ice queen. A sense of anticipation began to grow within her. The appointment was for seven o'clock.

When she arrived at his office, Tony began, "You realize, Katharine, that this application may stand or fall on your expertise." His eyes were glowing.

"That's most flattering, Tony." She met his gaze. "But isn't my role really just technical support?"

"Such modesty." He smiled and then turned to the cabinet for drinks. "It does become you." With a quizzical expression, he raised a decanter. She nodded, and he poured for both of them.

"Do you want to review my testimony for tomorrow?" Katherine asked.

"Indeed! I'm sure you know your stuff. It's the manner of delivery that concerns me."

"Really?" Katharine was genuinely surprised.

They sat together on the couch, placing their drinks on the coffee table. "Aldermen are a sort of subspecies of the human race," he said. Katharine began to laugh. His glance silenced her. "But it is imperative to give them the sense of being addressed as intelligent human beings. They love their little ponds. They relish exercising their small administrative powers."

He lounged back as though making distance for a thorough visual inspection of her. "Make them feel important and powerful. That's the key."

Katharine simply nodded. His examination of her was distracting. She wondered if he would touch her. He moved forward. Now he was so close to her that she could see the pulsating of his neck. She could feel his breathing close by.

She almost touched his hand, but did not. "Should we...practice?" she asked.

"Practice? And what should we practice, Mrs. Rowe?" He shifted back from her in surprise.

"Well, you did rehearse Archbishop Staunton." She felt the flush rising from her chest and neck. Her face burned.

His eyes were glowing. He waved dismissively. "Before we get into that, Katharine, I want to learn all about you. Do you have a husband?"

At last he was making his move. She paused to frame her answer. "Yes, but we live quite separate lives." She hoped her tone was encouraging.

His hand brushed her knee. Strangely, she had never noticed his smallest finger before. She stared in fascination. On his left hand, the smallest finger was deformed. In fact, from the last knuckle, the baby finger divided into two tiny, separate digits, each with its own small pink nail. It formed a tiny, perfect claw.

Dispassionately, Tony studied Katharine's face. First he saw shock, then fascination, which was followed by revulsion. Mother always wanted him to wear a glove to hide his ugly deformity. He knew Katharine was deeply embarrassed, just like Mother. He removed his hand. Staring at her, he withdrew a soft black glove from a pocket and slowly inserted each finger, one by one, into it. "Now you will not be distracted," he said quietly.

Katharine could not look directly at him. "No...I'm sorry. I..."

She knew he was talking to her as he drew her toward the window. He smiled broadly, his arm forming a sweeping arc that encompassed the city below. "One day," he began, so softly she had to strain to hear, "all this will be changed."

"How do you mean?" She forced herself to look away from his gloved hand and into his eyes.

"This city used to be called Hoggtown. Sometimes it still is." Tony sighed deeply, then continued. "In truth, it is an emerging form." With the gloved hand tucked into a pocket, he began to pace the full length of the expanse of glass with leisurely strides. He turned back toward her, and in the murky light, said, "But the city persists in contradicting itself. So many graceful, uncluttered lines, surrounded by scabby little pockets of rot."

Now Tony stood close to her. She saw the muscles tense along his jaw, around his lips. She saw his eyes. They bore into her as he whispered, "Someone with the necessary power must guide the city through its transformation."

"But doesn't the vitality of a city come from the people?" Katharine began. In the last fading light, she saw the flecks of amber fire in the irises of his eyes. She saw the pupils narrow and harden. She regretted contradicting him.

"You are mistaken, Mrs. Rowe. The greatness of the city creates the vitality." His tone was low and threatening, forbidding further comment. With a smile, he continued, "No one will stand in the way of the transformation." He beckoned her to join him at the window, and slid his arm about her shoulder. She leaned ever so slightly into his embrace.

"I want to show you something, Katharine." Quickly, he retrieved a leather case from his desk and returned to her side. "You can see this every night around this time."

From the case, he withdrew a black pair of binoculars. "Look!" He thrust them into her hands. "See, across from us, in the Old City Hall?"

Katharine saw that he had removed the glove. She raised the glasses. The old Victorian-style building possessed cavernous arched windows at least eight feet tall, each broad enough to permit half a dozen people to stand shoulder-to-shoulder across it. Most of the windows were darkened, but in the fading light, rows of pigeons could be seen on the ledges, puffing their feathers and squatting down for the night.

"You're wanting me to look at the pigeons?" She laughed.

"No, just raise the glasses and look in the window." His voice was light and playful.

"Ah! Spying, are we?" Laughing once again, she leaned back into him. Two wobbling tunnels of light popped into view. She lowered the glasses and focused them.

The window directly across and one floor down was lit with pale yellow light. It was a sparsely furnished office, with government-issue filing cabinets and two desks.

There was a wooden swivel chair at each desk. She tried the glasses again, but could only focus on the dark, curved forms of the pigeons on the outer ledge.

"There they are now," Tony whispered close by her ear. He tipped her glasses upward. She saw two people standing together at the window. Her hand was unsteady at first as the figures jostled before her eyes.

A man stood directly behind a woman. *Amazing, the detail you can see,* Katharine thought. A blonde woman, her hair pinned up in an old-fashioned style, was wearing a plain white blouse and a dark skirt. The man was much taller and larger than the woman. The top of her head touched his breastbone. Her face bore no expression. He was broad-faced and almost bald.

"Now watch what they do," said Tony.

The bald man reached over the woman's shoulder and roughly pushed his hand into her blouse, while his other hand undid the buttons. Katharine felt McKeown's breath, short and sharp on her neck. She was transfixed by the boredom on the woman's face. The man grasped the woman's nipples, and together they swayed gently back and forth.

Tony broke the silence. "They do this every night, about now. What small, sad lives they live," he sighed. "They think they are daring, adventurous, and romantic with their shabby little groping in a window. How little they know of the exhilaration of real danger."

Katharine was alarmed at the sudden rise and fall of Tony's chest. She turned back to the window and raised the glasses once more.

Dark forms filled the tunnels of light in the binoculars. A black streak sliced sharply through her line of vision. Lurching backward, she let the glasses fall. Swooping down from somewhere above was a huge and menacing bird, black against the sky.

Tony swiftly closed in on the window, grasping her arm so tightly that she cried out. He grabbed the binoculars and peered across to the ledge. "My God! It's a hawk!" he breathed.

Together they watched as the huge black bird rose swiftly into the open sky, with a pigeon clutched in its talons. Katharine glanced backward and into Tony's face. So completely absorbed was he in the swift and powerful flight of the hawk that he glowed with unguarded admiration. This time, she scarcely noticed when his naked claw finger traced along her collarbone.

In unison, they turned from the window. Tony approached his desk. "You know, Mrs. Rowe…" He paused and reached into a drawer.

Katharine felt his eyes, hard as stone, boring through her. "Yes?"

"I have a confession to make." His voice was flat.

"Really, Mr. McKeown?" Wondering what secret desire he was about to confess, she crossed the room to join him.

He snapped on the desk lamp, "I must confess to an incurably sweet tooth." He held out a bowl of hard candies. "Care for a Butterscotch Bit?"

Startled, Katharine laughed and shook her head. Smiling, he popped a candy into his mouth. He motioned her to a chair. "Now, Mrs. Rowe, shall we get down to business?"

For two hours, they reviewed the evidence and the manner of presentation. At the end, Tony asked, "Shall I walk you to your car?"

Briefly, Katharine debated with herself. Should she risk exposing her vulnerability to him, or should she present a strong and confident front? She decided upon the latter. "No, don't worry. I'll be fine."

His eyes lowered in hesitation. "It's just that there's a killer out there. The mad artist, committing horrific acts." He shuddered as his voice trailed off. "Are you sure you'll be safe?"

"Yes, I'm sure," she said with a smile, and left.

The lawyer settled at his desk and turned to the organization of his notes of their interview.

CHAPTER 12

▼

The Florist could not resist. Silently, he moved down the stairwell to the parking garage. He had to study Mrs. Rowe as much as possible. A photograph rarely captured the essence of a being.

The light between the rows of cars was dim. He could, without fear of detection, observe her from a distance as she hunted for her car.

There she was near the red-lit exit sign, pausing to search her purse for her keys. Foolish woman! Her keys should be in her hand. Now she was at her BMW.

Hidden in the shadows behind a concrete post, he sighed deeply. As she opened her car, her dark hair fell back, exposing her long and elegant neck. Such beautiful skin!

Memorizing the image, he turned away and swiftly mounted the stairs to the City Hall Square. If she were not more careful, he might have to follow her regularly, to save her for himself.

CHAPTER 13

▼

The next morning, Katharine's brother, Gerry, slipped up the back stairs of his dental clinic with a cup of black coffee. Struggling with his briefcase through the heavy fire door, he sloshed the scalding coffee on his hand and jacket.

Making vague excuses to his staff, he closeted himself in his office in order to make his lists. Gerry was good at making lists—all kinds of lists. He made lists of bills to pay, lists of problem patients, and lists of various coping strategies and of how to get from one hour to the next. At the end of his list-making, he would lapse into exhaustion and stare at the squiggles on the scraps of paper without comprehension. He needed an index of his lists.

Gerry was under a lot of pressure. Sometimes he couldn't remember things. He was often terrified that he might be blacking out.

He could not bear to look at the financial statements for the clinic. One glance at his bookkeeper's worried face was more powerful than any computer-generated graph. One word from the dreary accountant told him more than he ever wished to know about the bottom line.

"Am I insolvent?" Gerry recently asked his accountant, who looked uncomfortable and hastily prepared the check for his fees.

At first, Gerry loved his gleaming dental clinic, choosing to work long hours into the evening. Slowly, he would move from one examining room to another, each equipped with at least one hundred thousand dollars worth of equipment and fixtures—nothing but the best for Dr. Gerald Deighton. At first, his gentle touch had brought the patients in droves. He would tell them, "If it hurts, just take this mask and breathe deeply through your nose." At the first whiff of nitrous oxide, most patients usually became agreeable.

But their satisfaction did not last. Only months after he had shouldered the sky-high rent and signed the equipment leases, the practice turned sour. Larger premises and more equipment added to his staggering debt load. His monthly costs had risen to over seventy thousand dollars—more than he had paid last year for his new Mercedes. Under pressure, Peter grew abrupt with his patients. Of course, they began to complain. The patients missed the personal touch. In such grand quarters, they felt reduced to computer entries. And. of course, the fees were too high.

Just too much financial pressure, he thought. It might be starting to make him crazy. He shuddered. Sometimes he forgot really important things, like where he had been or what he had been doing. Maybe he should see a doctor—get something to reduce the stress.

Gerry's telephone rang. "Harold Jenkins on line one. Says it's urgent, Dr. Deighton."

"Who in Christ is he?" He snatched up the phone. "Yes, Mr. Jenkins?"

Although surprised at the abrupt tone, Harry strove for the right note of sympathy. "Dr. Deighton? I'm your aunt's solicitor. Have the police been in touch with you?"

"What?" Gerry sounded as if he were being strangled. "The police?"

"I have unfortunate news." Harry paused to clear his throat. "Your aunt Marjorie passed away yesterday afternoon."

Gerry choked. Again the coffee spilled. "No! What happened?"

"I found her at home. The coroner thinks she died peacefully in her sleep."

"Coroner?"

"Yes. I called the police. It *is* customary when someone is found dead."

There was such a long pause that Harry thought they might have been disconnected.

"Oh, God! I'm sorry, Mr. Jenkins. It's just hitting me now. I haven't seen Marjorie since her birthday party two weeks ago, and now she's gone."

"I'm terribly sorry, Gerry," said Harry carefully. "But I'm obligated to notify all the next of kin. Apparently, the coroner hasn't decided whether there will be an autopsy."

"An autopsy? Why?" Gerry demanded.

"It looked like a natural and peaceful passing, but they may perform one anyway. Just to be sure."

"Yes, of course." Gerry stopped, and then hurried on, "As I said, I haven't seen her for some time. Yesterday I was at the clinic until after six." *Shit! Why did I say that?* He chewed his lip. He was getting mixed up.

In surprise, Harry frowned and reached for his pen. He had called Gerry's office yesterday at five, and he had been told that Gerry had left at noon and had not returned. What a strange conversation. Could it be the simple guilt of a neglectful nephew? Harry made a note and finished the conversation with a mention of the funeral arrangements. Poor Marjorie. Such strange reactions to the news of her death.

"By the way, do you know the name of Marjorie's housekeeper, or her phone number?"

"Why?" Gerry demanded.

Taken aback, Harry continued mildly, "I understood she was coming back to Marjorie's in the evening. I left my number, and I haven't heard from her."

"I know *nothing* about her."

"Right. Thanks anyway." Surprised, Harry said good-bye.

When Gerry put down the phone, he couldn't stop his hand from shaking. *Fuck! Why did I say I hadn't seen her?*

But then, after some moments, he smiled. Undoubtedly, Marjorie had left him a third of the estate. At least for now, his money problems were solved. *Auntie, your timing is perfect.*

Yesterday, he had left the clinic on his lunch break, arriving at Marjorie's within fifteen minutes. He had found her seated alone at the far end of the dining room table. Rosie was serving her lunch.

"What a pleasant surprise, Gerry." Marjorie began graciously. "Have you had lunch?"

Gerry nodded.

"Some coffee, then?"

Gerry shook his head, but remained silent. He did not know where to begin.

"You've come for some purpose?" Marjorie prompted. Gerry looked at her blankly. Although he had rehearsed his pitch in the car, he was unable to find the words.

"Is it about Donnie? Your son, I fear, is a very troubled youngster."

"No. Not Donnie." Awkwardly, he pulled up a chair. She was not making it easy. Soon, she would be discussing Donnie, ad nauseam, if he didn't come to the point. "No. It's about the clinic." He rubbed his hands nervously.

"It's money, then?" Looking disappointed, Marjorie set down her cup.

"Yes. I'm experiencing some temporary cash flow problems. I'm sure you've helped Katie before."

"No, Gerry. I haven't. Katharine would never ask for money." Marjorie said coldly.

Gerry's shoulders slumped. His hands twisted underneath the tablecloth. After several silent moments, Gerry said bitterly, "Oh, of course not. My mistake, Auntie. Katie's perfect. She'd never ask for money."

"How much do you need?"

Gerry looked up hopefully at his aunt. "About two hundred," he said softly.

"*Thousand?*"

"Yes. As an advance against any estate interest I might have."

Carefully, Marjorie dabbed her lips with her napkin. She gazed at her nephew levelly. "I don't have that kind of money, Gerry. How did you get into this mess?"

Anger flared in him. The old bitch was sitting on a pile of cash and she was turning him down flat. He struggled for control. "It's not a mess. It's a cash flow problem! All businesses experience that occasionally."

"You needn't get angry with me, Gerry. I can let you have a smaller amount— say twenty thousand, right away. And yes, it would come out of your share of my estate."

Twenty thousand, thought Gerry. Twenty thousand wasn't even a Band-Aid. Gerry stood up so violently that his chair nearly toppled over. "Never mind, Auntie. So sorry to disappoint you by asking. I'll go now."

"Gerry?" said Marjorie.

He turned in the doorway. "Yes?"

"Don't forget the offer of twenty is still open." She paused. "And we really should talk about Donnie soon." Gerry nodded curtly and, brushing past Rosie, let himself out.

Donnie was trouble. Psychiatrists, special tutors, and therapists all cost ridiculous sums. What the kid needed was a good kick in the ass. He and his wife, Beth. had argued back and forth.

"Setting fires in the ravine is not normal behavior for a fifteen-year-old. Fuck, it's not normal behavior for any age," Gerry had raged.

"Dr. Hannah says he's dealing with his pent-up aggression," Beth insisted.

"He's damn well going to feel some of my aggression soon."

"Dr. Hannah says it's healthy." Beth stood in the doorway, hands on her hips. "Go ahead, Gerry. Destroy all the progress that's been made. You think you can solve all problems by hitting people. Dr. Hannah says we have to be patient."

Gerry's lips twisted with bitterness. "Right! Be patient and keep paying through the nose." He slumped into a chair. "Next time, he's on his own. I'm not paying some high-priced lawyer to get him out of another scrape."

He shoved Donnie from his mind. Fussing with the list in his office, he began doodling. Moments later, he stared at the page, now covered with a disgusting profusion of wildflowers and thorns. He examined his handiwork in bleak amazement. *What the hell? I hate flowers.*

Christ! Why didn't he tell Jenkins he had seen her yesterday? There was nothing wrong with asking for a loan. But she had turned him down and now she was dead. They must suspect something if they wanted an autopsy. Now cops and the coroner were crawling all over the place. Several times, he reached for the phone to call Jenkins back. He ought to tell him, but what could he say?

His nurse came in. "Your first patient has been waiting for half an hour, Dr. Deighton."

He hated the reproach in her voice. As he entered the examining room, fear clutched at the pit of his stomach. His imagination ran amok. In his nightmare last night, a patient had revealed row upon row of decaying teeth covering the entire roof of her mouth. His revulsion terrorized him.

He was losing his grip.

Only the promise of a whiff of nitrous oxide at the end of the day would see him through: so relaxing, after a tough day prying away at people's jaws. He had first started the habit when the nitrous had eased a muscle spasm in his back, after a particularly difficult root canal job.

He remembered that day with crystal clarity. After the last had patient left, he checked the outer office doors twice. Turning out all the lights except those in the furthest examining room, he carefully set up the tank and mask. What if he couldn't control the equipment? What if the cleaning staff barged in? He stretched out in the chair, holding the control in his hand. If he were discovered, what possible excuse would there be?

Gerry placed the mask over his nose. Everything would be all right. Nice and easy. He pressed the button.

Immediately, an almost imperceptible hissing began. Gerry breathed deeply and greedily, holding the gas in his lungs. He smiled, but did not laugh. He saw his body rising up, free and excruciatingly light, expanding to fill the room. Floating up through space and time, all in a soft white room, like a figure in a Marc Chagall painting. His breathing settled to a slow and rhythmic pattern. His mind began drifting back through the years.

Katie floated up from memory. *Ever since Suzannah came, Katie picked on me.* Always, sitting at the top of the stairs watching everybody else, as Mother and Aunt Marjorie took turns walking the baby behind a closed bedroom door. Gerry had felt abandoned. One day he watched her as she carefully cut the curtains until they hung in shreds.

"Whose baby is it?" she laughed, as she snipped first one curtain and then the next.

"It's Mommy's baby," Gerry insisted.

"No it's not, stupid. She never got big."

Katie's teasing, Gerry thought.

Mother made him tell on her about the shredded curtains. Gerry did not know if their father punished her, but anger raged in Katie's eyes. He tried to keep away from her, but it was no use.

Just days later, his friend Peter came over to play in the backyard. Friends were allowed either in the kitchen or down in the cellar, but the dining room and parlor were strictly out of bounds.

Peter and Gerry had been playing with their trucks in the sand pit behind the garage. A shadow loomed above them. Squinting upward, they saw Katie standing above them, with one foot on either side of the trench they had dug.

"Gerry, bring your little friend inside. You've got to see something in the front hall." Her tone made him wary, but he obeyed. Setting down his shovel, he motioned Peter to follow.

"We're not supposed to go inside, Katie. What if we're caught?"

Katie tossed her head back, laughing over her shoulder. "Don't worry, Gerry. You're in enough trouble already."

Gerry stood still on the veranda, before the open door. Looking from his sister to his friend, he said, "Me? What did I do?" He fought to keep the whine from his voice. They slipped through the kitchen.

Before them lay the tiled foyer. Gerry blinked as his eyes adjusted to the cool, dim light. A thousand shattered pieces of Mother's vase lay strewn across the tile floor.

"I didn't do it!" he stammered, afraid to look up at his sister.

Katie smiled wearily. "Gerry...Gerry. You know you did, running downstairs to see Peter."

"But, no...I didn't, Katie!" Gerry backed away. His voice rose in a childish wail. He knew it was no use. Shaking his head, he started to cry, "No Katie, don't say I did. You know I didn't."

"Shut up, you little sniveler! Do you want the whole house to hear you?" Peter looked from Gerry to Katie, and then wiped the sand from his face.

"Be quiet and come into the dining room," his sister commanded.

"But Katie, we're not allowed in there," Gerry protested as he trooped in after her with Peter. Carefully, she closed both sets of French doors. The dining room was dark and still in the mid-afternoon. A few rays of sunlight spilled onto the burnished dining room table, punctuating the gloom. Gerry always tried to hold his breath in this room.

Katie pulled out one of the sideboard chairs. "Peter," she asked gently, "what do you think that is?" Peter peered in the gloom and then shrugged, wiping his hand on his pants. On the floor between the buffet and the sideboard stood a leather-tooled canister.

"I don't know," Peter began uncertainly, taking a step backward. "Looks like some kind of fancy garbage can."

Katie smiled indulgently. "Yes," she said slowly, "sort of." She reached for Peter's hand and drew him closer. "And what do you think is in it, Peter?"

"A stick?" Peter looked up furtively at Katie, then down at his shoes.

"Very good, Peter! But it's a special stick. It's a cane!" She released Peter's hand and withdrew the cane. Looking only at Gerry, she continued, "It's for punishing children, but only when they're really bad." Katie's arm rose up and brought the cane down hard on the plush chair seat with a crack. Dust flew up. Peter lurched backward.

Katie was smiling. "Just like in the church, Gerry."

All of them became aware of a puddle forming, and then spreading at an alarming rate, on the hardwood floor around Gerry's sneakers.

Uncontrolled panic drove Gerry sobbing through the kitchen and out to the garden. Stumbling across the lawn, he reeled around the back of the garage and flung himself onto the sand pit. Deep shame flooded through his body. His wet pants were growing cold and prickly.

He stopped crying. Katie was above him, humming. "Look at me, Gerry," she said in her singsong voice.

"Where's Peter?" Gerry choked. If he kept crying, she'd only get madder.

"Gone home, of course."

"Did you tell him about the church, Katie?"

"Your secret's still safe. I collect and keep secrets, Gerry. I'm not a baby like you. I don't blab!" Gerry knew she was really mad. "I saved you that time and just maybe, I'll save you this time."

Gerry lay on his back, shielding his eyes against the late afternoon sun. Her shadow loomed above him. Quickly, she dropped to her knees. Pinning his shoulders down, she whispered fiercely, "You have to promise you'll never tell on me again. You're just a stupid little baby, so I'm going to forgive you—this time.

But from now on, you have to do exactly what I say!" She sat on him hard, squeezing out his breath. "Understand?"

"Yes, Katie, I understand," he had whined. "Please let me go!"

Assured of her victory, Katie smiled down on him indulgently. "I'm going to save you this time, Gerry. I'll tell them the stupid cat did it." Irrationally, a wave of relief swept over Gerry. Katherine reveled in the power. At eleven, she was master of the game, and Gerry was in her thrall.

Stretched out in the dental chair, Gerry released the button and the flow of nitrous oxide gas stopped. Nausea welled up from the pit of his stomach. The sense of lightness, which had expanded to the furthest extremities of his body, was now replaced with a crushing soddenness. The tingling in his extremities receded as he sat up. Katie never left him.

CHAPTER 14

▼

Suzannah Deighton felt swallowed up by sleep. On the day after Marjorie's death, she awoke, near noon, to a dull ache at the base of her skull. She fumbled for the bottle of pills at her bedside. It would take at least three of them to clear her head today.

Opening one eye, she desperately hoped to be in a different place and time. It was a game she had played as a small child. Katharine had always laughed at her. "Baby games," she had called them. "Close your eyes tight. Hide way under the covers." Imitating her childish whine, Katharine had taunted her: "Make it go away." Katharine was so smart, and she always let you know it.

Suzannah stared at the lipstick-stained glass of water next to her. She tried to concentrate. What Marjorie had asked was too hard for her to do. It wasn't fair, although Frank said it was no big deal. Struggling upward on the pillow, she tried to remember his words.

"You want to make Auntie suffer? Go ahead. But what about all she's done for you? She can decide when she wants to go."

Frank always made everything sound so easy and sensible.

She rose to the mirror and ran a brush through her long blonde hair. *Pretty, once upon a time,* she thought, as she struggled with the tangles.

Lighting a cigarette, she singed her fingers with the smoldering match. Thank God Frank had been too drunk for sex last night. Trying to climb onto her, he had simply rolled over with a groan. She toyed with the idea of going without the pills. Red for ups and yellow for downs.

Without thinking, Frank used up money like breathing air. The biggest fiasco was her dress boutique right on Yorkville Avenue, one of the highest-rent districts in Toronto. Ever since it failed, Suzannah could not plan for the day. If she stayed in bed, at least she might not sink further into debt.

"Think big, baby. Think big." Frank grinned.

At first, she thrived on his support. The store seemed to be her very first success in life.

Frank set up her books and managed the money. He was so sweet. He talked Harry Jenkins and that trust officer, McCrea, into advancing one hundred thousand on her trust fund for start-up expenses.

Only recently had the accountant said, in baleful tones, "The bank deposits do not tally with the cash-register receipts." Peering suspiciously over the rims of his glasses, he continued, "Ms Deighton, there's at least a seventy-five-thousand-dollar discrepancy. A lot of money has not been deposited. A tax auditor would have a field day."

That's why Grandpa's trust shrank so much! Frank was siphoning off the money. After a whole week, she still didn't have the guts to confront him.

The telephone rang.

"Hello?" she croaked, pushing a limp strand of hair from her face.

"Miss Deighton? Harold Jenkins here."

Suzannah shook her head to clear the fog. "Yes?"

Suzannah had always reminded Harry of a faded flower child. He hated to break bad news to someone who appeared always on the verge of silent hysteria.

"I'm terribly sorry to call with bad news, Suzannah." He softened his tone. "But your Aunt Marjorie passed away yesterday afternoon."

At first, Harry heard only silence, and then a low groan. "No...please say it isn't true." Suzannah began rocking back and forth on the kitchen stool.

"I'm afraid so, Suzannah. I arrived at her house for an appointment and found her." He hastened to add, "It appeared she had a very peaceful passing."

"How did it happen?"

"Apparently, she just passed away in her sleep. I found her lying on her bed. The police and the coroner came."

Alarm rose in Suzannah's voice. "Police? Coroner?"

"It's customary, Suzannah, to call them when someone's death is unexplained." He hesitated to continue. "They may do an autopsy—"

"Autopsy?" she gasped. "Was she murdered?"

"Oh, no! But when there is no obvious reason for the death—"

"Thank God!"

"Sorry?"

"There wasn't a note?"

"A note? No."

"Good," she said quietly.

"Should we have looked for one?"

"No, of course not." Suzannah's voice returned to a normal tone. "Mr. Jenkins?" She hesitated. "There weren't any bottles of pills lying around?"

"No." Harry was becoming alarmed at the strange line of inquiry. Did Suzannah think her aunt had committed suicide?

"Good. I was worried she might have overdosed. She was taking so many medications and was quite depressed this past year. I was worried that her depression had come back."

"You're concerned about an accidental overdose, not suicide, right?"

"Yes, of course. Marjorie was far too strong to think of suicide. I mean, she seemed quite happy lately. At least until her birthday party..." Suzannah's voice trailed off uncertainly.

Harry picked up his pen and began writing a note. "Gerry mentioned a birthday party."

Suzannah sighed deeply. "Yes, Gerry and Katharine were very unpleasant that night."

"Meaning?"

"Well, they were just their usual cold, unfeeling selves." Suzannah felt her anger mount. "I mean, Gerry's just waiting for the cash. I suppose he'll be happy now. And Katharine never gave a damn about Auntie anyway."

"What happened at the party?" Harry asked.

In an odd singsong voice, Suzannah told Harry about the evening. He took notes as best he could.

Coincidentally, all of them had arrived on Marjorie's front porch at the same time. Staggering under a huge gift-wrapped package, Gerry had come up the walk. Beth, his wife, tripped along in high heels behind him. As usual, she was the first to speak.

"This is dreadful...I mean, really dreadful." Beth's voice was a stage whisper. "We should be taking Auntie out for dinner, not imposing like this." Glancing about for support, but finding none, she pushed Gerry toward the front door.

Frank threw out his arms, nearly knocking Gerry's gift to the ground. "I know, I know!" Frank's laugh was ugly. "And we're only coming to filch a little money from the old girl. Why not treat her to dinner, like decent folk would?"

"For God's sake, shut up, Frank!" said Katharine. "Don't be such a bloody idiot! You can be heard for blocks."

"Truth hurts, eh?" Frank leered at Katharine, but stepped back. "Ballbuster," he muttered.

Roughly, he grabbed Suzannah's arm and pushed her forward. "Listen, babe," he hissed in her ear. "No back-talk from you tonight. I got a plan, and soon you're gonna thank me." Suzannah nodded. She was so easy to keep in place, he thought.

Rosie answered the single sharp rap of the knocker. Drawing back in the hall light, she beckoned them inward with a slow and distant smile. Her calm dignity made their nervous and boisterous chatter sound foolish. In the foyer, the women shrugged out of their coats and the men tramped in behind them. They cleared their throats, tuning up for an evening of loud conversation, necessitated by Marjorie's deteriorating hearing. Henry, the houseman, silently assisted with the coats. Because no one wanted to enter the parlor first, they all hung back, jockeying for last place.

No one saw Marjorie place a record on the old gramophone near the bookcase. Crammed into the foyer, all six of them startled in unison when the deep, resonant tones of "Pomp and Circumstance'" shook the house and made the chandelier sway.

Oblivious to their presence, Marjorie Deighton paraded the length of the parlor, waving a baton to conduct an invisible orchestra. Carried by the passion of the music, she swept her arms upward in a crescendo of bliss.

Suzannah beamed. Never had she seen her composed aunt so engaged with life and so vulnerable. Marjorie was breaking free, Suzannah thought, as a momentary pang of envy flashed through her. Any joy she derived from Marjorie's freedom was almost instantly extinguished by the identically pursed lips of her brother and sister. In their growing embarrassment, Katharine and Gerry looked to Rosie, as if for guidance. Rosie remained impassive.

On the upswing of the baton, Marjorie pivoted to face the unseen audience for the final orchestral crescendo. With her face suffused with joy and abandonment, her features were those of an unfettered child.

Suddenly conscious of her audience, she stiffened in mid-air. The deep pleasure on her face crinkled into horror. Suzannah's heart constricted. Marjorie rushed to the gramophone and yanked the needle from the record. The house was filled with a deathly screech, as if some wild and free animal had been mortally wounded.

Marjorie's shoulders shook and her hands trembled as she stared at the still spinning record. Suddenly, she burst into tears. Sniffling like a small child, she collapsed into a nearby chair and reached for a Kleenex in her pocket.

"You must think I'm just a foolish old woman who has taken leave of her senses and ought to be put away," she choked. "But none of you can imagine what it's like to be eighty-five." Marjorie looked searchingly at her guests hovering in the doorway, then continued uncertainly, "You long for life and fun, but you're so terribly weary."

She continued to stare at her hands, folded in her lap. "I have these dreams," she murmured. "I hear beautiful concert music in the distance beyond grand brass doors. I want, with all my heart, to run to it." She sighed heavily. "But I cannot." Moments later, she looked up, and with a brave smile said, "And so you see, I am stuck here."

With brisk and efficient movements, Katharine poured a glass of water at the sideboard and held it out to Marjorie. "Please, Aunt Marjorie, pull yourself together and drink this."

Smiling, Suzannah flew to her aunt, who remained oblivious to Katharine's outstretched glass of water. Kneeling before her, she clasped Marjorie's trembling hands and said, "Auntie, I just adore that piece! It's so stirring, isn't it?" Slowly, Marjorie raised her eyes to meet Suzannah's.

"When I was a young girl, my father used to take me to the symphony," Marjorie began, her voice faraway in recollection. "In those days, the women dressed in beautiful gowns, and the men in tuxedos, to go to the concert." Marjorie waved dismissively. "Nowadays, Toronto has no style."

With gleaming eyes, she continued, "Once, when the conductor finished that very piece, everyone in Massey Hall gave him a standing ovation. Such freedom and passion in the hall!" Her face was now wreathed in smiles. "The conductor was a very handsome man, and for weeks, the music went round in my head and I dreamt of him every night. What was his name?"

"It was Elgar…Edward Elgar!" Suzannah laughed, caught up in the moment.

"No, my dear," Marjorie shook her head sadly, "that was the composer's name."

"Aunt Marjorie?" Katharine said wistfully, "I understand completely your wanting to break free. You lived in a very repressive time, especially for women."

Marjorie Deighton looked sharply up at her. She said, "Yes, I did. But I wonder just how different it is today."

Katharine nodded slowly. "True enough. Women can't rise to the top without a battle."

Marjorie frowned and said, "It's more a matter of being allowed to be yourself." Then she appeared to draw inward, collecting scattered childhood memories. The reserved Marjorie Deighton reappeared to celebrate her eighty-fifth birthday. Suzannah saw her face shrink with the ebbing of life and pleasure. Katharine was relieved.

Beth spoke first. "Auntie, we've brought you a birthday gift."

Marjorie Deighton smiled with her usual reserved graciousness and nodded to Rosie to take the huge parcel.

Dinner was an awkward affair. Beth chattered incessantly, and Frank regaled the table with his exploits in the real estate market. Twice Suzannah excused herself and hid in the washroom. Staring at the prettily flowered wallpaper, she asked herself what Frank had done with her money. She still could not confront him.

After Henry, the houseman, removed the dessert plates, coffee was served in the parlor. Marjorie spoke "There may not be many more occasions when we are all together."

The room fell silent.

"I haven't been well for some time now." Hesitating, Marjorie sipped her coffee, then set the cup down carefully. "I want you all to know, that I have made two wills." She surveyed the puzzled expressions on her guests' faces. "One disposes of my property. It is safe with my solicitor, Mr. Jenkins, and the other is here." Marjorie reached for the sideboard and took an envelope from the drawer.

"Aunt Marjorie," broke in Katharine, "I thought you could have just one will."

"Well, this is a different kind of will. It's called a living will," Marjorie spoke stiffly.

"A living will? And what is that?" asked Katharine, struggling to attain a note of neutrality.

"A living will," Marjorie continued, "is one that sets out the manner in which I wish to depart this world. I want to take whatever precautions I can to minimize suffering and preserve dignity. When the time comes, I just want everyone to let me go as peacefully as possible. And so I have signed this document, which is a clear expression of my wishes in the matter." Marjorie sighed and sat back in her chair, closing her eyes, as though wearied by the effort of talking. Her guests nodded simultaneously.

Katharine reached out her hand for the envelope, "May we read it?"

Marjorie slowly lowered her glasses and peered at her niece.

"I want you, Suzannah, and Gerry to read it together. But not tonight." She smiled weakly. "After all, this is a birthday party." Then she handed the envelope to Suzannah.

Henry poured another round of coffee and took orders for liqueurs. Frank sat back, puffing on his cigar. Katharine drank down her liqueur in silence, while Gerry fussed with a stack of magazines.

At last, Marjorie said, "And now, my dears, I'm sure it's late, and I know what busy schedules you all have." She turned to Suzannah as everyone began to rise. "Suzannah, my pet, help me upstairs, would you? Your birthday is next, and I have something for you. You don't mind waiting, do you Frank?"

Everyone set down their cups and glasses as Marjorie stood unsteadily. "Now, all the rest of you, it's been lovely of you to come, but I know you want to get on your way."

With Henry's deft handling of doors and coats, they quickly found themselves at the front door, saying hasty good-byes.

Harry listened to Suzannah's story, vividly picturing Marjorie strutting the length of her parlor. Energy must have surged through her with each crescendo of the march. No wonder she wanted to run toward the music, and away from the weariness of her life. He hoped she got exactly what she wanted.

Distracted, he finally said, "So you think Katharine and Gerry are only after Marjorie's money?"

"No, Mr. Jenkins. Only Gerry. But Katharine couldn't care less about Auntie. She never did a thing for her."

"Suzannah," Harry began carefully, "would you know how to reach Marjorie's housekeeper, Rosie?"

"I have her number somewhere," she said vaguely. "I'd have to look and call you back."

"If you would, please," Harry concluded.

She hung up the phone abruptly and sat motionless on the kitchen stool. She bit into her knuckle and whispered, "God damn you, Frank!" She knew it was a mistake to tell him about the pills. She could not forget Marjorie's plea.

After speaking with both Gerry and Suzannah, Harry called the police.

"Will there be an autopsy, Sergeant Welkom?" he asked. "I'd like to know when to make the funeral arrangements."

Welkom sounded bored. "No. The coroner's office isn't requiring one. The body's ready for pickup by your funeral parlor."

Damn, he thought. Now he would never know for sure. He supposed the next of kin could demand an autopsy, but that was unlikely. He called the Tudbury Funeral Home.

Marjorie had organized every detail, from the hymns to the style of the mahogany casket. Some clients left their world in a mess when they died. She wanted a neat and tidy exodus. Perhaps she dreaded burdening her family.

Harry smiled. Some clients, driven by fear of exposing dark secrets, were meticulous in their planning of funerals and estates. Some simply loved control, dead or alive. In wills, the dead hand could rise from the grave, strangling countless generations with endless trusts—power from the beyond.

For Harry, the world of siblings was remote. His mind wandered off to his sister, Anna. She had been absent from his memory for years, existing only in a world long lost to him.

The summer when Anna died had been the worst year of Harry's life. It was near the end of her eighth-grade school year, when they had the traditional class picnic at Tolmey's Beach, just north of the city.

Mother had taken Anna on the stifling, hot bus downtown to Eaton's and Simpson's department stores to find a bathing suit. Anna had chosen a bright red suit with white piping on the edges and a flared skirt. That night, full of life, she had posed in front of the mirror, alternately smiling and frowning as she examined her thirteen-year-old body in the new bathing suit.

At the school picnic, six eighth-grade students contracted the polio virus. Three children were permanently confined to wheelchairs. Another two had to rely upon that hideous monster, the iron lung. Only one had died: Anna. The last time he saw her, she was surrounded by ugly, wheezing machines. Dying at the age of thirteen, Anna could do no wrong.

Anna and he used to play outside, waiting for Dad to get home from work. He remembered racing up the driveway and flinging himself into his father's arms. "Do an under-doggie, Daddy! Please!" Laughing, Stanley would lift his son up high and swing him down fast, landing him softly on the grass. As Harry sat in his office, the starchy smell of Dad's collar and the damp feel of his shirt on his back came back with piercing immediacy.

Ignoring convention, Dad said and did as he pleased. In the school where he taught downtown, the children were very poor. Sometimes he would invite a child and his parents for dinner at the house. Invariably, these people were pinched, lean, and wary when they arrived. By the end of the evening, they left the house with smiles of gratitude.

When Anna died, an enormous emptiness filled the house. His parents fell silent, as if the space between them had become an ocean. He worked harder at school than he ever imagined possible. His straight-A report card only drew wan smiles from his parents. Their love and life died with Anna.

Harry had settled many estate cases in which brother and sister battled to the death. Twenty-page affidavits would be filed in court, each one setting out the deficiencies of the other in blood-thirsty detail. Each one screamed, in tantrums of jealousy, "I am the better child." Strange words from the mouth of a forty-year-old!

After Harry's call, Suzannah was unable to sit still. She tried to tidy the kitchen, but it was no use. Frank had left too much of a mess. She sat on a kitchen stool and gazed out into the garden.

She remembered every detail. Upstairs, after the party at Marjorie's, Suzannah had drawn up a chair at her bedside.

"Suzannah, come closer, pet," Marjorie had said from her bed. "Is the door shut?" Without waiting for an answer, Marjorie continued in a low and rapid voice, sounding as if she were afraid time would prevent her from finishing. "You are the only one I trust."

Suzannah drew nearer and smoothed her cover.

"You and I are one of a kind. I have a far closer bond with you, my sweet, than the others." She grasped Suzannah by the wrist. "So you see, you're stuck with seeing me through to the end."

"Please, Auntie, it's not a matter of being stuck. I'll do anything I can. What do you want me to do?"

Marjorie's eyelids fluttered open. "That living will…" She pointed to the envelope lying on the bedcover. "It's really just rubbish! No one can be held to it."

She turned her face away on the pillow. Suzannah strained to hear her. "Suzannah, I'm so afraid. No…not of being dead, but of dying. Do you understand what I mean?"

Her questioning eyes flew open and she looked keenly at her niece. "The living will only says I'm not to be kept waiting, propped up by this and that machine. Just let me go."

Marjorie was silent for so long that Suzannah's fear began to grow. Finally, she spoke again. "If I am taken ill here, I want you to help!" Struggling to sit up, she squeezed Suzannah's hand. "The living will isn't enough. If the pain from the cancer becomes unbearable—"

"You have cancer?" Suzannah clasped her hand over her mouth in shock. Through tears, she said, "I'm *so* sorry, Auntie. I didn't know."

Marjorie waved dismissively. "And even if I can't speak sense, I know you'll understand. I want you to do this for me." Weakly, she motioned to the night table. "The pills are in this drawer. Open it."

Suzannah gasped. There were at least twenty bottles of medication lined up, with color-coded labels.

"You see, darling, I've been building my own little collection right here. All you need to do is follow the color chart and give them to me. This is my own way out, but don't worry: if I am able, I'll do it myself."

Weary with exhaustion, Marjorie slumped back on the pillow. Her voice was so low and muffled, that Suzannah could scarcely hear her.

"I told you about the terrible dreams, Suzannah." Tears filled her eyes. "I'm in a long, dark, narrow hallway. I'm in a wheelchair and can't sit up properly. So much crying and moaning, too." She shook her head helplessly. "Others are trapped with me. When I look down at my hands, I see the nails are long and yellow."

Marjorie's breathing became shallow and rapid. Her hand fluttered up in the air. In a soft but insistent voice, she continued, "Then suddenly I see the nails are really tubes and needles jabbing into my hands and arms."

Eyes closed, Marjorie began to gasp. Suzannah rose to seek help, but her aunt grasped her wrist with surprising strength. When her eyes flew open again, Suzannah saw the horror reflected in them.

"I wake up. I'm suffocating. I want to run down the hall toward the music in the distance beyond beautiful golden doors." Marjorie's eyes glistened. "But I can't, because I'm caught in the tubes."

Suzannah sat transfixed by the terrible vision her aunt painted.

"Promise me! Promise me you'll do it for me, if I can't." A single tear rolled down her cheek.

Cold seeped into the pit of Suzannah's stomach. The thought of administering an overdose to Marjorie was horrific.

Marjorie's glare was imperious, demanding an immediate answer. Suzannah glanced about the room frantically. She took the hand of the small, frail, yet powerful woman.

"But Auntie!" Suzannah felt as though someone else were speaking her words from a great distance. "Why me? Why not Katharine?" Suddenly, she felt like a small child again."Gerry? Couldn't he…?" Her voice trailed off as Marjorie's expression clouded over in disappointment.

"Katharine!" Marjorie jerked her head away on the pillow. "What does she know of suffering? She'd give the order to the doctor by phone, between meetings, without missing a beat. Besides," she continued wryly, "she admires me for my strength. She cannot stand weakness."

Suzannah flinched at her aunt's grating words. "And Gerry!" Marjorie continued with a sigh. "What does he know about anything?"

With a knowing glance at her niece, she said, "There's no one but you. You know what pain is and how it wears you down." Her voice dropped to a whisper. "We have a very special bond, my darling. In time, you will understand. Only you will know when I can't take anymore and just want to be let go."

She took Suzannah's hand and looked into her eyes. "Katharine is far too efficient and has had Gerry under her thumb ever since they were children. He can't think for himself, and, besides that…" Marjorie ventured a weak smile. "He has as much sensitivity as sandpaper."

Suzannah was startled by her own childish pride. *My God, I'm the favored one. And at the same time, the executioner.*

Marjorie glared at her. "Well?"

Suzannah opened the bedside drawer and ran her finger across the little plastic bottletops of pills. After a moment, she replied, "All right. I'll help you, Auntie."

"Thank you, my darling," was all Marjorie whispered.

Downstairs, Frank paced the foyer like a caged beast. Except for Henry's silent shadowing, Frank easily would have knocked an ornamental vase from a table. At last he saw Suzannah, pale in the faint light, clutching the banister. She descended the staircase.

"What took you so long?" he demanded.

Suzannah remained silent until they had left the house and entered the car.

"What'd dear Auntie want?" Frank was insistent.

At last Suzannah whimpered, "What am I going to do, Frank? She wants me to give her pills so she can die at home."

Frank was attentive immediately. "She's got pills to do it? Where?"

"In the drawer of her bedside table. There's got to be a least twenty bottles." Suzannah wiped her sniffly nose. She did not catch the eagerness in Frank's expression in the lights of the oncoming traffic.

"What did you tell her, sweetie?"

The question made Suzannah choke as she gently rocked back and forth. Frank pulled the car to the side of the road. "Listen, babe, you said you'd help her, didn't you? I mean, you can't make her suffer."

Suzannah did not understand why she trusted Frank. But when life frightened her, she always turned to him. She had no one else. When his voice became soft and concerned, she could not resist him. She let him put his arm around her while she leaned on his shoulder. "Yes, I said I'd help her."

"You did right, babe." He patted her head and swiftly jerked the car back onto the street. He turned on the radio to find some nice soothing music to get her in the mood. "Another victim murdered on the sand dunes at the Scarborough Bluffs. This is the Florist's fourth…"

"My God, Frank! They have to catch him."

His huge hands clutched the steering wheel. He'd have to settle her down to have any chance tonight. "I know, babe. It's awful." He caressed her neck and tried to sound soft and caring. His thick hand nearly choked her. She gasped and shifted away from his grasp.

"Don't worry, honey, they'll catch the bastard real soon," he said softly.

CHAPTER 15

▼

Harry left the office just before five to have drinks with his friend Stephen Barrett at the club. The Alton Club was a small stone structure located at King and Bay, the pulsing center of the financial district. Its heavy wrought-iron gate, adorned with a brass coat of arms, gave discreet protection from the curious eyes of the casual passerby. Only properly identified members and their guests were admitted.

Harry nursed ambivalence toward the club. It had always been the inner sanctum of the old moneyed crowd, and it remained one of the last bastions of class and unspoken sexism. Despite his egalitarian upbringing, Harry wrote a check every year from his business account for the exorbitant fees, and shaved a tiny amount of tax from the demands of Her Majesty.

Several years ago, Harry had taken his father for lunch in the dining room of the Alton Club. By then, Dad had become a shrunken man whose shirt collar gaped. His face was mildly contorted by a recent stroke. At the retirement home, he would not let anyone shave him, and consequently, his face was patchy with whiskers.

Why the Alton Club? Harry knew he could not impress his father. Besides, what man at his age still sought his father's approval? He could only try to make up for the lost years between them.

Dad sat in silence with his scotch, seeming to drift off into his other world. Harry reflected, with sadness, that watching senility creep over his father was like seeing lights turned off in a house one by one. Then, surprisingly, a light would snap on again and burn for a moment or an hour, until it flickered into darkness.

Their lunch was interrupted.

"Harry?" Harry lowered his menu as Jonathan Conroy approached the table. "Good to see you!" Conroy clapped him on the back. Ever since Harry had bailed him out of a professionally tight spot on a real-estate deal, he had been quite friendly. There could be no other reason. He was small potatoes next to a firm with a "Grand Corridor."

Harry rose and introduced his father.

"You must be very proud of your son, sir." Jonathan shook the old man's hand. "Were you a lawyer yourself?"

Stanley rose with only slight difficulty. "No, sir, I was a teacher." Harry was pleased: his father spoke with strength and confidence.

"Oh, that's grand! Which university?"

Stanley simply shook his head and smiled.

"Then at one of the boys' schools?"

"No, Mr. Conroy. I taught grade five at Dalton Public School downtown to forty children. I started in the Depression." Stanley paused and glanced around the paneled dining room of the Alton Club before continuing, "Those days, no one had a thing."

Harry knew the rest of the story, but could think of no way to divert his father.

"I saw little children crying each day in class because they were starving, Mr. Conroy." Stanley Jenkin's voice choked with memory. "They smelled. Some had no running water, you see. They had no warm clothes." Stanley held out his hands in a gesture of helplessness. "I could not understand why they had to suffer so, when a privileged few had so much."

The old man had begun to weep openly. Conroy was stricken with embarrassment. Harry patted his father's shoulder and eased him back into his seat. A waiter filled the water glasses. Conroy recovered. Hastily, he shook Harry's hand and bowed his way from the table.

That had happened several years ago. Today, Harry rang the bell. The Alton Club concierge peered out suspiciously. Once the door opened, the foyer brought Harry back into the last century. Massive portraits of founding members lined the paneled walls.

Since its inception in 1897, the Alton Club enshrined its world views in the minutes of the board's special and general meetings. Those weighty leather-bound tomes housed in the elegant library contained much of the club's illustrious history. At the 1939 annual meeting, it had been duly recorded that those of the Hebrew faith were to be denied membership. In 1953, after citing the Senator McCarthy hearings, they recorded serious debate about requiring new members to disavow any connection with the Communist Party. Interestingly, the issue of blacks becoming members was never even posed.

Over the ensuing quarter-century, women's rights groups had made major inroads at the club. Provided a lady had two male sponsors, she could be considered for membership. This year the club proudly proclaimed an open-door policy, although no male truly regarded a woman as a serious member.

From the foyer, Harry spotted the long, angular frame of his friend Stephen Barrett perched on a stool and silhouetted by the glow from behind the bar. As he handed his overcoat to the hall porter, Harry breathed deeply and prepared to settle in for a relaxing hour or so.

"So, how's the defender of the downtrodden?" Harry asked as they shook hands. Although Stephen practised only criminal law, he was the epitome of the sleek Bay Street corporate lawyer.

A tight-lipped grimace, which served as a smile, flashed across Stephen's face. "Not badly, thanks. How's the funeral business?" Harry chuckled. His friend persisted in referring to his estate practice in this fashion.

Friends since the early days of law school, they knew the easy repartee was always there. Surprisingly, "old school tie" Barrett had thrived in the underworld of criminal law. Stephen found that many of his future clients came from some of the city's best boarding schools, where he had been a student himself.

"Listen," Harry said, tapping his arm, "what can you tell me about money coming in from the Far East?"

"There's plenty of it. What else do you need to know?"

"Is it okay?"

Stephen laughed. "You mean *is it laundered?*"

"Yes."

"No, not yet. Canada's one of the best places in the world for that. There's hardly any restriction. Why?"

"I have a new client from Hong Kong buying up some land."

"So? That's hardly unusual. Most of the money is perfectly legitimate."

"I suppose." Harry's voice trailed off as he tried to pin down what was troubling him. "It bothers me that I'm not getting the whole picture from the client."

"Why should you, Harry? There are lots of things you're better off not knowing. In my practice, you never want to know too much."

"What's the usual procedure for money-laundering?"

"It's pretty simple. Dirty money from drugs, prostitution, porn—you name it—flows into the country from all over the world. It goes into banks, trust companies. And to lawyers and accountants, some of whom are innocent, unsuspecting dupes; others are in on the game. The money is used to buy legitimate businesses or land, so when they sell, the proceeds come out 'clean.' There's lots of methods to mask the game, but essentially, that's it." Stephen laughed. "We think we're getting tough by enacting reporting requirements of cash over ten thousand dollars. But lawyers are exempt."

Harry ordered a beer; Stephen ordered another scotch. They sat in silence for some moments, waiting for the drinks. Harry studied his friend, who had begun tearing his napkin into tiny strips.

"Something wrong?" Harry asked.

Drinks were delivered. Stephen stared at him and then shook his head. "You know, some days I think seriously about dumping this and sailing around the world."

Harry knew that Stephen could actually afford such an escapade. His tone suggested much more than wistful fantasy.

"Nobody plays by any kind of rules anymore—certainly not the lawyers. There aren't enough jails to hold all the criminals." Stephen shook his head sadly and gulped the drink in front of him. "Besides, the small-time operators aren't the real problem. It's the criminals up the line with all the money and power. Nobody ever touches them. For them, money-laundering is normal business."

Harry was attentive. Rarely did Stephen depart from his glib, acerbic attitude. Depression was unheard of for his friend.

"Sounds like you're getting a bit jaded." Harry offered, testing the mood. "Maybe you should take some time off."

Stephen did not immediately reply. After a long drink, he said, "It's just a revolving door. I've been defending the same dumb beasts for years. I started with real lowlifes, the ones who knock over convenience stores and shoot the cashier just for fun. Now I do all sorts of complicated frauds and murder conspiracies. Believe me, it's the same moronic thinking at work. Money may buy a veneer of civility, but it's the same vicious, dumb-fuck beast underneath."

"What do you think about these petal murders?" Harry asked.

"Now that's interesting, Harry. A brilliant murderer, or at least one with artistic sensibility. Rather shoots my theory down," Stephen concluded glumly.

"Why brilliant?" Harry asked.

"From what I've heard, this guy seems to agonize over his victims. 'Could that life develop into greatness, if spared?' Interesting sense of morality." Stephen grimaced. "At least that's what some psychologist on the news theorized."

"Really? I hadn't heard that. What I can't understand is how he can thinks he's creating when he's killing."

Stephen winked at him. "Don't forget, Harry: he's completely and utterly mad."

Harry shrugged. "Most of my clients are sane, I guess. They worry about whether they've paid enough tax."

"Sounding just a little bitter yourself?"

"Not really. Life's just getting a bit too predictable, although the money is better."

"Estate work's not exciting enough?"

"Maybe." Harry was suddenly weary. He thought of leaving, but then he said, "I think Laura's having an affair."

"No!"

"She's seeing someone at work. Not coming home that much." Harry never felt so tired.

Stephen was quiet for a moment. "That's tough, Harry. What are you going to do?"

"Probably try to keep going as is, at least for now. If I confront her, I have to deal with the consequences. I'm not ready for that."

"Time for one more?" Stephen was signaling to the bartender. Harry nodded. Suddenly, he didn't feel like talking anymore. It was a lousy mess—so bad he hadn't gotten around to calling Natasha yet, whose soft smile had caught him at the funeral, and whose intimacy drew him in. With Laura likely in the arms of Dr. Stover, why not?

Harry lit a cigarette and returned to his beer. In the mirror, he caught a dark reflection of a small, familiar figure gliding between the tables. To Harry, he certainly looked like Albert Chin. He sat down with someone Harry did not recognize, perhaps one of the members of the Hong Kong conglomerate.

Harry grasped Stephen's arm. "Look in the mirror," he whispered. "That's my new client over there."

"What's his name?"

"Albert Chin."

Harry was now turned three-quarters around on the stool to watch. Their end of the bar could not be seen from the lounge. Chin was hunched over the table talking rapidly and punctuating his words with sharp jabs of his finger. Their voices rose, but Harry could make out no words. The other man raised his hand, as if to calm Chin. From his briefcase, he withdrew a thick manila envelope. He slid the package across the table to him.

Albert Chin dropped the envelope into his briefcase as the waiter appeared with drinks. He threw his napkin down and shoved back his chair. With briefcase in hand, he marched angrily off toward the washroom.

Questions raced through Harry's mind. A payoff? What was going on? He slid off the bar stool and strode down the hallway in pursuit, leaving Stephen staring after him. He slowed his pace, then halted outside the washrooms.

Following men into washrooms was a bit ridiculous, but some instinct drove him onward. Taking a deep breath and straightening his tie, he opened the door and sauntered in. The coast was clear. Only one of the three cubicles, on the far wall, was occupied. Harry entered the one next to Chin.

Between the metal divider and the white-tiled wall of the stall was a space of about two inches. He saw the back of Chin's head through the crack. Harry watched him count out—what, thousands? hundreds of thousands?—of dollars from the envelope.

Was Chin getting some kind of payoff? For what? With just a twinge of guilt, he thought of the two hundred thousand he had tucked into the bank yesterday, and, of course, the trip to the Bahamas, courtesy of Mr. Chin and his conglomerate.

The door to the washroom opened.

"Albert?" The voice was low and angry.

Chin flushed the toilet and exited the cubicle.

Harry had no idea what his client and the other man said in Chinese, but he could not miss the underlying tones of angry insistence from both of them.

After they left, Harry headed back to the bar. and sat heavily on the stool beside Stephen.

Chin and his companion had left.

"That is *really* weird. Chin's just been paid off for something. He was sitting in the can, counting a huge wad of money."

Stephen shrugged. "Money flows in mysterious ways, Harry. Best not to ask too many questions."

It was after seven when Harry left Stephen. Moving slowly up Bay Street toward the car park, he tried to approach the Chin puzzle logically. Of course, nothing prevented his client from dealing with anyone he wished. But the cash had to be a payoff for something. No legitimate deposit or down payment would ever be made that way. At that point, Harry's thought process stalled.

With the evening to himself, he debated whether to pick up a couple of files from the office and bring them home. On the other hand, the baseball game was on television. It was a chance to relax.

On the broad plaza of the Old City Hall, a man with a guitar stood in the shadows beside a wheelchair.

"Mister?"

Harry knew it was a mistake to slow his pace. The man was young, his face thin and dirty. Except for the angelic smile, he looked like innumerable street people. He pointed to a black top hat on the seat of a wheelchair.

With messianic zeal, the young man spoke. "Do not fear to reach out from the invisible cocoon that you are forced to inhabit." His eyes seemed fixed on some world known only to himself.

Invisible cocoon? What the hell? Harry tossed some coins into the hat and hurried on. Abruptly, he turned in the direction of his office.

Out of the last rays of the setting sun, Harry buttoned his overcoat against the cold wind slicing into him. He picked up his pace as his building came into view. Something nagged at the edge of his consciousness.

As he spun through the revolving door, he could see Hakim, the night watchman. He was a huge man crouched on a tiny stool behind a desk, no larger than one in junior grade school. The remains of Hakim's lunch were spread out on the desk, covering the logbook.

Startled, Hakim looked up. "Mr. Jenkins. Thought you was still upstairs." He unearthed the logbook. "Your client must be waiting up there for you."

Harry stopped short in confusion. "Client? What client?"

Oblivious to Harry's mounting concern, Hakim bit into his sandwich and chewed slowly.

"Hakim, who's upstairs? Did he sign in?" Harry grabbed the book. Across from his suite number was an illegible scrawl. "I'm not expecting anyone."

Hakim stopped chewing and gulped hard. His round face darkened. "He say he have an appointment. I thought you was still up there."

Harry entered the elevator and jammed his finger into the call button. Fumbling for his keys, he watched the floor numbers light up with agonizing slowness. Each clang of the elevator reverberated in the silent building.

At last it opened at his floor. Immediately, he saw the office door slightly ajar. Lights were on inside. He strode down the dark hallway and flung open the door.

The waiting room was empty. A cool breeze wafted from his office. Heart pounding in his chest, he called out. When he saw the chaos in his office, his stomach wrenched. Filing-cabinet drawers were torn open. Files were pitched on the floor. Desk drawers were yanked open.

Neatly stacked in the center of his desk was a sheaf of papers. A silver knife was plunged through them, nailing them in place. Scattered around were handfuls of rose petals. The vase on the credenza held only stems of flowers.

Harry knew at once that the papers were the Chin offers. He drew closer. The papers were not damaged in any way, except for a neat incision in their center. Jonathan Conroy of Cheney, Arpin, had them returned in the space of only two or three hours.

A promising spring breeze filtered in through the curtains at the window. He leaned out over the fire escape. Twilight prevented him from penetrating the depths of the alleyway below, but he could just make out a slight, shadowy figure swinging from the last rung of the fire escape. He heard a body thud on the pavement below, followed by a low groan and curses. Then he heard hurried, hobbling footsteps back down the alley toward the street. Harry did not call out, but turned back into the room. Surveying the ransacked office, he telephoned the police.

Two officers arrived. The older one stared balefully at the disarray, and then slowly took out his pen and pad.

"Did you touch anything?" he began gruffly.

Harry shook his head. "Just the telephone to call you."

Stepping on the clutter, the officer moved behind Harry's desk. "This have anything to do with the Deightons, you think?" He gazed steadily at Harry.

"The Deightons?" Then Harry peered at the officer in the increasing gloom. Not until then did he recognize him as the one who had come to Marjorie's house. "No, I don't think so. I'm sorry, Sergeant Welkom. I didn't recognize you."

Welkom shrugged as if this were no surprise. "You must have a pretty interesting practice, Mr. Jenkins." He sat down heavily in Harry's chair. "What kind of work do you do?"   •

"It's an old family practice. You know, real estate, estates…a little commercial work."

"Got clients with money outside the country?" asked the sergeant blandly, as he eyed the knife in the desk.

"Oh, a few." Harry was beginning to feel uncomfortable. He resisted the invitation, created by the sergeant's silence, to continue.

"Any idea what they were looking for?" Welkom gestured toward the knife and the petals. "Somebody's obviously trying to give you a message."

Harry sighed deeply and sat down on a straight-backed chair. Welkom lounged in his chair behind his desk.

"It's a quiet practice," he began stiffly. "Ordinary middle-class people, buying and selling houses and making wills and dying. That's about it." He was surprised at his own belligerent tone.

Welkom stood up. The sergeant was at least six-foot-two. "You'd be real smart, Mr. Jenkins, to tell us anything you can think of. Whoever did this is telling you something, and I think you know what it is."

"Listen, I have no idea. My office is broken into, and suddenly I come under investigation. That's ridiculous!" Harry rose swiftly, determined to gain control of the conversation. "The man on the security desk signed the person in. Why don't you talk to him? Maybe he can give you a description."

"Like I said, Mr. Jenkins, somebody's telling you something. You'd be smart to be careful." Welkom nodded curtly. "Anyway, we'll talk to security now. If you find anything missing, give us a call."

Waiting with the other officer, Welkom punched the elevator button three times.

"You know, Samuels, something funny's going on with that lawyer."

"Sir?"

"Looks like a pillar of the community. But you can't trust lawyers." Welkom shouldered his way into the elevator. Closing his eyes, he leaned wearily against the back wall.

"What's wrong with him?" the young officer asked.

Welkom's eyes flew open. His lips curled downward. "My mother was cleaned out by a shyster lawyer. Even after he admitted it, she still thought he was a very nice gentleman." The elevator doors opened to the lobby. "Who ever heard of a con artist who wasn't? Right?"

Samuels nodded and stepped back for Welkom.

After they had left, Harry sat staring at the knife. Carefully, he lifted the corners of the offers. The vendor companies had signed the offers, but had increased the price. It would be most interesting to see Chin's reaction to the condition of his paperwork.

Harry lifted the phone to call Conroy. He left a message consisting of one question: who had delivered the counteroffers? Wearily, he turned off the lights and locked up. He would start the cleanup in the morning.

CHAPTER 16

▼

In fury, the Florist ripped up a dozen petal drawings made on the copies of Katharine Rowe's photograph and threw them on the floor. With his large, muscular hand, he could not catch the flow of the line. Such artistry evoked the entire range of human emotion. He stared bleakly at the torn pictures strewn on the floor.

He had actually seen Katharine Rowe yesterday in the parking garage. She was even more beautiful than her photograph. But maybe she really deserved the name "Katie," which he had read in the society column. So many grown women had childish names like Bunnie or Patsy. She was nothing but a high-class whore.

Still, her beauty demanded his very best design. Lifting another copy of her photograph from a drawer, he sought his finest drawing pen. More technical difficulties beset him.

A pen was not a knife. Paper was not flesh. The very first challenge of his art was to capture the freedom of spirit in the Matisse drawings. Only then could he hope to redeem these souls. A force beyond himself summoned the creator. Only withered souls refused the challenge. Katharine Rowe would be his masterpiece for the world.

Lost in thought, he considered yet another technical difficulty. To create such a beautifully evocative line, the victim had to be absolutely still. Should he immobilize her first? He could easily obtain drugs that paralyzed muscles.

He dismissed the notion. The pitiful thrashing was one of the most satisfying aspects of his art. The delicious dawning of terror drove him to intense, orgasmic delights of both mind and body. The deep pleasures of creation could not be achieved without pain, suffering, and challenge. No birth without blood. He would have to persevere until he could draw such a line under any conditions.

CHAPTER 17

▼

On the morning of Marjorie's funeral, Harry entered St. Timothy's Church and took a seat in the second pew on the left. Marjorie had stipulated the full Anglican burial service, which would last more than an hour. Shifting uncomfortably on the unforgiving wooden surface, he tried to settle in for the lengthy session ahead.

Reverend Sleem, rubbing his hands together, nodded and smiled at Harry. The church had been a beneficiary of Deighton charity for generations. Marjorie's departure might or might not bode well for it. The church abhorred the uncertainty of not knowing where it stood.

Angry restlessness possessed Harry. If it weren't for the indifference of the coroner's office and the lazy incompetence of the sergeant, there might have been an autopsy. Now it was too late. Folding his arms across his chest, he stared at the vaulted ceiling.

His anger mounted. The image of Chin, counting the cash, barreled into his mind. Damn it! With all his sophistication and charm, his client had gotten him into the conflict with Marjorie. And then his office had been ransacked. Who could have stabbed the offers to his desk? The vendors were a series of faceless numbered companies, so it could be anyone.

He glanced along the pew, only to see a man staring at him. Nodding politely, Harry decided it must be Bob, Katharine's husband. Katharine sat between him and her sister. Suzannah appeared pale and vapid in a long floral skirt. Clutched in her hand was a small bouquet, which had suffered considerably from her twisting fingers.

Frank, the depleter of trust funds, sat beside her, incessantly shifting his girth from side to side. He seemed to grow in bulk each time Harry saw him. But obviously he was unscathed from his encounter in the office with the man with the muscle, who must have been from the mob.

The church filled up rapidly. A slight figure hitched and hobbled up the main aisle to the head of the coffin. Harry could make out the pinched features of a young man. From several rows back, Harry heard a whispered voice. "It's Donnie...Gerry Deighton's son."

It appeared that the boy was about to address the assembled mourners. A hush settled over the church. Nervous coughs flitted through the silence. But it was not to be. Instead, Donnie simply spread his hands with great care over the head of the casket and stood silently, with his chin lowered to his chest.

Then Donnie raised his eyes, which were filled with anger. He scanned the first two rows of pews on either side of the church until he spotted Harry. The fury was so uncontrolled that the others in the pew turned to stare at him. Alarmed, Harry looked back at the boy quizzically. He could not imagine the cause of the rage. He had never seen Donnie before.

Gerry Deighton stood abruptly and approached his son. Grasping Donnie's arm, he attempted to lead him from the coffin. The boy held back, but then faltered. Seeing his father's angry look, he consented to be led back to the pew.

Donnie slumped beside his parents and bent his head. Marjorie Deighton was his great-aunt, but he called her "Gram." Now that she was gone, nothing mattered. He was the only one who really loved her.

Gram died last Tuesday, Donnie remembered. She was the only one worth talking to. His parents never listened. After school, he stayed in his room, hiding from his mother and her stupid bridge parties.

Sometimes, he would go to Gram's house to talk or to read to her. She seemed to understand him, even when he didn't understand himself. At least she listened. Every day started and finished in the black pit inside himself. It took all his energy just to get out of bed and get dressed. What was the point? The only good days were when the diving club met and when he saw Gram.

Something was different when he got to her house that day. A silver-gray Mercedes was parked in the laneway. Donnie stopped to run the palm of his hand slowly over the hood of the car, expecting any moment to be yelled at. Then he took his key and went in the front door.

A loud, angry voice bellowed upstairs. At the foot of the stairs, Donnie held his breath. Frank waved a bunch of papers and then tore down the staircase.

"What do you want, kid?" He squirmed into his overcoat, the papers spilling to the floor. Donnie watched in silence as Frank stooped to pick them up.

"Hey, by the way kid, Auntie wants her tea. It's in the kitchen, all ready. Take it up to her, willya?"

Donnie nodded, but said nothing. Glancing out the window, he saw a tall man sliding into the Mercedes at the side of the house. .

"Who's he?" Donnie looked at Frank, who peered out the window.

"I dunno," he muttered. "Must be someone from the church."

"Look, kid, go get Auntie's tea, willya? It's getting cold. She's waiting for it." Then he left, slamming the door behind him.

Donnie took the tea tray from the kitchen and headed upstairs. Gram stood before her window with the sun streaming in. She looked all faded. As Donnie shut the door, she turned.

At first, he saw the glint of anger in her eyes, but then she softened and said, "Ah! It's you, Donnie. Yes, put the tray down next to the bed, dear." Donnie moved some glasses and papers to the far side of the table to make room. He sat on one of the chairs drawn up to the bed.

"So, you've come from the diving club, Donnie?" she prompted.

He smiled gratefully and nodded. He could talk about the club and the dives he was working on. Maybe the team would get in the finals. He was sure that Gram had never dived into a pool.

She laughed, "When I was young, ladies were only permitted to go bathing."

He grinned at this. Smiling felt strange; he did it so rarely.

When he talked about his dives, she got this look in her eye and said, "I know what you mean. It's like breaking free—like learning to fly."

Sadly, he said diving would be over if they did not make the finals. "I don't know what to do Gram. Nothing seems worth doing, anyway."

Marjorie nodded. She always seemed to understand. "Both of us are weary." she said, "You at the beginning of life and I near the end."

He looked at her with apprehension.

She continued, "You're like my brother George. He tried to fill the shoes of his father, a decorated war hero. An impossible task. Consequently, only with great inner strength did George ever find his own way." She looked sternly at him. "You have that trait, Donnie. You will find your own way. Just as I will find mine."

Some of the things she said scared him. Not knowing how to answer, he silently poured her tea and handed it to her. She had lain down on the bed, propped up by pillows, and slowly sipped from the cup. Then she told him it was time to leave. Now she lay in the coffin and he had to keep on living.

Gram lived in a different time, when things were *simpler* and *people* were somehow more important. She stood for what was right. He couldn't believe all the stuff on the Internet about the Florist. Although Gram would never have understood that kind of person, Donnie did, at least a little bit. The guy's ideas about fire were really cool, especially the part about its cleansing power. Fire destroyed everything that was ugly. For all Donnie cared, the whole fucking world could go up in flames. Then he could start again. But he could hear Gram saying that the Florist was a madman. She was right. Carving people up and redeeming their souls was nuts.

From his pew, Donnie glanced over at Jenkins. The lawyer's eyes kind of darted around. Maybe he was crooked and wanted to steal Gram's money, just like Frank had said. But Frank was a slimy bastard. He couldn't trust him either. Donnie shoved his chin into his collar and closed his eyes.

A hush fell over the church. Reverend Sleem climbed up to the pulpit. Although Harry thought the clergyman resembled an unkempt Santa Claus, he sensed there was little mirth within the man.

Sleem smoothed his surplice and cleared his throat. Gazing out, he saw approximately a hundred people awaiting his words. In the first few pews sat the family, and behind them were several rows of gray heads, followed by the usual cluster of business associates. His duty, as explained to him by the archbishop himself, was to ensure that the next generation of Deightons was brought into the fold to continue the tradition of generous contributions. He cleared his throat and began intoning.

"I am the resurrection and the life, saith the Lord: he that believeth in me, though he were dead, yet shall he live; and whosoever liveth and believeth in me, shall never die."

Sleem was prepared for the rustling of the pages of the Common Prayer Book and the fumbling of those trying to find the page. He could spot a non-attender a mile away. In fact, he made it a game. *Fish out of water.* He smirked inwardly.

But by the time he had finished, saying, "We brought nothing into this world and it is certain we can carry nothing out," only the very slowest were still shuffling.

Reverend Sleem dove into such a lengthy recitation of Sir William Mortimer Deighton's contributions to the church that Harry began to wonder whose funeral it was. Had Crawford survived Marjorie, he would have brutally criticized the priest after the service for failing to give proper respect to the deceased. But the old man would have remained cool and circumspect, despite the passions roiling beneath his calm surface.   •

At last, the six pallbearers approached the casket. In unison, they shouldered the coffin, and in step, proceeded down the center aisle. Frank was a pallbearer at the rear.

A fine rain was falling outside, no more than a mist, although it made the steep steps of St. Timothy's slick and black. The pallbearers teetered precariously on the top steps and then descended with great care. The mourners hung back underneath the arched doorways and held their breath until the procession reached the sidewalk.

Swiftly, the pallbearers swung the casket around for entry into the hearse. Forced to dance backward, Frank stumbled and let go of his burden. The others desperately clutched the casket to prevent its slide from their shoulders. Other mourners pitched in to help slide it into the hearse.

Slamming the rear door of the hearse, Frank cursed furiously. With exaggerated motions, he dusted his hands and brushed off his clothing, oblivious to the horrified silence that had fallen over the gathering.

Harry was incredulous. Frank earned his reputation as a lout effortlessly. Looking up the steps, Harry spotted Donnie standing at the very top, near the doorway. He wondered if he should approach him. Tears streamed down the boy's face.

A few mourners tried to console Donnie, but he tore away from them and ran into the church. Sitting in the darkness of the last pew, he wiped his tears.

"Gram," he whispered, "I'm so sorry. Frank shouldn't have done that. Treating you just like a bag of garbage. I don't know what to do. Is that guy Jenkins really crooked? Please tell me what to do." He tried to stop sniffling so he could hear Gram's voice, but the church remained silent.

Donnie stalked outside toward the subway. He didn't want to go to the cemetery with his parents. His father couldn't wait to get her buried and get the cash. He slumped onto a park bench. He kept thinking about the Florist and what he'd found on the Internet. Whoever he was, the Florist was right about one thing: the cleansing power of fire. He had to admire the guy for saying that.

Following the burial, Harry headed to the reception at Katharine's home on Blyth Hill Road in Rosedale, where lawyers, stockbrokers, and those of independent means dwelt. He rolled down his misted window to read the house numbers. Deighton wealth made such a location possible.

He parked the car and mounted the front steps of the Georgian-style red-brick home. After being welcomed by a butler at the front door, he hung up his coat and was free to stroll the main floor.

When Harry visited the homes of clients, he liked to guess at their personalities from their surroundings. This interesting game often provided valuable insights. He suspected Bob had chosen the house and Katharine had decorated with a smothering vengeance.

Her foremost triumph was in the living room, where the furniture was low-slung and probably hard to get out of. The far wall was papered in a dramatic, bold stripe. On the opposite one hung several canvases splotched with fantastic colors. Despite the vivid slashes of red and orange colors across the canvas, the room chilled him.

Accepting a drink from a waiter, Harry wandered into the study, where Bob had established his own cluttered turf and small domain. The old oak desk was piled high with books and papers. More books were jammed into the bookcases lining the wall. Harry understood this warm, scattered peace. He sank into one of the leather armchairs. Never before had he witnessed such a psychotic clash of personalities expressed in two rooms under one roof.

The door behind him suddenly closed, and Bob moved slowly and deliberately into the study. Approaching the far side of the desk, he kept his eyes fixed on some distant point in the garden and did not see Harry. Heavy-set and compact, he was every man's notion of a learned professor.

Wearily, Bob extracted a pipe from a breast pocket and sat down. Staring out the window, he began to mutter. "What kind of mess are you in now? Oh, Katharine…you've made my life hell." A deep sigh followed.

To avoid further embarrassment, Harry had to announce his presence immediately. Shifting in the high-backed chair, he coughed discreetly. Receiving no reaction, he rose to introduce himself.

"Bob, I'm Harry Jenkins, Marjorie's lawyer." Bob spun around in his chair. His face was white. Extending his hand across the desk, Harry continued, "Sorry to surprise you. I just wandered in here and found your study so inviting that I…" His voice trailed off.

Bob stood up unsteadily to shake his hand. Worn creases of sleepless worry lined his face. "Please, Mr. Jenkins, do sit down. I've been a bit preoccupied lately, what with all that's been going on."

They sat in silence for several moments, and a waiter came in with a tray of drinks. Bob took a glass of wine. Harry declined.

"Listen, Mr. Jenkins—"

"Harry, please."

Bob removed his glasses and stared at the ceiling. "I wanted to talk to you about Marjorie anyway, Harry. She called here for Katharine the night before she died. She wasn't here, of course."

Harry could not miss the bitter edge to his words.

"She seemed very upset and wanted to speak to Katharine and Suzannah. From what I could tell, she wanted some advice about finances and maybe her will."

Harry was trying to reconstruct his last conversation with Marjorie. "You're probably right, Bob. She phoned me the day she died. I went to see her about changes to her will."

"And?"

"And nothing. She was dead when I got there. She had said she was seeing some people at two and would need my advice."

Bob stood up and turned on the desk lamp. "Did you ever hear her speak of a living will?" he asked.

"Only once or twice. I told her it wasn't easily enforceable, but if she wanted she could write one out herself."

"Harry, do you think there's anything odd about her death?'

To Harry, Bob's concern seemed genuine. "It's hard to say. She looked very peaceful. No signs of violence." Harry shook his head. "There was talk of an autopsy, but nothing came of it."

"Why an autopsy? Was there anything suspicious?" Bob's frown deepened.

Harry did not feel as certain as he tried to sound. "I don't know. I've left that up to the police." He decided against setting out his concerns.

"Could she have committed suicide?"

"I really doubt that. Why would she call me to discuss her will and then kill herself?

Bob shrugged. "I don't know. I just don't know what to make of this living-will business. Maybe she did want to die."

"Well, maybe she did. But as far as I knew, she wasn't in any pain or distress. She was probably just lucky. She got what she wanted: an easy, natural death."

"Well, I hope you're right, Harry." Bob glanced at his watch. "Thanks for the time. But I'd better see to the other guests." He patted Harry's shoulder as he left the study.

Puzzled, Harry rose and circled the desk to look out the window. Apparently a living will was blatant evidence of suicidal intent. Many clients would be alarmed at the thought. Reflecting on the conversation, he wandered into the hallway.

The living room was filling up. Not many of Marjorie's generation were in the crowd, Harry noted. *Must be business associates of Katharine and Gerry.* Murmurs from the corners of the room floated to him.

"I wish they'd catch that Florist, whoever he is."

"He must be terribly demented. Imagine! Thinking you're creating beauty when you're destroying life."

"It's fascinating from a psychological point of view."

Harry moved away. With all the media attention, the grisly murders hung in everyone's mind.

Frank was leaning against the mantelpiece, with Suzannah close at his side. Swaying slightly, she closed her eyes.

Donnie slouched in a chair and glared at Frank. Rising unsteadily, the boy limped painfully toward Frank. With Donnie at her side, Suzannah attempted to focus her eyes.

"Isn't it terrible, Donnie?" Her voice was softly slurred. Refusing to take his eyes off Frank, Donnie remained silent. With studied care, Suzannah placed her glass on the mantelpiece. To console him, she draped her arms around the boy.

"Poor dear." She patted his cheek. "You're the one who'll miss her most." His arms hung loosely at his sides. Under Donnie's glare, Frank shifted uneasily from foot to foot.

"Take it easy, kid. I'll talk to you later," Frank said moving away.

Suzannah released Donnie and sighed. She said loudly to the gathering, "Frank's so upset about Auntie, you know. He just has to have another drink." The bitter sarcasm in her tone caused everyone to look up. Frank kept walking toward the bar. She knew she would pay for baiting him, but she didn't care. Her voice grew louder rising above the general din. "No one knows what happened to Auntie. Even worse, no one even cares—except you and me, Donnie."

The guests were breaking off their conversations to listen. Retrieving her glass, Suzannah took a long drink and began drifting about the room.

"We didn't care about Aunt Marjorie when she was alive. She couldn't rely upon us for anything. She knew we were just waiting for her to die." In the silent room, her voice began an upward slide, ready to drift out of any normal key into hysteria. "Now that she's dead, we can divide up her money, and she's got piles of it—hasn't she, Mr. Jenkins?"

Shocked by the absurdity of the scene, Harry said nothing.

Katharine marched into the living room. The waiters stepped back to the corners.

"Suzannah, stop this instant. You're drunk and making a complete fool of yourself!"

Suzannah might have waited all of her life for the moment. Turning on her sister with a sweet and dreamy smile, she said, "Why, Katharine, dear! You of all people know it's true. When did you ever take time from your busy life to give Auntie a second thought? You and Gerry never paid her any real attention. You were just waiting for her to die."

Katharine slapped her sister hard across the face. Red blossomed instantly on Suzannah's cheek.

"When," hissed Katharine, "did you ever do anything except wring your hands and moon over her?" Katharine mimicked her. "But Suzannah, here's something you didn't know. Marjorie was strong and tough. She despised whining. You just wallow in it. You're way off base if you think Marjorie wanted your smarmy pity."

Katharine rushed from the living room.

No one knew what to do. Everyone set down their drinks and looked for the quickest route to the front hall closet. Confusion reigned as they searched for coats, hats, and gloves in the vestibule. Some hung back until the crowds thinned out. Within five minutes, the main floor was empty except for Harry, Suzannah, and the waiters.

Harry found his coat had been thrown on the floor. He let himself out the door. Suicide? Natural death? Murder? And now emotional neglect. Stepping outside, he pulled up his collar and hurried for the car.

Frank cornered Donnie on Katharine's back porch. "Where's the will, kid?"

Donnie hunched forward and pulled an envelope out of his windbreaker. "I got it here."

"The combination I gave you worked okay?"

"No problem." Donnie hesitated. "Frank, why do you want her will?"

"I told you already. That lawyer, Jenkins, is a real shyster. He's gonna rob your auntie blind."

Donnie thought Jenkins seemed okay, but he couldn't tell for sure.

"Did you create a distraction like I told you?" Frank reached for the envelope.

Donnie couldn't help but smile in recollection. "I trashed Jenkins' office. And," said Donnie, drawing himself up, "I stabbed a knife through some papers on his desk and tossed a bunch of flowers around them."

"What? Are you fucking crazy? Why?"

"To make it look like the Florist guy was there."

"Jesus! You must be outta your mind, kid."

Donnie's face darkened. "You wanted a distraction." Then he stepped back and threw the envelope at Frank's feet. "Here's the will. That's the last thing I'm doing for you, Frank." Donnie turned and limped down the driveway.

"Fucking little jerk!" Frank shouted, then he stooped to retrieve the papers.

After the funeral reception, Harry went home. Opening the front door, he saw Laura on the stairs.

"Hi." He set down his case. "When did you get in? I thought you'd be late."

Her smile was quick. "The meetings were canceled, so I thought I'd come home and take a bath."

"You want me to scramble us some eggs?"

"Sure, Harry."

Only then did he notice the bag at the top of the stairs.

"I'll go up and run the bath." She turned and hurried up the stairs.

"What's in the bag?"

"Just some old clothes I was going to drop off at the Goodwill."

In the kitchen, Harry got out the eggs. Pain across his chest made him sit for a moment at the counter. He breathed deeply until the spasm passed. He knew she was about to leave.

Half an hour later, they sat in the den with the dinner on separate trays. She snapped on the television.

"Laura? We have to talk."

"About?" She looked up innocently.

"Us. You, me…Dr. Stover."

"Harry, there's absolutely nothing to talk about. It's a strictly professional relationship."

He stared hard at her. "I don't believe you."

Laura rose swiftly, almost knocking over his tray. "Well, then that's too bad, Harry." She searched the drawer for a package of cigarettes.

"There's some in my jacket on the living-room chair." he said dully.

When she returned, she sat at the counter and lit the cigarette. "All right. There is a problem. But it's just us. We don't communicate anymore."

"Jesus! How can we, when you're not here most of the time?"

"My work—"

"God damn it, Laura! Can't we ever have an honest conversation?"

"This is a conversation? You're shouting at me." She slid off the stool and started cleaning off the countertop.

"All right," he sighed. Moving behind her, he tried to slide his hand underneath her breast.

She lurched away. "Don't. Just don't, Harry." She began to cry. He drew her close, and grudgingly, she laid her head on his shoulder.

"Laura? I'll do anything to save our marriage. But we have to start talking," he whispered. "We could try marriage counseling."

She sniffled, then moved away. "All right. Set up an appointment."

In silence, they cleared up the half-eaten dinner.

Laura went to bed at ten-thirty. He watched the news. On his way upstairs, he realized that neither of them had said "I love you."

Gerry Deighton did not go home with his wife after the funeral reception. Instead, he drove downtown to Yonge and Dundas Streets. Most of the dingy book and record stores had been mowed under to make way for gleaming new structures of glass and concrete. *Fucking desolate,* he thought as he parked the car and started walking north.

At last he came to his destination: Stress Relief Spa. Slowly, he climbed the stairs to the second floor, where a skinny kid sat with his feet up on the reception desk. Gerry booked an appointment with Ming Tao, expert masseuse. He was shown down the hall to a dimly lit room, where he undressed and lay on the table under a white sheet.

"Just call me Ming," the masseuse said when she entered and turned down the lights.

"Ming," said Gerry wearily, "I want everything tonight."

Ming laughed gently and pulled down the sheet. He groaned with pleasure as her fingers worked up and down his back. When he turned over, he had an immense erection. She covered him with a towel and began her work. When they were finished, Gerry sat up and reached for his wallet.

"Ming, did anyone ever tell you that you have the most exquisite skin?"

Ming smiled and pocketed the money. Gerry reached out and gently touched her face. She froze as he ran his finger along her neck and down her shoulder. "Very beautiful," he whispered. Ming backed swiftly out the door. Gerry sighed and dressed.

CHAPTER 18

▼

When Harry awoke next morning, he lay very still, for fear of losing forever the fleeting fragments of his dream. He had awakened with an erection, but now that was swiftly fading along with the dream. Once again, he closed his eyes. Soft, sultry shadows of a woman remained, along with an indescribable softness lingering over his entire body. Lying still in the warmth of the covers and conscious of his own rhythmic breathing, he tried in vain to recapture her presence and identity.

Laura was gone, and the far side of the bed was cold, rumpled, and empty.

Kicking off the covers, Harry padded into the bathroom and ran the shower as hot as possible. Billows of steam rose to cloud the mirror as he dutifully tossed his pajamas into the hamper. He turned his face upward into the pulsing jet of water and gasped in the heat. Frustration flashed within him, but receded almost as quickly, leaving him with a painful sense of longing. Slowly, he began soaping his chest.

Always toeing the line. Nose to the grindstone. And ever faithful to Laura. Last night, her packed suitcase had sat at the top of the stairs like rock-solid evidence of a failed marriage. What the hell did twenty years of a life mean, anyway? With a creeping sense of doom, he wondered where to find a marriage counselor.

Stepping from the shower, he grabbed a towel. What did he have to show for years of loyalty and duty to his profession and his clients? With his elegantly regal bearing, Crawford, the embodiment of professional propriety, was a notorious seducer of women. Battles of moral conscience were foreign to him. *Passion and thrall* were the last words he said as he pitched to the floor.

Harry grimly recited the very practical reasons for his obedience: mortgage, taxes, car payments, office expenses. The list had no end. Maybe it was time to cut himself some slack.

With a slow, circular motion, he cleared off the mirror. Then he remembered. A smile crept over his face. Today would be good. He had a ten o'clock appointment with Natasha to appraise the Deighton house. Within twenty minutes, he was dressed and out the door.

In traffic, he considered Marjorie's estate. He and the Gideon Trust Company were the co-executors. Quick and decisive action was required to gain the upper hand, otherwise he might lose control of the estate to the trust company. Without determination and speed, a poor solicitor acting with a major trust company might be relegated to the status of a flunky with a brand-new rubber stamp.

Harry knew their game well. Senior trust officers lured his clients with promises of prompt personal attention, and then concluded, in pitying tones, that only they had the resources to back up such promises. From then on, their teams of experts, their appraisers, and their investment counselors and accountants called the shots. The senior trust officer issued instructions after brief consultation with the poor solicitor on legal technicalities. But not this time, he vowed.

Years back, a hapless junior trust officer named Steinberg had attended Crane, Crawford and Jenkins for a meeting with the estate beneficiaries. In the library, the deferential Mr. Steinberg had been seated apart from the Deighton family. Nowhere could he rest his file in comfort. His papers persisted in sliding from his grasp and his constant efforts to retrieve them gave him a groveling air.

At one point, Steinberg requested the birth certificate of Miss Suzannah Deighton. Carefully, Crawford set down his gold pen. "I beg your pardon, Mr. Steinberg," he said coldly. Flustered the trust officer looked up.

Crawford's voice rolled like distant thunder "A cursory glance at your file, Mr. Steinberg, will confirm that the Deighton family is one of the most respected and prominent families in the city, whom I have had the honor of representing for more than thirty years. Are you implying, young man…?"

Mr. Steinberg was no fool. He stammered, "Certainly not, sir. I'm sure that's an unnecessary detail."

That was it. Control from beginning to end. Exercise the power at every opportunity, and never relinquish authority. This time he would seize the reins. He hadn't notified the trust company of Marjorie's death until after the funeral. That eliminated one occasion for contact with the beneficiaries. Now Natasha reported to him on the appraisals.

The few times they had met, her glance and warm smile made him hope that she felt his attraction. He tried to dismiss the thought. Plenty of women were warm and friendly, and it meant nothing. She seemed just out of his reach. But still, he hoped.

He pulled up in front of the church, just behind Natasha's red Porsche. She lowered the window and favored him with one of her brilliant smiles. Her phone was cradled against her sleek black mink. Swept with a desire to reach out and touch her soft and silky fur coat, he busied himself instead with his briefcase. She knew her business inside out, but never let a man think she was too expert. She had just a touch of vulnerability. Harry enjoyed her immensely.

She took his hand and stepped gracefully from the car in her long black leather boots. Her fur draped open, revealing an elegant red wool dress beneath. He longed to touch her glossy black hair, which curved softly to her shoulders and blended in with her mink.

"Harry!" She continued to hold his hand. "Such a pleasure to see you again! It was so crowded at Richard's funeral—we couldn't talk."

Intimacy. With the sense of being gathered into her confidence, Harry smiled and took her arm. "The pleasure is mine, Natasha. I'm really glad you can do this appraisal."

"I'm delighted. We must have lunch, once I've done the work." She leaned into his arm.

For Natasha, Harry was an intriguing prospect. Immediately, she knew from his eyes and his touch the depth of his attraction to her. But something was holding him back. Without a doubt, he was a gentleman. Perhaps he was truly in love with his wife.

Natasha was weary of coping with brutish male egos: those legions of professional men who assumed a quick lay on the office couch was simply their due for a promising referral. In her experience, men were generally a disappointment; women were an occasional temptation. Harry would be a refreshing challenge.

A sputtering Honda Civic pulled up behind Natasha's Porsche. Harry winced. The neat, square frame of Cameron McCrea, senior trust officer, emerged from the little car. With bustle and determination in every step, he marched toward them.

"Well, old chap, good to see you again," began McCrea. Harry bristled, but checked himself. He introduced McCrea to Natasha as one of the many trust officers at Gideon.

Natasha shook hands with him and then gazed up at the house.

"Oh, Harry," she sighed, stepping back close to him. "This residence...it has such majesty, such grandeur!" Glancing sideways toward the trust officer, she continued, "Aren't you enthralled with its charm, Mr. McCrea?"

Until that moment, McCrea had given little thought to the house, or, for that matter, the estate, except for a rough calculation of executor's compensation and Probate Court fees. What he saw was excess. For his taste, which bordered on the austere, he saw too many turrets and too many curlicues. He was plagued with a puritanical abhorrence of the flagrant spending of the wealthy. Furtively glancing at Natasha, he wondered who retained her.

"Mmm...well, I suppose," McCrea began, somewhat vaguely. "Looks like the turrets up there on the right-hand side could use some repair."

"Repairs?" Natasha's eyes widened. "But of course, Mr. McCrea, when even the finest of homes reaches a certain age, loving care and restoration is required to maintain beauty!"

Harry tried to suppress a grin. It was going better than he had hoped. Natasha had concluded that the trust officer was a dullard without beauty in his soul. Poor Cameron was already intimidated. The sun shone.

He took Natasha's arm and started up the walk. The windows in the upper stories glinted in the light. Clouds blotted out the sun, and shadows swiftly chased them up the walk, overtaking them before they reached the veranda. With them came a chill wind, causing Natasha to shiver, ever so slightly, against him.

Harry hadn't entered the house since he had found Marjorie dead. The lock was stiff at first, but after a moment, the door swung open.

Natasha's lips were close to his ear. Her breath was warm and stirring. "Harry," she whispered, "it really is magnificent, isn't it?"

He smiled and nodded, stepping back to let her in.

Indeed, the foyer was impressive. Suddenly, the sun burst through the clouds and light flooded in, setting the paneling aglow. The broad expanse of carpeted stairway led the eye upward to the now-quiet bedrooms. The door to the back stairs would have to be fixed, but Harry would leave that to McCrea and his many minions.

Through the French doors was the parlor. He could easily imagine Marjorie seated by the fireplace, with gentle Rosie serving her sherry. Harry knew Natasha was already formulating a marketing plan. Through her appreciation, he could see the house was a splendid residence that would attract the most discerning buyers. She would be able to excite a prospective purchaser with her vision. That was just one of her many talents.

Harry stopped in the doorway. Something was eluding his grasp. Only a few days ago, he had stood right there, straining to hear in the silence. He tried to recollect the sound in the upstairs corridor that afternoon. But then again, old houses always made noises. He proceeded into the parlor, eager to catch up with Natasha.

Transfixed, Harry stood watching Natasha. With the most casual of gestures, she draped her full-length black mink coat across the sofa, exposing its slashes of deep red tints. With that one motion, the dream of last night exploded in Harry's brain.

Natasha! What had he done to her—with her—time and again? Images flashed in his mind of her naked…of her dressed in tight black corsets with long garters, posing for him. Harry stood marooned in the living room, conscious only of the deep flush rising in him.

Cameron McCrea had set his briefcase down and was now inspecting the hallway, squinting upward in search of cracks in the ceiling. He pursed his lips and jotted furiously in his little black notebook every few paces. Next, McCrea scurried across the parlor and dropped to all fours. Craning his neck to see up the chimney, he fiddled with the damper. Natasha winked at Harry over the view of the trust officer's rear end. With any luck, thought Harry, soon the man would be examining the fuse box in the basement and double-checking for incontrovertible evidence of termites.

Drinking in the detail and atmosphere, Natasha moved gracefully through the principal rooms. A marketing strategy was beginning to form in her mind. Knowing that only a select few would be right for this home, she intended to target that group from the start. The purchasers would have a lifelong love affair with the bygone eras of the city.

Both of them heard McCrea tromping down the cellar steps. Natasha gazed at Harry. Why was he standing like a lost soul in the middle of the parlor? Gracefully, she circled about the room, immersed in viewing the chandelier, until she backed into Harry with a thud. Swiftly, she turned about to face him, finding herself within inches of his chest.

"Oh! Harry, I'm sorry!" Her fingers rested lightly on his tie.

Harry realized he was grinning foolishly at her. Breathing deeply, he took in her fragrance, the warmth of her touch and closeness. He wanted the moment to last forever.

She took his hand. "Come. Show me the upstairs."

Having lost his voice, he only nodded. Happily, he trotted up the stairs at her heel. In the dream, she had floated everywhere about him, and now she was above him on the staircase. He yearned to reach out and touch her. They paused on the landing.

Natasha suddenly turned toward him and sniffed. "My God, Harry! What could that smell be?"

"What?" Harry was shaken from his riotous fantasies.

"It must be from one of the rooms." She shook her head as if trying to catch its direction.

In unison, they ascended the remaining flight to the second floor. "It seems to be gone."

"Gone? What's gone?"

"That odd smell." For just a moment, they stared at each other, then simultaneously shrugged.

Natasha began her tour of the bedrooms. "Could you help me, Harry? I want to measure these rooms." She began to unravel her tape measure. The yellow metallic tape dangled halfway across the room. Harry stretched it to the far wall. They repeated the procedure, several times. She recorded the measurements and snapped the tape back in place. Mesmerized by her soft, deft motions, Harry hungrily drank in every detail.

Standing close to her, he glanced at the bed and flushed. Edges of his dream persisted in crowding into the room. There she was, laughing, drawing him down and further into her. Savoring each lacy bit of fantasy, he sensed both danger and freedom. He had not forgotten that his bed had been cold, rumpled, and empty this morning.

She smiled at him and waited. Most men would have slammed the door and dragged her down onto the bed. How bold did she have to be?

Was she really inviting him? Harry wondered. Surely he must have gotten carried away by his fantasies. It was crazy. McCrea was still bumbling about in the basement. How he loved the thought of that prissy old maid stumbling in on them. But it would be excruciatingly embarrassing to misread the situation.

As Harry wrestled with his circuitous self-debate, Natasha smiled and closed her case. Best not come too close just yet, she decided. He looked as if he could scarcely breathe. "I'll do the rest of the measuring later, Harry."

Briskly, she moved out into the hall. The moment was gone. Harry followed at her heels down the stairs. Below him, he saw her, all motion and light and life. Catching his breath, he was amazed at one thought. He would happily risk everything for just one chance with the lovely Natasha. Energy not felt in years flooded through him. Reckless joy and passion suffused his spirit. At last, he felt something.

From the dining room, she exclaimed, "Harry, come quickly! You really must see this!"

Desperate to recapture the fading moment, he strode through the parlor and into the dining room.

Natasha was gazing upward. "This chandelier is very rare."

Her smile faded. "Harry! Watch out!"

Something grazed his ear as he lurched sideways. A plate lay in tiny pieces at his feet, having inexplicably slipped from the wainscoting.

Natasha touched his cheek. "My God, Harry, are you all right?"

Staring at her, he nodded. Pure desire coursed through him. The space between them seemed to dance and crackle. At that very moment, he could draw him to her.

"Ghosts, I suppose." McCrea stood smirking in the doorway to the kitchen.

Furious at the intrusion, Harry said, "Let's look at the kitchen." Taking her arm, Harry guided Natasha past the trust officer.

"Truly in its original state!" laughed Natasha.

Compared to the other rooms, Harry thought, the kitchen was cramped. Set in one countertop was a single porcelain sink, which was badly stained. Cupboards were few and small, scattered in pairs about the walls. A small kitchen table sat under the high window.

"Sunday dinners of well-done roast beef, boiled potatoes, and overcooked vegetables," said Natasha.

McCrea looked befuddled.

"What we need, Natasha, is a pot of borscht bubbling on the stove," said Harry, touching her arm.

Cameron cleared his throat. "Shall we get down to business?" He pulled out his notebook. "Your opinion, Mrs. Boretsky?"

"Surely you understand, Mr. McCrea, that I must see the whole property and run some comparisons." She turned to Harry. "But listen, Harry, you do know that property values have escalated drastically in the last few years and that the church is applying to the city for rezoning."

"What's this about the church?" McCrea asked, leaning against the counter and beginning to fill his pipe.

Natasha continued, "The church is selling to a shopping-mall developer. They must get the zoning amended before the sale can be closed."

"Zoning applications are usually trouble, Ms. Boretsky. Commercial developers usually surround the last residence. Its value drops dramatically because it's no longer in a residential setting. The best you can then get is the land value," said McCrea.

Natasha smiled patiently. "I'm sure you know that it's very difficult for a developer to get commercial rezoning in a primarily residential area." She turned back to Harry. "I do suggest that if your clients want to sell, they should do so fairly quickly."

Harry only nodded. Natasha could look after herself. She knew her stuff.

It was hard for the trust officer, speaking for a mammoth corporation, to keep the scorn from his voice. Lighting his pipe, he continued, "At Gideon, we like to proceed with extreme caution in such circumstances. The last thing we want is a beneficiary pointing the finger at us and saying that we didn't get fair market value. You remember the Bingham estate, don't you, Harry?"

One glance told Harry that McCrea was hiding a smirk behind his damned pipe. He certainly remembered the estate and angrily scrawling across the file, "Never trust a trust company."

The Bingham family had owned several small but elegant apartment buildings in the city. The beneficiaries had sought to remove Gideon and Harry as co-executors, claiming improper accounting and loss of certain sales of the buildings. Endless appraisals and reports so befuddled the denizens of the trust company that some very attractive offers slipped by. Harry became Gideon's scapegoat.

"Let's not waste time with reminiscences. I want to show Natasha the rest of the house," Harry said, determined to maintain the upper hand with McCrea. His desire for Natasha was nearly all consuming.

"You know, Cameron, there's something upstairs that needs fixing. Perhaps you could send a man around to have a look."

Brushing past the trust officer, he strode into the hallway, saying, "After all, Gideon has *so* many resources at its disposal."

Pausing with one foot on the first step, he called to McCrea. "The landing door at the top of the stairs was jammed shut the other day." Harry was determined to impose a host of menial chores on McCrea.

He took the stairs two at a time. Halfway up, his eyes remained focused on the landing door. Behind that door, Harry knew was a set of dark and cramped back stairs connecting all three floors. As he neared the landing door, he was overcome with the odor he and Natasha had noticed earlier. He stopped.

Only days before, the landing door had been stuck. Expecting resistance, he wrenched the knob in a show of force. The door flew open.

A body, in a black-and-white maid's uniform, sprang out at him. Stiff, flailing arms smashed into his head and shoulders. Falling toward him was a black face contorted by rigor mortis into a mocking grin.

Desperately trying to fight off the attack, Harry fell sideways. Retching with the odor, he smashed against the banister.

Frozen in horror, Natasha and McCrea saw the black corpse chasing and beating Harry downward until both bodies lay heaped together at the foot of the stairs.

Natasha fought to pry the corpse away, but it had locked Harry in a deathly embrace. McCrea phoned emergency services as Harry drifted into a nether-world.

CHAPTER 19

▼

After several hours of surgery, two of Harry's ribs were reconstructed. Racing to the surface of consciousness, he cried out, "Natasha!" He gasped. The pain was intense.

Two nurses worked over him. "Mr. Jenkins? How are you feeling now? You've had a nasty bit of business, haven't you?" The voice was unbearably loud and cheery, Harry thought. Surely this was not a normal tone. He tried to open his eyes, but the light forced them shut.

Someone took his pulse and said, "We've been trying to reach your wife, Mr. Jenkins. You've had a bad fall, but the doctor says the ribs will heal well."

The nurse was very young. As the anesthetic wore off, her face became clearer. She looked just like his sister, Anna, at thirteen.

She placed his wrist on the bed cover and recorded all his readings on his chart. His head throbbed above his eyes and at his temples.

"What happened to me?" Harry asked, trying to turn his head on the pillow.

The nurse glanced up at him. "Remember, Mr. Jenkins? You were knocked down the stairs at someone's house."

Rosie's contorted face flashed before his eyes. She must have been dead.

"You had a visitor earlier," said one of the nurses as she adjusted the IV bag. Harry only murmured a reply.

"Very pretty, too," the nurse laughed.

Harry's eyes flew open. "Who was it?"

"She said her name was Natasha."

"Really?" Harry grinned. When he tried to sit up, he gasped with pain.

The nurse laughed. "Aha! We'd better get her back here. She'll bring you back to life fast enough."

"Where is she?"

"She had to leave, but don't worry: she said she'd be back." The nurse patted his hand and left.

Harry tried to concentrate on Marjorie and Rosie, but Natasha took over his thoughts. Sinking downward, he reached out to touch her. Her black mink coat slid silkily between his fingers. He knew Laura had not come. She was gone, like his sister, beyond his reach. He slipped back into sleep.

Harry could hear voices out in the hall. The door opened.

"What the hell happened to you, Harry?"

He felt a hand on his arm. Blinking his eyes open, he saw Stephen.

"I got knocked downstairs by a corpse."

"What?"

"I yanked a door open at the Deighton house," Harry murmured. "Rosie's corpse flew out. I lost my balance and fell." Harry smiled feebly. "Scared the hell out of me and Natasha."

Stephen pulled a chair up to the bed and sat down. "Jesus, Harry! That sounds like a really bad murder mystery."

Harry smiled wanly. "I know," he whispered. "But honest to God, it *did* actually happen."

"Who's Natasha? Rosie?"

Harry struggled to sit up, but fell back; the pain was too intense. He had to concentrate. "Rosie's the housekeeper for a client of mine. And Natasha...well, she's a realtor." He knew the anesthetic had not worn off. The painkillers muddled his thoughts, but did not stop his talk.

"I'm sick of this damned 'duty' stuff." Harry gasped in pain. "I'm stuck in a dead marriage and can't seem to live my own life." His head dropped back onto the pillow. "I want out." He felt his guard vanishing and he didn't care. "I'm completely fed up. I want..."

"What *do* you want?"

Harry was silent for some moments. "Life. Feeling...something. I don't know. Passion. Natasha."

"This is serious," Stephen laughed. He figured humor could do no harm. "Does she want you?"

The simplicity of the question intrigued Harry. "Yes—at least, I think so."

"Lucky man," Stephen grinned. "What's the problem?"

"I *am* married." Even Harry knew he sounded stuffy. "At least I used to be."

"I know. You told me about Laura. But Harry, not everyone's as duty-bound as you. Why not cut yourself some slack? If you don't, then you'll poison whatever good you have."

The image of a smiling Laura, in Dr. Stover's bed, came upon him swiftly.

Stephen smiled and patted Harry's shoulder. "Listen, pal, I shouldn't have to tell you this stuff. Get yourself out of here first and we'll go out for drinks." Harry watched as Stephen left. He started to snore, then drifted off to sleep.

Later, Harry thought it was only a dream. He recollected a soft kiss on his cheek and a gentle touch. A voice was low in his ear. When he murmured something unintelligible, Natasha smiled to herself and then left. She knew he would recover quickly. He woke, only for a moment, to see an empty bedside.

Hours later, the door banged open and the curtain flew back. Harry woke abruptly. A massive figure loomed over him.

"We keep running into each other, Mr. Jenkins. Welkom here." The sergeant spoke in gruff tones. "You got a pretty exciting practice for a family solicitor." Harry had no idea what sort of response was required. "What do you know about Miss Michaels?" asked the sergeant.

"Who's she?"

"The dead woman. Miss Deighton's housekeeper. Her corpse knocked you down the stairs."

"Oh, that's her last name. I only knew her as Rosie."

"She was strangled," said Welkom flatly.

Harry could not imagine anyone wanting to harm Rosie. "Was there a robbery?"

"Doesn't seem to be anything stolen, Mr. Jenkins. But then, it's hard to tell." Welkom paused as he searched for his pen. "Did you check your office? Anything missing from there?"

After the break-in, Harry had tried to put everything back in order. Nothing seemed to be missing. With everything dumped on the floor, it had been hard to tell. His head was beginning to pound again.

"The autopsy on the Michaels woman showed that she'd been strangled. Not just strangled, but her neck was snapped in two places. Must have been one hell of a mean bastard who did it." Welkom paused, then consulted his notebook again. "According to the autopsy report, the time of death was on the 16th, probably in the afternoon."

It took a moment for this information to sink in. "That's the same day Marjorie died. She must have been there when my secretary and I found Marjorie. That's why the landing door to the back stairs was jammed."

"Exactly, counselor." Welkom snapped his notebook shut. "But the worst part is that she was cut up real bad. Someone took a knife to her stomach and carved rose petals. Pretty crude stuff. Then he dressed her back up. Real neat."

"Jesus!" Harry breathed. Astounded, he struggled to organize his thoughts. "You mean the Florist killed Rosie?" His voice trailed off. "But what's the connection?"

The sergeant shrugged. "Who knows? Don't know if there is one. We're not sure it's the same person. The artwork isn't nearly as neat. Could be a copycat."

Harry frowned. "I don't see any connection between my client and the Florist."

Pen and notebook in hand, Welkom asked, "Who else, besides you and your secretary, could have been in the house that afternoon?"

Harry exhaled sharply. "Damn it all. I told you repeatedly that someone was there at two o'clock. The telephone was ringing off the hook. Why didn't you follow up?"

Ignoring his questions, Welkom said doggedly, "If Miss Michaels was strangled, your client was likely murdered, too."

"*Really*, officer?" Harry muttered. "That's hardly surprising." Still, it didn't fit. If Marjorie had been murdered, it must have been poison. Harry could not visualize the same hand carefully administering an overdose, and then snapping a neck in two places.

"Mr. Jenkins?"

Harry realized that the sergeant was shaking his shoulder. He must have drifted off.

"Why would anyone want to kill Marjorie?" Harry managed to ask. "She was such a great lady."

"You tell me, Mr Jenkins. You're one of her executors, aren't you?" Welkom's face loomed close to Harry's. "Who would inherit her estate?"

"St. Timothy's Church gets a legacy, and the balance is divided equally among the three next of kin."

"Lots of money?"

"Depending on the value of the house, between five and six million."

The sergeant whistled. "The family would do very nicely." Welkom stood abruptly. His form hovered over Harry's bed. "People have been murdered for a lot less, counselor." Although the area was cramped, Welkom began to pace. Turning on Harry, he said, "The knife, Mr. Jenkins."

Harry stared at him blankly. His only thought was the pounding in his head.

"The knife that was sticking in your desk," Welkom prompted.

"Yes?" Harry was having difficulty following. What did the knife have to do with Marjorie?

"It was clean: no prints on it at all. Who's Albert Chin?"

"Another client." Harry replied.

"For how long? Where'd he come from?" Welkom's jaw jutted out, almost touching the pillow.

Harry tried to turn away. Because of solicitor-client privilege, he could say nothing. "Sorry, sergeant. I'm sure you know I can't tell you about any other client's business." Harry sighed. Welkom remained silent for several moments. "Where does that leave things, then?" Harry muttered. His eyelids were beginning to droop.

"Nowhere, Mr. Jenkins. Not without your help. You see, I figure there are at least two connected murders so far. Besides, with that knife sticking out of your desk, haven't you thought somebody might be trying to give you a message?"

Harry's eyelids flew open. "Listen, sergeant. I don't understand your connection between the break-in, the knife, and the Deighton business. As far as I'm concerned, they're totally unrelated." But he could not dismiss the fact that Chin's purchases surrounded Marjorie's property. Also, the conglomerate wanted an option over her place. But how often was someone murdered over a real-estate deal?

Welkom smiled sadly. "Just a hunch, counselor. What I can't figure out, though, is you." Welkom scratched his head. "You told me she was just an old lady who died in her sleep."

"Who asked about an autopsy, sergeant?" Harry tried to raise himself up. "Who called you to ask about the housekeeper and the autopsy?" He fell back in pain. "Why wasn't all of this done in the first place?"

Welkom's face darkened. "*Now* it will be. You can count on it, counselor—and you can tell the nieces and nephew. I'm getting an exhumation order right away." Welkom stood and patted Harry's shoulder. "We'll talk again real soon, Mr. Jenkins." Then he was gone.

Nothing fit. How could the other murders on the news have anything to do with Marjorie? If she had been murdered, Rosie might have come across the killer and been strangled. If there were any connection between the Deighton murder and the break-in, it was the Chin land deals.

The nurse arrived, laden with a box.

"Mr. Jenkins! What beautiful flowers. A dozen long-stemmed roses," she exclaimed.

"Who sent them?" He hoped Natasha had.

The nurse opened the envelope and held the card up to the light. "It says here: *'Get well soon. Albert Chin.'*"

Harry grew very cold. He closed his eyes and gasped in pain. "Jesus! Can you give me something?" He clutched his side. "For the pain?"

After consulting the chart, the nurse adjusted the flow of morphine. Gratefully, Harry lapsed back into oblivion.

CHAPTER 20

▼

Several days later, Harry returned home from hospital. Although painkillers kept the thousands of knives from thrusting between his ribs, they coated his mind in a soft fuzz. Idly, he drifted through the morning, without much thought of anything. The telephone rang.

"Hello?" he muttered.

Miss Giveny's voice was a high-pitched wail. "Oh, Mr. Jenkins! Something terrible has happened. I knew only trouble would come from it."

Harry was awake. "What on earth are you talking about? What's happened?" Only a cataclysmic event could drive his taciturn secretary to such a frantic pitch. "Miss Giveny, tell me what it is." Harry spoke with as much authority as he was able to muster.

"Mr. Jenkins, the will is gone." The choking sound continued. "I've looked everywhere." Only loud sniffles could be heard. He hoped she was trying to pull herself together.

"What will? Surely not Marjorie's?"

An ominous silence followed. "Yes," said Miss Giveny in a hushed voice. "Marjorie Deighton's original will is gone."

Harry sat up. Pain ground into his side so violently that he gasped for breath. At last he said, "But we got it from the vault the day we went to see her. You made two copies, and we took them with us. You must have put it back, because you made more copies after she died."

But maybe it hadn't been returned to the vault, he thought. Likely it had been on his desk or hers. Over the next few minutes, Harry ran through a list of places to look. Each suggestion was met with the adamant reply, "It's not there!"

Things went missing. Invariably they were found later, misfiled or stored in some bizarre place for safekeeping.

Then he remembered. The night the office was ransacked, he had gone directly through the gloomy twilight of the foyer into the bright lights of his office. But only a dim light had been on in the outer office, where the vault had stood slightly ajar. Mesmerized by the knife stabbed into the Chin offers and the petals, he had forgotten the vault. The utter chaos of his own office had completely distracted him.

"I'll be there right away."

Harry called a cab and struggled into some clothes. Popping three painkillers into his mouth, he hunted down a glass of water in the bathroom.

Forty-five minutes later, he entered the office to see Miss Giveny with red-rimmed eyes and a Kleenex bunched at her lips.

"Oh, Mr. Jenkins." She was alarmed at his pallor. "I shouldn't have gotten you out of bed."

Harry walked gingerly to the vault. From the Rolodex, he confirmed the number of the will, and then methodically went through each of the twenty-five wills stored in the particular box. Yes, the envelope numbered 2625 was there, but empty. The office rule was to keep the envelope with the will at all times, so someone had taken it. Dizziness forced him into a nearby chair.

"Call the police at 55 Division. I want to speak to Sergeant Welkom."

Only Suzannah would benefit from the theft of Marjorie's will. In the previous one, Suzannah got the house outright at age thirty. In the missing one, she had to share it with her brother and sister. Frank's ugly, leering face rose up in Harry's mind. He cursed. Frank would stop at nothing.

"I've got the sergeant on the line," Miss Giveny called out.

"Sergeant, Harry Jenkins here. There is something missing, after all."

"Which is?"

"Marjorie Deighton's will. The original."

"When did you find that out?"

Harry seethed at the implication that he was withholding information. "Just now," he replied coldly. "My secretary went to the vault, and it was gone."

"Okay," the sergeant sighed. "I was coming over anyway."

Harry replaced the receiver and then redialed. He needed advice quickly. More attention paid in criminal-law class would have been helpful now, he reflected.

"Is Stephen Barrett in, please?"

"One moment. Who's calling?" came the cheery voice.

"Harry Jenkins. And tell him it's urgent, would you?" Harry eased into his chair. It hurt to sit. It hurt to stand.

"Harry, good to hear from you. What's up?"

"I need some quick advice, Stephen. How far do I have to cooperate with the police in revealing information about clients?"

There was a lengthy pause. "That depends," Stephen began cautiously. "Who's charged with what?"

"It's part of that murder investigation of Rosie Michaels."

"You have to cooperate. The police can ask any questions and look at any files regarding that client," Stephen said briskly.

"And the gray areas?"

"Refuse, then call me. Who's investigating?"

"Sergeant Welkom. 55 Division."

Stephen groaned. "Jesus, that guy should have been retired five years ago. Thinks he's the only real cop left. Very sloppy."

Harry could hear voices in the outer office. "Thanks, Stephen. I may be calling you about this later."

"Sure, anytime. But be careful, pal."

Harry hung up and rose stiffly from his chair. When Sergeant Welkom arrived, Miss Giveny ushered him and one other uniformed officer into the office. Sitting down, Welkom fished a sheaf of papers from his breast pocket. He tossed them on Harry's desk.

"What's this?"

"Read it. It's a court order," growled the sergeant.

For a moment, Harry stared at the neatly folded document. He could see the edge of the red seal poking out.

"We're going to exhume the body, Mr. Jenkins."

"It's about time the police did their work," Harry said mildly. He unfolded the papers and began reading. "Are you serving me with this?"

"Guess so, Mr. Jenkins. You're Marjorie Deighton's executor. You're responsible for the body, right?"

"Yes, I'm one of the executors. Gideon Trust is the other."

"I think you should get her next of kin together right away. The body will be exhumed in the morning for an autopsy."

"Good. It should have been done right away."

"Listen, counselor, stay out of police work. The coroner's office—"

Harry waved him off. "I'll arrange the meeting."

"Good. I'd like to be there. Might shed some light on the case."

Harry nodded curtly. "I'll let you know, sergeant. Now, about the missing will."

Welkom shrugged. "The officer here will take down the details."

"Only one person would benefit from the theft of the will. Suzannah Deighton gets the house under the old will. In the stolen one, she has to share it with her brother and sister."

Welkom could not overlook this information. He nodded to the other cop, who took out his notebook. "So, you're saying this niece, Suzannah Deighton, broke in and took the will?"

"Not her, sergeant. But her boyfriend, Frank Sasso, might have."

"Okay, we'll look into it." Welkom stood in the doorway. "Remember, counselor, to let me know about that meeting. I want to be there." Welkom pulled the door shut.

With intense pain in his side, Harry sank into his chair. Damn! He'd forgotten the painkillers. He buzzed Miss Giveny to set up a meeting of the beneficiaries that afternoon.

Ten minutes later, his secretary called out. "Mr. Jenkins? Do you want to speak to that Mr. Chin? He's on line two."

"All right," Harry sighed, picking up the phone. "Yes, Mr. Chin. What can I do for you?" The flowers were only a dark and hazy memory.

"I am most happy to see you are better. Did the flowers arrive?"

"Yes. Thank you very much." In the long pause, Harry could think of little to say. "It was very kind of you," he added.

"I understand the purchases will close tomorrow. After that, the conglomerate would like you to prepare an option to purchase the Deighton property, as soon as you are well enough. I have a further retainer for that work and certain rezoning work."

Harry cut him off. "I told you, Mr. Chin. I am terribly sorry, but I cannot act in that matter, because I am her executor."

"Surely, those are only technical concerns which may be overcome by—"

"I *am* sorry, but it's a conflict I cannot ignore. I could refer you to—"

"I see. That is most unfortunate. I will have to advise the conglomerate. They will be very disappointed. Good day, sir." Chin hung up.

Harry stared at the phone. *So much for that work,* he thought.

CHAPTER 21

▼

For thirty-five years, Mrs. Beatrice Clough had presided over the main reception hall of Gideon Trust. She was a pleasant, powdery person whose disposition mirrored the quiet elegance of her surroundings.

Mrs. Clough sat behind a huge cherrywood desk, the surface of which glowed in the reflected lighting of the brass lamps. According to her, quiet courtesy was the hallmark of refined and well-bred people. Trouble was usually announced with loud and boorish manners.

She checked the agenda for the afternoon. Mr. McCrea had hastily scrawled a two-o'clock appointment for the Deighton estate in the calendar, but had not listed the names of the expected visitors. The Deighton family were old clients. Lovely people. She anticipated with pleasure the arrival of the next generation.

A loud braying voice from the elevators interrupted her typing.

"I told you, Gerry, this estate's gonna be wound up real fast. No dicking around. Just wait and see." Mrs. Clough stiffened. The glass doors banged open. Here was a troublemaker.

The red-faced man approaching her desk was bursting out of his jacket. A man and two women raced to keep up with him. Wielding his briefcase like a weapon, he slammed it down on the cherrywood surface of her desk, almost knocking the brass lamp to the floor. Mrs. Clough reached for the red emergency button underneath the desk, but hesitated.

"We got an appointment with a Cameron McCrea on the Deighton estate. Tell him Frank Sasso's here."

Mrs. Clough nodded mutely and reached for the intercom. She'd buzz security if Mr. McCrea said so. Mr. Sasso removed his troop to the farthest sofa.

"Listen, Gerry, I got a surprise for this trust company. They've been nothing but a goddamned pain in the ass with Suzannah's trust." Leaning forward, Frank continued confidentially, "Them and that lawyer Jenkins are gonna be out of the picture in about five minutes."

"What the hell have you done, Frank?" Katharine sat in rigid fury next to him on the sofa. Gerry and Suzannah occupied the armchairs.

Frank smiled and grasped her wrist. "Listen, sweetie, I'm only doing what Auntie really wanted. Just watch."

Tearing her arm from his grasp, Katharine said, "If you've done something to her will, Frank, by God, we'll fight you to the end."

"Me?" Frank spread his hands out, as if to placate her. "You'll see. Auntie's only done what's fair to everybody."

McCrea bustled out of a side door of the reception. "Good afternoon, ladies and gentlemen." He ushered them swiftly down a hallway to the boardroom. Mrs. Clough sighed in relief.

The trust officer swung the door open and stepped back. Frank barged in ahead, then suddenly stopped. Expecting to see only Jenkins, he was surprised when a tall, balding man rose to introduce himself as Peter Thompson, vice-president of personal trust. Harry Jenkins nodded, but remained seated. At the far end of the room, a gray and weary man rose. Instinct made Frank stiffen and step back. *Fuck! Must be a cop,* he thought.

When all were seated, Peter Thompson began. "We've invited Sergeant Welkom here today because he has some important documents relating to your aunt and her estate." Thompson hated being dragged into these messy affairs. The police and trust companies were not natural allies.

"This is about Marjorie's will, Mr. Thompson?" Katharine wanted to get right to business. Frank snapped open his briefcase.

"Yes. Mr. Jenkins is going to take it from here." Thompson nodded to Harry.

Harry began distributing copies of the will. "It's usual to begin with a reading of the will, ladies and gentlemen. There's a copy for each of you. I'll answer any of your questions at the end."

"Just a minute now, Mr. Jenkins. Are you sure that's the latest will? What's the date on it?" asked Frank.

Immediately, Harry was on his guard. Trouble was coming from Frank, right on cue. "It's dated the twelfth of April, 1998."

"Nineteen ninety-eight, you say? You sure of that date?"

"Yes." Harry said. Frank was headed into his cat-and-mouse routine. For sure, he was involved in the missing-will business, thought Harry. Frank was lounging back in his chair, but he leaned over to rummage through his case. Harry hoped the chair might snap under Frank's girth.

"Well, seems like that's an out-of-date will. I got one right here that's dated just before she died."

Peter Thompson, Cameron McCrea, and Harry glanced at one another.

Thompson was the first to speak. "How do you happen to have Miss Deighton's will?"

Frank ignored the question and barreled on. "This will appoints another lawyer—not you, Jenkins—as the executor." Frank waved the document in the air. "That means, Jenkins, you and your cronies here at the great Gideon Trust are out of the picture." Frank's grin could not have been wider.

"Let's see it, then," Harry said impatiently. "It was made just a few days before Miss Deighton died?"

"So?" Frank pulled on his tie. "That doesn't mean it's no good."

"No, but it must be the one she wanted to change."

"But she didn't."

"True, Mr. Sasso. Only her death prevented that." Disgusted, Harry folded his arms across his chest. "And you still haven't told us how you got this will."

Still smiling broadly, Frank tossed the will along the table to Harry, who spent several moments examining it.

His gut sank. "Yes, that looks like Marjorie's signature." Then he felt his anger rise. "Just how did you get your hands on this, Frank?" He peered at him, wondering whether the bully or the wheedler would surface first.

Frank hesitated only for a second. "This lawyer, Fulford, gave it to me." His jaw jutted out. "Told me Marjorie made it fair and square, when she was of sound mind, and without any influence, either."

Harry saw Frank's weakness. Too rehearsed. Out of his depth. Probably Fulford had given him some rudimentary coaching. "You sound worried about something," Harry prodded. "Pretty defensive."

"What does it say?" asked Katharine. Her voice was low and threatening. "I know you, Frank. How did you get Marjorie to change her will?"

Harry held up his hand for silence. "This purported will makes major changes."

"Hey! What's this 'purported' shit?" Frank's grin began to fade.

Harry ignored him. Nodding in McCrea's direction, Harry continued, "Both Gideon and I have been replaced by a sole executor. A lawyer named James Fulford gets the job. The will leaves the house to Suzannah and divides the rest of the estate equally among the three of you."

"God damn it, Frank. You're a real bastard!" Katharine was halfway out of her chair.

Gerry rose to stand beside her. He held her arm. "Katie, don't. We can fight him, but not this way."

"Don't be such a wimp, Gerry." Tearing her arm away, she glared incredulously at her brother. "That's exactly what he wants. He's trying to sucker us into litigation. Spend the whole estate on lawyers. You want a fight, Frank? You've got one."

Harry was formulating a plan. Undoubtedly, Gideon would refer even the least contentious matter to their solicitors. "Cover your ass" was their motto. Months later, a four-page legal opinion letter would be tucked in the file, stating the obvious. An executor could be fired without recourse. Meanwhile, Frank, when no one was looking, would have pocketed the estate assets from the game board. With Gideon's glacial speed, a crook even as stupid as Frank could outsmart them. The whole situation reeked. The swiftest course was to take on Fulford.

Welkom rose. Circling the table, he went to stand next to Frank. "You can save this stuff for later. Right now, there's something a lot more important." He handed Gerry a sheaf of papers.

"What the hell is this?" Gerry asked, pulling out his reading glasses.

"It's a court order. Read it," Welkom said flatly.

"For what?" Frank was annoyed with the cop's butting in.

"To exhume the body of Miss Marjorie Deighton tomorrow morning."

"Why?" all three beneficiaries chorused.

"Our investigations indicate that your aunt was murdered."

Harry surveyed all three beneficiaries. The sergeant's statement had frozen them in place.

Katharine turned pale. "Who else was at the house that day?"

Gerry sank into his chair, muttering, "Jesus! This will hold up the administration, I suppose."

Katharine stood over Gerry. "Did you go to see her for money, Gerry? You've been talking about that."

"Me?" Gerry was enraged. "God damn it, Katie, are you accusing me?"

Katharine's voice cut the still air. "Of course not. You wouldn't be capable of that. But I know someone who is." Everyone in the room froze as she glared at Frank.

Suzannah spoke, for the first time, in a low and dreamy voice. "Why, Sergeant Welkom, I'm not surprised to hear you say that. It's about time someone thought about Auntie. I'm not doing anything about the estate until we know what happened to her."

Frank glowered at Suzannah, but said nothing.

"Frank!" Katharine hissed. "What in God's name did you do to make Marjorie change her will?"

"Absolutely nothing." Frank grinned. "She did it of her own free will. You just can't stand the idea that she loved Suzannah more. What'd you ever do for Auntie?"

For just a moment, Katharine was speechless.

Harry held up his hand. "Suzannah is right." He looked directly at Frank. "Obviously, anyone implicated in Marjorie's death in any way should not benefit from her will. Even though I only knew her as a client, I still want to know how and why she died. I'd think *all* of her next of kin would feel the same way."

In the reception room, Harry watched Katharine push past Frank. He grabbed her arm. "Listen, Katharine. Marjorie only did what's fair and right. Sometime, when you've settled down, you'll understand."

"Get your disgusting hand off me!" Katharine wrenched away.

Seeing Frank's face darken with fury, Harry almost stepped forward. But Katharine, her words dripping like acid, said, "Frank, you're a sleaze and too stupid to pull this off."

Frank hesitated, but then stepped back. Katharine entered the elevator and was gone. The woman was more than able to look after herself, thought Harry.

Anger drove Harry up Yonge Street to his office building. Lawyers like Fulford poached on clientele for a living. It was time to pay him a visit. But as he walked along the hallway from the elevator, the painkillers began wearing off and his knees almost gave out. With his shirt matted to his back, he tried to straighten his shoulders, but the pain was too intense. Fumbling with the knob, he smashed his briefcase against the office door with such force that he could hear Miss Giveny's muffled shriek inside. He pushed the door open, only to find his secretary standing halfway in the foyer, armed with a heavy staple gun.

"Mr. Jenkins! It's you!"

"Of course it's me. Put that thing down."

"You look like death warmed over." She followed him into his office.

Harry struggled out of his jacket and sat down. Propping his elbows on the desk, he said, "Please don't just stand there gaping. Get me the Deighton files, please." Then the room started to swim.

Quickly returning with the files, she seated herself across the desk from him.

"Miss Deighton has made a new will," Harry began, as sickness welled up in his stomach.

Miss Giveny stiffened. "What does it say?"

"She's appointed a new executor. Unless the beneficiaries contest, I'm out of the picture." Harry could not contain his bitterness. Rising from his chair, he began to pace, but found he could only limp in pain.

The law did not allow an executor to protest if he lost his job. A court would undoubtedly appoint an independent administrator in the event of a battle. Even so, the best strategy was to scare the new lawyer off.

"Who gets the estate?"

"She gives the house to Suzannah outright," said Harry. "The rest of the estate is split equally among the three of them." Harry shoved his hands in his pockets and stared out the window. He sighed deeply. "St. Timothy's still gets its legacy." Lost in thought, Harry let his voice trail off.

"But that's almost the same as her old will," Miss Giveny said.

"Exactly! They'll argue that Marjorie simply wanted to return to her old pattern of distribution. Because Suzannah is over thirty, why not give it to her outright?" Harry returned to his study of the alleyway below. "By the way, did you ever see the secret trust? I never found the instructions in the file."

Miss Giveny shook her head slowly, then asked, "Did she name Gideon Trust as the executor?"

Harry was overwhelmed with weariness. Helplessness was settling over him. He leaned on the windowsill. "No. Gideon got tossed out, too. Some lawyer named Fulford has the executorship now."

"Fulford? He's called three times this afternoon.

Harry turned abruptly from the window. "He has?"

"Yes, James Fulford. He's demanding all the Deighton files."

Harry kicked hard. The full wastebasket shot across the room. Both of them watched the contents fly everywhere, then slowly flutter to the carpet. Harry slouched into his chair.

"That bastard has no right to my files," he whispered, after a long while.

Miss Giveny rose to go. From the file, an aged, tattered envelope slid onto the desk. Harry retrieved it. "What's this?" he asked.

Her hand shot out. "Nothing. Let me have it for the file."

The desperate note in her voice alerted Harry. "What's in it?" Slowly, he began opening the envelope.

"Please, Mr. Jenkins, don't!"

Harry was alarmed. "Is it to do with the Deighton file?"

Miss Giveny's lips pursed into a knot. "Yes," she admitted.

"Then I shall open it." He tore the remains of the envelope and spread the sheet on the desk. He began to read carefully.

Dear Suzannah,

I love you with all my heart, in a very special way. Conventions and restrictions of my time have forced me to keep a secret. Now that I am free, I can tell you. You are my only child, whom I have loved from a distance. My heart has ached constantly throughout the years to tell you. As a young woman, I was governed by passion. The times were very restrictive. I fell deeply in love with an older married man: Richard Crawford, my lawyer. You can understand how a woman can be swept away by a man. Thralldom makes you risk everything, without fearing loss. You were born of my secret passion, and I have always known we are one of a kind. We yearn to break free. But I greatly fear for you. You are bound by fear, not passion, to Frank Sasso. I have always wanted you to have this house for yourself, but I am worried that he will cheat you out of it someday. I cannot let him do that. Be sure to ask Harold Jenkins about the secret trust. It is your safety and your freedom, my darling. In time, you will break free of that man.

With my enduring love,

Your mother,
Marjorie Deighton

Slowly, Harry looked up at Miss Giveny. "You were keeping this from me?" he asked quietly. Almost overwhelmed, he remembered Crawford's drawings and his declarations of love, or rather lust, just before he pitched onto the floor. *"If you have not experienced the passion, the thrall, you have not lived."* He should fire Miss Giveny on the spot.

Gladys Giveny's reaction was unexpected. Her face was red with blotches. She bunched a Kleenex up to her nose. "Yes," she spat out angrily.

Surprised, Harry peered closely at her. He struggled for calm. "But why?" he asked. "Surely you understand how important this is. It explains why Marjorie left the house to Suzannah." He felt the anger rising fast within him. "What explanation could you possibly have?"

The woman's eyes flashed. "You'd never understand! I had to protect Mr. Crawford from such accusations. Besides, Mr. Crawford swore me to secrecy."

"And you kept this from me out of some misguided notion of privilege?" Harry's voice was rising fast. His face was flushed. Miss Giveny cringed. "Jesus! Who else knows this?"

"Nobody." she insisted.

"Not Suzannah?"

"Of course not."

"What about Katharine and Gerry?"

"Who would tell them?"

Harry pondered his legal position. In his hand, he held the evidence substantiating Suzannah's claim to the house. Regardless of the executorship, he would have to reveal it.

Miss Giveny bowed her head and began muttering darkly, "No man could have resisted her. That brazen hussy flirted shamelessly with him."

Harry struggled to visualize Marjorie Deighton consumed with aggressive, libidinous intent.

With tears glinting in her eyes, Miss Giveny said, "I typed up the paternity agreement. Mr. Crawford put fifty thousand dollars in trust for that baby, although there was not a shred of proof it was his. George and Mildred Deighton agreed to raise Suzannah as their own. I'm the only one still alive who ever saw that agreement." After a pause, Miss Giveny continued fiercely, "Mr. Crawford was a true gentleman. It might have been anyone's child. But he didn't complain. He took responsibility."

"Do we still have the paternity agreement?"

"No. I destroyed it after Mr. Crawford died."

Harry caught his breath. "Good God! What other evidence have you hidden or destroyed?"

She looked up at him. When she spoke, her voice was strong. "None!" She glared at him. "What do you know about these things, anyway? You've lived with your wife all these years. You've no idea what it's like to love someone from afar, but work with him every day. I loved Mr. Crawford. I had to protect him."

Only then did Harry understand the depth of Miss Giveny's lonely passion. Visions of Merle slipped into his mind. If he tried, he could feel sympathy for the woman trembling across the desk from him. *I suppose I should fire her.* It certainly was more than warranted. But where would she ever find another job? It would be like turning an orphan out on a cold winter night.

Quietly, he said, "Get me Fulford on the phone."

Fulford's voice was high, reedy, and quavering. Harry had an instant picture of an absurdly thin and mottled crane wavering in a pond.

"I assume you are aware, Mr. Jenkins, of Miss Deighton's new will?"

"And I assume you're aware, Mr. Fulford, that you've got a fight on your hands."

There was a short pause, and then Fulford continued briskly, "The will is completely valid, although I can understand why some people may be angered by the changes."

"I want to meet with you."

"When? Let me get my book."

"Now. I'll be there in twenty minutes." Harry hung up.

Fulford's office was in an old but stylishly renovated house on Bloor Street; tarted up to look like a British barrister's chambers. A brass knocker and name-plate adorned the oak door, and fake gas lamps were set on either side. With some malice, he imagined the Deightons' horror of such grand quarters.

Fulford was foolish to keep Harry waiting. Flipping through old magazines, Harry had plenty of time to develop his strategy. When the lawyer finally beck-oned him from the hallway, Harry recognized him instantly. It was none other than Jimmy, also known as "the Inflator," for his outrageous fees. In court, Harry had seen him wring his hands in supplication to wrest the last nickel of compen-sation out of each estate.

Harry sat in the wing chair in front of Fulford's desk. He pushed a file to one side and set his briefcase down. Fulford remained standing behind his desk. Glancing at his watch, he said, "I haven't much time, Mr. Jenkins. What can I do for you?"

"How did you get involved with my client?" Harry demanded, snapping open his briefcase.

"That's scarcely your concern now, is it?" Fulford's thin lips drew into a tight line. Harry was close enough to see his nostrils twitch.

"Yes, it is. I couldn't place you at first, but now I can."

"Meaning?"

"Meaning that you're the lawyer with the creative approach to estate account-ing. Listen, Jimmy, I was in court the day Judge Farley lit into you. Weren't the beneficiaries alleging doctored appraisals?" Harry gazed benignly at Fulford. Compensation for executors was calculated on a percentage of the value of the estate assets. A good photocopier made it easy to increase the value of appraisals.

"Get the hell out of here, Jenkins!" Fulford rose to his full height behind his desk. He towered over Harry, but he was trembling.

"Listen, Jimmy," Harry said in the most soothing tone he could find. "You know this Deighton estate won't be easy money. There's bound to be a nasty fight. Sit down and we can fill each other in."

Fulford hesitated and then sat down. Harry continued, "Now, how did you get involved in this one?"

"All right, but there's not much to tell. I got a call from the vicar at St. Anne's Parish Church."

"That's not Marjorie's church."

"No. Apparently the vicar had been contacted by a man named Frank Sasso, I think." Fulford made a show of consulting his notes. "Sasso wanted him to recommend a solicitor to do a simple will for Miss Deighton." Fulford shrugged. "I was called and went to see her."

Harry took a long yellow pad from his briefcase and began making notes.

"When I got there, the housekeeper let me in, and I met with Miss Deighton in the living room."

"Anyone else in the house?"

"Not that I know of."

"How did Marjorie seem?"

"You mean, did I think she was competent?"

Harry nodded, not wanting to interrupt. Fulford consulted his file.

"Yes, she was alert—well aware of her assets and who would be the natural objects of her bounty. Actually, she was quite concerned about the family members."

"Do you have any notes of your interview?"

"Of course." With a mildly offended air, Fulford turned to the few pages in his file. "I asked if she had made a will before. She smiled at me rather sadly, I thought, and said 'too many.'"

"Did you ask to see them?"

"No. Miss Deighton made it quite clear that she simply wanted to instruct me, after which I would prepare the will and return for her signature. Which I did."

"Then you went back on the eighth?"

"Yes."

"Why did she appoint you as her executor?" Harry held his breath, steeling himself for the answer.

"She didn't want you to know about the changes." He looked at his notes and continued. "In fact, she thought you'd try to talk her out of them."

Harry was astounded at Fulford's candor.

"Also, she said, and I quote, 'He's a dear, patient man, but not incapable of telling me I'm a foolish old woman.'"

Harry smiled. Indeed, that was something she might well say. She must have felt pressured. That was why she had turned to him on the day she died. There was evidence of suspicious circumstances surrounding the making of the new will. But was there enough to make a case of undue influence? Frank was the instigator: that alone was more than suspicious. But suspicious circumstances were only small clouds casting shadows; Harry needed a thunderstorm. He stood and began to pace. Fulford watched in wary silence.

"What did she say about the family?"

"Not a lot, really. She did say that she'd left the house in trust for Suzannah in a prior will and now she wanted to give it to her outright, after what she had undertaken to do. Those were Miss Deighton's words. Suzannah apparently made some sort of promise."

"Which was?"

Fulford shrugged. "She didn't say."

Harry turned on Fulford. "Didn't she tell you that the most recent will divided the estate equally three ways?"

"No, she didn't." Fulford seemed genuinely surprised. "Had she said so, of course, I would have inquired further."

Pompous little prig, thought Harry. But he was pleased. The will had been prepared without complete information, maybe under duress. If not, there were at least lots of suspicious circumstances. Her words could be interpreted to mean that she had replaced him as executor against her better judgement.

"Did you know she called me in on the 16th to make another will?"

"She did?" Fulford seemed surprised, but this time it might have been feigned. "What happened?" he asked.

"I found her dead." Harry stared at Fulford, who was now twisting his fourth paper clip into a knot. He debated how much to reveal. "At first, the police thought it was a natural death, but since they found the body of the housekeeper, they think it's homicide. They've got a court order to exhume the body tomorrow."

Fulford stared back at Harry in shock. "But who would murder her?"

"You guess, Jimmy!" Harry snapped. "Lots of funny things happen in estates, especially when there's plenty of money to fight over." Harry waited to let him digest everything. Although very pale, Fulford gave away nothing.

Harry said quietly, "I think you've been used." He had succeeded beyond his fondest dreams. Fulford was scared. No doubt he knew more than he let on.

"Yes, it is a terrible mess," Harry continued casually. "First, there's a murder investigation. The niece and nephew left out in the cold will certainly challenge the will. There's even a big chunk of money to fund the litigation. Their lawyer will have fun cross-examining you."

Fulford tossed the knot of paper clips onto the desk and shut the file. He massaged his temples, but remained silent.

Harry prodded further. "I expect the police investigation will drag the administration out." He concluded softly, "The executorship is hardly worth all the trouble, is it?"

Fulford's eyes flickered. "Of course, that's what you're after, isn't it, Jenkins?"

"Well, of course. She was my client," he answered mildly.

Fulford shook his head slowly and sighed. "I'm prepared to renounce the executorship. But we'd better come to terms first." He picked up a pen and pad.

"What terms?" Harry was on his feet.

"Under the circumstances, I think twenty-five percent of the compensation is fair."

"For what?" Harry demanded and strode around the desk.

Fulford lurched back in his chair.

Harry was within inches of the man. "Listen, you son of a bitch! You just don't get it, do you? You're sitting in the middle of a contested will case and a murder investigation. And somehow, like it or not, you're personally involved."

Fulford turned white.

Harry returned to his seat and shook his head in amazement. "You're either stupid, or you're such a greedy bastard that you just don't care! You sign a renunciation before I leave this office, or I'll make sure this case gets dragged out before Judge Farley!"

Twenty minutes later, Harry strode from the office with the renunciation in his briefcase and a broad grin on his face.

CHAPTER 22

▼

Traffic crawled up the parkway in the early twilight. Frank sang along with the radio as he followed the string of red taillights. A perfect day. Time to celebrate.

Thinking of Jenkins and McCrea, he chuckled. They'd looked like they'd been kicked in the balls. He, Frank Sasso, had outsmarted them all.

The best part was getting back at that ballbuster Katharine. The frigid bitch was just like ice. *Madder than hell about the will, too.*

So what if dear Auntie called Jenkins about her will the day she died? She didn't change it. Fact was, Suzannah promised to help her make an exit, if and when, she wanted. *That ought to be worth a fucking house,* he chuckled.

He fingered the buttons on his cell phone. With one quick call, he would settle the bitch down. He reached Katharine's voice mail.

"This is just a friendly warning," he said. The lights of the oncoming traffic made his face look pale and distorted. "Keep this crap up about lawyers and you'll get what you're *really* dying for. But next time, babe, you're gonna get hurt real bad, if you don't stop this shit." Laughing, he hung up.

Auntie's timing had been perfect. She'd just died real peaceful in her sleep. Making the new will upset her so much, she just croaked. There was nothing to show up in the autopsy.

"Dear sweet Marjorie," Frank sang out. Smartest thing he'd ever done was to visit her the night after her birthday party. She was too sick to come down, so he just went right up to her room.

"What brings you here, Frank?" Marjorie had asked suspiciously when he drew a chair up to her bed. "Where is Suzannah tonight?"

"She's been out looking at nursing homes."

Marjorie struggled to sit up. "What? For whom?"

"For you, Auntie dear." Frank laughed at his own mimicry of Suzannah.

"You're lying, Frank." Marjorie reached for the telephone, but he caught her wrist.

"Don't bother calling. She ain't home."

"But why would she be looking for homes?" Marjorie asked uncertainly.

A sly smile crept over Frank's face. "I know what you asked her to do, Auntie. We gotta keep you from popping all those pills."

Marjorie was horrified. "She told you?"

"Yup." Frank grinned. "Didn't you know assisted suicide is a criminal offence? You want your *favorite* niece to go to jail?"

Marjorie slumped back on the pillows. If Suzannah had told Frank, he must have bullied it out of her, she reasoned. "Well, what do you want Frank?"

"Now that's a good girl. I always said you was smart. Me and Suzannah don't ask much. You want her to help you? Then you gotta give something in return. That's fair, right?"

Marjorie remained silent.

"All Suzannah wants, Auntie, is the house. Not till you're dead, of course."

"That's it?"

"So that it's free and clear from Katharine and Gerry."

"And if I refuse?"

Frank smiled and shook his head. "You don't want to do that. Believe me. We'll put you into a nursing home for the criminally insane. We'll tell people this nice little old lady is off her rocker, dancing around and collecting little bottles of pills." Frank opened the bedside drawer and whistled. "My, my! Look what we got here, Auntie."

"All right, Frank." Marjorie sighed deeply, turning her head away from him on the pillow. "I'll do it. Get a lawyer to draw up the will, and I'll sign it."

Frank grinned. "Right away, Auntie. I'll take care of everything. I knew you'd see reason. You're really a very intelligent woman."

Marjorie raised her head from the pillow. "You've got what you came for, Frank. Now, leave!"

"Sure. I'm going." He bent to kiss her cheek, but she pushed him away.

"Still got some fight left, eh?"

Marjorie drew herself up. Momentarily, anger flared, but quickly she was flooded with over-powering weariness. Where was the Deighton strength, she wondered? She knew she was too tired to fight him. Perhaps Suzannah felt the same.

"See ya, Auntie. I'll be back with a good lawyer for you." Frank slammed the bedroom door shut.

In his air-conditioned car, Frank began to sweat. The day was *not* perfect. He could not forget his meeting with the Chinaman, Albert Chin, that morning.

He had carried the leather satchel up two flights to the Sunrise Trading Company on Spadina Avenue.

The Chinaman, with great care, counted every bill.

"Mr. Sasso? There is not enough money here. The gentleman in Buffalo said he was sending over eight hundred thousand." Chin's eyelids flickered.

"Look, Chin! Every goddamned penny is there. Believe me, Benny only sent over six hundred."

Chin reached for the phone.

"No...Al. C'mon. I'll check and see. If there's anything missing, I'll get it to you by Friday at the very latest. You'll see."

The Chinaman scared Frank. He steepled his long, thin fingers, seeming to go off into some crazy trance.

"I promise, Al. Don't call Benny."

"Your job, Mr. Sasso," Chin began with a low tremor in his voice, "is to bring *all* the money with *each* delivery to the conglomerate from Buffalo. There is a serious problem if any is missing." Chin stood up and bowed. "You have until tomorrow at noon, sir."

Returning home from the meeting at Gideon Trust, Suzannah sat on the couch in the darkening living room, drinking. By early evening, the bottle of scotch was half-empty.

At first, just a tear or two trickled down her cheek. If she had not told Frank about the pills, Marjorie would still be alive. He must have given her an overdose. But how did he make her change her will? It couldn't be very hard. Frank liked it when things were easy.

She tried to reason. With the house, she had a hope of freedom. Marjorie would have told her to throw Frank out, but what did Auntie know about men like Frank? Katharine wouldn't put up with crap from any man. Secretly, she hoped Katharine would fight the will and fix Frank once and for all. Sometimes she wished she could just disappear. Suzannah knew about running. Once she had worked in the church mission house for street kids on the run, serving soup and handing out blankets. Struggling upward on the sofa, she reached for the light, but slumped back.

She had a brilliant idea. She could use Marjorie's house for homeless kids. She sat up straight. That would be doing some good. But Katharine would probably laugh at her. So expert at everything—always talking about her work with battered women at Emma's Hostel.

More tears slid down her cheeks. Maybe she could buy Frank off with her share of cash in the estate, if he promised to leave. *Ridiculous!* It wasn't just the money; he needed somebody to hurt.

As he pulled into the driveway, Frank picked up the champagne on the front seat. Suzannah's car was there, but all the lights in the house were out. Probably she'd dozed off, he thought. Taking too many Valium, and with all the liquor, her mind was like a soggy Kleenex. But it made it easier to keep her in line. He heaved himself out of the car and banged the front door open.

"Hey, babe! Where the hell are you?" Frank shouted from the hallway.

Suzannah could not breathe in the still living room. She could run out the back door, but her legs would not move.

"In the living room, Frank," she said quietly.

Frank stood in the doorway. "What the Christ you sitting in the dark for? You know how to turn on the lights, don't you?"

She knew that tone: half humorous and half menacing.

Frank circled the coffee table, tossed off his jacket, and then sat beside her on the couch. "You okay, babe?"

She nodded.

"Listen, sweetie, I brought us champagne. Time you and me had a little celebration."

He grasped her thigh. "Been into the scotch, eh?" His tone was light. "Hope you can still see to cook the dinner."

He shoved his hand up under her skirt and jammed his thumb into her thigh. Encircling her neck with his other hand, he dug his fingers in and wrenched her around to face him.

"What's the matter, babe? We haven't done it for at least two weeks." He shoved his tongue between her lips. His weight on her was crushing.

"Frank, no. Wait." She struggled out from under him. "Listen, let's have dinner first. Drink the champagne and then go to bed early."

He stopped and studied her.

"You'll see, Frank. I'll be good tonight. We can do anything you want tonight. But let's eat dinner first."

He sniffed suspiciously, "Don't smell nothing cooking. You'd better not be playing games with me."

"Honest, Frank, you'll see." She squirmed to the far end of the couch, fixed her hair, and said, "Let me pour you a scotch. Dinner will be on the table in no time."

Moments later, she set the drink in front of him. He grabbed her wrist and pulled her down. She struggled away. He pinched her hard. "You are one fantastic piece of ass," he said, laughing. "Too bad your brains aren't as big as your tits."

Suzannah took two lasagna dinners from the freezer and set them in the microwave. With a paring knife, she cut up some lettuce and tomatoes and tossed them into a bowl.

Fifteen minutes later, Frank occupied his chair at the head of the table and stuffed a napkin into his collar. She served the lasagna, salad, and bread. Retreating to her end of the table, she poured herself another scotch.

"Well babe, we're on easy street now." Frank grinned. He broke off a chunk of bread and reached for the butter. "No more money worries. No living from one deal to the next, hoping the money's gonna be there."

"What do you mean, Frank?"

"Auntie's property must be worth at least two million."

"Really?"

"In this market, no problem." Frank crammed a piece of bread into his mouth and chewed. "But listen, sweetie, don't you trouble your head about that kind of stuff. I'll get the money into the highest-return investments. We'll be all set then, just you and me."

Frank spooned more lasagna onto his plate. His napkin trailed into the serving dish. "This is our chance, babe," he began wistfully. "People are gonna start showing us respect once we got money. Just think of that sister of yours." Frank lounged back, smiling in recollection of the meeting at Gideon. "Katharine's gonna understand, real soon we're not some trash she can laugh at." His mouth tightened in frustration. He seemed to speak to himself. "I'm sick of them looking at us like we crawled out from under some rock. With their fancy degrees, they're always laughing at us."

Suzannah stared at her fork. She knew he would never change. "Frank?"

"What?"

"Auntie's house is mine. You've no right to tell me what to do with it," she said quietly. She hated her wheedling tone.

Frank stopped chewing. "I think your poor little brain has forgotten something, babe." He tossed his napkin down. "If it wasn't for me outsmarting all of them, that house would not be yours. You'd be sharing with your sister and that wimpy brother of yours."

It was too dark in the dining room to see Frank clearly, but there was no mistaking his tone.

Suzannah continued blindly, "What did you do, Frank, to make Auntie change her will?"

Frank spoke calmly. "Your aunt is not a stupid woman. She can see reason."

"I'll bet you reasoned with her, all right!" Suzannah's breathing was short and sharp. "What did you threaten her with, Frank?"

With exaggerated patience, Frank said, "Listen babe, I'm not going to tell you this twice. You are going to forget this crap about the will, and you're going to do exactly what I tell you."

"Forget it, Frank!" Suzannah's voice rose shrilly. "I'm sick of the way you think you can kick me around. You've no right!" The scared faces of the street kids flickered through her mind. "I'm not going to sell Auntie's house. It's mine! I'm going to turn it into a halfway house for kids!" She tried to fight back the tears back, but it was no use. Too late, she heard the stem of Frank's wine glass snap.

He grasped her hair and jerked her neck back. "A halfway house, is it? And just how did your pea-brain come up with that?" he taunted. "Don't you mean a half-wit house for people like you?"

Frank slammed her hard against the table. Awkwardly, she teetered. With one hand, he knocked her to the floor. He towered over her, with her plate of lasagna in his hand.

"Listen, you moronic bitch!" He dripped the lasagna onto her head. "Get this into your brain: I'm selling the house and investing the money."

He kicked hard at the side of her head and threw the plate to the floor. Fragments of china stabbed her cheek.

Suzannah was very cold on the floor. She drifted into unconsciousness. When she awoke, she could hear Frank snoring in the bedroom. Finally, she got to all fours and raised herself to a standing position. In the bathroom, she wiped the congealed blood from under her eye and around her mouth. She thought she looked dead. Not bothering to change, she fell asleep on the living-room couch.

CHAPTER 23

▼

As soon as Harry entered his house, he called out for Laura. There was no response. In the kitchen, he saw a note propped up against the coffeepot. It read: *I'm having dinner with Martha tonight. Don't wait up. L.*

He sank onto a kitchen chair. Restlessly, his eyes roved about, taking in the barrenness of the house. People who had a life together put photographs of happy times on the wall, and magnets and calendars on the fridge. Angrily, he tossed the marriage counselor's appointment card beside Laura's note.

Looking into the dining room, he saw a large wicker basket on the table. Laura must have put it there when she had dropped by. He knew immediately, without reading the card, that Chin had sent it. He was almost afraid to open the green, glistening cellophane wrap. Inside, he could see boxes of cookies and chocolates. At last he opened the card.

Dear Mr. Jenkins,

I have discussed our conversation with the conglomerate. We do hope you will reconsider. We are willing to pay handsomely for your services, as we know you will complete the work in a timely and expert manner. Please reconsider your position carefully.

Sincerely,
Albert Chin

Harry crumpled the card and flung it into the kitchen wastebasket, then dialed his client, only to encounter a voice-mail recording. He said, "Mr. Chin, I'm very sorry, but as I explained, I cannot act in the Deighton offer as I am already the estate solicitor. Oh...and thank you for the gift basket, but please do *not* send anything more. Good night, sir." Surely, by God, that should be clear enough.

He opened the refrigerator. In the pale white light, he saw a small selection of neatly packaged carrots, lettuce, and tomatoes. Further back was some cold meat and a tub of tofu. The sparse stock undoubtedly reflected the thin spirit of their marriage. A world without pleasure now enveloped them.

At the kitchen table, he thought of their long, leisurely dinners, years back, filled with wine and conversation until midnight. In bed, their lovemaking was first as soft and sensuous as shadows, then as wild and violent as August storms. Then they would lie exhausted in the dark. Desperately, he wished for a return of such passion. Surely such a love could not simply evaporate. Unable to swallow, he set down his sandwich and snapped on the television.

The six o'clock news was on. Hunger drove him to try again to eat. Over the last few days, it had been painful to move, eat, or breathe. He forced his mind back to Marjorie.

No doubt Frank had procured the new will, but Harry was puzzled about Suzannah's promise. It was likely that she had agreed to nurse Marjorie at home if she were to become really sick. Marjorie did have a justified horror of nursing homes.

Frank was in the center of the mess, but Harry had to prove at least undue influence. Just because Frank was a money-grubbing fraud, that didn't necessarily mean he murdered her. He couldn't envision Suzannah as someone involved in a murder. She seemed to wander dreamily from one day to the next. Perhaps she didn't know a thing. If someone knew about Marjorie's call to him about the will, he or she might have decided to get rid of her fast. Unless Marjorie had spoken about the appointment, no one else would have known of it.

Rosie had been badly cut up with ugly petal designs. Welkom, for what it was worth, thought the work wasn't artistic enough to be that of the Florist. And Harry was at a loss to understand why Rosie might have fallen prey to the mad Florist. If the two deaths were connected to the Florist, why on earth would he poison one and strangle and carve the other? Maybe Rosie had come back early from her free afternoon and interrupted the killer, who had attacked her in a brutal rage. Theories ran rampant in his mind, but nothing added up.

On the television, two gurneys with bodies shrouded in black were being removed from a house somewhere in the east end of the city. Against the backdrop of the street, the reporter spoke.

"In this modest bungalow on Pape Avenue, two young women, Deirdre Jamieson and Linda Lee Hong, were brutally slain. Both were paralegals in the law firm, Cheney, Arpin. The question on everyone's mind? Has the Florist struck again?"

Photographs of the two smiling women appeared on the screen. Slowly, Harry set down his sandwich and squinted. *Good Lord.* He knew Deirdre Jamieson. She was the pretty one from Cheney, Arpin who had come to the land registry office to complete the Chin deals.

The closing had been difficult. All the documentation had appeared to be in order, but there had been a few missing items. When it came to real estate, Harry was a stickler for detail. Usually, the vendor directed the purchaser, in a formal document, how to make out the checks. Deirdre had given him a direction signed by Zaimir Heights on behalf of all the numbered companies. Not satisfied, Harry had called Chin, who had immediately instructed him to pay the funds to Zaimir and close the deal. Only now did Harry remember that McKeown was the lawyer behind Zaimir. Harry dumped the remains of his sandwich into the garbage and poured the rest of his beer. The telephone rang.

"Hello?" Harry swallowed hard.

"Sergeant Welkom here."

"Yes, sergeant?" Harry was on his guard.

"Need you down at forensics."

"What for?"

"To identify something for us." Welkom's tone was flat, revealing nothing.

"If it's something to do with the break-in," Harry said, checking the annoyance in his voice, "can't it wait until tomorrow?"

"No."

Harry sighed. He knew to be careful with the sergeant. "All right. Where are you?" Resigned to his task, he wrote a note for Laura and set it beside the coffeepot. *Missives passing in the night,* he reflected sadly.

The forensics lab was temporarily housed in the cavernous medical building on the University of Toronto campus. Looking for parking, Harry drove slowly along the road circling the broad, grassy playing field. On the crescent, only the medical building was lit up. The other turreted structures rose up dark and menacing in the fog.

As he mounted the steps, the sweet, sickly smell of formaldehyde wafted into memory from his undergraduate years in science at the university. The hall must have received a new coat of paint in the last thirty years, but it was the same putrid hue of green. The steel door of the elevator was narrow and heavy, but the brass inner gate clanged open easily. By the time the elevator had risen to the third floor, Harry had read the fine print of the elevator license twice.

The upper hallway was well-lit. At the far end, two policemen sat on wooden chairs, drinking coffee and chatting. As he approached, one of the officers stood.

"I'm looking for Sergeant Welkom, officer," Harry said.

"Your name, sir?"

"Jenkins, Harry Jenkins."

Harry was immediately motioned inside. The immense lab was all too familiar. Globe lamps hung from the high white ceilings, and a pale and eerie light was diffused throughout the room. The windows were high and blackened by the night. People felt dwarfed in these rooms.

Welkom appeared at the far end of the lab, walking stiffly toward him between the tables equipped with sinks and stools.

Without preliminaries, the sergeant said, "Want to show you something, Mr. Jenkins." He guided Harry past the rows of stainless-steel autopsy tables. He ushered him into a small room at the far end, which was dim and very cold. Harry heard the whir of a fan.

The sergeant switched the light on. Two stretchers were lined up on either side of the white-walled cubicle, with scarcely two feet between them. A body, covered with a sheet, lay on each gurney.

"Why have you brought me here?" Harry cleared his throat. There was a chemical odor in the air. The sergeant eyed him and did not answer for a moment.

"Hope you have a strong stomach, Mr. Jenkins. This is pretty ugly."

Harry had seen more than his fair share of corpses in his line of work. He liked to believe in the existence of the soul and an afterlife. Corpses reminded him of empty, scattered cartons and drained tins. The contents were gone and only the packaging remained.

Harry's stomach lurched as Welkom drew back one sheet, exposing the body to the waist. It was Deirdre. Just days ago, she had been young and very pretty. Now there was a huge gash above her left breast and smaller wounds all over her torso and arms. Harry closed his eyes once more and reached out for the edge of the stretcher to steady himself. He felt hot.

"There's more," the sergeant said, turning down the sheet to the girl's knees. In contrast to the violent gashes, a neat incision, performed with surgical precision, ran from her navel to her pubic bone. On each side of this incision was etched a garland of rose petals.

Harry turned away. "Why are you showing me this, sergeant?"

Welkom did not reply. He pulled the sheet up over the body and turned to the other stretcher.

"This one was strangled," Welkom continued impassively, as he drew down the sheet. She was an Asian woman, and she had the same petal design etched on her cheek. Her fine neck was darkly bruised and crushed. Immense force must have been used. Her head lolled to one side at an odd angle. From the navel downward was the same precise incision, decorated on each side with a profusion of rose petals. Harry fought against the nausea welling up inside him.

The sergeant followed him out. Touching Harry's shoulder, he said, "You remember Rosalind Michaels? She was strangled and cut in sort of the same way, but it wasn't as good as the Florist's earlier work." Welkom waited while Harry took this information in, then said, "The drawing on these two women is *simpler*." Welkom seemed to be struggling for words. "More *artistic...*in a way. The first four women were cut up like the two women here tonight."

"So the Florist did a poor drawing on Rosie and then, for these two, returned to his usual style?"

"Well, maybe."

"Or, sergeant, the Florist did not attack Rosie. As you said before, it could have been a copycat killing."

Ignoring Harry, Welkom ploughed on. "Do you know or recognize either of those women?"

Harry took a moment to answer. "Yes, one of them. They were the ones on the news tonight, right?"

"Right. Deirdre Jamieson and Linda Lee Hong." Welkom took out his notebook. "Which one do you know?"

"I don't really know either of them, sergeant."

"You just said you did, counselor."

"I met Deirdre Jamieson on one occasion. She closed out some land deals at the registry office with me." Harry said.

"The Chin deals?"

Harry nodded.

The sergeant tapped him on the shoulder. "We're not finished yet, Mr. Jenkins. Got more to show you. Follow me."

Welkom shut the door and motioned Harry toward a seat. Opening a white enamel cabinet, he took out a plastic package. "Exhibit One, counselor." The light cast an orange color across the sergeant's face.

Harry leaned forward in order to see better. From the package, Welkom extracted a small silver knife, covered in blood. "Look familiar, Mr. Jenkins?"

"It looks like a thousand other knives."

"No, counselor, it's like the one in your office that was stabbed through the papers. We found this one next to Deirdre Jamieson, all covered with blood. Real messy."

"As I said, sergeant, it looks like a thousand other knives." Although it was cool in the office, Harry felt flushed. The two men were silent for some moments.

"Maybe you should tell us what's going on, Mr. Jenkins," the sergeant said quietly.

"Going on?" Harry was genuinely alarmed. "I don't know anything about these murders." Seized with a growing claustrophobia, he stood up. "And certainly nothing of the previous murders." Then anger flared in him. "You're struggling to make ridiculous connections because the police haven't done their work."

Welkom did not try to disguise his sneer. Harry sat down again.

"There's more." Welkom consulted his notebook. "Chin Fong Hue. That name mean anything to you?"

Harry shook his head.

"The house where these ladies lived is owned by a Chin Fong Hue. Telephone's in that name too."

"So?"

"Your client's name is Chin."

"For God's sake, sergeant! The name Chin is as common as Smith."

Slowly, the sergeant rose from behind the desk and stood behind Harry. He gripped his shoulder and said, "Listen, Mr. Jenkins, I'm going to do you a real favor and tell you how we see it. You're sitting in the middle of one hell of a mess."

Harry shook his shoulder free of the officer's grasp and swiveled around in his chair.

"First, counselor, I find you at the Deighton house. Your client's dead and you're telling me that she's just an old lady who's died of natural causes."

"What? Damn it, I was the one demanding the autopsy! But nothing happened."

Welkom waved dismissively and continued, "Then your office is broken into. A small silver knife is sticking out of a bunch of land offers. Rose petals are strewn around. The offer is from an Albert Chin for properties all around the Deighton house. And who's the purchaser's lawyer? None other than you, Jenkins. Next, you're knocked down the stairs at her house, by a corpse."

"I'm supposed to be responsible for that? That's ridiculous," said Harry. "When are the police going to start doing their job?"

Welkom ignored him. "Then we find the Michaels woman carved up a lot like the first four."

"So? Everything you've said adds up to a random killer.

Welkom barreled on. "Before we know it, Miss Deighton's will's been stolen. And now, counselor, we're looking at two carved-up young women. You just happen to know one of them: Deirdre Jamieson. Met her closing the Chin deals. And what a surprise! The murder weapon's just like the knife in your desk."

Welkom stood above him, his arms folded across his chest. "Jesus Christ, Jenkins! It don't look good. Either you're up to your ass in all of this, or else you're too stupid to see that you could be lying on that stretcher next."

"What am I supposed to say to all of that?" Harry nearly shouted. "I don't know anything about those women. As far as Albert Chin's concerned, I doubt I'll ever see him again. All his land deals are closed." Harry bit his lip. He had to be careful. Solicitor-client privilege prevented him from speaking of Chin. Welkom was standing over him.

"So now he owns all the property around the Deighton house and the church?"

"A search at the registry office will tell you."

"You've been paid?"

Harry did not answer.

"How much?" Welkom took out his notepad.

"That's my business, not yours."

The sergeant smiled sadly. "Listen, Jenkins, it's no problem for me to get a look at your bank accounts and your trust statements." He waited.

Harry knew the sergeant was right. "I was paid well enough."

"How well?"

"About a hundred."

"Thousand?"

"Right." Harry sighed. The only way out of this was simply to get up and walk out.

"Isn't that kind of rich for five or six deals?"

"There was a lot of work."

"Really? That's more than fifteen thousand a deal. Glad my lawyer doesn't charge like that!"

"Listen, sergeant. I don't have to answer these questions." Harry's voice was quiet and even. "I have nothing more to say to you."

"Okay, okay. But don't make us do things the hard way."

Harry nodded and rose to leave.

"Let's just hope you're not next." The sergeant smiled. "Oh, by the way, the autopsy report for Marjorie Deighton came back."

Harry waited.

Welkom took a sheet from an envelope. "Says here…high levels of barbiturates in the blood. Time of death on the 16th between noon and three."

Harry nodded curtly. "Glad to see you've gotten the job done, officer." Then he left.

Alone, the sergeant cursed under his breath and opened another envelope. It contained the reports of interviews of people around the Deighton house on the 16th. A silver-gray Mercedes had been parked in the laneway between the house and the church that afternoon. Its license had been traced to none other than Fong Hue Chin.

Welkom stretched back in his chair. So Mr. Chin was at the Deighton place that afternoon. Rose petals were carved on the Michaels woman and the two young paralegals who lived in Chin's house. Chin must be the Florist. All the pieces were adding up nicely, he thought. He was not troubled by the other murders. Pretty soon he'd have enough to nail the bastard.

Unsteadily, Harry started for his car, overcome with visions of precise carvings on young, unblemished flesh. Fog hung low over the playing field and obscured the other buildings. Street lamps, smudged by the mist, dotted the crescent.

Welkom's words chilled him. With pain flashing up his side, he hurried, head down, into the deepening fog. He stopped under a street lamp to catch his breath. He could not erase the memory of such malevolent artistry. It was one thing to read about these grisly murders in the press, but to see it was more than he could bear.

He sought to make sense of the quagmire. The rose petal was the killer's trademark, linking the murders of Rosie, Deirdre, and Linda Lee, and maybe four other women—but, thank God, not Marjorie. Nothing made sense. There might be no connection whatsoever to the Florist murders. Why would the Florist poison Marjorie?

Rosie had interrupted Marjorie's killer, who then turned on her in a brutal rage. Welkom suspected Chin for two reasons. First, he stupidly thought the murder weapon looked the same as the knife that had been stabbed through Chin's offers. Anyone could have broken into his office and impaled the offers to his desk—and why would Chin attack his own paperwork?

Chin was also suspect because he was buying up the properties around Marjorie's. It didn't make sense to murder for a land deal, no matter what was riding on it. Besides, Chin solved problems with money, and Harry thought Chin's delicate physique disqualified him from the role of a rapacious murderer.

Harry was betting that Marjorie's killer was close to home. The nonsense over the wills certainly suggested Frank Sasso. There was no known connection between Frank, the paralegals, or the Chin deals, much less the other women. It was a dead end.

With smirking insinuations, Welkom had drawn an odious portrait of him at the center of a maelstrom of murder and fraud. Abdul Mudhali, the assistant manager, was only the beginning of his dishonor. Despite minimal involvement in the Chin deals, he had been paid an exorbitant amount. His complicity in murder and fraud had been purchased with that money. Only greed could explain his abysmal lack of judgment.

Harry had reached the other side of the crescent, and he saw his car parked beside the turreted University College. A light rain fell. Why was it always about money? Laura had forced him into the invisible cocoon of her wealth, where money was the only yardstick.

He stopped. What the hell? Those were not his words. He stared at a row of industrial trash cans in a huge and haunting doorway, and then he remembered. The guitar player with the black top hat and wheelchair had said in his seductive, insistent voice, *"Do not fear to reach out from the invisible cocoon you are forced to inhabit."* Standing alone on the darkened sidewalk, Harry knew his time for escape had come.

Strolling toward his car, he thought of his father, who had simply ignored convention. He had spoken to whomever he wished in whatever way he wished. That is, until Anna had died, and then he had spoken to almost no one, not even his wife and son. Meeting Chin, Harry had seen only the money. In his lust for wealth, he had turned a blind eye to danger. Throwing aside his usual caution, he had become a dupe. No wonder Welkom was suspicious. Dad would not have been blinded by Chin's wealth.

Look where faithfulness to his wife had gotten him. Despite years of strict adherence to the canons of his profession, one misjudgement had landed him in a mess. Shaking his head, he muttered, "Jesus! I must still be waiting for my Sunday-school prize."

Suddenly, he grinned. Natasha! Her loveliness made him yearn to break free. With car tires hissing by him on the crescent, he imagined her touch, her smile. Fantasy could become reality. With life in his step, he rehearsed the lines he would use to call her to invite her to dinner. He knew he could make it happen.

When he turned the ignition of his car, the headlights did not come on. After fiddling with the switches, he remained sitting in the dark. He got out and checked the front of the car. Both headlights had been smashed in with a crowbar, which lay on the sidewalk.

He looked about. In a row of ten cars, only his had been touched.

Getting back inside, he suddenly saw an envelope neatly placed on the passenger seat. For long moments, he stared at it. Finally, he carefully slit it open and read: *We are very disappointed in your refusal. We trust you will reconsider.—The Conglomerate.*

Harry stared straight ahead. A shadowy figure walked slowly past his car. Harry locked the doors and held his breath. Chin was getting desperate *and* dangerous. After dealing with Welkom, he had no appetite for calling the police. He would have to meet with Chin alone. When the figure started down an alley between the buildings, Harry climbed from his car.

Shivering, he pulled up his collar. It would be quicker to cut across the field, but the path now seemed desolate. Instead, he chose the lighted sidewalk down to College Street to catch the streetcar to the subway. He heard the muffled screech of the streetcar on its tracks near the corner. Traffic was light, and he easily crossed to the concrete island in the middle of the street. But he had been too slow. The doors wheezed shut, and the streetcar glided away. Harry stood alone, watching the flashing yellow light in the fog.

He decided to have his car towed to a garage to repair the headlights. Forget the insurers—they would want a police report. He could only try to reason with Chin and reach some sort of agreement.

CHAPTER 24

▼

The elusiveness of the Florist cast a pall over the city. Although he loved the media attention, he derided the dull and unimaginative souls who debated the nature of a person who could create and destroy in one moment. For him, their small minds had no understanding of greatness.

Perhaps he should send them a drawing and a note to explain the task he had undertaken. Soon they would understand that only his artistry could redeem the souls of these women.

His responsibility was to make a moral judgment about the worthiness of an individual life. He had to guard against his passion blotting out his vastly superior reasoning power and intellect. When appetite overcame rationality, tragic consequences could result. Passion could blind his judgment.

CHAPTER 25

▼

Cheney, Arpin was shell-shocked. Jonathan Conroy was bilious. Snatching a handful of antacids in his private washroom, he swallowed them down with a glass of water. All three morning papers were spread across his desk. Deirdre Jamieson and Linda Lee Hong had been strangled and stabbed with unimaginable brutality. Rumors were rampant that the murderer was connected to his firm. Was the mad artist, the Florist, in their midst? Jonathan Conroy, senior partner and Treasurer of the Law Society, had to chair the emergency meeting of the executive committee.

Such a catastrophe could poison the very lifeblood of the firm.

The two women were not much older than his daughter. For several months, Deirdre had worked with him on a number of real-estate deals—most recently, the Zaimir and Chin transactions. *So pretty and capable.* Now she was dead.

His hands shook as he gathered the newspapers and carried them into the small boardroom next to his office. Seated in the leather high-backed chair at the far end of the table, he waited for his partners.

Peter Niels entered first. White-faced and grim, he slammed his case onto the mahogany surface so hard that it skidded almost to the other side.

"This mess," Niels began, gesturing in the direction of the newspapers, "could not have happened at a worse time." As he helped himself to coffee, his cup rattled in its saucer. "Look at the papers, especially the *Sun.*" Niels pulled out a chair and set down his cup. Shaking his head, he continued, "You realize, Jonathan, they're saying someone in the firm was involved." Niels shook his head. "You have to squelch this shit right away, or else the firm will lose big time."

Jonathan stared at Niels in profound shock. "Did you know the girls at all, Peter?"

Niels seemed surprised at the question. "No, can't say I did. Why?"

"Peter, we usually display some sense of loss and sadness."

Niels grimaced and waved Jonathan off. "Sure, sure. I know, but we can't have the cops all over the firm."

"We have to cooperate with the police investigation, Peter." Jonathan said quietly. "I realize they might cause some inconvenience, but we have nothing to hide."

Arnie Rosenberg marched in, followed by Bill Cawthorne. "Jesus, Jonathan!" Arnie was red-faced and breathing heavily. His glasses had slipped to the end of his nose. "The cops are going to be crawling all over us. We have to limit their investigation, or else the firm will be brought to a standstill."

The corners of Conroy's mouth tightened downward. "Your only concern is inconvenience, Arnie? What about these poor girls?"

Arnie waved him off. "Fine! Of course it's awful, but I, for one, am not putting up with idiot cops asking all kinds of stupid questions. We have to set some rules."

Cawthorne took a seat on the far side of the table and laced his fingers together. He was a quiet man, given to lengthy silences before expressing an opinion on so much as the weather.

Niels continued testily, "I'm only thinking of the firm's reputation, Jonathan. We can't afford to be associated with this kind of mess!" He looked about the room for support.

Conroy was shaken by his partners' callous indifference. "Gentlemen." Slowly he shifted his gaze from one man to the next. "The first order of procedure is to express formally our sincerest condolences to the families of these poor girls."

Rosenberg shook his head impatiently. "Sure, sure, Jonathan. My secretary can organize all that kind of stuff. Send flowers from the firm for the funeral." He leaned forward in his chair and jabbed his finger at Conroy. "But we've got to get in touch with whoever's investigating and reach an understanding. The police can't go rummaging through all the files and taking up time with questions."

Conroy shook his head. Niels and Rosenberg were sad cases, he thought. *Not one iota of humanity in their sleek carcasses.* "None of us has anything to hide," said Conroy, looking at his partners. "We have a duty to assist."

Silently, the door opened. Tony McKeown stood before them, his shoulders sagging. Conroy was shocked to see him so ashen and stricken with grief. All watched as he took a seat, closed his eyes, and massaged his temples.

"Gentlemen, I cannot think of a sadder day," he said at last. "Such horrific events are totally beyond human imagination." Choking, he continued, "Those poor women! To meet such a grotesque fate..." His voice trailed off. "I trust, Jonathan, that we will personally convey our sympathy to the families, and that all of us will attend the funeral. We should also tell the police that we want to give our fullest cooperation in the investigation. I knew the girls only slightly, but I think we should tell the police anything we can about them."

Finally, Conroy thought, a strain of decency had been voiced. The other partners shifted uncomfortably in their seats. Conroy knew McKeown's reputation as a tough guy, but was now delighted by Tony's sense of honor and decency. In the past, he had been disconcerted by the hunger and depth of calculation in the man's eyes, but had put it down to healthy ambition.

Everyone was silent.

"You've all seen the photographs?" Tony asked, his voice faltering. He spread the newspaper open, as if arranging a shroud. "Those poor women," he sighed. "Only a mad beast could have ravaged them. The families must be in grave distress." He rose to pace. Everyone was silent. "We must help in any way we can."

McKeown had never really fit in, thought Rosenberg. Always the lone wolf, never a team player. Here he was making everyone look like cheap shits.

Cawthorne was quick to take his cue from McKeown. "Tony's right, gentlemen. We've all been remiss." Steepling his fingers together, he continued in his most judicious tones, "It matters not a whit whether anyone in this firm is implicated. We must cooperate fully with the police."

"That goes without saying, gentlemen," said Tony, with his back turned on them. He stared out the window onto the cavernous windows of the Old City Hall. "And we must do whatever we can to comfort their families."

Fascinated, Conroy watched McKeown turn from the window. With the light on his face, he seemed pale and tentative. *A stricken soul,* he thought.

McKeown stopped. He gripped the boardroom table. The others saw him shake his head as his eyes grew flat and unseeing.

"You all right, Tony?" Conroy reached out to touch his arm.

McKeown did not speak for several moments. "Gentlemen! What if the Florist is within this firm?" He looked at each member of the committee, one by one.

Conroy drew Tony into the chair next to him. "I know, Tony. It's beyond contemplation. But rest assured, we'll do whatever is necessary to help."

Conroy was convinced of one thing. Despite the nasty rumors about Tony's greed and questionable practices, there was a solid, decent human being within.

Back in his office, Tony slumped into his leather chair and stared out the window. The pigeons were waddling along the ledges of the Old City Hall. He remembered the rush he had felt the other night when the hawk had swooped down.

"Mr. McKeown?" his secretary called. "Archbishop Staunton is on the line."

"Yes, archbishop." Tony spoke quietly. "The church application for rezoning was dead as of yesterday.

"What happened? I testified just as you said. Why did we lose?" demanded Staunton angrily.

"It was as I told you, Archbishop. Staunton. The ratepayers were very much opposed from the outset. And you, sir," Tony said, lounging back and smiling thinly, "were imperious, overbearing, and ultimately ineffectual."

Staunton choked. "What is the church to do now?"

"I promised that I would have an offer for you."

"When?"

"Soon, Archbishop Staunton. Despite my disgust for the church's irresponsibility in condoning the behavior of its priests, I shall not abandon it."

Staunton was immediately defensive. "The church cannot supervise each and every one of its clergy all the time."

"Listen, sir. Please do not try to excuse the abuse of innocents. It disgusts me."

There was a long pause. "Call me when you have the offer," said the archbishop. Then he hung up.

Tony took his binoculars from the desk drawer and began scanning the windows of the Old City Hall. It was amazing what you could see in broad daylight.

CHAPTER 26

▼

The next morning, Harry's mind was still beset with images of mutilated flesh. Seeking the world of normalcy, he decided to call Natasha first. But on his desk lay a scrawled pink message slip. It read: *Mr. Tony McKeown called. Offer on 42 Highland about to expire. Call at once.*

"What's this message from Mr. McKeown?" Harry called out to Miss Giveny. "What offer is he talking about?"

"It's on your desk."

"Why the hell didn't you tell me about it?"

"I was going to last night, but you were kicking wastebaskets about and then storming out of the office," she said stonily. "He called again just before you came in this morning."

Thoughts pounded in his brain. It was time for a change. A new secretary—one who did not hide evidence from him. Despite his newfound sympathy for her, he was getting sick of her crankiness. But if he were to fire her, what would happen? Immediately he pictured her and Merle eating cat food, in a kitchen with no heat.

The offers were at least twenty percent over his estimation of the present market value. He rang Natasha.

"The appraisal report is ready, Harry." Natasha's voice lifted Harry's spirits.

"I have an offer on the property. For two-point-five million dollars."

"That's way over market value. Who submitted it?" she asked.

"A numbered company. A lawyer, Tony McKeown, acts for the purchaser." In the silence, Harry was unsure if she was still on the line. "Natasha?"

"It is a fantastic offer. But who is behind the company?"

"I don't know yet, but I'll find out." Harry paused. "Natasha? Do you have time for a quick lunch today?" Harry caught his breath. "I mean, I would like to see your report."

"Certainly, Harry. I'd love to." After making the necessary arrangements, Harry dialed McKeown's office.

Harry began, "I realize your client has given us until five this afternoon to respond to the offer on Highland, but I need more time to get the beneficiaries together."

"Take your time, Harry. Take another forty-eight hours, if you like. My client's in no hurry. I'll fax you a letter confirming the extension."

Harry sank back in relief. Time limitations gave lawyers nightmares. If some critical date whizzed by, the unfortunate lawyer was in the soup.

The telephone rang again. Miss Giveny was not picking it up. Passive insurrection was one of her fondest guerrilla tactics.

"Harold Jenkins here."

"Harry, it's me." Laura's voice sounded distant.

"Hi, me." Habits of intimacy died hard.

"Harry, I have to go to Montreal for a conference."

"Oh?" Suddenly, he felt too weary for anger.

"For the museum. I didn't mention it earlier, because I forgot to put it in my calendar."

Harry said nothing. Laura was driven to fill silences. "Is that all right, darling?"

When did she last call me darling? "It's part of your work, isn't it?"

"Yes. I have to go," she said hastily. After a pause, she said, "I got your note about the appointment tomorrow with the marriage counselor."

"I can rebook it if you want."

"Let's talk about it when I get back."

Nothing decided. Everything postponed. His voice broke in frustration. "What the hell is the point? Be honest, Laura, you don't have the slightest interest in our marriage." Harry was amazed. At last the words were out of his mouth.

"I didn't say that!"

"No, of course not." Restless with fury, he did not want to stop. "That would be too straightforward for you. Games. Always games."

Her voice rose sharply. "What are you talking about?"

"Forget it! Just go, but don't expect me to sit around waiting."

"What's that supposed to mean?"

"Nothing." Harry simmered. "I suppose Stover's going?"

"God damn it, Harry, of course he is. He's my boss."

"Fine. See you when you're back."

"I'll be at the Ritz-Carlton, if you need me."

When Harry hung up, he realized he was smacking his pencil on the receiver. Most of the stuff on his desk was from Laura: glossy, slick, impersonal items, suitable for anyone. He shook his head. Normally he was not an ingrate. Closing his eyes, the room at the Ritz-Carlton on their honeymoon floated in his memory.

With determination, he forced himself to concentrate on work. He instructed Miss Giveny to set up an urgent appointment with Katharine, Suzannah, and Gerry for the afternoon. As a solicitor, he was obligated to present McKeown's offer to all concerned parties, despite their arguments over the wills. Then he tackled the other phone messages. He crumpled up Mudhali's latest message and pitched it in the garbage. Pretty soon he'd have a case against the bank for harassment.

Natasha had suggested they meet at an Italian restaurant several blocks east, past the park and the cathedral. Stepping into the dimly lit restaurant, his spirits rose. It was a romantic atmosphere, certainly not suitable for reading lengthy contracts.

He saw her in a booth near the back, and waved. Harry had been faithful to Laura throughout their marriage.

"Great to see you." They shook hands. "I wasn't at my best at our last meeting at the house." He slid into the booth across from her.

Natasha smiled slowly. "The last time I saw you, Harry, you were in bed."

"Pardon?"

"You should see your face," she laughed. "I came to see you in the hospital."

"Ah…so it wasn't a dream after all," he sighed.

"No. I really was there. You had nurses all around you, so…"

"Thank you for coming," he managed to say.

He ordered a carafe of red wine from the waiter, and they picked up their menus.

"So, Harry," she said, "you have such good news. That's a marvelous offer. Will it be accepted?"

"Well, the house isn't necessarily for sale. It's up to the beneficiaries to decide."

"Will your clients want to expose the property to the market?"

"Quite possibly. And if they do, I will recommend you *very* highly." Harry sought to divert the conversation to a safe topic. He could not discuss the mess with the wills. "How's the market for these properties?" he asked.

"Excellent, Harry. The Deighton property is in a prime location, and it is of the highest quality. It will go very quickly, I think."

Only once did Harry lose his train of thought, as his gaze floated from her lips to her collar line.

She reached for her satchel. "I have the appraisal here for you." She handed him the binder.

For a moment, he could not take his eyes from her. He estimated that Laura was probably catching the plane to Montreal. The details of their room eighteen years ago at the Ritz flooded his mind again. And here he sat, with another woman who was turning him inside out.

"Harry? You look so far away."

He shook his head. "Sorry, Natasha." He loved to say her name. "I was just thinking about the offer."

"But there's so much flipping of properties," she said.

"A hot market?"

"One that is about to explode. There's a lot of money moving about."

"What do you think is its source?"

"From everywhere. You know Toronto well, don't you Harry?"

"I've lived here all my life."

"I think every race, religion, and nationality is represented here."

"Yes?"

"So that's the number of sources."

"Have you lived here long?"

"Since I was about twelve. We lived in the east end, above a store on the Danforth. My parents escaped from Russia in the fifties. They lost everything. They were so grateful to arrive safely in Canada." She spoke with quiet reflection. "They always said this country was the best place in the world." Smiling sadly, she continued, "Sometimes we think life is hard here, but unless you have lived in a country where your family can be dragged out in the street and shot, you do not know how truly lucky you are. My father always said that if you lost everything once, you needn't ever be afraid again."

They ordered lunch. The waiter poured more wine.

Natasha asked, "What's your wife's name?"

"Laura," he said quietly. "We've been married for almost twenty years."

The waiter came with the salads.

"You're married, Natasha?"

When she shook her head, he wished he could reach out and touch her lustrous, dark hair.

"No, I'm not." She smiled and sipped her wine. *Of course such a man would be married, but he looks so sad when he speaks of her,* she thought.

"So…Mr. McKeown is acting for the purchaser?" she continued.

"Yes. You know him?"

"Only by reputation, really," she said carefully.

"And?"

"He's brilliant, and…ruthless." She reached across the table and lightly touched his hand. Her gaze held him. "Before you told me about this offer, I would have recommended listing it for sale at 1.75 million, Harry. But now, who knows?" She shrugged. "The surrounding properties have just skyrocketed. Do you know what is going on?"

Natasha had done her job well. She knew from the title searches that he had acted for Mr. Chin, and she had spotted the potential conflict of interest.

"Natasha, I know the titles to the properties may show that I'm in a conflict of interest." He drank down his wine. "I wish I knew what was going on, but I don't."

"I'm not worried about you, Harry." Her gaze was soft. "But men like Albert Chin can be trouble. You don't want to get too close."

"What's wrong with him?"

"All I have is hearsay, but apparently, he has huge sums of money behind him and is a very determined man."

With her perspective from within a tight-knit real-estate community, Harry hoped she might shed some light on Frank. "Ever hear of a broker, Frank Sasso?"

"Is he involved in this deal? If he is, that spells trouble. Sasso is a very small player. He does what he's told by Chin."

After lunch, she kissed his cheek. Not much more than a peck. "I believe you, Harry, but watch out. I care about you." Briefly, her fingers traced the pattern on his tie.

"I'd like to see you again, Natasha."

"You have a wife, Harry."

He thought she spoke rather sadly. "Yes, but…"

For Natasha, Harry was very unusual, but she understood his hesitation. Loyalty was a rare trait.

Standing in the glare of sun on the sidewalk, Harry grinned as she walked away. But then, as if clouds had rolled in, he felt chilled. The possible connections between Chin and Sasso led to a swamp of conjecture. And now McKeown, the lawyer for the church, was further involved.

CHAPTER 27

▼

At a quarter past three, Harry entered his office library. Copies of the offer and the two wills were neatly stacked at the end of the table. He massaged the back of his neck and contemplated the onslaught of the Deighton beneficiaries. No doubt a major confrontation was brewing.

Crawford's roguish visage glowered down upon all potential proceedings from the wall. Beside it hung the portrait of Crawford's senior partner, the mild-mannered Geoffrey Crane. Although Harry never knew the man, he wondered how Crane had coped with the young Turk, Crawford. To Harry, Crawford was an aberration in the firm. He toyed with the notion of removing the picture, and smiled at the realization that he was still haunted by old ghosts.

The purpose of the meeting was to effect some settlement among the warring factions of the Deighton clan. There was nothing like will changes to drive families apart. Rational clients usually shuddered at incurring gargantuan legal bills simply to make a point of principle, but a stubborn few could drain the estate coffers just to settle an ancient family score.

The library door rattled. Opening the door, Harry was confronted by a fuming Miss Giveny, bearing a tray with a coffeepot, cups and saucers.

"Where should I put this?" she asked, plunking the tray on the library table. "Those Deightons have been nothing but trouble for the firm," she said in her most spinsterish tone. "I'm sure one of the children knows what happened to Marjorie." Glancing significantly at Harry, she trundled from the room, muttering, "Those Deightons will never agree on anything."

Voices floated in from the foyer. *Good grief. Ten minutes early.* In his heartiest Crawford manner, Harry strode into the foyer.

"Good afternoon," he said, beaming and taking Katharine's hand. Her smile was brief and professional. Gerry stepped forward to shake hands, then hung in the background.

"We're the first ones here?" Katharine asked.

"Yes. I expect your sister any moment."

"Could Gerry and I speak with you alone, Mr. Jenkins?"

Harry hesitated. "Yes. But it's customary to meet with all the interested parties together, Mrs. Rowe. Whatever I say to one should be said to all."

"Mr. Jenkins, Frank Sasso has a stranglehold on my sister. We need to speak before he arrives."

"He's coming?"

Katharine smiled patiently. "Suzannah is rarely let out on her own. She can't stand up to Frank."

"I'd normally exclude an outsider from our meeting."

"That would only make matters worse."

Harry nodded and ushered them into the library. Intending to avoid the semblance of secret dealings, he left the door ajar. In hopes of forestalling incriminating conversations, he offered coffee. They declined.

Taking his seat, Harry began uncomfortably, "You understand, Mrs. Rowe, I'm somewhat in the middle here."

"Meaning?"

"Any estate lawyer has to be impartial in dealing with the beneficiaries."

Katharine nodded and said, "Don't worry. We're not asking any special favors from the estate. Gerry and I have retained a lawyer."

Anyone cut out of a will ought to get legal advice, but Katharine's speed suggested a preemptive strike. "Shouldn't your counsel be here?"

"Not yet. We'll make it clear to Suzannah that this is her only chance to settle with us, otherwise we bring in the lawyers and sue for undue influence. You saw Frank gloating over the new will he got Marjorie to sign. We won't back down on undue influence. Frank's in for a very expensive battle." Katharine's smile was cold and brittle. Gerry slunk back in the shadows. *A well-coached client,* thought Harry.

"Whom have you retained?" Harry asked mildly, picking up his pen. He was not prepared for the answer.

"Mr. Tony McKeown, of Cheney, Arpin."

Slowly, Harry set his pen down. McKeown was into everything. An offer submitted on Marjorie's house. Representing the church in a rezoning application.

And now, acting for two beneficiaries over Marjorie's will. Closing his eyes, Harry saw shark fins cutting too close.

"Mrs. Rowe. Mr. Deighton," he began stiffly, "I must advise you that Mr. McKeown submitted an offer on behalf of one of his clients to buy your aunt's house."

Katharine's lips froze into a perfect "O."

Gerry covered his face with his hands and said wearily, "That's just terrific, Katherine. See what you've gotten us into?"

Harry recognized Miss Giveny's peremptory knock. "Come in," he said absently, his mind still lost in thickets of possibilities.

Miss Giveny made way for Suzannah.

Gerry was immediately on his feet. "Suzie! For God's sake, what happened?"

Katharine gasped. Tears of fury sprang in her eyes.

Wavering in the doorway, Suzannah tried a weak smile. "It's nothing. Just a bit of an accident." Frank loomed behind her. His massive hands dangled at his sides.

Suzannah's face was swollen. Her left eye was partially closed. Deep purple and yellow welts rose to her hairline and down into her cheek. Her lip, split open several inches, had required stitching.

Harry was swept with rage. At the sight of Suzannah, every sinew in his body screamed. Visions of the hideous carvings and bruising on the paralegals leapt to his brain. "What in hell is going on here, Frank?" he demanded.

Immediately, the pleading in her eyes silenced him. At last he understood why beaten women stayed with their men: gut-wrenching fear.

"Good God!" Katharine bit her lip. "What have you done to her, Frank?" she hissed.

Gerry pulled out a chair. Frank guided her to the table. He spoke as if she were a small child. "I always tell her to be real careful around the house. Tell them what you did this time, honey!"

She brushed strands of hair from her blackened face and whispered, "It really was stupid of me." She twisted a Kleenex around her fingers. "I was trying to wallpaper one of the bedrooms. I was up on a ladder. I reached over too far and fell off." She shrugged. "That's really all there is to it."

She glanced up at Frank.

"Poor baby!" he said. "You just have no sense of balance with heights."

Katharine had witnessed the same fear and pleading in other women's eyes at the shelter. Those victims rarely broke free of their men alive.

Satisfied that no further challenges were coming, Frank continued, "Now what's this meeting all about, counselor? How come you still figure in this?"

"Before we continue, Frank, everyone must agree to your presence."

Everyone looked about uneasily.

"It's up to Suzie," said Gerry. "If she wants him here, then it's okay with me."

Suzannah twisted her Kleenex and said, "It's all right."

Katharine simply nodded.

"I still figure in this, Frank, because James Fulford has renounced the executorship," Harry said.

"What does that mean?" Frank was wary.

"It means he doesn't want the job. He's signed a renunciation. I have a copy for all of you."

"Now, wait a minute! That doesn't mean the new will's no good."

"No, Frank, it doesn't. But now there are two wills and an offer on the house. The more recent one gives Suzannah the house, and the balance of the estate is split equally among the three of you. The prior will divides the whole estate, including the house, equally among the three of you."

"Let's see the first will," said Frank.

"I can only show you a photocopy of it."

"How come?" Frank shifted in his chair. "Where's the original?"

"I don't have it, Frank."

"You mean you've lost it?" Frank could not suppress a grin.

"I didn't say that," Harry said quietly.

Momentarily, Frank looked uncertain.

"Just what *are* you saying, Mr. Jenkins?" asked Gerry. He glanced at Katharine, who was rigid in her seat.

"I'm saying it's gone. Taken from this office," said Harry blandly. Instinct told him to tread carefully.

Frank said, "Seems like you got yourself a bit of a problem, Mr. Jenkins."

"How so?"

"The will was in your office, wasn't it? Even in your vault. You're responsible for a client's will, aren't you?" Frank's fists clenched as he spoke.

"I'm saying that the will was stolen. My office was ransacked. I called the police. I'm told they're following up some interesting leads. Somebody wanted it very badly."

"Where does that leave us now?" asked Katharine.

Harry shrugged. "It's not all that serious. The court will approve the will, under these circumstances."

"You're telling us a court's gonna allow a copy?" Frank pushed back his chair.

"Yes, of course. Particularly if the original has been stolen."

"Well, just a minute. I hear different!" Frank was on his feet, looking down on Suzannah. "Listen. I talk with some of the best legal minds in the city, you know. And…" Frank stopped. "Well, they're always saying you gotta have the original of anything for court!"

"Good thinking, Frank. That's probably what the thief hoped," Harry added mildly.

"Listen, Jenkins—you accusing me of taking it? Why would I take an old will, when she'd already made the new one, fair and square?"

Gerry interrupted. "Look! This is a waste of time. If a copy of the old will is as good as the original, what does it matter? I thought we were here to look at an offer." Gerry glanced about the room for support. "We could all use some money now, couldn't we? I know I certainly could."

"We *can* look at an offer, can't we?" Katharine asked.

"Of course. If all the beneficiaries agree, then the property can be sold and the proceeds held in trust until the issue of the wills is decided in court," Harry replied, distributing copies of the offer among them. "The offer is far above the estimated fair market value of the house. It is submitted by a numbered company through the law office of Cheney, Arpin, courtesy of Mr. McKeown. The problem with a numbered company is that it's very difficult to ascertain the true owners of the company. We don't know whom we're dealing with. The sale is to occur on June twentieth. The purchase price is two million, five hundred thousand dollars. If accepted, the value of the estate will be over five million."

Suzannah's voice broke the dead silence. "Don't any of you understand? We must think about Aunt Marjorie. She's not just dead; she's been murdered. Yet here we sit, fighting over the spoils, without a thought for her. I am not going to decide about the wills or the offer until we know who murdered her. And that's final, Frank."

Harry intervened. "Suzannah is making an important point. I'm sure everyone here cared for Marjorie and wants to know what happened."

Katharine spoke. "Suzannah, I'm sure you are acting out of loyalty to Marjorie. But I want to be perfectly clear about one thing. I'm not waiting to straighten out these wills. I have an appointment to see my lawyer, Mr. McKeown, immediately after this. You'll be hearing directly from him." Katharine pushed back her chair and stood up. "Gerry, I'm going to do this myself. You don't need to come with me."

Relieved, Gerry nodded dumbly.

At the door, Katharine turned on Frank. "Touch Suzannah again, Frank, and you'll have to deal with me."

After the others had left, Harry stretched and massaged his neck. Suzannah was right. Marjorie was still at the center of the maelstrom. Settlement was impossible until they knew who killed her.

Miss Giveny appeared in the doorway. "Your corporate searches were just delivered," she said.

Harry took the envelope and rifled through the searches. After several moments of study, he examined the connection between Zaimir and the numbered company. He said, "Sit down, Miss Giveny, please. What do you think of Frank?" he asked.

Miss Giveny's eyes widened. "He's a very dangerous man."

"Capable of extreme violence?"

"Anything could crawl out of that skin, Mr. Jenkins."

Harry simply nodded. "Do you think he beat up Suzannah?"

"Who else? Only a fool would believe that story of falling off a ladder."

"Who do you think murdered Marjorie?"

Miss Giveny made a face and quietly said, "Frank. Who else?"

Harry stared into space.

At last, Miss Giveny cleared her throat loudly. "Mr. Jenkins?"

"What?"

"You look like you're lost in a brown study. Do you want me for anything else?"

"No, that's it. Thank you." Pocketing the key to Marjorie's place, Harry rose from his desk, found his coat, and headed out the door for her house. The secret trust had to be the missing piece in the puzzle of Marjorie's wills.

Harry swore he would find the secret trust, even if he had to tear the house apart.

He took the steps two at a time to her bedroom. It was still exactly the same as when he had found her. There was a slight depression in the bedspread where she had lain. Even the wastebasket was full. Carefully, he smoothed the crumpled papers on the desk. There was nothing but discarded shopping lists and birthday cards.

After searching her drawers, he decided to try the parlor. His eyes rested upon a side table with a locked drawer, but no key. Running his hand underneath the drawer, he came up dry. He reached behind the mantelpiece clock, and there it was—a small silver key.

The drawer opened with surprising ease. He saw neatly organized packets of papers, elastic bands, and paper clips, along with a deed, a survey, her living will, and a journal from a trip. About to close the drawer, he noticed a small black metal box at the very back. He unfolded the papers inside, and read.

SECRET TRUST OF MARJORIE DEIGHTON, TO BE READ WITH ANY VALID WILL OF MINE:

IN THE EVENT OF MY DEATH, any interest in my estate, whether a conveyance of my house, or a share in the residue of my estate, or any legacy in favor of my daughter, Suzannah Deighton, shall only be given to her PROVIDED THAT she is not living with or in any way influenced by FRANK SASSO. The determination of these issues shall be made at the sole and absolutely binding discretion of my solicitor, HAROLD JENKINS, (regardless of whether he is an executor of my estate or not) of the firm Crane, Crawford and Jenkins, whose judgment and diligence I implicitly trust. IN THE EVENT THAT the said HAROLD JENKINS determines that my daughter is living with FRANK SASSO or is influenced by him in any manner, he may instruct any executor of my will to hold such interest in trust for her and pay out only income in such amounts and from time to time as the said HAROLD JENKINS sees fit in his sole and incontestable discretion.

Harry stared out the leaded glass windows of the parlor. Yes, Marjorie had signed and dated the trust several years back. He'd had her confidence, right from the start. Richard Crawford was too personally involved to exercise sound judgement. She had probably witnessed Richard's increasingly bizarre behavior at very close quarters. Laura never understood how much Harry valued the trust and confidence of a client—nor did he until he read Marjorie's secret trust.

According to the secret trust, Suzannah would get no interest if she had anything to do with Frank. Since the trust applied to any will, Marjorie had felt safe in changing it. Slowly, he inserted the document into his breast pocket, and then locked up the house.

C H A P T E R   28

▼

The ritual gave the Florist great pleasure. Every Thursday night at eight o'clock, he took a small gold key from his bureau and unlocked his den. His mother had died at precisely eight o'clock on a Thursday night, almost twenty-five years ago. With growing apprehension, he wondered if she would speak to him tonight. It was so frustrating. Sometimes he felt as if she were right in the room with him. At other times, out of spite, she refused to appear.

The lock turned and the door silently swung open. The room was in stark contrast to the rest of his apartment, which was sparsely furnished in a minimalist style. Three wooden tables were stacked high with chinaware. On the walls hung rows of prints of African masks, frighteningly primitive.

According to ritual, he took five measured paces toward the window and then drew open the drapes, letting the moonlight sweep into the room. Light shimmered across the three wooden tables stacked with chinaware, the finest Spode, in a variety of floral patterns.

The artist examined the round and heavy soup tureen (mother's favorite), then caressed a sugar bowl, and then a creamer. With loving care, he set the pieces down and faced the window.

"Mother, you would be so proud of me. Despite my deformity, I am becoming a very fine artist. I have worked very hard."

Holding the sugar bowl up, serenity crept over his features. Swiftly, he snapped the handles from the little bowl. He spoke softly, as if in prayer. "Mother, I have met a woman. Her name is Katharine Rowe and she is perfect. I want you to see her."

He carefully placed the shards of china onto a snowy white napkin and wrapped them up.

"Goodnight," he said. "I love you, Mother."

CHAPTER 29

▼

Donnie dragged himself up the stairs of the Dundas subway station. Tears ran down his face. Last night, he had talked to Frank when he was drinking and in an ugly mood.

"Listen, kid," Frank shouted, "I didn't hurt your precious Gram. She just died in her sleep."

"But you made her change her will. My dad says so," Donnie insisted.

"She left Suzannah the house, fair and square, after she promised to look after her."

"My dad says she died of an overdose."

"Well, I don't know nothin' about that." Frank shoved Donnie aside.

He could tell, by the way Frank's eyes were all shifty, that he'd poisoned her tea and then, worst of all, used him to deliver it. Frank was going to pay big time.

In the chat rooms, they were talking about the Florist and the cleansing power of fire. But that guy used a knife. Donnie loved the smell and crackle of fire, but that was no way to get rid of Frank. He knew he was too small and weak for a knife. It had to be a gun. But how could he get one? The next day, he asked around at school. The Flamingo Restaurant, he was told.

Most of all, he wanted the bastard to suffer. Smiling, he decided to make Frank crawl on the floor with his fat ass waving in the air. *Make him beg.* He met the man selling guns in the back room of the Flamingo. It was easy! He gave them the money and he got the gun. Already, he could hear Frank pleading.

On the morning Donnie got the gun, Frank drove to Buffalo to see Benny. He was at the Burlington Skyway. Below the high bridge, the bay glistened, but on the Buffalo side, heavy clouds made the water a dirty gray. *Jesus!* Chin had told him to see Benny about the missing money. A few years back, he'd met the Chinaman on some downtown condo sales. And when he had needed cash fast, he had introduced him to Benny. No problem. He could earn it by delivering bundles of cash from Benny to Chin. He kicked himself. It had been stupid to take a loan from the last delivery. Now he had to explain fast.

Benny's office was at the back of a convenience store. Frank parked in the back laneway.

"Hiya, fat boy!" Frank did not move. "Benny's expecting you. We're going in the side door." Two men led Frank down an alleyway and into an alcove. "Put your hands against the wall, fat boy."

"Come on, guys," Frank said, but he set down his briefcase and leaned into the wall. He craned his neck around to see them. The first blow was the worst. Screaming, Frank crumpled to his knees. Writhing in the rubble, he almost blacked out from the pain radiating from the small of his back. A boot slammed into his neck, cutting off his air. Hot breath was on his cheek. The pavement scraped his chin.

"Frank, Frank. The boss don't like his men taking unauthorized cuts." There was a low chuckle. "Just a friendly warning, fat boy. It's payback time."

They dragged Frank to his feet and opened the door. "The boss is gonna see you now, Frank."

A dim light was at the end of the hallway. Frank stumbled and touched his wet cheek. When he reached the light, he saw blood smeared on his hand. He tried to catch his breath. A door opened. Benny sat at his desk. Except for the eyes, he could be anybody's grandfather.

"Listen, Benny, I'll settle up with you next week. Honest."

"You've been stealing, Frank." Benny said quietly. "I'm very disappointed."

"Benny, I swear to God I'll pay you back. Just give me another week," Frank pleaded. The other men moved closer to Frank. Benny waved them off.

Frank wrestled his briefcase open. "Maybe we could make a deal. I got an offer on a hot property. Somebody wants this land real bad, Benny. Give me a little breathing space and I'll sign it over to you." Frank wiped away the blood dripping from his eyebrow.

"An offer on a house? What good is an offer on a house to me?"

"Everybody's bidding on it, but I'm in there first," Frank lied. "When I flip it…"

Benny's eyes flickered, but he remained silent. One of the men said, "You don't understan', fat boy. Benny wants the money now."

Benny stood up and glided around the desk in his slippers. He rested his hand on Frank's shoulder. Softly, he asked, "Are you a family man, Frank?"

Frank shook his head.

Benny stood back in surprise. "You mean you got no kids?" He took out a pipe and began to tap it on his palm. "You know, Frank," he continued softly, "my biggest pleasure in life is taking the grandkids to the park, getting them ice cream on a Sunday afternoon." Benny smiled broadly in recollection. Turning, he said sadly, "Don't let one of life's biggest pleasures pass you by."

Frank grinned in relief. Benny was giving him time. "No Benny. For sure—"

"You're still a young man, Frank. There's still time."

The men crowded close to Frank.

Benny's eyes narrowed. "If you steal from me, maybe you're never gonna be a papa. Understand me?"

"I swear to God, Benny, I was strapped." Frank trembled as he reached for the offer. "I tried to call you to ask, but—"

One of the men stabbed a gun in Frank's back. "Shut up, you fucking liar!"

Benny spoke quietly as he patted Frank's shoulder. "I don't like liars, Frank. You get me the money—all of it, today. Okay?" His smile was gentle as the men grasped Frank's arms.

"Sure, Benny. I'll get it for you right away."

"How you gonna do that, Frank?"

Frank threw out his hands and grinned. "Don't worry. I got resources. I'll be back this afternoon with it. Just a matter of freeing up some capital."

Benny's mouth tightened into a straight line. Frank backed out of the room. Benny nodded to the two men.

At the family cemetery, Donnie slid onto **a** bench. He tried to figure out how to load the gun. Nobody except him and Aunt Suzannah cared about Gram. They were just like a bunch of bugs scurrying around mindlessly. His father spent all his time cramming his hand into people's mouths and counting up the cash. His mother was always wondering what people thought. It was a useless existence. But today he would do something that mattered.

He whispered, "Gram, I got the gun. Today's the day." He held the barrel up against the sky. It was starting to rain again. "See? Here it is. I did something right."

In the laneway, Frank squeezed behind the wheel of his car. Gasping, he frantically searched for the keys.

"Hey, Frank!" One of Benny's men dangled the keys just outside the window. Leaning in and grinning, he said, "Don't forget this afternoon, fat boy!" He tossed the keys ten feet from the car. Frank squirmed out and picked them up. As soon as he pulled away from the curb, the men got into a blue Buick and followed him.

After Frank cleared Canadian customs, the Buick disappeared. His breathing began to ease. Tilting back the seat, he turned on the radio. Somehow he could scrape some money out of his realtor's trust accounts.

He saw a blue flash. Instinctively, he wrenched the steering wheel to his right. His head slammed against the dash as he desperately braked. The car swerved violently raising a cloud of dust behind it. Dazed, he fought for control of the car. A concrete abutment rose up ahead of him. Careening to a stop, he narrowly avoided slamming into the guard rail. From the blue Buick, Benny's boys waved up ahead in the distance.

"So what's the deal?" asked one of Benny's men.

"We kill the fat boy at his office or his house. Wherever he goes. And we don't use guns."

"What?"

"No guns. Just a knife."

"Benny doesn't use knives."

"This time he does."

The other man whistled and looked out the window at the city looming up ahead. "I don't like this kind of shit. A bullet through the head would be just fine."

CHAPTER 30

▼

On the way back from Marjorie's, where he had found the secret trust, Harry heard the news in the car. "An arrest has been made in the murder of Marjorie Deighton." Harry turned up the volume and gripped the steering wheel.

"Last night, shortly after midnight, police arrested Mr. Albert Chin on charges of the murders of Miss Deighton and her housekeeper, Miss Rosalind Michaels, and two employees of the law firm Cheney, Arpin, Deirdre Jamieson and Linda Lee Hong."

Harry caught the voice of Sergeant Welkom.

"The investigation has followed along the normal channels, in the usual manner. Good, careful police work has enabled us to make this arrest on all four murder charges."

Harry snapped the radio off. They had arrested the wrong man.

Jesus! Good solid police work, he thought. *Don't call in forensics. Don't do an autopsy. Ignore everything I've said. Don't follow up with Frank.*

Chin couldn't weigh more than one hundred and forty pounds, and Rosie weighed at least two hundred pounds and was four inches taller. Already, he'd seen Frank's handiwork. *Poor Suzannah!* Like an animal, Frank had torn and pounded her face. And he had plenty of reason to kill Marjorie. Harry knew he owed it to Suzannah to set the police straight.

When he stepped out of his car at the police station, reporters swamped him. Flashes blinded him as the reporters crowded in with their mikes and cameras.

"Sir? Are you Harold Jenkins?" a reporter shouted.

"What about the Albert Chin case?"

"Me?" Harry was flabbergasted. "How do you know me?"

"The police want to talk to you about some land deals you made with the accused."

He pushed past the reporters and hurried to the front desk.

Trailing behind him, one reporter shouted, "Sir? Wasn't Marjorie Deighton a client of yours? How is her murder connected to the two women from Cheney, Arpin? Were they in on the deals too?"

Harry demanded to see Welkom. He was surprised to be immediately ushered through the swing gate and down a corridor to an empty office.

Harry sat down on a chair, scrunching his knees under a small table. Moments passed. He looked out the window onto the parking lot. He stood up and leaned on the windowsill covered with grime. Not until he began pacing did he realize how small the room was—just like a cell. *Typical intimidation by the police.* What in hell had Chin been saying about him?

"Afternoon, counselor. Good of you to drop in. I've been looking forward to our little meeting." Welkom tossed a binder on the table. Two more men crowded into the room.

"This here is Officer Riley." Welkom gestured toward a man, who took a seat and grinned at Harry. "And here's Officer Cominskey. They arrested our Mr. Chin early this morning."

Welkom pulled his chair so close to Harry that their knees bumped. Riley leaned over the back of Harry's chair. Cominskey sat motionless, staring at him. Swept by a wave of claustrophobia, Harry shoved his chair backwards, banging against Riley, who still grinned down on him.

Then anger surged in him. "It's completely ridiculous. You've arrested the wrong man."

"How so, counselor?" Welkom looked intently at him.

"I told you Frank Sasso should be investigated. He has plenty to gain from my client's murder."

"Like what?" Welkom asked.

"Marjorie's house for his girlfriend. He forced Marjorie to make a new will, and likely stole the old one from my office. And I saw his girlfriend, Suzannah Deighton, today. There's no doubt in my mind he beat her up. Besides, just look at Chin. He's half Rosie's size."

"Where would we find this Mr. Sasso?" Cominskey asked mildly.

"He's a realtor. His office is out on the Danforth."

"A realtor? How well do you know him, sir?"

Harry was disarmed by the tone. "Well enough. For years, he's been in my office trying to get money out of Suzannah Deighton's trust fund."

"What makes you think he did this?" asked Cominsky.

Harry leaned forward and spoke intently. "Frank brought Suzannah to my office today. Her face was bruised and scraped raw and her lip had been split wide open and stitched up. Until I saw her with him, I wondered why beaten-up women didn't just leave." He paused, then continued more quietly, "But after seeing them together, I know why. It's gut-wrenching fear, plain and simple."

"Frank admitted that?" asked Cominsky.

"He didn't have to. It was obvious." Harry replied.

"Why didn't you call the police?"

Harry sighed. "If you saw the pleading look in her eyes, you'd understand."

"So this guy Sasso's in real estate." Welkom's jaw jutted out. "Trying to pick up more commissions, counselor?"

Harry's mouth dropped open. "What?"

"Well, counselor," began Welkom, setting his cigar on the edge of the table, "Mr. Chin says you've had some real interesting land deals together."

"I already told you about those, Sergeant Welkom."

"In fact, he says you masterminded and drew him into a massive money-laundering scheme, demanding some *very* handsome secret commissions. And that you stole part of his retainer to cover some bank debts." Welkom turned the page in his binder. "Says you even demanded a trip for you and your wife to the Bahamas."

In shock, Harry said nothing.

The officer sat back and stared at Harry. "I hear the Atlantis Resort is a pretty fancy place. Most honest folk would have to save up for years to stay there."

Harry knew he had turned a blind eye. Of course—what else could Chin have been doing other than laundering dirty money, and setting him up to take the fall?

Welkom squinted at him. "Says you put the whole deal together, so when Marjorie Deighton died, you'd sell him her house and pocket another fat commission."

Harry spoke evenly. "Are you charging me with something, sergeant?" No one in the room responded. "Because, if you are, I want to call my lawyer."

"What makes you think you're being charged, counselor?"

"Obviously, your questions, sergeant."

Cominskey spoke for the first time, in placating tones. "They're just questions in the normal course of our investigations, Mr. Jenkins. Anything you can tell us might be helpful."

Mutt and Jeff routines, thought Harry, glancing at the young officer. "I'll say nothing until I speak with my lawyer."

The sergeant gruffly slammed a phone down in front of Harry, who dialed Stephen immediately. Stephen's voice was chilling. "Harry, keep your mouth shut until I get there."

Within twenty minutes of Stephen's arrival, Harry was released. They stood squinting in the sunlit parking lot.

"For Christ's sake, Harry, stay away from the police. They've got nothing on you about the murders, but they'll follow up on the money laundering. *Don't* talk to them at all without me present."

Shaken, Harry thanked Stephen. He had unwittingly walked right into the trap Chin had set for him. He got into his car and phoned his office. Laura had left a message. Back from Montreal, she wanted to talk over dinner. To regain some shared intimacy? No, probably to tell him she loved another man.

CHAPTER 31

▼

Donnie walked slowly across the Bloor Street viaduct to Frank's office. Tires hissed across the broad expanse of concrete and asphalt. Up so high, it was lonely and ugly. But looking over the bridge, he could see the budding trees creating a green and yellow haze over the valley below. He shut his eyes tightly. Donnie had heard of people, especially kids, jumping off this bridge. Once he got Frank, he'd come back and look over the edge.

Moving slowly along Danforth Avenue, Donnie looked up. The sign on the second-storey window read "Procon Realty, Inc." It was Frank's office. Without any particular plan, Donnie hobbled around to the back lane and climbed up the fire escape. The washroom window was open a couple of inches.

Looking down, he wondered about the blue Buick with New York plates parked below him.

Two men ran out a back door. Donnie coughed. One of them stopped and looked up.

"You hear something?" Slowly, the man drew his gun.

"Jesus, Sam! Get the fuck in the car!" They spoke in hoarse whispers. Donnie could see faces in the dim light. Their eyes seemed to drill into his. Jumping in the car, the men slammed the doors and lurched into reverse, shooting out of the lane.

Donnie climbed through the window and inched the washroom door open. It was almost too dark to see. He squinted in the gloomy office.

It was almost entirely dark, but Donnie could see well enough. Filing-cabinet drawers had been yanked out, and files were strewn on the floor. The telephone receiver dangled from his desk. Frank lounged back in his chair, oblivious to everything.

Lazy bastard. Time to wake him up and have some fun.

Gently, Donnie tipped the chair back and placed the barrel of the gun to Frank's right temple.

"I've come to settle a few scores," he whispered close to Frank's ear.

He touched Frank's shoulder and felt a sticky wetness across his back. He shook him, but jumped back when Frank's head wobbled at a funny angle.

"Frank!" he whispered fiercely, pinching his cheek. "Wake up. It's time to pay." Grinning, he put his face down close to Frank's. "This is going to hurt as much as I can make it."

The streetlight outside the window flickered on, illuminating the office in a sickly yellow glow and revealing a huge gash across Frank's neck from ear to ear. Blood still flowed. His shirt was completely soaked.

"Jesus," choked Donnie, jumping back. With the gun hanging limp in his hand, he gazed at Frank's lifeless eyes. "No!" he wailed. Then he vomited onto the floor.

He scrambled out the window and down the fire escape. At the street, he hailed a cab. He couldn't go home, not with all the blood covering his hands and clothes. Donnie laid his head back on the seat of the taxi. Did those guys with the Buick do it, or had the Florist beaten him to it?

He could hide out at Gram's house. The cabbie kept glancing at him in the rear-view mirror. The swish of the tires on the glistening pavement lulled Donnie in and out of consciousness.

"Hey, kid? Sure you don't want me to take you to the hospital? You don't look so good."

Donnie sat up as straight as he could. "No. Please, just take me to 42 Highland Avenue. It's my grandmother's place." The driver shrugged and headed west on Bloor Street.

At Gram's house, Donnie slipped through the kitchen window and pulled himself inside. Stumbling through the darkened house, he reached the attic stairs. He could hide under the eaves for the night.

CHAPTER 32

▼

At home, Harry showered and shaved, trying to preserve a shred of optimism against the sinking in his gut. Surely they could get counseling and work it out.

Half an hour later, he sat on the patio in the sun and smoked a cigarette. The house needed a new roof. Maybe a patch on the driveway would do.

It was almost five o'clock. A breeze was up, and it was getting chilly. Harry went inside and called Laura's office, only to get her voice mail.

He glanced at the hall table and wondered why he had not seen the envelope before. Sinking onto a dining-room chair, he slit open the envelope, noticing the shadows creeping throughout the room. Although he already knew the message, he read carefully.

Dear Harry,

While I was going to meet with you tonight, I thought it better to write instead. We have not, for years, been going in the same direction. It's as if we can never speak, one person to another. We are so different, and we always have been. Harry, I have found someone I truly love. Likely, it will come as no surprise that it is Peter Stover, at the museum. I have decided to move out and live with him. Consequently, I will come to the house tomorrow and take my clothes and a few personal items. (Please don't make this difficult.) After that, I think we should communicate only through our lawyers. I wish there were some way to make this easier for you, but I know only time will do that. You're a kind and reasonable man, Harry, so I hope I can count on that.

Laura

Tears stung at Harry's eyes. Blindly, he shouldered his way out of the house and into his car. Never had he been so cold on a spring day. His fury piloted him in unknown directions. Somewhere on the highway east of the city, he admitted his part. Somehow they had simply drifted apart. Or was that true? No contented wife could be seduced against her will. Surely he could have prevented it. A floodgate had opened, and his mind was filled with useless waves of recrimination. There had been no huge argument, only skirmishes, followed by long silences. Over what?

When he pulled off the highway, he realized his direction. He was going somewhere isolated from the world, where he could think. The Scarborough Bluffs wound round the eastern edge of the city. He had been there many times as a child. From the beach, the city skyline was barely visible. No one would see him on the deserted stretch on a weekday afternoon.

He parked the car. Behind him were the high, sandy cliffs, set one against the other. The broad gray lake spread out to the horizon. Anyone watching from above would be surprised to see a solitary man in a business suit marching past bulrushes as tall as men, and onto the beach.

He trudged through the soft, sinking sand westward, toward the city. The constant wind swept down from the hills, cutting through his jacket. He longed for the cold to anesthetize him.

Up ahead, a dog ran in circles around a pile of rock and driftwood. Gulls dipped over the water and called out in eerily human-sounding voices. Harry stared out onto the rolling waves of the huge lake. Bereft, he wished he did not know the truth.

The cliffs ahead rose sharply straight up from the water. The afternoon sun shimmered on the smooth and sheer rock face. On the horizon, his city lay reduced to a tiny black smudge, as if it had floated away from him forever. With Laura gone, the city he once loved existed only in a jumble of memory.

Suddenly, Harry began to run. His leather shoes squished on the damp sand as he neared the pile of rock and wood ahead. Wincing at the pain in his side, he stopped not ten yards from his destination.

The driftwood, piled high, looked like a prehistoric monster. Harry kicked away some garbage and bent to examine the wood. Seizing a long piece of driftwood, he held it up in the unceasing wind. The knot in the wood stared skyward like an ancient, wizened eye.

The heft of the wood aroused an unexpected sense of power in him, then murderous frustration swept through him. In sudden fury, he swung the driftwood upward and felt his body stretch to its limits. With all his strength and power, he smashed the blind, gnarled eye on the rocks. The reverberation stunned him. The splintered wood shot along the beach. Elated, he shook with his own long-buried fury and smashed another piece of wood, and then another. He sank to his knees on the deserted beach, isolated by rock, wind, and water. At last, he was spent.

Quietly, he returned to the car. With the wind roaring in his ears, he acknowledged the emptiness within. It was strangely familiar. Somehow, he had always known his marriage would end this way.

CHAPTER 33

▼

When Katharine left Harry's office, it was only three-forty-five. Her appointment with Tony McKeown was at four-thirty. She had half an hour to fill.

From the bright sunlight, she entered the cool, dim arcade. Squinting, she slowed her pace, until her eyes adjusted to the softly filtered light from the vaulted ceilings of glass. Then, driven by the specter of her sister, she marched blindly down narrow corridors, surrounded by marble and brass. Soon she was lost in a maze of tiny shops.

She stopped for coffee on the mews. From her purse, she took a pen and notebook and laid them on the table set with white linen and silver. She had to organize her thoughts before meeting Tony.

Her sister's face floated into her mind again. The stitching and the bruised, puffed disfigurement enraged her. Suzannah was no different from the women at Emma's shelter. That female, self-effacing deference nearly drove her mad. When she told them to be strong and stand up for themselves, they just looked blankly at her. How could you build confidence and strength when there was nothing to work with? They were only little children. Looking up, she stared at pigeons strutting and puffing along the intricately scrolled ledge.

The white-coated waiter's face was bland and smiling as she ordered coffee. She gazed down the mews at the rows of stone columns in shadows, and shivered. Women were traditionally subservient. Caught in dependency, they made easy and convenient targets. But why had violence increased as women gained their independence? Her coffee arrived, and she sipped it. Women still flocked to the shelter in droves. Her thoughts returned to Suzannah.

Through tears, Suzannah had said only several weeks ago, "Frank will never leave. He needs someone to hurt."

"For God's sake! Why do you let him?" Katharine demanded.

Suzannah shook her head slowly and said, "You can't get rid of men like Frank. He enjoys hurting people too much. It's *that* simple."

Katharine never understood women's weakness, but she could grasp glimmers of the pleasure of domination and submission. Few men frightened her. None had been physically brutal. With her own strange sense of power, she had frightened a few herself.

Years back, she had been with a senior cabinet minister in the government. Although soft and more than middle-aged, he had radiated power and charm. He had commanded her to undress and lie on the bed. As he watched her satisfy herself, she had thought he would ignite. Katharine reveled in a strange, shifting mixture of domination and submission. After all, it was only a game, which ought not be taken too seriously.

She turned to thoughts of Tony. He had intentionally put himself in a position of conflict by acting for St. Timothy's, submitting an offer for a client on Marjorie's house, and advising her and Gerry. She would find out why.

CHAPTER 34

▼

Harry took the slow route back into the city along Kingston Road. He passed long stretches of broad, desolate roadway fringed with scabby motels and wrecked cars. Suddenly, he was pulling up in front of his house. A car sat in his driveway.

He almost wept. Were they here already? He could not bear the sight of Laura with Stover. He had always pictured the man with a pretentious goatee and a pipe, fat and out of shape, with little darting eyes and a fake English accent.

A man stepped from the car. He was alone. Did Laura lack the guts to come herself? Did she send her lover out to do her dirty work? The man bent to see Harry through the car window.

"Harry. It's Bob Rowe. So sorry to disturb you, but..."

Harry was slow to understand. When he at last realized he was not confronting Stover, he shook his head and asked, "Bob, what are you doing here?"

Bob tugged on his goatee, "I'm afraid it is really urgent, otherwise I wouldn't have come. But I have to find Katharine. I understand she had an appointment with you."

"Yes, this afternoon, along with Gerry, Suzannah, and Frank." Harry ushered Bob into the house.

In the living room, Bob sat on the edge of his chair and began fiddling with his tie clip. "Did she say where she was going?"

"Why don't you tell me what's wrong, Bob?"

Staring out the window, Bob spoke in a distant voice. "Katharine's been threatened."

Harry sat up. "By whom?"

Bob turned into the darkening room. "By Frank Sasso."

"With what? You mean over the will?"

Bob shrugged helplessly. "It's on the voice mail at home. Yes, he said he would hurt her if she didn't stop the fight about Marjorie's will."

"You're sure it was Frank?"

"Yes. He's called the house before. I know his voice."

"Did you call the police?"

"No, if they're involved, Katharine would be furious."

"But that's ridiculous."

Bob held up his hand. "You don't know Katharine. She'd think I was spying on her."

"What? When her safety's at stake?" Harry thought he was less amenable to calling the police himself.

As if deciding whether to continue, Bob sat silent for some moments. "Katharine sometimes goes off. I mean, she has friends...men...that she meets."

Harry saw Bob's shoulders sag. He wanted to find words to console him, but could think of none.

As if a dam had burst, Bob turned to him. "Harry?" He fumbled for his pipe and polished its stem. "The only way I can make sense of it is this: I still love her. She's strong, capable, brilliant, and tough. But she's so strong that she can't trust enough to love anyone. One part of her is at war with another." His voice choked. "I'm afraid she's doomed." He buried his face in his hands. His voice came to Harry as if from a hollow void. "That's why she does it...she's always hoping to find the one she can trust enough." At last, Bob looked up at him. "That's why I'm always there to pick up the pieces," he said softly. "Since she knows I'll always be there, she takes me for granted."

With sadness creeping over him, at last Harry spoke. "Well, she had an appointment right after she left my office, with another lawyer, Tony McKeown."

Bob removed his glasses and massaged his temples. "Can you call him for me, Harry? It's all we have to go on." Harry nodded and lifted the receiver.

CHAPTER 35

▼

Tony had canceled a meeting to accommodate Katharine.

Seated on his deep leather couch, she struggled to maintain an assertive air. She knew her anger was evaporating. Every movement of the man was smooth and disarming; every word was soft and insidious. From his office window, she could see black clouds creeping over the city.

Tony smiled blandly as he handed her a scotch and sank beside her on the sofa. Casually, he gestured toward the window. "Magnificent, isn't it?" He edged slightly closer to her. His left hand, the one with the tiny claw finger, rested on his knee. Katharine shifted forward on her cushion and concentrated on her drink. He caressed the razor-thin crease of his trouser leg with the little claw. She sipped her drink and then set it on the coffee table. She was drawn to him one moment, repulsed by him the next.

She endeavored to marshal her logic, her plan of attack. Although he was now lounging against the deep pillows, she knew it was only a pose. McKeown never relaxed. In the growing silence, it was difficult to collect her thoughts.

"What can I do for you, Katharine?" It was a simple question. Any lawyer might begin with it. But his voice caressed her name. In the dim light, she saw his eyes dance with amusement. The way he tapped that delicately deformed finger doubled her tension. He was waiting for her. In the light, she hoped he would not see the flush spreading up her throat. Her skin prickled and her clothing felt rough. It was her move.

"Surely it can't be so terrible, Katharine, that we can't talk."

She was certain he was taunting her. He sat forward slowly and set his empty glass on the table.

"Is it about your aunt's estate, or something else? After all, you and I should be able to talk about almost anything." His questions hung in the air.

She found her voice. "Yes, it's about Marjorie's estate." Katharine stood up and moved away toward the window where it was cooler. "Listen, Tony," she began, "the family just had a meeting with Harold Jenkins this afternoon. There's an offer from one of your clients on the house."

"Isn't that a good thing?"

"Well, yes, but how can you still represent me and Gerry? That's certainly a conflict." She hesitated, then raced on. "Isn't it?" Immediately she hated the quizzical tone in her voice. It was just like Suzannah's.

McKeown rose and joined her at the window. "Well, I won't. Not if you don't want me to."

"But shouldn't you have told us that at the outset?" she persisted.

"Well, I'll certainly withdraw, if that's what you want. But it is a good offer, isn't it?"

Katharine was surprised at the question. "Yes, it's a very good offer."

McKeown stood back from her, laughing. "Now I understand why you're here!" Touching her shoulder, he guided her back toward the couch. His hand grazed her hip. "You're trying to jack me up, right?"

He sat down again. "Katharine, it's an excellent price. In fact, it's twenty-five percent over the market value. My client desperately wants the land and is ready to outbid, if necessary."

She was disarmed by his frankness. "Then your client isn't the church?" she asked. McKeown appeared to find this very amusing.

"No, certainly not."

"Then how many different interests do you represent?"

"Listen, Katharine, I can't answer all your questions." McKeown lounged back again. Like an electric shock, she felt the jolt of his appraising eyes wandering up and down her legs. "Why don't we have dinner together? Maybe I can answer some of them."

The telephone rang in his inner office. Until then, Katharine had not been aware of the adjoining room.

In one lithe movement, he rose from the sofa. "Excuse me for a moment," he said, smiling. "I'd better take that call." Glass in hand, he strode into the office beyond.

Katharine watched as he turned back and carefully set the door just an inch or so ajar. She sighed and tried to relax in the deep cushions surrounding her. She knew she was drawn to him. She tried to distract herself by leafing through several art magazines that were neatly stacked on the coffee table. She found a strange assortment of photographs and paintings of African masks. Running her finger over the glossy surfaces of the pictures, she shivered. Some were ugly, crude, and primitive. Others, with their simple, almost primordial lines, evoked an ethereal sense of calm, as if from another world beyond her experience. Suddenly she was seized with the desire to enter it.

Tony turned on a lamp in his small office and answered the call.

"McKeown," he said softly. In the dim light, his eyes glimmered green and yellow.

"Mr. McKeown, it's Harold Jenkins."

A small smile broke over Tony's thin lips. "Harry. Good to hear from you. What's up?" He moved from behind the desk and opened the door just a crack more. Now he had a perfect view of Mrs. Rowe, pretending nonchalance as she examined his magazines. The line of her neck and shoulder was tense. She had not quite given herself over to him. In time, she would.

"A Mrs. Katharine Rowe left my office at about three forty-five this afternoon," said Harry.

"Yes?" Again, Tony glided across his office. Peering around the corner, he opened the door just a bit more. He held his breath. *She is lovely,* he thought.

"She said she was going to your office."

"Oh?"

Harry knew McKeown would be loath to reveal that Katharine was a client. "I'm calling because her husband, who is with me now, is quite concerned about her whereabouts."

"I can certainly understand his concern. With that mad artist on the loose, I'd be worried too," said Tony softly. Distracted by Katharine's pacing in the outer office, he watched her gaze out upon the city hall. A touch of restlessness possessed her. "She did have an appointment with me, Harry, but she called to cancel just a few minutes beforehand."

"That's odd. She seemed so intent on seeing you about the Deighton estate." When Tony did not reply, Harry continued, "She didn't say why, did she?"

"No, Harry." Tony touched his cheek and then his chin. He would have to shave.

"Or where she was going instead?" Harry persisted. McKeown's nonchalance was irritating.

"Harry, my secretary took the call," Tony replied. "Not the first one to not show up, though." He chuckled. "I hate to let the pretty ones get away."

"Pardon?"

"Just joking, Harry," Tony said with unusual energy. With his claw finger, he circled the rim of his glass. His sleeve knocked a pen from his desk. Deft as a panther, he sprang to retrieve it.

Through narrowed eyes, he gazed through the opening of the door. There she was framed in the light. He blinked his eyes. He could tell by the way she crossed her legs and smoothed her skirt that she was waiting for him.

"Tony, if there is anything more you can think of…"

Tony sat up straight. "You sound really worried, Harry. Any specific concerns?"

"Her husband tells me she has received a threatening phone message."

Immediately, Tony was interested. "Really? From whom?"

"A man, Frank Sasso."

"I think I've heard that name. Who is he?"

"He's the boyfriend of Katharine's sister, Suzannah."

Tony silently moved toward the door. Holding perfectly still, he watched Katharine intently, his head cocked to one side. *Such a lovely red dress.* Then, softly, he opened the door another inch.

"Harry? I think I know who he is. If I'm right, he's a pretty nasty thug. You know the type. Grabs whatever he likes, regardless of right or wrong."

In surprise, Harry stared at the receiver. McKeown was scarcely known for his ethics.

"What did he threaten?"

"If she didn't cooperate, she'd get hurt. Or words to that effect."

"That sounds like Frank. A dangerous bully."

Harry was surprised at the vehemence in Tony's voice.

"You know, Harry, I've heard guys like him hang out at a place called the Gold Coin," Tony hesitated. "I think it's a bar somewhere around College and Spadina. But, of course, I can't say for sure."

Harry wrote down the information.

"You might try there…" Tony's voice trailed off as Katharine paused to examine herself in the mirror on the far wall. He caught his breath. She was ready. He hastened to end the conversation. "Harry, old man, I've got to run. But I'll be sure to call if I hear from her."

Harry stared at Bob for a moment. "Apparently Katharine canceled her appointment with him. He suggested we look for Frank in some bar."

Bob covered his face and swore.

Sinking with weariness, Harry saw himself marching along the beach at the Bluffs. He felt the reverberation up and down his arms from smashing wood on rock. From the depths of his own wretchedness, pity for the man overtook him.

Bob's few words had painted a nightmarish world. Katharine went off sometimes with people…other men. "Bob, where does Katharine go?" Harry swallowed hard.

In the growing shadows, Bob sighed deeply. "I don't really know, Harry. You'll not think much of me as a man, but I've known for years that Katharine finds…" His voice was choked as he continued, "…what she thinks she cannot find with me. She's sick, Harry. She thinks she can find satisfaction elsewhere. The truth is she has never found it anywhere."

Harry did not know what to say. Two sad men, he thought, with two unsatisfied women. At last he asked, "Has she gotten into difficulties before?"

"Yes, and I always pick her up and try to go on." He smiled bravely up at Harry, then lapsed into silence.

Weary as Harry was, simple humanity demanded that he help Bob.

"Rather than looking for Katharine, we might try to find Frank," Harry suggested. "Not much point in hunting in bars for him. If he's after Katharine, he won't be there."

Bob nodded. "Should we phone his house and office again, just in case?"

"Sure. Call Katharine, too. She may be home or back at her office."

Frank's line was busy. The other calls to Katharine turned up nothing.

"Let's go to Frank's office. If his line is busy, he's probably there."

Together, they headed for Procon Realty on the Danforth in Harry's car.

In Tony's office, Katharine glanced at her watch and then at the door to his inner office, where a soft light glowed. During her wait, she had decided to seduce him tonight.

At last Tony entered and sat beside her on the sofa. "Sorry for the interruption. Shall we have dinner?"

She put down a magazine and saw the flicker of green and yellow in his eyes. His very presence aroused her. A frisson of danger shot through her. He was the right combination of roughness and…what? Katharine could not place it. She realized she was staring at the tiny claw: two tiny, perfect digits in one. Amused, he was waiting for her.

They had dinner together in the Long Bar overlooking the city hall square. The city shimmered. Tony was at his charming best. Losing count of the times the white-coated waiter appeared with yet another drink, Katharine felt her tension ease.

The restaurant dissolved into hazy darkness as she focused only on Tony's face. It was a rough face, not a kind one, but full of life. She struggled to remember what they were talking about. Something about the house.

"Yes, of course your client's offer is a good one," she heard herself say. "But my dear sister, Suzannah, is about to ruin everything for us." The face across from her was quizzical, impelling her to continue.

"There are two wills, you know. If Suzannah gets the house under the second will, she's going to donate it to charity—that is, if Frank doesn't kill her first." She reached out and touched his hand. He was impassive. "So we can't accept an offer yet."

Tony said quietly, "If Suzannah's the problem, perhaps Frank will have to use a little more persuasion."

Katharine had no reply to his words, which were so softly seductive, yet so chilling.

Tony brightened. "You have a nephew, don't you?"

Katharine was surprised. "Yes. Why?"

"I've seen him once or twice with Frank. He seems like a smart kid."

"He's Gerry's son."

"The dentist?" Tony smiled.

Katharine nodded. Vaguely, she wondered at his interest in the boy.

"I'd like to talk to him. If he has any interest in the law, we have some good summer programs at the firm for bright students. How would I contact him?"

"He's only fifteen, Tony." Katharine was lost, unable to fathom the connection with Donnie.

McKeown shrugged and smiled. "Well, it's never too early. I've seen him a couple of times, once at your aunt's house."

Tony's face sharpened into focus.

Maybe he is the right one, she thought.

Her husband was frightened of her, as though she might eat him up…devour him. "Insatiable," he had called her. Bob was so timid. He thought she was some psychological freak. Never once satisfying her, he had stopped trying.

Tony's brooding smile floated off and dissolved into recollections of Frank's scowling face.

Never again. Not Frank! She must have been drunk when that had happened. Frank, with his fat sausage fingers pressing on her thigh, had loomed over her, grabbing and bruising her arm and then her leg. Swollen, piggish fingers pressing and prodding. But no feeling.

Then thick hot fingers wrapping round and round her neck. Flickers of panic, building to flames of fear. Choking with rage and revulsion, Katharine had fought him off. Her voice was like a whip. It was easy with Frank. Her words, so corrosive, deflated him. Frank was a nobody.

Tony would be different. His magnetism and power were cold and cruel. He demanded and then he took. She could see it in his eyes. He was a brilliant and worthy catch.

With great precision, Tony slit the cellophane wrapper of his cigar with his claw. His eyelids flickered as he saw that she was transfixed. Briefly, he puffed on the cigar until its tip glowed.

Katharine sipped her wine. Men had always been drawn to her. There were really only two kinds. Some tried to storm down the door, demanding their due, coercing, thrusting, and cursing. Men like Frank, vicious if refused, but ultimately ineffectual. McKeown was different.

Then there were the others. The touch—slow and tentative, then increasingly frantic. As they approached the ice queen, they were chilled and their touch became furtive and then groveling. Imagining the sensation of his tiny, perfect claw, she caught her breath.

He saw her across the table, caressing her lower lip with her tongue. He knew what was on her mind. It would be easy. She was begging for it.

When the waiter had cleared the table, Tony said, "We will go to the Royal York Hotel. I've made a reservation." It was not a question.

She assessed the possibility of danger. Katharine knew how to look after herself. She was not like Suzannah. She smiled slowly in agreement.

Outside Frank's office, two police cruisers blocked off the corner of Danforth and Coxwell. Harry felt his stomach sickening as he pulled off onto a side street and parked. As he and Bob approached the corner on foot, the rotating light of an ambulance swept through the crowd. Harry knew at once that the police were in Frank's office.

With Bob behind him, he pushed his way through the crowd. An officer was questioning a witness: a small woman, wearing an old-fashioned pillbox hat, tugging on the constable's sleeve.

"He was just a young kid, and he kinda limped along the sidewalk over there. Then I saw him get into a cab. Just a kid, you know."

"Where'd he come from, ma'am?" asked the officer.

"Like I told you. I seen him jump from that fire escape round at the back. Then he come limping out to the street."

"So he came out of that window around at the back."

"Well…I think so."

"Were you at the back too?"

"Well…no."

The officer took down the woman's name and phone number, then snapped his notebook shut.

Harry pressed further into the crowd. Words swirled around him. "Guy up in that office's been murdered. Real messy. They slit his throat."

"Who was it?" Harry asked the man beside him.

"Cops said it was the mob that killed him. A realtor named Sasso."

Harry dropped back into the crowd and found Bob. He tugged his sleeve. "Listen. I think Frank's just been murdered."

"What?" he exclaimed.

Harry had no desire for more dealings with the police. "Let's get going. Obviously, Frank's not after anyone tonight."

They drove slowly back along the Bloor Street viaduct. Harry squinted in the flash of lights from oncoming cars. If Frank were dead, did that mean Katharine was safe?

Bob slumped in his seat, radiating hopelessness. It would be easy just to call it a night and drive him back to his car. Then he could get into a hot shower. He knew at once that he could not bear the emptiness of his own house. Loneliness nearly overtook him.

He had to do something. Suddenly he said, "Bob, I'm going to call McKeown back." He did not know why.

Reaching for his cell phone, he dialled McKeown's office. After ten rings, a woman answered the phone.

"Mr. McKeown's office."

"Is Tony in, please?"

"No, he's left for the day."

"Really? Is there anywhere I can reach him? I'm a solicitor, Harold Jenkins. It's urgent I speak with him."

"I don't know where he is, Mr. Jenkins." The woman sounded bored and vaguely annoyed. "He left about an hour ago for dinner with a client."

"A woman?"

"Yes."

"What did she look like?"

After a long pause she said, "I don't know. I'm sorry, but I can't help you any further. Good night."

Harry stared at the phone. Obviously, it could be anyone. But the secretary had indicated that it was a female client.

Katharine and Tony checked into the Royal York Hotel. Together they strolled along the red-carpeted corridor to the elevator. Violin music floated out from a far-off dining room. His pleasure was beginning to build. How trusting she was, coming with him. He pushed the elevator button and then stood back. Her skin was as smooth and white as porcelain china, but soft.

Not until the elevator door shut and they were alone did she wonder when he had arranged a room. She liked the self-assurance and command. Facing the front of the elevator, both of them watched the progression of the lighted floor numbers in silence.

When the elevator stopped at the ninth floor, they stepped into the corridor. Tony drew the key from his pocket. He wondered if she would struggle. Thrashing and writhing definitely increased his pleasure. In a caress, he drew her lustrous black hair gently back to expose her neck. He took the key and opened the door, standing back for her to enter.

He knew her weakness. He would circle endlessly, prolonging his pleasure. At a moment of his own choosing, he would swoop down and place his mark. It was odd how few things in life were truly permanent.

Katharine stepped through the doorway.

The room was ready; the bed covers were turned down. A bottle of champagne rested in ice on the coffee table.

With great deliberation, Tony drove the deadbolt into place, then he carefully chained the door.

"Don't worry," Katharine laughed, "I won't try to escape."

Pocketing the keys, he said, "You don't know, Mrs. Rowe. You may want to." His voice was flat and his face was stony, but he smiled as he set his case on the bed and snapped it open. He said softly, "In fact, you may beg me to let you go."

Like a careful artist, he had brought only his finest instruments.

Gently drawing her to him, he touched her face, then traced her lips with the claw. Circling her ear, he trailed the double finger down to her shoulder and breast.

For Katharine it was an odd sensation, and it made her body quiver. She reached up around his neck and drew him down to kiss him. His lips were hard and taut.

He held her out at arm's length. "Are you repulsed by this little finger?" He held it up to her within an inch of her nose. "I will wear a glove if you wish."

"No," she lied. "Don't."

"Good." He fixed her with his gaze and slowly began unbuttoning the top button of her blouse with his claw, then, more rapidly, the second and third buttons.

"Silk! How soft and lovely. Just like your skin," he whispered as he buried his face in her breast. Through her blouse, he grasped her nipple, now erect.

She winced. Tony would be very rough, but pain was her only chance to feel some pleasure.

He pushed her away. She wondered what she had done.

"Take off all your clothes, Mrs. Rowe. Then lie on the bed." His voice was hollow, distant, and commanding.

Katharine laughed uncertainly. She was used to more preliminaries: the kissing, the fondling, at least the pretence of seduction. But the prospect of making herself utterly naked and open to him was the ultimate arousal. The furtive groveling of legions of men in darkness had never stirred her. Perhaps he was like her senior cabinet minister.

"Yes, sir!" She sought to make it a game—maybe a striptease.

Tony stood stiffly apart from her. He caressed his claw with his thumb. He could read her mind; he was tearing away at its layers. Soon she would be raw and exposed to him.

In her best provocative manner, Katharine slowly opened the last buttons of her blouse to reveal a filmy pink lace brassiere. Slowly, she shrugged one arm and then the other from each sleeve, letting the blouse float to the floor. He did not move. She was hoping at least for a smile, at least.

Arching her back, she undid one hook and then the other, letting the bra slide slowly down. Exposing first one nipple and then the other for him, she paused to judge his reaction. His eyes bore into her, commanding her to continue.

Beyond him, she could see herself in the full-length mirror. *Not bad,* she thought. Her breasts were full, but not too heavy. She paused to catch herself at just the right angle. Engrossed in her own image, she did not see the disgust growing on his face.

Pleased with her appraisal, she casually tossed the pink lace brassiere for him to catch. He did not stir. The brassiere lay dangling over the edge of the bed, untouched.

Heedlessly, she slid from her skirt. Her smile was seductive as she tossed her head, letting her hair fall onto her shoulders and back. What was he thinking? Surely by now she should have aroused him.

The bitch was strutting, but not for him…for herself. Already, he imagined her pleading. Good. It would only drive him to new heights. Mrs. Rowe had no idea.

Again she turned to catch her image in the mirror. Her legs had always been good, she thought.

She could have slid the lace panties off at that moment; it would have been the natural climax to the show. Later, she wondered why she had not. Instinct would be the only answer. Instead, she approached him on the bed, her arms folded across her breasts.

Tony's excitement grew as he reached into his briefcase. Her body was sleek, but the flesh of women her age would begin to buckle and sag in a few years, becoming not nearly so enticing.

Instinctively, she had wrapped her arms around herself. *Good.* She was sensing danger. Terror always took his breath away.

With a bold smile on her lips, she reached out for him. He moved away to study her. At last he spoke coldly. "Lie on the bed."

Katharine was stunned—her vanity required some appreciation. But she obeyed. She crouched to retrieve her clothing. His dark form rose swiftly in the mirror. He circled behind her, fully dressed in his dark suit.

By the line of her shoulder, he knew she was beginning to sense danger. He stood over her, crowding her.

She looked up at him, a question forming on her lips. When had he put on the gloves? Weren't they the clear, latex kind?

"Before I touch you," McKeown spoke in an imperious tone, "I must examine you."

Katharine froze. She had heard those words before. Frowning in confusion, she tried to rise, but he clutched her shoulder.

Confusion spread across her face. Her lips contorted in fear. He saw the very first delicious dawning of terror. Driven closer to ecstasy, he saw her mouthing strangled words. Soon she would plead with him.

He pushed her shoulder roughly downward. The texture of the gloves strengthened his grip.

Her thigh muscles quivered as she struggled to rise. In dawning horror, she remembered the girl in the washroom. The girl had been crying, "He said he was going to examine me, and then he hit me!"

A glimmering silver knife was in his hand.

Dear God! Tony is the Florist. She tried to struggle away across the floor.

Tony pulled her straight up by the hair. With the gloves, his grip was hard and sure. Momentarily, her strength and will to resist deserted her.

Clutching her arm, he held her out from him like vermin. "You will submit!" Then he flung her like a rag doll onto the bed.

Panic consumed her. Blindly, she raised her arms to ward him off, but it was no use. He bore down on her sprawled, defenseless body. Vainly, she fought to rise.

Instantly, he was on top. The naked hatred in his eyes filled her with terror.

She had no voice. "No, stop!" It was no more than a strangled whisper. The gloved hand clapped over her mouth. She could not breathe or cry out.

He was driven to prolong his ecstasy. Although she was strong, her legs were beginning to twitch and flail beneath him. Pleasure surged throughout him. *Lambs to the slaughter.* He gagged her mouth. At last he saw the pleading in her eyes.

Even with the gag, Katharine could breathe well enough. Desperate energy surged through her. Twisting one leg free, she pushed hard against him.

Surprised, he teetered on the edge of the bed. A little fight added excitement.

Swiftly swinging up her other leg, she caught him hard in the stomach. For a moment, he could not breathe. He slumped forward. Wrestling her left arm free, she clawed at his eyes with her nails.

He saw her left hand fluttering upward like a small bird. The nails were blood-red. He clutched her wrist, drawing it down sharply, while his other hand seized her throat. At the very moment of his own choosing, he could crush her. She crumpled underneath him.

Katharine saw only the red, swollen features of his face. The room was disappearing into blackness. He was too strong.

Thick twine was knotted around her neck. Rope cut and burned her ankles as she fought to breathe. He wrenched her over onto her stomach. Gasping for air, she twisted her neck on the pillow.

Slipping from consciousness, she had only one thought: *She had only ever wanted someone to trust enough to love.*

He bound her arms tightly in place and fitted a rope around her ankles.

She was falling into darkness.

Astride her, McKeown held the knife high. He would carve his finest design for her. He stopped to admire the skin, so soft and white, laid bare for him. *Such purity.* He hummed a gentle lullaby and stroked her neck to calm her. To undertake such delicate artistry, she had to be quiet. Soon she would be ready.

The nape of her neck lay exposed for him, the fine hairs damp. Carefully, he turned her head to expose the cheek. He cocked his head to one side, like an artist considering his next brushstroke. With a small knife, sharp and precise as a scalpel, Tony carved a perfect petal on her cheek.

His features choked with ecstasy as he regarded his creation. But he had to go further. *The artist must rise to the challenge.* With great concentration, he visualized the flowing lines of Matisse. Then he drew long and graceful lines down her neck and shoulder.

Katharine dropped swiftly into darkness.

Shock was merciful to her. She barely clung to consciousness. A cold, sharp instrument traced circles on her shoulders and downward on her back. She knew there was no help. She had only wanted to trust someone enough to risk love.

There was a surprising amount of blood from his work. The last desperate twitching rippled throughout her body, followed by a few brief shudders.

Pain floated somewhere outside her body. A garden wall covered with vines and masses of tiny white flowers appeared before her. It was at least six feet high, with a wooden gate set in it like a door. When she opened the gate, sunshine streamed through.

A child's singsong voice led her into a formal garden with winding walks and shrubbery shaped like soldiers at attention. A golden light illuminated strangely docile animals she had never seen before. There she saw a little girl with blonde hair to her shoulders.

"Here we go 'round the mulberry bush," the child sang, as she pushed her doll carriage along the garden path. Then she turned toward Katharine and said solemnly, "Shut the gate. There's a bad lady on the other side." Turning to attend to her doll, the child said simply, "We cannot let her in."

Katharine knew she was dying. So much time had run out. She could hear a scream and then soft moaning from the other side of the wall. The bad lady's body was being twisted and turned and bent. She knew it soon would be dark.

The little girl smiled now as she chattered to the doll. Katharine knew she would be called in from her play. In the distance, she could hear sobbing and pleading. She turned back, and the little girl was gone. Katharine was alone in the garden. Darkness rapidly cloaked all that she could see.

Tony kneeled astride her twisted body. The blood seeped onto the floor. With a towel, he staunched the flow, gently patting her skin. It was amazing how much blood could come from his artistry. She was a truly beautiful woman now that she bore his mark. There was no birth without blood.

His fist knotted her black, silky hair. With the thick lock of hair, he twisted her neck to view the side of her face.

Slowly, he inserted the knife in its leather sheath and placed it, along with the twine and the gag, into his briefcase. He dismounted from her and sat beside her on the bed. Grasping her shoulders, he turned her onto her back. Her head lolled to one side. Bruises were appearing on that long and beautiful neck.

He studied her chest. It did not rise or fall. He touched her breast. With his perfect claw, he circled her flat nipple. It did not respond. She must have suffocated in the pillow. Now she was dead. With a gentle smile, he carefully drew the cover over her. Standing before the mirror, he brushed off his suit with meticulous care, then left.

A chambermaid found Katharine when she came to deliver towels. The paramedics and police rushed her to the Toronto General Hospital.

Hours later, Katharine awoke to blinding white hospital walls. The garden wall was gone. A safe, familiar voice filtered through to her. Her eyes blinked open. Bob was there. She was safe.

"You're in the hospital. Thank God, Katharine," came her husband's voice. "You've been terribly cut. Your neck was almost broken! Who did this to you, Kate?"

Katharine did not answer. She was quickly sinking backward and downward, hoping to find the garden once more. His persistent tones followed her. "Who was he?"

She turned her head on the pillow in the direction of his voice. She did not open her eyes, but murmured, "I don't know. I can't remember."

"You mean…" Bob could not find the words. He buried his face in his hands. "You picked up another stranger?" He choked back tears. "Kate, you're sick. I don't know what to do. You've got to get help." He fell silent. Once again, Katharine slid into the blackness.

Harry leaned against the wall of the hospital corridor. He had seen more than enough. Driving back from Frank's office, Bob had received the call from the police telling him that that Katharine was nearly dead.

Harry would never forget how Katharine looked as she lay on the gurney under the stark and sterile lights of the emergency room. Her once-sleek body lay crumpled under white sheets. Ugly red welts encircled her wrists and ankles. Violent deep-purple marks were scored along her neck. But worst of all was her cheek. On it was cut, with cruel precision, an intricate petal design. Ugly lines were etched down her neck and shoulders. Whoever had caused this desecration had murdered Rosie, Deirdre, and Linda Lee. His theory was destroyed. Frank was dead; he could not have attacked Katharine. Another hand was at work…the Florist, after all.

Harry found his way to the cafeteria. Eating food was impossible to contemplate. He waited while the coffee machine drizzled out the coffee. Given what the secretary had said, maybe Katharine had gone to McKeown's office. In the barren coffee room, lit only by the light of the vending machines, he drank his bitter coffee. Then he crumpled up his cup and tossed it into the basket.

CHAPTER 36

▼

Harry finally went home to his empty house. Every inch of him ached. He tossed his coat onto the hall chair. In the kitchen, he stood in front of the refrigerator and drank the rest of the orange juice from the container. With Laura gone, nothing seemed to matter much.

He switched on the television to catch the local news. A reporter stood at the corner of Danforth and Coxwell Avenues. The twirling lights on the cruisers and ambulance illuminated the street in garish reds and yellows. Frank's throat had been slit. He could not have attacked Katharine. And Chin was in jail. Rosie was marked. So were Deirdre, Linda Lee and now, Katharine. Another hand had carved those grotesque petals. A wrathful god was on the loose.

Tony McKeown was everywhere. He represented the church in the rezoning application. He represented Katharine and Gerry in the will dispute. His client, whoever it was, had submitted an offer for Marjorie's house. Yet nothing suggested a direct connection with Albert Chin.

Picking up the phone, he dialed Stephen's home number. As the phone rang, his eyes drifted about the room. The upholstery on the chair, once so comfortable, was frayed. In the lamp's light, he could see a layer of dust coating the coffee table. Suddenly the whole house seemed worn and shabby from years of neglect. The phone continued to ring. He wanted Stephen's advice: something, anything about Tony.

He gazed out the window at the garden. Dark images of McKeown swooping downward like some mindless bird of prey came to him. At first, his face was friendly enough, but then shadows slipped across, so that only the eyes burned from the dark. Such dazzling eyes could paralyze a victim, he thought.

It was only a hunch. There was no proof of any kind, but Harry's suspicions hardened. Tony was the killer. But he had nothing to go on.

He dialed Natasha. He yearned for the comfort of her soft and reasoned tones. "You have reached…" Harry hung up. She was not in.

He knew he was on his own.

Tomorrow morning, he would pay a surprise visit to Tony's office. With a growing sense of dread, he climbed the stairs to the silent rooms above. Without turning on the lights, he lay on the bed. Exhaustion swept over him, and instantly he fell into a deep sleep. At four in the morning, he sat up. Twisted in the covers, he fought to free himself.

At ten o'clock that morning, Harry arrived at Cheney, Arpin without an appointment. The reception area dazzled in the morning light. Beyond the expanse of glass, the lake glared brilliantly, hurting his eyes.

Striding toward the rosewood reception desk, he tried to push thoughts of the rusting fire escapes outside his own office windows to the back of his mind. Earlier he had debated the wisdom of simply appearing at Tony's office. The man would either see him or not. Crawford had always extolled the virtues of surprise and rear-guard action.

Last night, Harry had imagined dragons and gargoyle-faced keepers at the gate, but the receptionist greeted him with a welcoming smile. How could such a hideous being as Tony exist in the midst of such normalcy?

"I'll just see if he can squeeze you in, Mr. Jenkins." In moments, Harry was whisked down corridors to McKeown's office, which had a miniature reception room of its own.

"Please have a seat, Mr. Jenkins. Mr. McKeown will be with you shortly," said the secretary. Harry sank into the sofa. The room was elegant and spacious, with dark paneling and a floor-to-ceiling bookcase filled with yards of law texts. It had all the accoutrements of a highly successful law practice.

I have nothing with which to confront him, only a hunch. He will escape. He thought of leaving, but he had no excuse for such behavior.

Harry was fascinated by the photographs of African masks lining one wall. Some were rough-hewn and primitive. Others, with fine flowing lines, were ornately carved and decorated. Harry took out his reading glasses and peered more closely at one. It showed a bronze mask with tiny, agonized faces carved into its chin. Along the cheek and up to the forehead, the tiny faces grew more serene, as if they had been released from purgatory. Harry pocketed his glasses and resumed his seat.

Ten minutes passed. Rising to pace, Harry checked his watch.

The secretary smiled at Harry and said, "We'll just knock on his door to see what's keeping him. Come with me."

Harry stood behind her as she tapped softly. She turned to him with a brief smile and said, "Mr. McKeown is such a wonderful man, but sometimes he gets so involved with his work." Receiving no reply, she opened the door.

Harry saw Tony seated at his desk. The strangeness of the scene fascinated him. In the morning light, the lawyer's features seemed afflicted with remote and private suffering. Oblivious to them, he slid a soft black leather glove on his left hand. Carefully, he fitted it onto each finger, one by one. Then he held out his gloved hand as if to admire it. His face grew serene as he picked up a silver knife.

The secretary coughed discretely. As if awakened from a dream, Tony startled. When he looked up, his expression was feral, like that of an animal disturbed while devouring its prey. Cold certainty swept over Harry. He had met the killer in his lair, and he had come with nothing.

Swiftly, Tony tore the glove from his hand and buried it and the knife in his pocket. His eyes gleamed with a brightness Harry had not seen before.

Recognition flickered in Tony's eyes, replacing the malevolence. A masking smile spread across his face. Tony sprang from his chair. "Harry, old man! What can I do for you?"

They shook hands, and the secretary withdrew.

"Do sit down." Harry took the chair across the desk. "Coffee?"

Harry shook his head. "I've come about the Deighton estate."

"Are your clients going to accept the offer?"

"I doubt it. The beneficiaries have a lot to sort out first."

The telephone rang. Tony reached for it.

Harry was transfixed. On the smallest finger of McKeown's left hand, he saw a tiny, perfect claw. *What a strangely beautiful deformity.*

"Yes, send them in," said Tony, "I need the research for this afternoon." Hanging up, he turned to Harry and smiled broadly. "Sorry, old man. Some students are bringing material I need. Won't take a moment."

Tony inspected his pant leg. With meticulous care, he picked several pieces of lint from one knee. The door opened. Two students struggled inward, carrying stacks of books and briefs. One of them was becoming red-faced from his exertions.

"Gentlemen," Tony began pleasantly, "I'd like you to meet Harold Jenkins, a colleague of mine. Harry, this is Brian Willoughby and Mark Goldberg."

Harry nodded and smiled. The students breathed heavily under their burdens.

"Sir? Where should we put the texts?"

The other asked, "Where do you want the Chin purchase and rezoning files?" Harry caught his breath. *Chin files?*

Tony nodded absently toward a table in the farthest corner. As Willoughby hoisted his pile, one book popped out from his stack and flipped open as it fell to the floor. Harry saw Goldberg freeze. Willoughby cursed under his breath.

Swift and deft as a panther, Tony was instantly on the floor beside the unwitting law student. Crouching, he scooped up the volume and rose to tower over Willoughby, who appeared unaware of the senior lawyer's cold anger.

McKeown ran a fingernail down the spine of the book, then motioned both of them over for closer inspection. "Mr. Willoughby," he began in bland tones, "how much do you think this volume cost?"

Harry, entranced by the growing flatness in Tony's eyes, caught his breath.

Willoughby shrugged. Harry winced. The boy was foolhardy.

"Mr. Willoughby?" The edge in McKeown's voice was sharp.

"Yes, sir?" Willoughby deigned to flash a charming smile.

"What value would you put on this book?" McKeown held the leather-bound legal text out to the law student.

The boy shrugged again. "Well, I really don't know, sir."

"With your carelessness, Willoughby, you have cracked the spine."

"Me?" The student's eyes widened in surprise.

"I saw you drop it," McKeown said flatly.

"Really? If I did, I'm sorry. I didn't realize—"

"How much, Mr. Willoughby?"

Momentarily, the young student appeared flustered.

"You don't know, do you?"

"Not exactly, Mr. McKeown." Willoughby cleared his throat. "I'm terribly sorry, sir. I'll certainly pay to replace it."

McKeown turned from the law student and sat at his desk. His low chuckle filled the room. "You don't have the slightest idea of its value, do you, Willoughby?"

Harry sat paralyzed by the spectacle.

McKeown began brushing his trouser leg. He spoke in a soft, lilting voice. "Mr. Willoughby, isn't money wonderful? If you have enough, there are never any real consequences in life. Wouldn't you agree?"

Brian Willoughby stared at the senior lawyer. Reaching into his breast pocket, he retrieved his checkbook. "Tell me how much you want, sir," the student said as he uncapped his pen.

Momentarily, McKeown appeared amused. "Put that away, young man." His voice grew quietly chilling. "This time, money is not enough."

Harry wanted to to intervene, but his fascination with the grotesque scene rooted him to the spot. *The pornography of another's humiliation at the hands of a master,* he thought.

"Sir?"

A smile broke out on McKeown's face. "You've always been protected from any consequences, isn't that so, Willoughby?"

Harry was stunned. His mind swung in wild arcs. He was about to witness a crucifixion. And he could neither intervene nor turn away. Willoughby had no idea he was being led to the slaughter. The boy smiled tentatively.

McKeown swung out of his chair and stood close to him. "You're fired, Mr. Willoughby. That's a real consequence money can't fix."

Willoughby turned pale in the darkening office. He stammered, "You can't do that, sir."

Harry, deeply embarrassed, gazed out the window.

McKeown spoke coldly. "You are clumsy and incompetent."

Panic struck the boy. "You can't fire me. There's a committee. I'll appeal to the committee."

McKeown said quietly, "Mr. Willoughby, I *am* the committee."

Willoughby's shoulders sagged. Goldberg tugged on his sleeve. Silently, they headed for the door. Harry turned away. Fascination, like that with the carnage of a traffic accident, suffused him.

McKeown smiled benignly at Harry. "Students these days. You have to scare them witless to make any kind of impression."

He ushered Harry over to the coffee table. "You're on your own, Harry? No partners or students?"

Harry shook his head. "No. I prefer it that way."

"Wise man, Harry." Tony stroked his finger and continued reflectively, "You don't have the responsibility of teaching these useless young minds. You don't have to get involved in your partners' lives. Just be your own man."

Harry was disgusted. McKeown was trying to draw him into his world of pain and humiliation by inviting him to take part in his cruelty and pleasure.

"So, what about the Deighton estate?" asked Tony.

Harry stared into McKeown's eyes. They reflected calm after an outrageous storm, as if nothing had happened. "It's about Katharine Rowe."

Other than a slight flicker of the eyelids, McKeown betrayed no reaction. "Yes?"

"She's in the hospital. If she lives, she will be terribly scarred."

"Oh, my God!" said Tony softly. "Was she in an accident?"

"No. She was attacked."

"By whom? Where?" Tony's breathing became sharp and shallow. Fury burned in his eyes.

"Nobody knows." Harry leaned forward. "But she was found in a room last night in the Royal York Hotel. She'd been bound, gagged, and beaten. A peculiar design was carved with a knife on her cheek and down her neck and shoulders."

Tony was absolutely still for a moment before speaking. "What demented person would do such a horrific thing? Do you think it's this fellow in the papers?" Tony paused, as if trying to recall. "The Florist…or the Mad Artist? Whatever they call him."

Harry shook his head. "I don't know. It's beyond belief. But I'm here because you told me last night that she canceled her appointment with you."

"Yes, that's right. But she didn't say why or where she was going. You were worried about Frank Sasso." Tony nodded his head energetically as if recalling their conversation in detail. "I told you about some bars he hangs out in."

Too smooth, Harry thought. "Frank was found dead yesterday afternoon."

"What…? What happened to him?"

"His throat was slit. The police found him in his office."

"Jesus!" Tony covered his face. "Then Frank couldn't have done it."

"Obviously not."

"What an awful world." Tony looked beseechingly at Harry. "Who could have done such a thing?"

Harry shrugged. "I called back here around seven to see if you'd heard from Katharine. Whoever answered the phone said you'd left with a female client around six."

Tony's eyes narrowed for an instant, then he sat back and sighed. "True enough." Harry was amazed to see him blush. "I didn't want this to get out, old man, but I'm having an affair with one of the partners' wives."

Harry remained silent.

"That's who I was with." Tony flashed a smile. "I'm sure you understand."

Harry refused to be drawn in by his boyish charm. He studied McKeown's guileless expression.   •

Tony laughed. "That's what I meant about getting involved in your partners' lives."

At last Harry spoke. "Katharine's badly cut up. Her neck was almost broken."

"What kind of cuts?" Tony asked.

"Similar to those on the bodies of the paralegals at your firm."

"You mean Deirdre and Linda? You think there's a connection?"

"I certainly hope so. I wouldn't want to think more than one person was doing this."

Tony rose swiftly. "Indeed. Do the police know?" he asked.

"Of course. It's hard to miss the similarity."

The secretary tapped on the door and entered. "Mr. McKeown? Your overseas caller is on the line. Do you want to take it in your other office?"

"Listen, old man, I'd better take this. Mind waiting a few moments?" Flashing a smile, Tony opened a door to a small interior office. "Be back in five minutes. Just relax here."

When he was gone, Harry swiftly moved to the desk with the files. The tabs read *Chin/Zaimir/St Timothy's rezoning: Chin sale of 6 properties surrounding Church and Deighton lands*. All the property purchases he had completed for Chin had been flipped to Zaimir.

Harry thought he heard McKeown laugh in the interior office. Swiftly, he closed the files and resumed his seat. Moments passed. Harry rose and started on the next files.

Chin offer on Deighton lands and church. After Harry had refused, Chin had used McKeown to make the offer on Marjorie's house. No doubt all parcels of land would soon be owned by Zaimir.

McKeown's voice came from the outer office. The door remained closed. Harry opened the last file: *Offshore Transfers*. What possible explanation could he give, if McKeown walked in?

Lists of fund transfers squiggled down the pages in tiny columns: the slosh of money back and forth at ever-escalating prices. Chin was reporting money-laundering to Tony. Harry glanced over his shoulder. He turned the page. At the top of the first column, he read: *Cheney, Arpin/Zaimir/Buffalo #487693*. Heading the second column was *CCJ #690566*. His firm trust account.

Stephen was right. *"Dirty money from drugs, prostitution, porn—you name it— flows into the country from all over the world. It goes into banks, trust companies. And to lawyers and accountants, some of whom are innocent, unsuspecting dupes; others are in on the game."*

There it was—the proof that he was a dupe. More likely, an idiot.

The door began creaking open. Swiftly, Harry pocketed the page and resumed his seat. Either it was incriminating evidence or something very useful for his defence.

Tony bustled in. Harry resumed his seat.

"Sorry, old man, to keep you waiting." He smiled broadly.

Thank God he'd not been seen, thought Harry.

Tony continued to stand at his desk. The meeting was over. Harry gathered up his case.

"Thanks for dropping in, Harry, and keeping me posted. I'll send some flowers to her. What hospital is she in?"

"Toronto General."

Tony smiled genially. Harry had come unarmed. He was being shown the door.

"Let me give you my card, Harry. It's got my home number on it. Please call anytime." Tony moved to his desk. Harry followed.

As McKeown was searching for a card, Harry glanced down at his agenda, which was lying open. On it, he saw an intricate design of a rose petal.

McKeown's eyes dropped to the book. Swiftly, he shut it. Harry was acutely conscious of his own breathing and the rough feel of his clothing on his skin. McKeown was the Florist.

He looked up at Tony and into his eyes. True monsters had no special quality, Harry thought calmly. The man possessed no strange and frightening aspect, setting him apart from the rest of humanity. If anything, he exuded charismatic charm. Brilliant, handsome, engaging, he stood at the pinnacle of the legal world. But Harry could see at a glance that some fundamental building block of a human being was absent. Having no centre, the Florist was a jumble of sharp-edged jigsaw pieces from a dozen different puzzles. Where humanity should have been, Harry saw only the chaos and banality of evil.

"Are you all right, Harry?" Tony was smiling uncertainly.

"Of course. Why?"

"God! You look like you've seen a ghost." Tony handed him his card. "Listen, do you want some water?" He reached for a bowl on his credenza. "Have a hard candy to suck on."

Harry shook his head. "No…thanks. I'm fine." He watched as the lawyer popped a candy into his mouth.

"They're very good. Called Butterscotch Bits." Tony continued to hold out the bowl. "I have a confession to make," he said solemnly.

"What?" Harry caught his breath.

A sly smile crossed Tony's face. "I must confess I have an incurable sweet tooth."

"Really?"

"Yes." Tony laughed, revealing a row of brilliant, white teeth.

Harry steadied himself and glanced once again at the agenda, now closed, where he had seen the rose-petal drawing.

"See? I cannot resist indulging in innocent pleasures." Tony popped another candy in his mouth. He clapped Harry on the arm, propelling him toward the door. Tony slipped on his glove, and the two men shook hands.

The Florist was also the mastermind of the money-laundering fraud.

Harry was determined to go to the police, but first he wanted to see Katharine. He wanted to see those ugly floral patterns swirling on her cheek. Although there was no law against drawing flowers, the design was sickeningly familiar.

As he headed off to see Katharine, Harry was left with one thought. Chin had been fronting for McKeown all along, and poor Frank was just the bagman. McKeown was the Florist. At last he knew who had murdered poor Marjorie.

CHAPTER 37

▼

After Harry left, Tony shut himself in his inner office and gripped the edge of his desk. Intense pain always preceded his pleasure. Zigzag golden light flashed above his right eye; white fire burned at the base of his skull. Sometimes voices came from nowhere, followed by images of women, almost always women. Their shrieking inflamed his sense of cruelty and power and drove his pleasure deep into a world far beyond common lust. As the lights subsided, their moans grew fainter. When the visions departed, he was exhausted, and thought slipped away like water through fingers.

He was surprised to see that his legal pad was covered with intricately drawn flowers. The pen had been used with such force that the paper was cut. Bleak puzzlement overcame him. Only a deranged being would draw such things. Flowers were for funerals.

Tony's mother had died when he was ten. At the funeral parlor, he had hid in a corner, but his uncle had dragged him across the room to the casket.

"Show respect for your mother, boy. Say good-bye to her. Give her one last kiss." Shoved toward the casket, Tony tried to cling to a chair. Figures dressed in black drifted about him. He peeked over the edge of the casket and saw a wax doll.

"It's not my mother!" he cried out. But of course, it was.

The black figures closed about him and chorused, "Kiss! Kiss! Give her a kiss!" His stomach lurched with the sweet, sickening smell of banks of flowers. When he broke free, the black figures floated off in disgust. He took his pen-knife from his pocket and with careful artistry, etched a single rose petal on the gleaming oak casket. With his tiny, perfect claw, he touched her stone-cold hand and traced another petal.

Mother always wanted him to hide his deformity, but he was secretly proud of his claw. It set him apart from the ordinary and gave him a sense of power.

To clear the memory, Tony shook his head. He stretched, and wandered toward the vast expanse of glass window. Benny's men had reported that Frank Sasso was dead. Tony could not abide deceit. Frank had stolen from Benny's cash deliveries to Chin. The detailed description of Frank's wounds gave Tony a jolt of pleasure. He imagined Frank's dingy office tinged in red. Blood always fascinated him.

Donnie's pale and wavering form floated upward in his mind like a nagging, worrisome spirit. He could be real trouble. He had seen him with Frank at the old lady's house.

His private telephone rang.

"Yes?"

"The kid's hiding in the house, Mr. McKeown."

"Good. Leave him for me," he said softly.

He would deal with the boy immediately. Lounging back on the sofa, he tried to recall all the details. Frank was colossally stupid, but he had been the perfect pawn. The world would not miss him. He had used Frank and the kid to get close enough to dispose of the old lady. It had been a necessary killing. She had gotten in the way.

It was hard to remember all the women, but the killing of the housekeeper and the two Cheney, Arpin women stood out as supremely gratifying. His excitement had mounted sharply as blood spurted. Those bitches asked for it. Deirdre and Linda knew too much about the land deals and asked too many questions. In a way, they were also necessary. But with the skill of an artist, he had lured them onward to their most suitable fates. Blood spurted.

Only Donnie could place him at the scene. Although his killing was necessary, perhaps he could derive some pleasure from it. Another thought intruded. Some quality in the boy had caught his interest, perhaps a special intelligence that separated him from the commonplace.

Tony pressed his fingertips into his temples. That bitch, Mrs. Katharine Rowe, deserved it most. She tried to wheedle from him information about the offer. A perfect victim, she believed it was a love tryst at the hotel. With her seductive smile, she strutted with her long legs. She tried to save herself by seducing him with mere sex. In agony, she had lain crumpled on the bed. His mark was on her cheek. Harry tried to convince him she was not dead, but he was no fool. She was dead. Not even the undertaker's make-up would ever conceal those finely etched petals.

Tony determined to derive pleasure from this evening. Slow and careful preparations were key to his enjoyment. Having only killed women before, the prospect of killing a male was tantalizing.

The private elevator carried him down to the underground garage. He waved to Felix, the security guard, in his booth.

"Knocking off early, Mr. McKeown?" asked Felix, grinning and looking up from his lunch. Years of Felix's life had been wasted, crammed into his little box to operate the cash register. There never had been a climax of sheer terror demanding bravery or daring. The world was filled with dead souls like Felix, whose lives were a long, unbroken string of gray days. To be alive, a soul had to seek challenge and respond with great imagination and daring, otherwise it would shrivel into a useless appendage.

But was it wrong to kill a child? The complexities of the question intrigued him. Should a first draft of a manuscript be destroyed? Should a sketch for a painting be dismissed as crude and without merit? A simple tune could develop into a concerto of stirring beauty. Such questions plagued the artist. At what point should a life be judged worthy?

He stopped in front of his red Jaguar. Carefully, finger by finger, he slid on his leather driving gloves. Unlocking the door of the car, he paused to admire its sleekness. After several years of ownership, the leather interior remained spotless. A flick of the wrist with the key, and the Jaguar responded with the low growl he loved. Grinning, he saluted Felix, who strolled in front of his box as if on a leash.

At street level, Tony turned sharply onto a deserted Richmond Street and into the glare of the sun hanging low in the sky. Pleasure crept through him as the Jaguar responded smoothly. Caressing the steering wheel, he turned south, into the shadows of tall buildings on University Avenue, toward his harborside condominium.

McKeown's condo was on the twenty-fourth floor, facing the lake. He hated clutter, so the living room was furnished in the minimalist fashion. The color scheme mirrored the shades of pink, blue, gray, and charcoal in the sky, which blended with the shimmering expanse of water. Tonight, he studied the skyline to catch each transition of light and color. Later lights would begin to twinkle and flash at the island airport, not a half-mile offshore.

It was five-thirty. A timetable formed in his brain. He should be at the Deighton house by seven. With deliberation, he walked along the hallway, past the den.

Stopping, he checked the door. As always, it was safely locked. Part of his ritual of pleasure was a visit to the den.

As he entered his bedroom, the image of Donnie, pale and scrawny, arose in his mind. The skin on his face was his most striking feature. It was whitish, almost waxy, and pockmarked. He shuddered at the prospect of the rest of the boy's skin being cold and sweaty. Women's skin was soft and warm. It bunched and bruised. Donnie's neck would be hard and bony, like a chicken's. Although he lusted for the kill, he struggled for dispassionate consideration of Donnie's fate. Controlling the balance of reason and passion was essential, otherwise tragic consequences could occur.

Tony stood before his racks of suits and shirts. Reveling in finery, he caressed one sleeve and then another. For him, lack of appreciation of art indicated a dead and withered soul. Watching himself in the mirror, he removed his trousers. He lined the creases up and hung them in the closet. His charcoal suit was a bit too dressy. He laid the soft gray flannel suit on the bed and selected a shirt with a thin pink stripe. Satisfied, he put on a terrycloth robe and went into the bathroom.

He thought of business. His scheme was deceptively simple. With funds brought in from Buffalo and Hong Kong, through Zaimir, he acquired blocks of land in prime locations across the city. But St. Timothy's nearly upset the whole scheme. The archbishop wanted to sell the church to a legitimate and unrelated company. Of course their application to the rezoning committee had to be scuttled and one of his own companies brought in.

Naked, he stood before the mirror. Billows of steam rose from the shower and fogged his reflection into shadow. He addressed Mother.

"Does it surprise you, Mother, that most women find me very attractive? Despite my deformity, some have called me an Adonis. See my tiny, but perfect claw? You hated it and made me wash it repeatedly, as if cleanliness would erase an imperfection. But you are wrong, Mother. It is no imperfection. I am so marked as the one chosen to deliver judgment."

He snatched a towel from the rack. "All right, Mother!" He turned on the shower, setting the water at full-blast and very hot. "I will tell you why Marjorie Deighton had to die. She symbolized the dull complacency of sheep. When she refused to sell, she called me a charlatan who would defile her city." He flung his razor on the counter. "By God, I will trash those ancient structures erected by her bovine class. I will transform this city with cool, sleek lines."

He stepped into the shower. Gasping in the hot water, he began to soap his face and neck. He spoke with calm patience. "The money is only the byproduct of my calling. The more lots we buy, the more money can be made clean. Don't worry, Mother. The police have charged Chin with all of those murders. He will be convicted, and I will be free to deal with all the money."

He began to chuckle. "That other lawyer, Harry Jenkins? The world is filled with dull souls who hunger for more, but have no idea how to get it. He has such limited vision that he cannot comprehend what he really wants, much less what he needs. With his weakness, he made the perfect dupe. Besides, the internal audit department at Cheney's was asking too many questions. We had to use the trust account of a truly honest innocent."

He reached for the shampoo and began to lather. "What's that word you're using? Compassion? Of course I know what it means. But what does that specific emotion feel like? Am I not compassionate when I release a soul from the tyranny of a corrupt body? Why is that not compassion?"

He stepped from the shower and slammed the door. "What good is compassion to me? I have work to do and judgments to make. I will not shirk my duty, nor be sidetracked by such vague considerations."

Wrapped in a towel, Tony returned to the bedroom. He remembered the Deighton house clearly. It was similar to the one he had grown up in, but hers was much bigger and finer. Since Mrs. Rowe had forgotten to get her key back, he could walk right in. The house had all sorts of interesting nooks and crannies—excellent hiding places for the boy.

If Donnie possessed cunning, shrewdness, and feral instinct, a most interesting evening lay ahead. Brushing talc on his chest, he wondered if he would be clawed. The last desperate flailing was the best part. There wasn't much to Donnie. He could probably let it go on a bit longer than usual. If the boy failed him, he could, at a moment of his own choosing, easily slice into that meager throat. Either the boy would prove himself superior or die.

Finally dressed, he still had time to visit the den. With a small gold key in hand, he strolled down the hallway to the den. He turned the key. Silently, the door swung open.

Anyone entering the room might think he had stepped into a small warehouse of fine china. So stunning was the contrast with the simple, sleek style of the other rooms that anyone might believe he had mistakenly entered a room belonging to an entirely different person. Numerous tables, all laden with stacks of chinaware, were crowded together The first impression was one of a jumble, but precise organization rapidly became apparent. The den was brimming.

In neat rows and categorized piles, dinner platters, bread and butter plates, teacups and saucers lined the tables. Several massive soup tureens squatted on various tables. All was laid out not with great imagination, but with a view to displaying wares for sale.

Tony quietly closed the door behind him. He had not been in the room since the night with Mrs. Rowe. He went straight to his favorite set of place settings. His mother loved chinaware, particularly the delicate floral pattern of Spode. Tony loved china, too. In fact, he had spent several summers in England searching for replacements of the broken or chipped pieces.

Momentarily, a sense of peace settled upon him. Before he killed the boy, he had to choose the right piece. First, he picked up the sugar bowl and turned it to the light. *Too precious.* Tony caressed a teapot's rounded side, so cool and smooth to the touch. Donnie had poisoned his aunt with tea. Holding the elegant pot up to the lamp, he grasped the spout firmly. With one quick wrench, he snapped it off. Slowly, he ran his claw finger over the edges. The break was clean and smooth. Carefully, he placed the broken pot and spout on the table and covered them with a snowy white napkin.

As he slipped a razor and a knife in his pocket, he heard the chant from the dark figures. *"Kiss…kiss. One last kiss!"*

"Good night, Mother," he said softly. "One day, you will be proud of me. Perhaps I will learn compassion." He turned out the light, and was gone.

CHAPTER 38

▼

Katharine lay completely still in the narrow hospital bed, as if the slightest movement might destroy any shred of sanity. She tried to comprehend the dawning of her new world after last night. Thoughts like dark shadows hung over her, forcing realization. Her strength was no longer sufficient to protect her. Love and trust had been missing from her life all along. Such an understanding brought her façade crumbling down. She had to begin somewhere.

After leaving Tony, Harry telephoned his office. Surprisingly, Katharine Rowe wanted to see him as soon as possible about Marjorie's estate.

Startled by the urgency of his own footsteps down the tiled hospital corridor, he felt clamminess creep over him. Impatiently, he edged by a cleaner's cart blocking his way. Even if her room had been sunny, he would have had trouble recognizing Katharine. For fear of disturbing her lifeless-looking form, he moved silently toward the bed.

She looked even worse than she had in the emergency ward last night. The bruising encircling her neck had deepened to a dark purple, gashed with violent red burn marks. Although most of her cheek was covered in gauze, he could see the petal design etched in flaming red—so like the pattern on McKeown's agenda. Punctured with a needle, her hand lay on the cover. What an unholy price to pay for her strange passions!

As he set his briefcase down, she turned her head slowly on the pillow. Her swollen eyes flickered open. Recognition was mirrored in her dark, intelligent eyes.

"You've come, Mr. Jenkins. Thank you," she whispered.

He nodded. "What can I do for you, Katharine?"

"About Marjorie's estate," she mumbled. Her face, swathed in bandages, was like a death mask. "So hard to concentrate on anything…" Her voice trailed off, as if it pained her to speak.

Harry pulled up a chair and waited. "Do you remember what happened?"

"No." There was a long pause. "Yes, at least parts of it."

"Who attacked you, Katharine?"

She turned her head away from him on the pillow. "I don't remember. It's like a dream…you only get bits and pieces."

"Was it Tony McKeown? You were going to see him."

"I don't know," she whispered. "It must have been the Florist." She began to weep silently.

Harry stood up and looked out the window. Rain spattered down over the parking lot. There was not much to see in the dreary view. Considering the horrific attack, no wonder her memory was poor.

Katharine began, "About the estate: I want out. Suzannah can have the house. I know how Marjorie felt about her daughter." Her tone was flat, not bitter.

"So you knew."

"Of course."

"What about Gerry?"

"Gerry will go along with whatever I say."

Gerry stood in the door clenching a bouquet of flowers. "What will I go along with, Katie?"

Katharine turned her head at his voice. "Is that you, Gerry?" she asked.

"Yes, it's me." Setting the bouquet on the bed, he peered down on her. "Jesus, Katie!" he whispered. "What happened?"

"She was attacked by a man last night," Harry said.

"Holy shit! The Mad Artist? The Florist?" Gerry's face flushed. "Who did this to you, Katie?"

"I don't know. I can't remember."

Gerry glanced at Harry. "She has amnesia?"

"So it seems," answered Harry. "But I suspect her memory is coming back slowly."

Gerry turned back to Katharine. "What am I to go along with?"

"Nothing, Gerry. You can do what you want." Katharine closed her eyes. "I'm just tired of fighting about the estate."

Harry stepped forward. "She wants to withdraw her opposition to the second will."

Every muscle in Gerry's face tightened. "So Suzannah will get the house?"

"That's what she's told me."

Gerry threw his coat on the chair. "God damn it! You can't do that!"

"Do whatever you want, Gerry. I'm not stopping you," Katharine said weakly.

Gerry leaned over and hissed, "Thanks for your permission. But without you, you know I'm dead."

"Gerry, you'll have to fight your own battles."

"What? You're dumping me just like that? You know I don't stand a chance alone."

"I'm tired, Gerry, of always protecting you. You're too dependent on me. Look out for yourself, if you need the money that much."

Pure hatred suffused Gerry's features. "So you still see me that way? You bitch!" Reflexively, Gerry clenched his fist.

"Gerry, take it easy." Harry moved toward the bed.

Gerry's hand fell to his side. "Just like when we were kids. Nothing's changed, has it?"

Katharine's eyes hardened. "Gerry, I looked out for you all along. I can't do it anymore."

"Listen, this dental clinic's destroying me. I've got a wife who spends like crazy and a son whose psychiatrist bills are sinking me. I have to have that money."

Katharine seemed to withdraw. Her eyes grew flat and lifeless.

"Answer me! Why are you giving up?" Shaking his head, Gerry backed away. "Just like you, Katie. You won't say who attacked you." Gerry started to pace. "You won't say why you're giving up on the house. You just collect your dirty little secrets and keep them to use someday." He stood over her, jabbing his finger. "Just like you've always done. No big surprise some guy did this to you."

Katharine suddenly raised her hand. "Oh my God! I remember. We were in a restaurant."

"Who was, Katharine?" Harry asked. "You and who else?"

Fright grew in her eyes. "He was asking me about Donnie."

Gerry swung around. "Donnie? What about him?"

"He wanted to hire him as a summer student," she moaned.

"God damn it, Katie. Who?"

Harry shook his head at Gerry. "Be quiet. Let it come back to her." He took her hand. "What restaurant were you in?"

Recollection sparked in her eyes. "The City Bar and Grill, overlooking the City Hall Square."

"Who were you with?" Gerry demanded.

Turning her head on the pillow, Katharine sighed. "It was McKeown, Tony McKeown. He's going to hunt down Donnie." Her eyes were bright. She clutched Harry's hand. "He'll kill him!"

"Jesus, Katie. We haven't seen Donnie since the funeral. Where is this guy?"

Harry reached for the phone and called the police. Minutes later, he was still on hold, waiting for Sergeant Welkom. Slamming down the receiver, he asked, "If Donnie hasn't come home, where would he go?"

"Marjorie's. He has a key," said Gerry.

"We'd better get there right away." Harry grabbed his case and with Gerry in tow, headed for his car.

CHAPTER 39

▼

Donnie lay under the eaves in darkness for almost an hour. Wrapped in Gram's fur, he was comforted by the warm, perfumed aroma. Now he struggled to be free. Through some loose shingles, he peered out onto the lawn and sidewalk. The goons in the Buick with the New York plates were walking up from the church.

Huddled together, the men talked and looked up at the house. Donnie held his breath to hear what they were saying. The fur tickled his nose and almost made him sneeze. The men climbed up the veranda steps, where he couldn't see them.

"You think he's still in there?" one of the men asked, twisting the doorknob.

"We saw him come in and he ain't come out," the other said flatly. "He's probably hiding in the basement." The man lit a cigarette.

"What's this McKeown guy like, Bill? He's a lawyer, right?"

Bill nodded. "I've done a few jobs for him. A real mean bastard. He wanted a complete report on Sasso's execution." After a pause, he concluded disapprovingly, "He's a real sicko." Bill tossed his cigarette over the railing and pushed past the bushes to the back of the house.

When the back-door buzzer erupted, panic shot through Donnie. They'd be looking through the kitchen window, ready to smash their way in. Donnie felt for his gun. If he hid behind the trunks, he'd shoot them when they opened the door. But they'd slashed Frank's throat ear to ear. They could do anything.

Tony sat in his Jaguar in the church parking lot. Caressing the stickshift, he watched the house. In the rearview mirror, he saw the Buick with the New York plates, parked in the vicar's space behind the church. Moments before, he had seen them struggling through the bushes at the side of the house. Climbing onto the back porch, they knocked a garbage can to the driveway and whispered loudly. Tony was disgusted with their ineptitude. Returning to their car, the two men disappeared out the laneway to the street. His message to call them off had gotten through to Benny. The boy was his.

Donnie dared not move from his cramped spot. Pulling back the shingle, he watched the Buick's taillights pull out of the laneway. The car passed slowly up the street. When his breathing returned to normal, he shoved the gun into his pocket and headed downstairs.

Getting out of the Jaguar, Tony decided to concentrate on his pleasure. If Donnie were an intelligent boy, it would be amusing to match wits with him. He gazed at the house. There were plenty of windows on the ground floor to look into.

He would give the boy time to relax and breathe his last sigh of relief. On the sidewalk, he loosened his tie and then began circling the block at a leisurely pace. At the corner, he glanced up at the church. The massive oak doors were securely shut, presenting an implacable face to the world. Rather like the archbishop, thought Tony. And the archbishop wondered why church attendance was dropping. A chilly, light wind stirred the trees.

Tony turned up the alleyway toward a side door of the church. The thought of buying a church amused him. With the plans for the development of the shopping mall scuttled, the church had to sell out to him. Soon the whole area would be one prime block of real estate under his control.

A voice boomed out of the darkness. "Stop right there, mister. Where ya think you're goin'?"

Tony's eyes darted about, but he saw no one. Swiftly, his hand sought the razor in his pocket. Detecting a false note in the voice, he hesitated.

"This is private church property, mister, so get goin' or I'll call the cops on ya." Still he could see no one.

Tony was expert in ferreting out weakness. Somewhere hidden in the voice he detected a pleading note.

"I said...get the hell out of here, or I'll..." A massive figure loomed from behind the bin. Spotting a lead pipe in the man's hand, Tony sprang back.

"Mr. McKeown?"

Shocked at hearing his name, he saw the arm go limp. Relief swept over him as the pipe clattered to the pavement.

"Jeez, Mr. McKeown, what are you doing here?" The huge man lumbered toward Tony and grasped his hand. "I hope ya understand, I was just doing my job. I gotta do my job looking after the church."

John, the church caretaker, a half-wit, was almost twice his size. As the man wrung his hand, Tony was almost overcome by the smell of alcohol. Dropping the razor into his pocket, he stepped back. He didn't want to kill him, but the idiot could place him at the scene. *Another necessary killing.*

McKeown's voice was sharp. "John! Have you been drinking again tonight?"

"Ah, Mr. McKeown," he whined. "Please, I was just out back for a minute—I wouldn't let nothin' happen."

Tony fingered the razor in his pocket. "Look, John, you know I work for the archbishop."

John looked skyward and then fastened his eyes on Tony. "Please, Mr. McKeown, don't tell nobody," John implored. "I gotta keep my job!" He almost cried.

"John, you're a good man." Tony reached up to pat him on the back. "So I'm going to trust you with a secret."

John's moon face bent close to his.

"I'm here on very important business for the archbishop. Can you keep that a secret?"

John nodded vigorously.

"Okay." Tony tugged at the man's sleeve. "Now listen carefully," A sly expression slid over the caretaker's face. "If you swear to keep it secret that I was here tonight, I won't tell the archbishop about your drinking." Tony stepped back to gauge the effect on him.

The simple man's face broke into smiles. He nodded vigorously. "Sure, Mr. McKeown! As God's my witness, I won't tell nobody. But wait right here! I'm coming back!"

John broke from Tony's grasp and ran to the back door. Tony strode after him into the church. The idiot was nowhere in sight. Rows upon rows of darkened pews confronted him.

"Mr. McKeown? Over here!" Across the church, in the far aisle, sat the caretaker. "I was just gettin' a Bible, Mr. McKeown."

"A Bible? Jesus Christ. What for?" McKeown sat in the pew next to him. "Look, John, if you're playing games with me, I'll—"

"Games? Why, no, sir, not me." John's tone was injured, his face innocent. "I thought you wanted me to swear, Mr. McKeown. I wanna swear I won't tell nobody you was here, so I gotta have a Bible to swear on, don't I?"

Tony rested his back on the pew and studied him. The moon broke from behind cloud cover and cast a pale light on John. His broad, round face was utterly guileless. Tony caught his breath. His skin was just like a child's: smooth, soft, and hairless.

Summoning his best cross-examination manner, he said, "All right, hold the Bible in your right hand." John grasped the book and faced Tony solemnly.

"Do you swear, John, that you will forever keep the archbishop's secret that I was here tonight?"

"Sure, Mr. McKeown, I swear I never saw you here tonight."

"If you tell anyone, you'll lose your job, and when you die, you will burn in hell."

A tear trickled down John's smooth, round face. He clutched the Bible to his chest. "Honest to God, Mr. McKeown, I swear it! I'll never tell," he whispered.

Tony gazed at him, then smiled in satisfaction. He patted the caretaker on the shoulder and said, "Except for the drinking, you're a good man, John."

After McKeown left, John rocked back and forth in the pew. "Never saw the lawyer. Gotta keep my job," he muttered.

Tears rolled down his cheeks. Didn't Ma always say liquor was the devil himself? For sure, he was going to burn in hell. The church was so spooky at night, he wanted to turn the lights on, but the vicar would get mad. John lumbered up the aisle and opened the doorway to the hall.

Tony stood on the step outside and permitted himself one small cigar. Although he had scared John badly, if questioned, he would cry like a baby and tell all. He puffed on his cigar and looked up at the night sky. He could not forget the caretaker's soft skin. There was more than reason for taking care of the simple man.

A musician must explore all tonalities; an artist must master a broad palette of color. To become a virtuoso, he had to be fearless. Until now, Tony had only left his mark on women. It was time for a man. But John was huge. Although John's strength was superior, Tony expected his own speed and intelligence would win out. He saw his knife cutting male flesh. It would not be so different, surely. Heart pounding, he reveled in the intensity of his curiosity and the pleasure of his excitement. If he could set his carving on the caretaker, Donnie would be easy. Tossing his cigar into the alley, he entered the church.

John was almost back to the office when he felt a cool breeze at his ankles. He turned around and peered down the darkened hall.

"Who's there?" he whispered. "Please, you gotta come out."

He heard the door closing and a swishing sound far behind him. There were footsteps, too. Wishing he had the lead pipe, he swung around. For moments, the huge, stooping man strained to hear. Soaked in fear, he forced himself to walk to the office down the hallway, dimly lit only by the red EXIT sign.

Once in the office, he felt better. At least there was a good light and a radio. Carefully unwrapping his ham sandwich, he tucked a napkin under his chin. He chewed methodically, stopping every so often to take a swallow of milk. With a trembling hand, he set down the sandwich. He stood up and opened the door wide.

"Who's out there?" His voice quavered. Again he felt the cool breeze. In panic, he slammed the door on the faint swishing noise coming from the far end of the hallway. He'd check on the scary sounds later. He sat down and switched on the radio. To shut out his fear, John turned his chair back to the door.

Tony peered through the glass in the door. John was alone.

The caretaker was busy with the radio dial and did not hear the door creak open. He did not even see the shadow of McKeown's tall figure cast on the wall.

When Tony silently stepped into the room, a strange sensation passed over him. Was this what Mother spoke of? As if disoriented, he stopped and shook his head. Was this compassion?

Unaware, the caretaker chuckled at some mindless tune on the radio and clumsily tapped his fingers in time. Turning slowly in his chair, John looked over his shoulder.

"It's you, Mr. McKeown!"

His smile radiated a sweetness Tony had never seen before. He saw the muscles of the huge man flex; John's damp white shirt was matted to his skin. He saw the thinning but baby-fine hair, neatly combed in place. Suddenly he saw the simple man as more than an obstacle in his path. He thought that life could not have been easy for such an imbecile, or for his mother. He felt a flash of her pain from years of protecting such a simple soul, so easily wounded.

John was a true innocent, incapable of guile or meanness, a child forever. He should be spared. *Mother would be proud*, Tony decided, despite the great danger to him. It was an act of compassion.

"Am I ever glad to see you, Mr. McKeown." He clasped Tony's hand. "I was real scared." He hesitated and then said, "I ain't got much, but you want some of my ham sandwich?" He held it out to Tony. "I know how to make coffee too."

Tony shook his head and backed out the door. Softly, he said, "No, John. Just wanted to remind you about the archbishop."

"Yes, sir!" John grinned. "I won't forget."

Waving good-bye, Tony closed the door gently behind him. *Let him be,* he thought. *The Church has already damaged too many innocents.* In a fleeting moment, he had judged this simple soul with true compassion. Confused but elated by the sensation, he strode up Highland Avenue toward the Deighton house.

Donnie slid down the back stairs to the kitchen. A draft came at his ankles from the pantry. Maybe the men had come back. The back door was slightly open. Slamming it shut, he drew the bolt. He was so hungry that his stomach hurt. He snapped on the ceiling light and rooted in the cupboard for a tin of beans or soup.

After John, Tony had trouble concentrating on his next mission. He sought within himself to catch that fleeting sense of compassion, but it had gone. From outside the window, he watched Donnie. Although the boy's neck was long and spindly, his fair hair and skin gave him an attractive innocence. There was nothing special about the boy, no strength of spirit to save him. Once again he was lusting for the moment of judgment. It would take all of his concentration to determine Donnie's fate. *Let him have his food in peace,* he thought, stepping back toward the bushes.

Donnie ate the beans from the can, without pause. In his mind, he kept seeing Frank and the huge gash in his neck. Someone had gotten him back big time. He imagined Frank at the table, grinning at him.

Gun in hand, he pretended to slip up behind him. "I'm gonna kill you, you son of a bitch!" Donnie's voice was a shrill giggle. He pretended to strangle Frank with his arm and hold the pistol to his head. "Beg, you bastard! You poisoned her tea."

Tony heard Donnie shriek, and saw his convulsed solitary figure through the kitchen window. Perhaps he had underestimated the boy. Caught by the passion that contorted the boy's features, his admiration grew.

Raising the gun with both hands, Donnie pressed the trigger. Nothing happened. He slumped down in his chair and set the gun on the table. He must not have loaded it right. He lost himself in a study of its parts. The dark kitchen window loomed high above him. The ceiling light flickered. His reflection in the glass was pale and wavering.

From the back porch, Tony watched the boy with interest. He was very thin and deceptively frail. Despite his ineffectual air, Tony suspected he possessed the necessary feral instinct. Perhaps he could unleash the boy's furious lust for life.

But he could still snap that scrawny neck with his bare hands. He would take his time to decide his fate.

After reloading the gun, Donnie made his way to the dining room. The chandelier hung from the ceiling, casting a warm glow throughout the room. Tony moved from the back porch to just below the bay window of the dining room. He watched the boy set the gun on the glossy surface of the mahogany table.

Donnie was lost in a study of photograph albums, which he had found in the top drawer of the buffet. Grave faces peered up at him. The pictures were stuck in with dried-up black corners, and some of the brown-and-yellow photographs curled upwards at their edges. He tried to identify them. In one photograph, a bald, bearded man, erect in his chair, stared back at him: Uncle George. To Donnie, he looked like some kind of royalty. He had seen that glint in Gram's eyes too. Although she was soft, warm, and kind, her anger had a sharp steel edge. He saw toughness and strength in George and Gram. Hadn't she said that he was like George? It was in the Deighton line, she had always said. As he looked up, he caught his reflection in the window: skinny and weak. He pulled the drapes shut and switched off the dining room light. The silent house scared him. Gun in hand, he returned to the kitchen.

Just as he pulled down the kitchen blind he heard a creaking at the side of the house. His cheeks burned and his breath stabbed sharply into his chest. Paralyzed, he strained to listen for the next sound in the still house. The old gate at the side of the house was being pushed open. Bushes scraped against the brick wall. Someone was moving slowly along the path underneath the dining-room window. There was an odd swishing sound. The gate slapped shut. A low whistling came from the back step.

In three strides, Donnie was at the door to the back stairs. Scrambling upward in the darkness, he reached the door to the upstairs landing. He opened the door a crack and could see down the broad staircase to the front door.

Tony peered in the dining-room window. The boy was gone. He felt for the front-door key in his pocket and leisurely retraced his steps along the path at the side of the house to the front veranda.

Donnie clutched the gun. A tall, bulky figure peered in though the oval glass of the front door. Opening the landing door another inch, he raised the gun. With a click in the lock, the front door swung open.

In the car, Harry tried to form a plan. McKeown was probably in the house by now. He could only hope to get in and talk Tony out of harming Donnie. Gerry broke the silence.

"That kid has been nothing but trouble right from the start…" Gerry Deighton's voice trailed off in frustration. Red taillights on the cars up ahead illuminated his angry, twisted features. Harry shook his head. What kind of parent would be complaining about his own child in such danger? Still stuck in traffic, Harry cursed. Edging to the side of the road, he squeezed past the line of taillights curving up around Queen's Park Crescent.

"Thank God Katharine remembered Tony asking about Donnie," Harry said. "Call Marjorie's."

Gerry dialed the number on the cell phone. "Disconnected," he said dully.

Harry had been right about the drawing. He could see Tony's broad and easy smile when they had shook hands. *The Florist.* Harry thought about the African masks. McKeown could slip his mask of sunlight on in a second. Harry made an illegal left turn onto Bloor Street. They still had miles to go to reach the west end, in Friday night traffic.

Donnie saw the man switch on the hall light. He touched the trigger, but his hand was shaking so badly that he couldn't aim the gun.

Squinting in the light, the man looked upward. He called out, "Hello? Anyone here?"

Relief nearly made Donnie drop the gun.

"Am I ever glad to see you, Mr. McKeown." Donnie set the gun on the stairs.

"Hi, Donnie. What are you doing here?" Tony smiled up at him as he removed his leather driving gloves. Leaving the gun behind, Donnie grinned and limped down the staircase toward him.

The words tumbled out of his mouth. "Mr. McKeown, who'd you get the key from? You really scared me, you know. I've been here all alone and two guys came banging on the door, but I hid and didn't let them in."

Relieved at Donnie's greeting, McKeown smiled again. If the boy had any suspicions, they would be easy to allay. "Listen, son, your Aunt Katharine gave me a key and asked me to keep an eye on the house while it's empty."

Donnie nodded vigorously. He shoved his hands in his pockets to stop the shaking.

Tony removed his overcoat. As he looked up into Donnie's face, he felt for the razor in his suit pocket. In the shadows, the boy looked quite ordinary. He was not like John.

Now that Donnie was on the bottom step, Tony could see him more clearly. The kid was better-looking than he had remembered. He hadn't noticed the fineness in his features before. Benny's men had scared the boy so much that he was twisting his hands in his pockets.

"Was someone trying to break in?" Tony asked.

"Yeah," the boy barely whispered. He licked his lips and gulped hard. "Mr. McKeown, I saw something really bad tonight." Donnie sank down on the steps. Tony waited for him to continue. •

"It's Frank. He's been murdered."

Slowly, McKeown slid onto the steps beside him. The boy's shoulders began to shake, and he sobbed like a little kid.

"They cut him real bad." Donnie struggled to control his voice. Tony was fascinated by the tears coursing down his face, but he was also disappointed. The boy was a dullard, but not an innocent like John. It would be too easy. He held out a handkerchief.

"Where was this?" Tony asked.

Donnie blew his nose hard. "In his office. He was killed in his office."

McKeown was alarmed when Donnie broke into a wail. Worse still, he was tilting over, threatening to rest his head on his suit.

"Blood everywhere! They slit his throat. His shirt was soaked."

Awkwardly, Tony patted the boy's shoulder. "Listen, Donnie, you didn't see anyone else? I mean, you didn't see who did it?"

Donnie's face was buried in his arms. He nodded vigorously, without looking up. "It was the great big guys who came here," he whispered. "They were following me, I guess."

"Did you get a good look at them?"

"No."

Tony sat back, relieved. He wanted to know what the kid knew. It would be helpful information when he negotiated the cost of the assignment with Benny.

"I thought Frank used me to kill Gram. He poisoned the tea and got me to take it to her." Donnie looked as if he might burst into tears again.

"Really? Good God!"

Between sniffles, Donnie continued, "But now I'm not so sure. I don't understand why. I mean, she was probably going to die soon. She'd been pretty sick for a long time. I thought for sure Frank murdered her. But why would those guys kill Frank?"

Donnie looked searchingly up at him. Tony sat back from him on the steps. His hands would easily go around the kid's neck. He caught his breath as he imagined the sensation. A devoted artist must rise to the challenge, he thought. Unlike John, there was nothing here worth saving. John was a sweet innocent, with no knowledge of his own suffering. Donnie was a dullard who ought to be able to rise above his own ordinariness.

He shrugged. "Who knows? The city's filled with all kinds of weirdos these days." He was getting weary of the boy. The surge of power was fading and his head was beginning to throb. "Listen, son, did you report it to the police?"

Donnie shook his head incredulously. "No! Those guys might have been around. I just wanted to get away." After a long pause, Donnie looked up and brightening, said, "You're right, Mr. McKeown. I should tell the police. If the cops find out why Frank was killed, maybe they can figure out why Gram was murdered. Maybe it's all connected."

As he listened to the boy's drivel, Tony was transfixed with the pulse beating in the scrawny neck. He could do it right now, but he needed his gloves.

The boy rose swiftly. "You're right. I'm going to call the cops." He headed down the hallway for the kitchen. Desperately, Tony dove his hand into his pocket for the razor. The boy reached for the receiver.

Tony struggled for his voice. "You can't, Donnie." Donnie stopped and slowly turned around.

"Why not?"

"Because they won't understand, son."

Donnie considered this thought and then shook his head.

Tony slumped into the kitchen chair. The pleasure was quickly evaporating. If he had to kill him now, it would be a necessary killing without gratification. The boy possessed no special spirit after all.

"But those guys are going to come back," Donnie said. Lifting the receiver, he continued, "They must have cut the line." He held out the phone to the lawyer.

"The phone was probably disconnected after your aunt died." Tony took the receiver and hung it up.

He turned on the boy. "Don't you see? The cops will connect you with two murders. First, your great aunt's because you gave her the tea. And with Frank dead, you can't prove he had anything to do with her murder. You were at his office. They'll probably charge you with *his* murder."

Donnie shrank back against the wall. "He poisoned the tea," he insisted, "I didn't!"

Tony smiled wearily. "Donnie, Donnie. With Frank dead, you've got a real problem." He frowned and wagged his finger. "Statements by a person now deceased are subject to strict evidentiary rules. No judge will allow them." Sighing, he resumed his seat. "You're in kind of a mess, Donnie."

With hopelessness sweeping over him, the boy slumped onto the kitchen chair.

"Besides Donnie," Tony continued, "You were at the house the afternoon she died."

Donnie sat up straighter. "How did you know that?" he whispered.

The lawyer shrugged. "Frank told me."

But with him dead, there's no way proving the tea was poisoned by him." He smiled. "The police will say you poisoned her."

Cold seeped into the pit of Donnie's stomach. He'd never thought he could be accused of murdering Gram.

Gauging the effect of his words, Tony continued, "Believe me, Donnie, I know cops. They're always desperate to pin murder on someone." Tony leaned back in his chair, appraising the boy. He knew weakness intimately. "You'd make an easy mark."

The lawyer's corrosive words dripped like acid on the boy slumped in the chair. The cops would charge him with two murders, he thought.

"What do I do now?" Donnie's voice was bleak. McKeown extracted a thin cigar from his breast pocket, crumpled the cellophane and lit it. Fascinated, Donnie watched. He had never noticed the lawyer's baby finger on his left hand. He wiped his upper lip with his sleeve. The tiny double finger revolted him. Distracted, Donnie missed the calculating eyes fixed on him.

"Trust me," Tony said simply.

The boy's eyes lowered. Tony eased himself forward, quickly gaining a confident tone. "We have to find some proof that Frank did kill her."

"There isn't any." Donnie had never felt so alone and hopeless. The silence stretched out.

"Come upstairs with me to your aunt's bedroom, and we'll have a look." Tony reached across the table and placed a hand on the boy's shoulder. The kid was grossly stupid, with no spine. John was an innocent. Once he got Donnie into the bedroom, he could easily do it.

McKeown was almost gentle as he guided Donnie into the hallway. "You never know, son. The police aren't always so careful in their investigations." He was disappointed with the scrawniness of Donnie's arm.

Harry sped past dark, scabby buildings on Bloor Street and stopped in traffic at the intersection of Dufferin Street. Low, squat structures created a desolate scene. He visualized the rose petals. Such exquisite design and execution suggested a master who derived very special pleasure from the act. His final touch was like the signature of an artist. All the victims had been women, and the petals had a feminine flair. In some murky depth, McKeown must obtain intense gratification from his artistry. Had he ever marked a man or boy in such a fashion?

McKeown and the boy climbed the stairs into the darkness. In the upstairs hallway, Donnie leaned heavily against him. Fumbling for the light, Tony felt a rasping in his chest. His excitement began to mount. There was no point in saving such a dull child. He would make no great contribution to the world.

The lamps in the bedroom flickered on. As Tony guided Donnie through the doorway, the cool mustiness of the room crept around him. The familiarity of the scene rapidly became depressing. *Just like Mother's room, before she died.* The high, finely scrolled mahogany headboard dominated the room. Scatter rugs lay in oval pools about the burnished floor. Two small cut-glass lamps illuminated the dressing table with a rosy glow. The mirror above it reflected Donnie's slouching figure.

"Has anyone been through your aunt's papers yet, Donnie?"

"I don't know." Donnie sank on the bed. "Why?"

"Maybe there's some evidence implicating Frank in the murder."

"He must have wanted her dead to get her money."

Tony shrugged. The boy was becoming annoying. "That's not good enough." He sat heavily on the bench before the dressing table. "Presumably, Frank wouldn't inherit anything directly from her." Tony stroked his double finger. He saw attraction and repulsion warring within the boy.

Donnie slowly shook his head. "I don't know." Absently, he scratched his arms. His head hurt. If only Gram could tell him what to do. He had to trust the lawyer. There was no one else. He vividly imagined a life in jail for crimes he did not commit.

He looked up from the bed. The lawyer was looking at him strangely. Donnie licked his lips. His throat was dry. Rising quickly, he picked up a magazine from the table and sat on the edge of the chair in front of the window.

Tony watched the boy move. His form was not unpleasing—lithe and long, like a swimmer's. With Donnie seated on the chair, he would be able to get behind him. Tony moved to the window. The lamp bathed Donnie's neck and face in soft light. He reached into his pocket for the gloves.

"Donnie?" Tony spoke quietly. "Let's look for your aunt's will. Would she keep it in this room?"

"It's not here. I got it from Mr. Jenkins' office."

"Yes, I know. You gave it to Frank, along with the knife you stabbed into some papers. But maybe he put it back in the house somewhere."

Donnie stopped flipping through the magazine.

"Think back to that afternoon, Donnie. After you left, you kept calling her on the phone. How long did you keep that up?"

"How did you know that?"

"I know everything, Donnie."

Craning his neck, the boy looked up at the lawyer.

Tony continued speaking in a soft, lilting voice. "You've really been a very busy boy, haven't you, Donnie? First you break into Jenkins' office and steal the will, stab the papers on his desk with the knife, and scatter petals about. My, oh my. Then you kept calling her. Why? To be sure she was dead? You're right in the middle of it, aren't you?" Tony smiled down on the boy as he tried to twist around to see. "The police will be very interested. Someone will have to get you out of this scrape." Quickly, Tony slipped on the gloves.

The lawyer was in front of the window, behind Donnie's chair. Donnie tried to stand.

Tony's fingers were cold as they drove into Donnie's windpipe. The room danced and blackened for Donnie as he heaved backward. The glove smashed against his throat and mouth.

Calm flowed through Tony as he held Donnie fast against the back of the chair. Pleasure spurted throughout his body when he saw the spindly legs thrashing. He heard the screaming women in the distance. Deirdre had shrieked and begged. Linda had pleaded before her last breath. And there was John—the sacrificial lamb that he had spared at the very last moment, at great risk to himself.

Searing pain shot up Tony's arm, and he howled and jerked backward. His own blood oozed inside the glove. The boy's teeth had cut right through. Dumbfounded, Tony stared at him. The boy had spirit after all.

Sprawled on the floor, Donnie scrabbled to the door. Before the lawyer could reach him, he had slammed the door behind him. He knew how to jam the lock. Even though McKeown was strong, maybe he could keep him locked up, until he got to the basement.

Gram's voice rang in his mind as he slid down the back stairs, reminding him that there was toughness and strength in the Deighton line. He dashed to the basement, where Gram kept a tin of gasoline for the lawnmower. Just once, he could do something right.

Gently, Tony peeled off his glove. In the washroom, he held his hand under the cold-water tap, then bound it with a towel. Swiftly crossing the bedroom, he tore at the door handle. It spun uselessly in his grasp.

"Fucking little bastard!" Tony backed away and stared at the knob in his hand. He hunched down and tried to peer out. The kid had jammed the lock. Slamming his fists against the door, he howled in pain. He cradled his bleeding fist against his chest and kicked at the door. The boy was a worthy opponent after all.

Harry turned sharply onto Highland Avenue, while Gerry sat slumped in his seat. They were only minutes to Marjorie's. He remembered McKeown popping a Butterscotch Bit into his mouth while confessing to a passion for sweets. Had he been tantalizing him with possible admissions of heinous crimes? It wasn't that at all: that would have required awareness and a sense of irony. The man was a jumble of sharp-edged jigsaw pieces from a dozen different puzzles. He had no center; there was nothing connected inside. Monsters had no special added quality. An integral piece was missing. With Tony, all Harry could see was a great yawning void. Stephen was right—the banality and utter chaos of evil.

Halfway down the cellar steps, Donnie heard the crashing from above. The gasoline tin had to be in the cellar. It was dark and cramped downstairs, but he knew the terrain with his eyes closed. He scrambled to the cupboard.

Tony rose from the floor. The bleeding had stopped. He would outsmart the kid. He would tell him the penalties he would face for murder. His story about Frank was not credible. Frank was a businessman with no interest in the Deighton estate. Marjorie's death would give him no direct benefit in her will. He inserted the knob carefully into the lock and labored steadily.

Donnie pried open the cupboard latch. McKeown was at the center of it all. The door would not hold him back forever. Reaching for the gasoline tin, he felt silky, soft cobwebs surround his hand. Liquid sloshed in the tin as he lifted it onto the floor. There wasn't a lot, but there was enough.

Tony pitched the knob onto the floor. He hunted for something thinner and finer to pick the lock with, and found a nail file. He stopped for a moment at the dressing table and traced the scratch marks on his face. The boy had done a bit of damage. The memory of twitching arms and legs renewed his pleasure. At the door, he inserted the nail file. Easing it further, he held his breath. There was a scraping sound and then a click. The door swung open.

Adjusting his tie, Tony silently closed the door behind him. He polished the razor with his handkerchief. Soberly, he considered the fate of the boy. His excitement rose at the prospect that Donnie's life hung in the balance between his own reason and passion. But, was it wrong to kill a child? Should he feel compassion?

He tried to reason. Sculptors discovered innate beauty within a mass of stone. Great symphonies began with a simple tune. Perhaps Donnie was an unformed lump of clay, awaiting the hand of the master to reveal his strength and beauty. Given time and proper guidance, the boy might cultivate that special, powerful animal instinct and mesh it with a superior intellect. But did he possess that necessary intelligence?

The awfulness of the act of judgment nearly overcame him. The child was a miserable disappointment. He had whined like a dull, ordinary being whose life would only be a long string of gray, uninspired days. He struggled to capture that moment of compassion when he had looked upon John, but the sense, the feel of it eluded him.

Suddenly, Tony slumped against the door. Sweat poured down his face. Dark dreams pressed in upon him. He gripped the razor so hard that it cut his flesh. Passion swiftly mounted to blot all reason out. Conscious thoughts slipped from his mind like tiny beads of rain racing down a windowpane. He saw the black figures swirling around his mother's coffin. *"Give her a kiss. One last kiss,"* they chorused. He found no compassion within him, only lust for the kill.

Harry pulled up in front of Marjorie's. The house was ablaze with light from top to bottom.

"Thank God he's in there," muttered Gerry. "When I get a hold of him, I'll—"

"Shut up and wait here. Call the police. I can see someone in the upstairs window." Harry jumped from the car.

Donnie listened at the foot of the cellar steps. He cradled the tin of gasoline, the matches, and a small bottle of turpentine against his chest and ran to the main staircase. He would make the lawyer confess. McKeown might be waiting behind the door, which was silhouetted by the bright light of the kitchen. Donnie willed himself upward. Knowing every creaking step, he silently weaved his way to the top.

On the main staircase, he worked quickly and silently, soaking each of the twelve steps in gasoline. The heavy fumes worried him. McKeown might figure it out from the smell. Checking his pocket for the matches, he hid behind the cloakroom curtain at the foot of the stairs.

Harry ran up the front steps. The front door swung open easily. Immediately, the stench of gasoline stung his nostrils. "Donnie! Where are you?" he called.

Tony strode to the top of the stairs. Blood dripped from his hand. His eyes were glazed. Driven by the visions of dark chanting figures, he had entered another world.

"Donnie?" Tony called softly. "I know you're still down there. I can hear you even when you're not breathing. You are a dullard, but no innocent."

At the top of the stairs, the lawyer stopped and sniffed. He shook his head as if to dismiss his senses. Overcome with his lust for pleasure, he did not recognize the stench of gasoline. His madness drove him down the first set of stairs to the landing.

"You can't hide anywhere, Donnie. Not from me." McKeown removed his jacket as he stood on the landing. "I thought you had spirit. If you had, I might have spared you. But the world will not miss another tawdry, ordinary soul like you."

Searching for his quarry, the lawyer cocked his head. "A little sniveler, like you, would want to know why I had to kill your precious Gram." He smiled broadly. "She got in the way."

Lunging from behind the curtain, the boy screamed, "You goddamned fucking greedy bastard! You killed her just like that? For no reason?"

"Why, Donnie," the lawyer said, smiling, "you *do* have spirit. Come here, boy." He beckoned Donnie with his claw finger. "I'll tell you more."

Harry moved carefully toward the banister. "Forget it, Tony. Leave the boy alone. This is between you and me. You've done enough."

"Why, Harry, old man! How good to see you." McKeown's smile was broad, but his eyes gleamed brightly with the madness of another world. He brandished the razor. "I know every thought in your head, Harry. I know your weakness intimately."

"Maybe so, Tony. But leave the boy alone." Harry moved closer to the staircase.

Donnie wished he had the gun. He had to know what happened to Gram. Jenkins wasn't going to stop him. He shouted, "Okay, McKeown! Why did you kill her? I'm listening!"

Tony smiled, "It's really so simple. She stood in the way." His voice rose in swift anger. "She was a stupid, arrogant old lady who refused to listen." He paused, then said, "Donnie, you are just as thick-skulled and obtuse as she was." McKeown shook his head sadly. "Ah, Donnie! Had you not disappointed me, you might have lived." Tony folded his jacket neatly over the banister, then sat down on the top step. Blood seeped onto his cuff. "Your wonderful aunt wouldn't sell at any price. She stood in the way of progress. Just like the whole lot of her class—stupid and pig-headed right to the end. Just like you."

McKeown continued conversationally, "Frank tried to reason with her. That was pointless. But then again, he was just a pawn. Too stupid himself to be effective."

He shook his head in disgust. "Jesus! Marjorie Deighton! You know the type. Head like granite. So sure she was right. With her moronic stubbornness, she threatened to screw up the whole scheme. Just a dull, ordinary, but necessary killing." McKeown shrugged. "Frank was too dim to poison the tea. I was at the house. I did it. But it was terribly disappointing. Poison is so boring."

Harry had to protect the boy. He said, "Tony? Why not put the razor away? Come on down and we can talk it over." When Harry tried to lead Donnie to the door, the boy wrenched away.

Harry sought to engage McKeown in conversation. "I know what you mean about the old lady. Damned stubborn." Harry chuckled. "Head like granite."

McKeown's eyes blazed. "Don't you interrupt me, Jenkins!" he shouted. Then, as if caught up in a dream, he continued more quietly, "That housekeeper. Beautiful woman. Such lovely, soft skin. And Deirdre and Linda, so pretty. They were getting suspicious about the scheme. Too smart for their own good. They were going to go to the police. I had to put a stop to them." Suddenly, he laughed. "And you, Donnie—you and Frank were perfect. The two of you made it all happen."

McKeown stopped. His tone became cold. "First time you ever did anything right, kid!" Tony stood up and stroked the razor in his palm. "And now, Donnie, you know you're going to die." After a silent moment, McKeown's laughter rang out. Harry held out his hand. "Come on, Tony. He's just a kid. Let him alone." He doubted he could stop McKeown, but he edged closer.

Tony smiled. "Harry, old man, you just don't understand. Have you ever experienced that spurt of life at the very last? The thrashing? The pleading? Stuck in your tedious little life, Harry, when did you ever experience the real thrill of a life in your hands?"

Donnie was furious, determined for revenge, and Jenkins was not going to stop him. He reached into his pocket for the rag and matches.

McKeown looked downward through the darkness. Below, he saw the boy. "Are you ready, Donnie?"

Donnie spoke quietly at first. "Her death wasn't useless. Not if it stopped you." His voice rose. "She was good. She stood for all the things that matter. You pollute everything you touch with your filth. All your fancy buildings and designs. What good are they, except to make money? You greedy bastard! You just bulldoze anything good out of the way."

McKeown took two more steps downward. The razor lay open in his bloodied palm, its gleaming blade exposed. "You know you're going to die, boy. Soon that scrawny neck will be slit open, just like Frank's."

Donnie lit the rag. The single flame glowed and caught the lawyer's patient smile, which became a look of confusion. McKeown grasped the banister. Donnie crouched. Desperately, Harry grabbed the boy's arm, but he had already touched the flaming rag to the carpet.

Searing heat flashed upward. Donnie dove across the floor. The explosion knocked Harry down. Flames danced red, blue, and yellow up each step. The banister crackled and sparked in the heat. Curtains, engulfed in flame, funneled black smoke up the staircase.

Through the conflagration strode the lawyer's blackened, blazing form. His laughter rang out as he reached the bottom step. With the razor flashing, he cried out, "You're going to die, boy!"

Donnie scrambled to his knees. Shirt aflame, McKeown towered over him. His eyes glowed with madness, as he sang softly, "Time to die, boy. Just like all the others."

Suddenly, Tony staggered in confusion. Pounding his chest to kill the flames, he dropped to the floor.

Donnie rolled away. McKeown's hand shot out and clutched the boy's leg. A foot kicked Harry on the side of the head.

The lawyer's smouldering form rose up. He was on top of Donnie. One hand ripped back the boy's neck and fixed his chin. The other held the razor high. Harry struggled to catch his arm, but fell back choking in the smoke.

Donnie grasped the small bottle of turpentine. Fingers dug into his neck. He was fading. Soon he would be unconscious.

Tony brandished the razor. His hand swooped down, but Harry caught his wrist.

Tearing one arm free, Donnie thrust the turpentine bottle high and doused the lawyer's hair, which caught on fire. Harry pulled him off the boy.

A piercing scream was followed by low keening. "What a great artist the world has lost!" he gasped.

Tony's body ignited, stiffening straight upward. With his hands clutching his head, his body wavered for a moment in the flame. The acrid smell of blazing hair filled the house.

The lawyer's eyes rolled upward. His body shuddered, then slumped to the floor. Harry threw his jacket on him.

Donnie struggled to his feet. The blackened body convulsed and twitched as the fire burned upward. The lawyer's shrieks rose above the crackling blaze. The razor dropped from his hand and his eyes grew flat and cold.

Donnie sagged to the floor. Everywhere, he saw black. Unable to breathe, he clawed at the air.

Gerry threw open the door, with the police behind him.

Struggling for air, Harry dragged Donnie outside onto the veranda, where he lay gasping in the cool night air. In the billows of black smoke, he saw his father. Before the blackness of the oxygen mask, Donnie knew he was safe.

CHAPTER 40

▼

Harry stood on the front porch of the Deighton house. The street was jammed with fire trucks, an ambulance, and police cars. The blaze up the main staircase had been easily contained and doused. Severely burned, McKeown was loaded into the ambulance by the paramedics and rushed to the emergency ward. Donnie was also taken by ambulance to the hospital with his father. The fire trucks shut down their slowly twirling amber lights and started up their engines.

After giving the police his statement, Harry locked up the house. Overcome with weariness, he carefully lowered himself to the front steps of the porch. His shirt was torn and blackened; his pants were badly singed. McKeown had been at the center of the maelstrom all along. Harry's thoughts were a jumble.

McKeown had murdered Marjorie, Rosie, and the paralegals—and God knew who else. The man was untouched by any kind of restriction devised by law or the soul. Some puzzles could never be pieced together.

Nothing to go home to, he thought bleakly. With Laura gone, he felt utterly drained and empty. So shattered was he that he scarcely knew what to do next. For several moments, a cool spring breeze caressed his face. Slowly, he felt his spirits begin to rise and his energy return.

Glancing at the house, he thought of Natasha, and the day they had met for the appraisal. Too much restriction had deadened his soul. Without any particular plan, he headed down the sidewalk to a phone booth at the corner. He fished a couple of quarters from his pocket and inserted them into the slot. She *had* said to call anytime. He dialed. It rang twice and was answered.

"Natasha?"

"Yes."

"It's Harry. Harry Jenkins." He felt lightheaded.

"Harry?" Her voice was full of concern. "Are you all right?"

"Yes. Yes, I'm fine." He paused. A streetcar screeched by on its track, making it hard to hear, hard to think. "May I see you?"

"Now?"

He caught his breath, then said, "Well, yes."

"Certainly, Harry. I'm not really dressed, but please come."

He scribbled down her address. The trip from the phone booth to her apartment door took him less than fifteen minutes.

"My God, Harry! What happened to you?" She touched his cheek. For a second, he held her fingertips in his hand. Ushering him into her apartment, she took his jacket. He followed her into the living room.

Natasha was concerned. Harry looked pale and worn, and filthy. "Harry, are you hurt?"

With great effort, he produced a wan smile. He shook his head. "No. Really, I'm fine. I just wanted to see you." There, he'd said it. She smiled gently. "I'll tell you in a bit about my evening."

His eyes traveled absently about the comfortable room. Somehow, it was warm and intimate, despite the grand view of the city skyline.

"I just needed to talk to you," he concluded rather lamely.

"Would you like a drink?"

He gazed at her. She was gorgeous—the deep-cut red silk blouse and the black leather pants; the gold sandals and the red nail polish. And here she sat at last, not two feet from him.

She was waiting patiently for a response. Suddenly he realized that he had not replied. "No. Thanks. At least not yet. I'm still a little bit woozy."

"Something to eat?"

He nodded. "May I clean up first?" She showed him to the washroom off the hall.

"Come into the kitchen when you're ready, Harry. I'll make us a late supper."

In the washroom, he took a cloth to clean the worst of the black streaks from his cheek, then scrubbed his hands.

In the kitchen, he perched himself on the stool at the counter.

"Talk to me, Harry. I'm going to make the dessert first."

He watched as she took strawberries and peaches from the refrigerator. She reached across him and took a banana and an apple from the basket on the counter.

Suddenly he found himself talking. He heard the weariness and frustration in his own voice. First, he told her of his discovery that Tony was the Florist. He told her about Donnie, Tony, and the fire. Then he spoke of Tony and Chin and the money-laundering scheme. He suspected that it pervaded the whole firm.

In frustration, he slapped the countertop. "I turned a blind eye to the fraud and got sucked in." He swung around and faced Natasha. She set the fruit bowl down to listen.

"I should have known right from the start that Chin was laundering money through my trust account."

"But how could you have known, Harry?"

"There were signs, all right. Why would Chin come to me? I don't do land-assembly work. The land titles were the tip-off. Nobody conveys properties back and forth at ever-increasing prices unless they're creating some kind of scheme. You spotted it yourself. But I took on the work, thinking this was my shot at the big time." Harry was silent, overcome with disgust. "I'm just as greedy as they are."

Natasha regarded him evenly. "So," she said quietly, shrugging, "you're human, not infallible. That's not surprising. Besides, turning a blind eye to possible evidence of fraud is scarcely the same as planning and executing one, no?"

Harry looked up at her in surprise. He laughed. "You'd make a great defence lawyer, Natasha. I'll probably need one."

Smiling, she continued her work. He watched her, gaining pleasure in her soft, deft motions and her closeness. Sadly, he realized how long it had been since he and Laura had shared intimate moments of conversation. Now he was hungry to fill the emptiness within.

"Then you agree, Harry?" She held out a bunch of deep purple grapes to him. He took one.

"I suppose." He shrugged.

"To me, there is a world of difference. But even so, now that you know, what are you going to do?" Natasha asked.

"When I blow the whistle, I'll open myself to a lot of questions from the police and the Law Society."

"I know, Harry. You put yourself at risk by exposing them. But what choice have you?"

"None," he said.

Natasha reached for the peaches and was within inches of him as she continued, "I knew you would say that."

"Why?"

"Because you are that kind of man."

He gazed at her and nodded. "If McKeown dies, it will be harder to prove the fraud. Did you know him very well, Natasha?"

For the briefest of moments, she looked away. Turning back to him, she said quietly, "Fortunately, I met him only once. A frightening and dangerous man, without any soul."

Harry was about to ask more, but he stopped. The thought of all the female victims in McKeown's trail silenced him. Awkwardly, he reached for her hand. She smiled sadly and then withdrew her hand to continue her work.

She ran the water very hot and held the peaches in a strainer underneath the spray. The fuzzy skins of the fruit puckered and loosened in the heat. Drying them off, she peeled the skins, then cut each peach open to remove the dark brown pits. Harry watched as she cut the fruit into tiny slivers. Thin crescents of peaches lay glistening in the crystal bowl.

Next they were talking about Marjorie's house and the Deighton family and the wills. He laughed when she recollected Cameron McCrea looking on all fours in front of the fireplace.

In the sink, she washed the strawberries and sliced off their green tops. Turning, she popped one strawberry into his mouth. Her finger lingered a fraction of a second on his lips. He was not fantasizing this time.

Slowly, strip by strip, she peeled back the skin of the banana. Then she sliced the pale yellow fruit into small wheels. At last, she mixed the fruit in the bowl with Grand Marnier and spooned whipped cream over it.

He caught some of the whipped cream on his fingertip and licked it off. He realized he had not eaten all day as the sugar rushed through his body. He watched intently as she decorated the bright, creamy surface with five small cherries.

For their supper, she made an omelet with tiny bits of cheese, green peppers, and mushrooms. Sitting side by side at the kitchen counter, they ate, and drank the white wine.

With each mouthful, Harry felt strength and energy flowing within him. His words tumbled out.

"You know, Natasha, I've always wondered about you."

"Me?"

"You must deal with a lot of lawyers."

"Yes, sometimes I think far too many."

He chased the last morsel of egg about the plate, saying, "So what's your opinion of the profession?"

Natasha set down her fork and paused. She decided to give his question serious consideration. She saw beside her a good and decent man, who was different from any other lawyer she had known. To her, Harry brought careful intelligence to every thought and deed. But he seemed trapped in his own decency and desperate to break free.

"I think most men in the profession," she began, "are self-centered bastards. Little boys always demanding their due." Her eyes flashed. Their deep brown color was speckled with amber. "And if they are denied, some can get very nasty. I don't know much about the women in the profession. To survive, they may have to become like men."

She took the dessert from the refrigerator and spooned the fruit into small silver bowls.

"You know," began Harry after tasting the peaches, "in my practice, I've never gotten into the big money. I guess I thought it was a privilege to practice law and to serve people. And that the rewards would just naturally flow from that."

"That is the proper way, Harry. At least I think so. Most lawyers are out to get whatever they can, however they can. But you're different, and that is what makes you such a gorgeously attractive man."

She set down her spoon. Now her hand was resting on his knee, moving up his thigh. If she were going to have this man, she would have to take charge.

Harry sat close to her on his stool, afraid to move, afraid to dispel this dream. Her face was very close to his.

"Do you want me, Harry?"

"Yes," he breathed, then added, "Please."

She was laughing. "Such a gentleman." She slid from her stool. "Come with me into the bedroom, Harry." She took his hand, and he followed.

In the darkened room, she touched his cheek and kissed him. It was a simple kiss, but one that aroused him from the depths of his being. Gently, he wound her glossy black hair through his fingers to bring her closer once more.

"No, not yet, Harry. Lie on the bed, and I'll be back." She switched on the bedside lamp, which cast a warm, soft pink glow throughout the bedroom. She propped up the pillows, and he obediently stretched out on the covers.

He was determined to keep the image of Laura from rising within him. Anger would douse his ardor faster than anything. For once in his life, he deserved to savor this pleasure. Consumed with desire, he twisted onto his side. Lovely Natasha.

Soon she returned dressed in a filmy black gown. He reached out to pull her gently down to him. He would melt away with her touch.

"No, wait, Harry," she whispered close to his ear. Harry was about to collapse in frustration, but she smiled and with her fingers began the slow unbuttoning of her silk gown.

Giving into pleasure, he watched as the black silk fell away from her shoulder.

Natasha's breasts were scarcely contained in the wispy black lace brassiere. The gown fell, floating and wafting to the floor.

Harry felt a strange sinking sensation. Everything seemed to be falling away. At last, he floated free. With her back turned, she unhooked her brassiere and tossed it to him on the bed. He jumped to catch it in mid-air. In delight, he laughed as she glowed in his appreciation. With each of her lovely and sensuous movements, Harry felt layer after layer of inhibition falling away.

She turned back to him. Swollen with pleasure, he could not contain his delight as he fingered her frilly lace garter belt. The garters were deep crimson and edged in black, snugly pressing into her thighs. Silently, she commanded him to undo their buttons. At last he unhooked the black lace stockings. Heightening the moment to its peak, he slowly drew the stockings down, one by one. Euphoria. In his eagerness, he fumbled with her panties, but at last she was naked.

She took his hand and drew him from the bed. Stunned by her beauty, he followed her to the bathroom. After turning on the shower, she slowly undressed him. Together, they entered the shower. The soft skin, her entire being, overcame him as the hot jets of water pulsed down on them.

After they had dried off with thick white towels, Natasha took him to the bed. He lay back and she straddled his thighs. Bending low over him, she gently cupped his chin and gazed at him. In his intensely blue eyes, she saw a man she could trust enough to love, a man confident enough to be only himself.

With her tongue, she slowly circled each of his nipples. His skin tasted salty.

Harry could not speak as he held her fast against him. Kissing him deeply, Natasha gently moved back and forth. She dimmed the lights and took his hand to guide it downward from her breast.

Natasha was soft, warm, and lovely. She enveloped him completely. Harry could wait no longer. Guiding her hips, he shifted above her. Years of denial of pleasure fell away. Harry rose and gently laid her on her back and entered her.

This time it was not fantasy. She was really there. Many times he had imagined the moment, pictured her with him, but never like this. For an eternity, Natasha prolonged him, teasing and arousing him further time and again. Then, all in one moment, Harry discovered the beautiful Natasha and himself together.

Much later that night, he woke. She was there beside him, breathing slowly and deeply. The sky was beginning to lighten over the lake. Reaching out to touch her smooth black hair, Harry marveled at her warmth and closeness.

She stirred and drew him close. "What is it, Harry?" she murmured.

"I have to decide something." She raised herself on one elbow and touched his cheek. He was surprised at his readiness to speak and her willingness to listen. Laura and he had not talked in bed for ages.

"You have to decide what to do about Cheney, Arpin and your involvement. Am I right?"

Harry was delighted at the opportunity to talk.

"I have to think quickly about that. Then I have to figure out the rest of my life."

"Coffee?"

"Please."

She smiled and rose from the bed, pulling a silk dressing gown about her. He lay on the bed without moving until she returned with a pot of coffee and the cups. Her graceful movements gave him immense pleasure.

"So, what are you thinking?" she asked as she poured the coffee.

"A lot of different things," he said, shrugging, hesitant to put his disjointed thoughts into words.

"Such as?" She handed him his cup and saucer. Harry immediately set the coffee on the night table and sat up.

"I've been wondering," he began slowly, "why I didn't peg Chin as a crook right from the start. I can tell myself that I was blinded by wealth, but still that doesn't answer the question."

"And?" Natasha said, after some moments.

"I didn't see beyond what Chin represented to me: a chance, maybe a last chance, to make some real money." Harry turned away from Natasha's gaze, then continued, "All my life, I've thought that if I played by the rules, my reward would come. I stupidly saw Chin as my legitimate payoff, so I clung to that perception of him."

Such honest reflection in a male was new for Natasha. Most men she had known were blindly self-confident and aggressive. She began carefully, "Harry, I think all of us grow from our own roots. We can't help that. At worst, you may have been a bit naive."

Caught up in his analysis, he continued, "My father would have pegged Chin. He wasn't trapped in any preconceptions." Harry's tone was becoming bitter. Natasha searched for words to avert a slide into self-pity.

Harry twisted angrily in the bedcovers. "Crawford would have spotted Chin the instant he walked in the office."

"And you're still letting old ghosts haunt you, Harry?"

Sighing, Harry settled back on the pillow. "Yes, I suppose so."

"Listen, Harry," Natasha began, "what matters is what you do next, not what happened years back. So what if you were blinded? You aren't now. You have to act on what you know now."

Harry knew she was right. Self-recrimination was useless. He shrugged. "I'll turn my files over to the Law Society and brief them on everything." He sipped his coffee. "But I have to talk to Conroy first."

"Why?"

"He's the Treasurer of the Law Society. I don't think he knew what he was involved in. I think he deserves some forewarning."

"Harry, do you understand the McKeowns of this world and the people who allow them to operate?" she asked.

"No, thank God. Do you?"

She smiled. "No, not personally. And that is fortunate." Natasha knelt beside him on the bed. Harry was distracted by her closeness, but she spoke with such force and intensity that his attention immediately returned to her words. "To see McKeown as an evil sickness divorced from humanity, is a serious mistake, Harry. Unfortunately, he is a part of our world. Civilized behavior is meaningless to his kind. All of us have our dark currents, but we learn to control and mask them. Tony doesn't even try. For him, there are no rules or lines because he simply does not care. *But* he is a human being."

"But, Natasha, Conroy is not McKeown."

Placing one finger on Harry's lips, Natasha continued, "Tony seduces and captivates those around him, who then become willing participants. I would not warn Conroy. Perhaps he did not know, but you must acknowledge McKeown's power. For his evil to spread, it must have been nourished."

"And where does that leave me?" Harry said bitterly. "Right in the midst of corruption—either a participant or a fool."

"You are neither." Natasha shook her head in annoyance. "Your naïveté and the prospect of wealth blinded you. That's very human. But leave that behind; what you do next is what counts."

Harry knew she was right. He could simply walk away from his old ghosts, and they would lose their power over him. Lost in thought, he remained silent for some moments.

"But something else is bothering you?" she asked.

"Yes. Have you ever felt a sudden shift in your life, so that everything you once thought to be true no longer seems so?"

"Yes, It's a sense of loss, of change." She touched his hand. "It's a feeling that you, yourself, have changed fundamentally."

"Something like that."

"I thought so, Harry. It's in your eyes and in your touch."

He sighed and lay back on the pillow. "My wife's gone. The police have accused me of fraud, lining my pockets with fat commissions. My professional life is in danger and my life's been threatened." He stared at the ceiling. "Two weeks ago, my life seemed dead and boring. Now everything's upside down."

"You love your wife a great deal, Harry. Such a loss sometimes stays forever."

"So you learn to live with it?"

"Yes, you never get over it." Suddenly, she sat apart from him on the bed. "I will tell you a story about a very young man. He was a crazy kid." There was laughter in her voice, but then she sobered and said quietly, "I loved him very much. One night, we were in a club with friends. There was a band, and too much drinking."

She looked away, out the window. "A fight broke out, with a lot of pushing and shoving. A bunch of guys knocked a boy down and began kicking his head. The crazy kid knew none of them, but he tried to drag them off the boy on the floor. As I said, he was crazy to think he could stop four men."

Natasha seemed to withdraw within herself as she clasped her hands around her knees. They watched the sun break from the lake's horizon, and then she continued. "Two of them grabbed the crazy kid and marched him out to the street. His eyes were frightened, but still defiant." She looked directly at Harry. "On the street, they shoved him up against a wall and drove a knife between his ribs. They ran off, laughing. The crazy kid bled to death on the sidewalk before help came."

"My God, Natasha! Who was he?"

"He was my brother, Harry."

There was nothing Harry could say. He watched as she rose to pour more coffee. "That was twenty years ago. Had he lived, he would be about your age."

At last he said, "You can never recover from that."

"You can only hope the pain will subside enough to learn something from it. What I saw in their eyes was mindless evil. So I do know the McKeowns of this world."

Both of them lay back on the pillows and watched the sun climb into the sky over the Islands and the first ferryboat of the day set out from the dock. Without further talk, she drew him under the covers.

"Do you want me to make love to you, Harry?"

"Yes." Softly, his hand caressed the length of her thigh. "Please."

CHAPTER 41

▼

As soon as Harry entered his office next morning, he knew something was different. He stopped and set his briefcase down in the foyer. He sniffed the aroma of freshly brewed coffee. On the table was a bouquet of cut flowers. Strangest of all, a cheery humming came from the kitchenette. *Miss Giveny?*

Cautiously, he tiptoed to the kitchen door. Holding his breath, he peeked around the corner. Miss Giveny's back was turned to him. On the counter sat a tray with a cup and saucer and a cream pitcher. He could not imagine what miracle had lifted her from her usual state of crankiness. He took refuge in his office.

The last few weeks had taken its toll on his practice. Expecting to face a desk run amok, he had already resigned himself to buckle down to boredom. When he entered his office, Harry gasped. Warily, he approached the desk. At the far right corner, files were neatly stacked. Each one had a yellow sticky note on its cover. His agenda was open to the correct date, and several dozen pink message slips were neatly clipped to the page.

A soft tap came at the door. "Yes?" he responded cautiously. Miss Giveny backed into the room, with a tray in hand and a newspaper under her arm.

"Good morning, Harry," Miss Giveny said, smiling.

A beaming secretary was a shocking sight for Harry. And to be addressed by his first name! Could he ever learn to call her Gladys?

Miss Giveny did not wait for a reply, but set the tray down and proceeded to pour the coffee, just as if she had been doing so for years.

"You're a hero, Harry," she said, handing him his coffee.

"For heaven's sake, what are you talking about?"

"Here." She handed him the paper. "Take a look."

Harry took a deep breath. From the front page of the city section gazed Harold Jenkins.

Not a bad picture, he thought, taken for the fifteenth anniversary of his membership in the Alton Club. There was not that much difference—maybe a little less on top and a little more around the chin. All in all, he was pleased. Next to his photograph was the trim and devilishly handsome McKeown. Harry read.

ATTEMPTED MURDER AT DEIGHTON RESIDENCE

Anthony McKeown, a senior partner of Cheney, Arpin, has been charged with the attempted murder of Donald Deighton. Several weeks ago, Marjorie Deighton was a victim of premeditated murder. According to authorities, Harold Jenkins rescued the boy after McKeown threatened him with a knife. Sources indicate that McKeown is connected to the Florist murders. The Toronto Police Department also believes that McKeown was at the center of a major real-estate money-laundering scheme. Partners at Cheney, Arpin were unavailable for comment; however, firm sources reveal that Tony McKeown was already the subject of an internal investigation by their security and audit departments.

Setting the paper down, he said, "Maybe they will get to the bottom of it, but you can bet the firm will distance itself fast enough from McKeown."

"Aren't they already doing that with their internal investigations?"

"More likely, covering up."

Miss Giveny held out a pink message slip. "Jonathan Conroy has been calling this morning. He wants to have lunch at the Alton Club to discuss a potential merger of firms."

Harry was stupefied. "A merger? You can't be serious. That's like being swallowed by a boa constrictor. I'm a speck of dust compared to them." He tossed the message onto his desk. *And a troublesome one at that,* he thought.

"Why don't you find out what they're up to?"

"They're wanting to silence me."

"Aren't you curious? You might get some useful information."

He gazed at her thoughtfully and said, "All right. I'll call them, but I'm pretty sure I know what's going on."

Five minutes later, he had Conroy on the line and lunch was set for noon at the Alton Club. First, he had copies made of all relevant documents and correspondence on the Chin files. Then he made an appointment for eleven at the Law Society.

CHAPTER 42

▼

The private dining rooms of the Alton Club were located off a long paneled corridor running from the main dining room past the library. The executive committee of Cheney, Arpin had been closeted in the furthest room since nine o'clock, Monday morning. Any calls or visits from members of the press had been flatly turned down.

Jonathan Conroy sat at the head of the table, flanked on either side by Bill Cawthorne and Arnie Rosenberg. He popped an antacid pill into his mouth. He had slept little since early Sunday, when the press had called for a reaction to McKeown's arrest for murder and fraud. God help them—it looked like McKeown was the Florist. Nightmares had spilled over into reality.

Bunnie, his wife, had been mystified. In her books, unless you were stupid enough to get caught with a smoking gun in your hand, or worse still, with your pants down, there was no trouble.

"For God's sake, Jonathan. What is your problem?" she had demanded.

"I'm accountable," he fussed. "I'm the Treasurer of the Law Society."

"So? You didn't steal anything. You didn't bump anyone off."

"Yes, but I should have seen McKeown was trouble." He sank onto the bed clutching his stomach.

Jonathan was beset by the subtle shades of gray. Actually, he had known plenty and had turned a blind eye. And so, all Sunday and into the night, Jonathan weaved a tortured path through the realms of his distraught conscience. Fortunately, the fraud seemed to be contained within McKeown's practice. The firm could cope with one bad apple.

Looking down the boardroom table, Conroy cleared his throat. "This money-laundering scheme of Tony's..." Jonathan drove to the heart of the matter.

"Alleged money-laundering scheme, Jonathan." Arnie Rosenberg corrected him.

Jonathan merely nodded. "How in hell did it get past our accountants? I thought we had every conceivable check in place."

Rosenberg shrugged. "We don't know yet. We're just learning too."

"Well, what part did Jenkins play in it?"

"Tony used him as a front." Peter Niels said. "Apparently, it was better to use his trust account as a conduit for the funds."

"So he was a dupe. He knew nothing," Conroy persisted.

"Not at first," said Rosenberg. "But he immediately took a big chunk of the retainer, before he'd done any work." His eyes darted to Niels. "I'd say that implicates him big time."

"How does that establish his knowledge, his willing participation?" asked Conroy.

Arnie spoke patiently, as if to a half-wit. "He had to know what was up, otherwise he wouldn't have dared rip Albert off."

Steeves broke off from his doodling to say, "Our guys are not forensic accountants. Who knows? Tony was brilliant, you know. He could hide just about anything." Steeves' admiration was scarcely concealed in his wistful tone.

"Did Tony set up that chain of companies himself?" Conroy asked.

The simple, straightforward question demanded a forthright answer. Aware of the uncomfortable silence, the Treasurer of the Law Society glanced down the conference table. A moment passed.

"Well, Peter?" Conroy tried again. "You're head of the corporate department."

Peter Niels had begun twisting his third paper clip, and Cawthorne, suddenly developing a tickle in his throat, reached for the water.

Rosenberg spoke. "Who the hell knows, Jonathan? Tony didn't exactly tell us everything he was doing. Probably those paralegals did it for him. They were just dummy corporations."

Cawthorne at last silenced his cough. He leaned forward, resting his elbows on the table. All present listened intently.

"Jonathan, I must confess, that I did."

Steeves dropped his pen.

"What? Did what, Bill?" Conroy asked.

"Set up Tony's companies." Cawthorne's paleness grew with every word. "I didn't know—how shall I say it?—the precise purpose of the companies."

"Shut up, Bill!" Arnie Rosenberg's voice was a low, commanding growl.

Cawthorne removed his glasses and began polishing them with great care. No one spoke. Not until he replaced them did he continue to speak. "Arnie, I'm not prepared to live like this, wondering when the other shoe is going to drop."

Niels sprang from his chair and stood over his partner. "Listen, Bill. You're not going to screw everything up for the rest of us just because you've got some over-developed conscience!"

Arnie yanked Niels's sleeve. "Shut the fuck up, Peter! You're as stupid as he is!"

Jonathan looked down to see his dead-white knuckles grasping the table. He forced his next words out. "Gentlemen, does this mean you're all involved?"

Cawthorne pushed Niels away. "Yes, it does—and so are you! Ever heard of Zaimir Heights, Jonathan?"

"Yes. It's one of the firm's management companies. We're all shareholders in it," Conroy answered carefully.

"Well, our cut of the money clients launder gets channeled through Zaimir," Cawthorne continued.

"And out pops a big, fat dividend check with Jonathan Conroy's name on it," said Arnie, wrestling to his feet to approach Conroy.

Conroy saw blackness swiftly closing around the edges of the room. His heart raced. He struggled to shake off the nightmare. At last his vision cleared. He heard his own voice choking, "You mean we're getting laundered money directly?"

Arnie's laugh was a bark. "Wake up, Jonathan."

"How could you not know?" Niels said, smirking.

"Like it or not, you're in just as deep as we are," said Arnie.

"But I didn't know!" protested Conroy.

Rosenberg stood over Conroy. "Well, you should have. Director's fiduciary duty and all that bullshit." Then, more quietly, he continued, "You're a big boy, Jonathan. Don't get all high and mighty with us. Maybe we set up the companies, but who closed the Chin deals?" Rosenberg paused to assess his effect. Jonathan was almost green. "Better believe it, buddy: you're in exactly the same deep shit we are, unless you cooperate and stonewall this one."

As if as an afterthought, Rosenberg turned back on Cawthorne. "And that goes for you too, Bill. Just keep your mouth shut, and everything will be fine."

At last Jonathan understood. It wasn't just McKeown. It was all of them. He saw Rosenberg and Niels in a new light. Their sharp, flickering eyes darted about the room. Cawthorne and Steeves were quiet, but white as sheets. *Willing participants.*

Jonathan took great stock in civilized and gentlemanly behavior. There had to be a way out. Jenkins was the problem.

"How much does Jenkins know?" Jonathan asked.

Rosenberg answered, "Probably not much. He's just a family solicitor, a general practitioner; it would be way over his head."

Jonathan was desperate. If Jenkins could be persuaded to remain silent, the firm might be saved. But, by God, he'd read the riot act to his partners! No more screwing around with scams.

Feeling his strength return, he said, "Gentlemen! This firm needs strong leadership. We are not going down on this one. We knew absolutely nothing. McKeown got us into this mess and he probably won't survive." Jonathan looked at each of his partners in turn and said, "Mr. Jenkins is going to join the firm, whatever his price."

Both Rosenberg and Niels smiled with relief. Sanity was returning. Steeves and Cawthorne were mute. All of them nodded in agreement.

A sharp rap came at the door. The manager of the Alton Club opened the door and then discreetly withdrew.

Harold Jenkins strode into the room.

Conroy, bluff and gracious, rushed forward to shake his hand.

At once, Rosenberg assessed the opposition. Hiding a smirk behind his coffee cup, Arnie noted the suit. Jenkins was dressed conservatively in a gray three-piece suit and a solid blue tie—at least six years out of date. *Could do with regular workouts at the squash club too.* The briefcase was old and scuffed. Rosenberg was examining another species of lawyer: the family solicitor, the old family retainer. A glance in Niels's direction confirmed his view.

Harry remained standing. Surveying the conference table, he saw the litter of crumpled napkins, drained coffee cups, and dirty plates.

"Am I late, gentlemen?" He looked about the table, only to see the blank expressions of the executive committee. "I understood this was a luncheon."

A flush grew from the collar of the Treasurer of the Law Society. At least Conroy had the decency to be embarrassed, Harry reflected as he settled into a chair.

"Why, of course, Harry. The waiter will be along in a moment to set the table and take orders. Would you care for a drink first?" Conroy had recovered sufficiently to become the genial host.

"That would be very nice. Perhaps some wine, to aid the digestion, of course."

In unison, the executive committee broke into nervous laughter.

Harry looked surprised. "I'm sure we've all had a lot on our minds for some time. It doesn't help the stomach much."

Rosenberg glanced at Cawthorne, who bit his lip and studied his fingernails. Steeves continued his erratic doodling. Conroy summoned the waiter.

Harry looked about the room with his best bland expression. Momentarily, the image of Natasha floated into his mind. She had given him the courage to proceed when the risk to himself was so great. *Restore the balance,* she had urged.

Turning directly to Conroy, Harry said, "Well, you invited me here. Something to do with 42 Highland or Albert Chin's deals?"

Conroy shook his head, as though trying to recall. "Albert Chin? 42 Highland?"

Harry unsnapped his briefcase and shuffled through the papers. Finally he extricated two large files and spread them on the table.

"Surely you've not forgotten!" Harry gestured at the files. "Just look at the size of them. Lots of billable hours there."

"What's this got to do with us?" broke in Niels.

Harry waved him off. "Jonathan knows. Here's my correspondence to him enclosing the offers." Harry rooted about for his reading glasses. Adjusting them on his nose, he peered at Conroy. The room was silent.

"Don't you remember? I sent the offers from Albert Chin to you, on his specific instructions." Harry tossed the offers, which had the slice in them, along the table to Conroy. "Deirdre and Linda Lee worked on these files with you. Remember?" He glanced at Niels and Rosenberg.

"And look! Tony McKeown submitted an offer on behalf of one of his client's companies to the estate of Marjorie Deighton on 42 Highland."

No one in the paneled boardroom moved.

Harry held up another sheaf of papers. "My title and corporate searches. Funny how all the surrounding properties are flipped back and forth at ridiculously inflated prices, within a space of a year. And each company was incorporated by Cheney, Arpin."

Conroy was white. Rosenberg was livid. He leaped to his feet. "What the hell are you suggesting, Jenkins?"

Smiling gently, Harry sat back to assess the effect. When Rosenberg's left eye twitched, he knew he was on the right track.

"As I was saying, Jonathan," Harry continued, "there's Tony's offer on 42 Highland." Harry leafed through his searches. "Then there are all these numbered companies."

He sat back to assess the effect. Yes, it was going very well indeed. Natasha would be proud. All members of the executive committee stared at him. None of them took a breath.

"And then there's Zaimir Heights." Harry paused. "It took me a long time to unravel that one. I'm sure one of your paralegals could have traced the chain faster than I did. Everything comes back to Zaimir. It's a good name. Only trouble is, it's so good, it sticks in your mind."

Harry shook his head and chuckled. "You know, it was just a lucky break, really. But finally, I found the names of the directors and shareholders of Zaimir. Tough to trace. But, gentlemen, all of you, including Mr. McKeown, are the shareholders and directors of Zaimir.

"Another interesting point, gentlemen!" Harry withdrew a single sheet of paper from a slim file marked *Offshore Transfers*. "When I was in Mr. McKeown's office several days ago, I obtained this ledger sheet." Harry frowned as he studied the columns on the page. "A lot of money has been funneled from these numbered companies through my firm trust account, to Zaimir Heights." Harry threw up his hands. "I was a very useful dupe."

Harry glanced around the room. Rosenberg was looking for an opportunity to pounce. Niels looked like he might run for the door at any moment. Conroy was confused: out of his depth and sinking fast. The room was silent. Harry smiled blandly.

"Of course, gentlemen, although the chain is convoluted, it does become clear. All of you have received laundered funds directly from Mr. Chin's and Mr. McKeown's escapades. And just in case you're wondering, I've taken the precaution of copying the whole file for the Law Society."

Rosenberg spoke up. "So what? And you, Mr. Jenkins! We know you have Albert's two hundred grand. Or should I say you had it? Probably it's all gone."

He rose from the table and started pacing. "So you've benefited too, right?" Not waiting for a reply, he jabbed his finger at Harry. "That money, Harry, was very nice to have. Got you out of a lot of debt, didn't it?"

"Yes, it did." Harry replied.

"You never saw so much money in your life, did you? You knew right from the start what was going on, didn't you Harry? Your practice has been dying on the vine ever since Crawford packed it in." Rosenberg had rounded the table and was now standing over Harry. "You're in this shit just as deep as we are." His face was within inches of Harry's. "So don't play innocent with us!"

Harry sighed deeply. "Arnie, you're absolutely right. It has been a struggle."

Niel's eyes glimmered. "We're going to straighten this out with you, Mr. Jenkins. Once and for all."

"Peter, you remind me of your client, Albert Chin," Harry continued blandly. "Albert threw many temptations my way: first, a trip for two to the Bahamas, then thoughtful little gifts of flowers and food baskets. But as soon as I refused to act further, my headlights were smashed in and then Chin, when he was arrested, tried to frame me."

Natasha had talked about trusting his instinct and taking risks. Harry turned to Rosenberg and spoke quietly. "But Arnie," he said, "there's something I just don't get."

There was nothing to connect Cheney's with Frank's murder. Staring at Rosenberg, with his darting eyes, Harry forged on. "How do those guys from Buffalo figure in all of this, Arnie? I mean the ones who slit Frank Sasso's throat."

A flash of pure hatred crossed Rosenberg's face, but there were no words from the man.

"Jesus!" said Conroy. "What's this all about, Arnie? What's this about Buffalo? Who in hell is Frank Sasso?"

Taking another chance, Harry answered Jonathan. "Poor Frank! He was the low man on the totem pole. He brought the dirty money from Buffalo to Chin, who delivered it to Tony. Frank was stupid enough to steal from the mob, so Tony ordered his execution."

Arnie retreated and took his seat. He said quietly and evenly, "I had nothing to do with Buffalo. That was McKeown's department. I dealt only with Hong Kong and…" His voice trailed off as he looked down the table to see Conroy's shock. Slowly, the significance of his own words set in.

Conroy rose abruptly. His voice was strained. "You mean, you knew, Arnie?"

Arnie sat in silence, his head bowed.

Harry broke the silence. "He'll tell you nothing, Jonathan. But you should understand, by now, that your firm uses men like Benny and the mob."

"Arnie, is this true?" Arnie did not speak. The revelations had staggered Conroy. His face grew ashen.

Slumping into his chair, he could hear Bunnie warming up. *"You didn't stand up to some two-bit lawyer? Jonathan, you are a gutless wonder. Ready to throw everything we've worked for down the drain."*

He had to save the firm and himself. After taking a long time to light his cigar, he finally spoke.

"Look, Harry," Jonathan began wearily, "Seems like we're all in this together. Let's fix this up." His hand was on Harry's shoulder. "After all, nobody outside this room has to know a thing."

Harry marveled at the swiftness of the Treasurer's recovery. Natasha was right about Conroy.

The Treasurer's smile grew as he pulled up a chair next to Harry. "Besides, both our firms have a fine history. Surely to God we can't sacrifice that."

Harry could see the lines of red in the senior partner's eyes. Conroy paused in hopes of a reaction from Harry. Since none was forthcoming, he stumbled on. "Listen: you keep the money, Harry. I'm sure you can use it as much as any of us. And move your practice in with us. Keep your own clients, and we'll see you get five hundred thousand a year!"

Harry said nothing; he only smiled. A look of confusion crossed Conroy's face. "What, you want more?" He laughed, looking desperately at his colleagues. "Tough negotiator, isn't he, boys?" The room was silent.

"Listen, Harry, name your price! Whatever you want, it's yours. McKeown was real trouble. I see that now. If he murdered the girls and the Deighton woman, then I'm not surprised he had this Sasso killed. But McKeown's probably going to die, Harry. As God is my witness, Harry, I knew nothing of that part of it!"

Harry spoke quietly. "That's very interesting, Jonathan. Are you prepared to put that offer in writing?"

The silence grew. Jonathan grabbed Steeves's pad and tore off the sheets of black circles so hard they flew to the floor.

"I most certainly am!" Jonathan said, scrawling a number of lines on a clean page. "I know it's hard to make a go of practice these days, Harry. Isn't it time for you to relax a little and enjoy some of the rewards of our profession?" He shoved the pad across the table for Harry to read.

No one moved. Harry took his time in reading the lines several times. There it was—an offer, signed by Conroy—five hundred thousand a year and a signing bonus of one million.

In an instant, Harry could picture the good life offered by Jonathan and his cronies: the mansion in Rosedale, the summer residence in Muskoka, never a worry about money. Laura had always wanted him in on the real money. How ironic! Now that she was gone, the real money was offered.

But money was someone else's yardstick, and the measurement was constantly shifting. He had yearned for more. But more what? Certainly not what Conroy offered.

Funny thing about money, Harry thought. *Once you construct the good life, would you ever really have enough? And how much is enough?* Harry smiled. Natasha understood evil. She had predicted the offer of hush money, a bargain for one's soul.

Carefully, Harry set down the pad. He extracted a pen from his breast pocket. The executive committee watched as he took his pen, then slowly and gently pushed the pad back to Conroy with the pen. No one in the room moved.

"You can't buy me or your way out of this, Jonathan," Harry said quietly.

Conroy was almost gasping. "Harry! What's wrong? It's a fantastic offer."

Harry settled back in his chair. "I want to tell you a little story, gentlemen." He gazed up at the ceiling. "Before I came for lunch, I took a walk over to the Law Society. You know those wrought-iron gates, built more than a century ago to keep out grazing cattle? As I squeezed my way through those gates today, I thought of how we all got into this profession. It wasn't easy. Remember? Like going through the eye of a needle. But once we got through the gates, we found a beautiful garden inside. All sorts of advantages were given to those who made it through the gates. The good life. A very good life."

Harry continued to look at each member in turn. Niels and Rosenberg were huddled to one side. Conroy and the others sat rigidly in their seats, mouths agape.

"I like to think," Harry continued, "that lawyers are supposed to tend that garden and preserve its beauty. To help clients, not take advantage of them for our own personal gain." Harry smiled at the confusion on their faces. "Of course, for any of you having trouble understanding me, I speak metaphorically."

His voice grew in strength as he rose from his chair. "That may sound old-fashioned and idealistic. But it isn't just a question of a little fraud, or misrepresentation, or laundered trust funds. That's just money. This is about killing people who get in the way."

He turned and spoke directly to Conroy. His voice was hushed. "Do you get it now, Jonathan? Everything in your firm reeks. The most serious crimes have been committed here. But instead of coming clean, you want to hide the evidence. And you want me to help."

Harry reached across the table and retrieved Jonathan's pad. Everyone in the room watched in silence as Harry tore the page containing the offer from the pad.

Carefully, he folded it and inserted it in his breast pocket. "I'll just keep this offer, gentlemen, for the Law Society to reflect upon."

Harry shook his head sadly. "No, gentlemen, we can't work together. We belong in different worlds. The Law Society has a copy of the file. I'm sure you'll be hearing from them, as well as from the police."

Placing the file in his briefcase, he smiled and nodded to the executive committee. "I'm afraid I can't stay for lunch, gentlemen. My appetite is a little off today."

Suddenly, Rosenberg stood before him. His small, sharp face was contorted with rage. "Jenkins!" he hissed. "Don't give us all this high-and-mighty shit! You walk out of here without a deal, and maybe our friends will pay you a visit!"

Harry stared at the man, then glanced over his head to Conroy. "You see what you have in your midst, Jonathan? I don't envy you!"

Opening the door, Harry turned back into the room. "Good day, gentlemen." He shook his head sadly. "I'm afraid we're too many miles apart to do business."

Harry walked slowly across the City Hall Square in the sunshine. Suddenly, he picked up his pace. He was hungry after all. He bought a hot dog from the vendor under his red-striped umbrella, then sat on a bench near the pool and munched voraciously. Although he felt stronger than he had in years, he saw that his hands were shaking. What about the threat? He pushed Rosenberg's twisted features to back of his mind. Never mind. Back to business. The Deighton estate fees would more than cover any shortfall from the return of the Chin money. A thousand thoughts raced through his mind. One of them was Natasha. She had been right all along. He could not wait to tell her.

Life surged in him. Thinking of Marjorie Deighton marching to the strain of "Pomp and Circumstance," he smiled. He knew exactly how she felt in wanting to break free.

As he entered the office, Miss Giveny greeted him at the door. Her brow was furrowed with concern. "How was the lunch?"

"There was no free lunch, Miss Giveny. I had a hot dog on the square."

Determined to satisfy her curiosity, Miss Giveny followed Harry into his office. "But what did they say?"

"We were absolutely right. Corruption top to bottom. And yes, they did try to buy me off."

Righteous triumph flashed in Miss Giveny's eyes.

Harry smiled. His secretary was no fool. He put up with her crankiness because she was an essential part of the firm. But they need not be doomed to toil in such dreary circumstances.

"Get the newspaper, please. The office rentals section," he said. Glancing about the office, Harry continued, "We can afford better than this. It's time we left these old ghosts behind."

Miss Giveny's eyes widened. She scurried from the room, to return within moments with the paper. "Yes, Harry, it's time," she said.

CHAPTER 43

▼

From the warmth of the late afternoon, Harry, laden with two briefcases, struggled into the foyer of the Alton Club. Each case contained a copy of the Chin and Deighton files. Immediately, he felt the cool air conditioning creep around him.

Mumford, the concierge, hurried to his side.

"So good to see you, Mr. Jenkins," he said as warmly as his gravelly voice would permit.

Harry was surprised. Never had he received more than a curt nod from the concierge at the desk.

"Quite a shake-up around here, sir."

"How so?"

"Mr. Conroy has resigned his post at the Club to go on an extended vacation." Mumford winked and said, "Thought you would want to know." Smiling blandly at Harry's confusion, he concluded, "Mr. Barrett is waiting for you in the lounge, sir."

Briefcases in hand, Harry proceeded across the cool marble foyer toward the bar. At first he didn't see Stephen, who was seated off in a darkened corner. All the curtains in the bar were drawn against the sunshine of a lovely early-summer day.

"I brought the complete files and a copy of them for you." Harry set down the cases. "I want you to turn them over to the Law Society."

Stephen nodded and held up his hand for the waiter. "I have an appointment with the counsel for the Discipline Committee in the morning."

"I hate this kind of thing," Harry grumbled as he pulled out a chair. "There'll be no end of questions."

"What you're facing is nothing compared to Cheney, Arpin. Besides, the senior partners have the police to worry about as well."

"What about my position?"

"There's absolutely no evidence of intent on your part. That's essential to prove criminal fraud. The ledger you took from Tony's office, showing the flow of funds, helps to establish that you were used."

Stephen ordered the drinks, then said quietly, "It's not the law I'd be worried about, Harry."

"Meaning?"

"Your biggest problem is the guys behind Cheney, Arpin."

Harry fumbled for his cigarettes. "You mean, Benny?"

"Yes. Conroy didn't leave town because he's ashamed of himself."

"So the Buffalo guys are after him? Jesus!" Harry breathed. "That means me too?"

The waiter returned with the drinks. Stephen shrugged. "I think you'd better give the two hundred grand back, Harry."

"Gladly! I don't need that kind of trouble."

Stephen nodded briefly. "Good. I'll arrange it."

Harry looked at his friend carefully. "You know these people, Stephen?"

"I know enough not to cross them." Stephen sighed and then said, "Tony died this morning."

Harry's shoulders sank. "That will make it harder."

"For the police, maybe. But for the Law Society, I hear there's a pretty good paper trail."

"What are the charges against Cheney, Arpin?"

"Conduct unbecoming a solicitor."

"And me?"

"There aren't any, and my job is to ensure there never are. The less you have to say, the better. You knew nothing. You were duped. That's your defence."

The waiter delivered the drinks.

"Funny, I was so sure Frank was Marjorie's murderer—Rosie's too. And Welkom was just as certain it was Chin. But both of us were wrong. I was so convinced, I almost missed the connection of the petal designs."

Stephen leaned across the table and said quietly, "You're the one who put it all together, Harry." He chuckled. "I heard you had quite a session with the senior partners of Cheney, Arpin this morning."

"How did you know?"

"Bill Cawthorne called me this afternoon. He wants to testify at any hearing."

"Ah, a decent soul?"

"Perhaps." Stephen smiled wryly. "More likely, he hopes it will help if he cooperates with the police and the Law Society. But if he does, he could be in trouble."

Harry gulped his drink. "Then what about me?"

"Give the money back and keep your mouth shut as much as possible. You have no details about the connection with Buffalo. You were an innocent, drawn into something you did not understand."

Harry grew clammy. After the past two weeks, he had hoped to be in the clear. The prospect of guys like Benny after him was chilling. Dull estate practice was becoming more attractive.

Stephen continued, "They searched McKeown's apartment and found some very strange stuff. An extensive collection of silver knives and razors, lots of different gloves, coils of rope, and a few whips." Stephen lowered his eyes. "A lot of photographs of women with petal designs."

Harry took a swallow of his beer. "The guy is really sick! But he's so polished. It's like coming face to face with the devil." Harry tapped Stephen's arm. "When I saw the petal drawings in his agenda, he popped a candy in his mouth and confessed to an incurable addiction to sweets."

Stephen raised one eyebrow. "There's plenty more, Harry. He kept a locked room devoted to the display of chinaware. In a drawer, he kept broken pieces of china, each wrapped in tissue paper and tied with a ribbon. Each package had a woman's name on it: 'Marjorie Deighton,' 'Rosie,' 'Deirdre and Linda.'"

"Does that help to establish him as their murderer?"

Stephen smiled and shrugged. "Definitely. But listen." His face darkened. "There were three packages with other women's names: Jennifer, Megan, and Karla."

Harry was silent for a moment, and then said quietly, "So he really was the Florist?" Suddenly he felt weary.

"Tony left a book," Stephen said.

"You mean a diary?"

"No. More like a treatise on pleasure and death. Pretty cold and gruesome stuff, all about his duty to judge a life. Apparently, he thought he was redeeming their souls. Complete madness."

They sat in silence for several moments.

Stephen continued, "The most recent entry was the strangest. He wrote that his mother always accused him of having no compassion in his soul."

"That's for sure!" Harry said.

"*And—*" Tony held up his hand. "That more than anything, he longed to experience that emotion."

"Good Lord. That would be like trying to describe 'blue' to a color-blind person." Harry shook his head and stared into his glass. "God damn it. If I'd thought more about Chin at the outset—"

"Don't be ridiculous." Stephen grew stern. "If I'm going to represent you, stop beating yourself up. Believe me, Cheney, Arpin will try to spread the blame anywhere they can—so you needn't target yourself for them. And tomorrow, bring a draft for the two hundred thousand, and I'll get it delivered."

Harry nodded. *Thank God,* he thought. He still had at least one hundred and fifty of Chin's two hundred in his trust account. "Of course. I want to get rid of it as fast as I can." Then after several moments of silence, he asked, "Did I tell you Laura's living with Stover now?"

"No, you didn't. When did this happen?"

"Almost a week ago."

"Sorry, Harry."

Harry shrugged and tried to smile. He sipped his beer, and then pulled back the curtain at their table. Shafts of sunlight penetrated the gloom of the bar. Beyond the leaded-glass window, he saw a young woman glancing in her compact mirror. The woman waved at her girlfriend crossing the street. Chatting together, they turned up the steps and entered the Alton Club, unaccompanied.

Harry smiled. "You know, Stephen, I'm seeing Natasha."

"Wonderful. You like her?"

"Yes. A lot. I'm hoping it's for real."

Stephen nodded slowly, then winked. "Good for you, Harry. You need somebody."

CHAPTER 44

▼

Later in the week, Harry stood at his library window, staring down into the alleyway below. Only another month and he would be out of the premises, which the firm had occupied for more than fifty years. He would not miss the gray, rusted scene of fire escapes, peeling paint, and garbage cans. He shook his head, as if to dispel years of apparitions.

Within the hour, Suzannah, Katharine, and Gerry would meet in this room to settle Marjorie's estate. Copies of her wills were stacked on the boardroom table. The first one divided the estate equally among the three of them; the second gave Suzannah the house and split the cash three ways. Natasha thought the fair market value of the house was two million, five hundred thousand. With the cash adding up to three million, there was plenty to fight over. Would they insist on litigation to settle ancient family scores?

Harry strode from the library. "Miss Giveny?"

"Yes?"

"Please have coffee ready for the Deightons. I'm going to take a walk before they arrive."

Outside, he turned east toward the grassy lawns around the cathedral, where office workers were packing up remains of their lunches and heading back to work. The street shimmered in the early-afternoon heat. Harry turned northward up Victoria Street, seeking the shade of the buildings. He watched as an ambulance pulled under the portico of St. Michael's Hospital. Further north, parking lots sprawled on either side of the road, creating a desolate scene.

He stopped and smiled. Only a block further, he saw the large overhanging street sign. *Massey Hall,* it read in huge gold letters on black. It had been one of

Marjorie's favorite places. Suzannah had recounted her aunt's haunting dream so vividly that he saw it before him. She struggled to be free of the tubes snaking about her, to rush to the door of Massey Hall. *Running toward the music.* He breathed deeply and thought of Marjorie marching to the sounds of "Pomp and Circumstance" in her parlor.

He loved her spirit, her desire to be free. Marjorie, the maiden aunt, had fallen helplessly in love with an older married man, his partner. When he had gazed at her face, peaceful and stilled by death, he had not been able to conceive of such wild passion stirring within her breast. But then, it needn't make sense to him. Despite the restrictions of the Victorian era, she had found her own way. After bearing the child, Marjorie had made proper arrangements for her and remained close at hand as she grew up. Reflecting on the upheaval in his own life, he knew how hard it was to break free, to be yourself. He opened the tall, heavy doors of the concert hall, to see a lone figure sweeping away paper cups and empty soda cans.

Beyond the next set of doors, he could hear the somber tones of a chamber ensemble in rehearsal. Sometimes his life seemed spent in doorways, looking beyond to the future, longing to step forward into the light, but fearing to do so. And so he had spent years clinging to a dead marriage and a hopeless position under Crawford's thumb. What was the old adage? *The only regret is the risk not taken.*

Gently, he pressed his hand upon the ornately scrolled door. Silently, it opened. Smiling, he gazed into the auditorium, darkened except for the stage. The music stopped. The conductor began to laugh at some wonderful private joke. The musicians set down their instruments and began laughing quietly with him. Soon their jokes and comfortable chitchat rippled within the auditorium. Delighted, he let the sounds flow over him for long moments, and then closed the door and hurried from Massey Hall.

With the horrendous events of the past two weeks, he thought, *surely to God, some good can come from such an unholy mess.*

When he arrived back at the office, Gerry Deighton was in the foyer, fussing with his calculator.

"Gerry, it's good to see you," Harry began warmly. "Is Donnie all right?"

"Donnie?" Gerry seemed surprised. "Oh yes, fine…I suppose." He broke off and stared down at his shoes. Then he looked up, with his chin jutting out. "Are we going to settle this estate once and for all?"

The office door opened. Harry drew his breath in sharply. Suzannah entered first, guiding Katharine, who wore a soft green-and-gold scarf tied around her chin, dark glasses, and a broad-brimmed hat. Her movements were pained and tentative.

A broken spirit, was his first thought.

With surprising authority, Suzannah preceded her and shook Harry's hand. She acknowledged Gerry with a brief nod. "So, Mr. Jenkins, we've managed to get here." She turned to Katharine. "This is the first time my sister's been out since…"

"The attack," Katharine murmured. "Where shall we meet, Mr. Jenkins?" Katharine asked, not quite looking at Harry. "I'd like to sit down, please." She removed her dark glasses.

Everything in Harry screamed with outrage. Around her nose, the bruising was particularly black. Over the cheekbone, the injuries had begun to yellow. He caught just an edge of the petal design under the scarf.

Suzannah led her into the library. Only when she had difficulty seating herself did he realize that her vision had been affected.

"Is your eye injured?" he asked.

She gave a slight smile. "It's too early to tell yet. Hopefully it isn't permanent."

Harry looked away, then motioned the others to the chairs. Beside her sister, Suzannah seemed to radiate light, softness, and youth. Her creamy silk blouse and tailored skirt gave her an unaccustomed elegance. Seated furthest from the window, Katharine seemed dark and angular. Two completely different women, Harry thought, yet strangely well-paired.

Suddenly he knew what had to be done first. "I am hopeful," he said, "that we can come to a settlement of Marjorie's estate. I know she would want that."

Underneath the table, he could see Gerry's pant leg flapping as he jiggled his right leg incessantly. Suzannah smiled tentatively. Katharine remained impassive.

"But first I must give you some important information." He reached for a file. "While it affects all of you, it pertains most directly to you, Suzannah." Harry withdrew two envelopes from the file and handed them to her. "Marjorie addressed them to you."

Alarm flashed in Suzannah's eyes, but then she began to open the first envelope. She spread the single sheet out before her and began to read. The room was silent. Suzannah's mouth dropped open, and her breath came in sharp draughts.

"Oh, dear God!" she cried.

Gerry bit his lip and leaned across the table. "What is it, Suzie?" he demanded.

Tears trickled down Suzannah's cheeks. Katharine stared at her bandaged hand.

"God damn it! What's the matter?" Gerry shoved his chair back.

Suzannah, wide-eyed, looked up at Harry. "Mr. Jenkins, I did not know."

"Suzie?" Gerry nearly shouted. Suzannah slid the paper across the table to Gerry.

Harry saw every muscle in his face tighten. Gerry grew pale, and his hand shook violently. "You're her daughter?" Marjorie's secret trust lay open on the table. "Jesus! That really does it. So you get the house after all."

Katharine spoke quietly. "That does seem fair, doesn't it, Gerry?"

Her brother turned on her. "And I suppose you knew all along, Katie."

Katharine nodded.

Gerry's mouth twisted. "Just like you too. You and your goddamned secrets. Why the fuck didn't you tell me?"

Katharine lifted her bandaged hand and set it on the table. "Because, obviously, that is what our Aunt Marjorie wanted. I respected her wishes."

Gerry slumped down in his chair.

"That's why she asked me," Suzannah whispered, staring at the trust and the letter.

"What do you mean?" Harry asked.

"She wanted me to help her end it all, if it got too hard for her." She twisted her fingers together. "She had all these pills, Mr. Jenkins."

"Wait just a minute!" Gerry shouted. "You mean she asked you to assist in suicide?"

Suzannah nodded, her eyes brimming with tears.

Gerry jumped up and towered over her. "And did you?"

"Me? Of course not, but…" Suzannah began to groan. "I told Frank and I think maybe he got them. The pills, I mean."

"What? You mean Frank poisoned Marjorie?"

Fearing Gerry might lose all control, Harry stood up to intervene. "No! Sit down, Gerry. That's not what happened. Tony McKeown, the Florist, confessed to her murder. I was there. I heard every word of it."

Katharine fingered her bandaged hand.

Gerry continued. "The Florist? I thought he attacked Katie. What's he have to do with Marjorie?"

"He was at the root of everything. He murdered and ravaged. He nearly slit your son's throat. And he poisoned Marjorie, because she resisted him. She refused to sell her property to him."

Gerry was stunned. "She was murdered because she refused to sell her house?"

"Perhaps she wanted to have it to give to Suzannah," Katharine said quietly.

Harry tried to settle Gerry back into his chair. "No. There's much more than that. McKeown was assembling the whole block of land, including the church, as part of a money-laundering scheme. The man was totally unhinged, and when Marjorie refused to sell him the last piece in his scheme, he got rid of her."

Harry sat back and regarded the three of them. Suzannah's only mistake was telling Frank. She wasn't involved, and Frank was dead. No good could come from their knowing Tony had used Frank as a pawn, just as Frank had used Donnie.

Harry saw Gerry's eyes gleaming through narrow slits. He could read his thoughts. If Suzannah had any part in Marjorie's death, he would argue that she should not benefit from the estate. *Time to step in.*

"Listen, Gerry, Suzannah acted solely from compassion—an act of kindness, if you will. We all like to think we'd do the so-called right thing at any given moment, but that's only clear in hindsight. Can you honestly say you would have done otherwise?"

Gerry fussed with his notepad. "If she hadn't told Frank, maybe—"

"That's ridiculous. Frank didn't murder Marjorie," Harry said quietly.

Katharine spoke. "That's beneath even you, Gerry. Suzannah loved Marjorie. She only wanted to comfort and reassure her, which is more than either of us did." Katharine suddenly sat forward and with one swift motion, she removed her scarf. The ugly petal design was only beginning to heal.

"Marjorie was extremely intelligent. She would not fall prey to McKeown's charms. She stood up to a true monster because she was a principled woman." Slowly and with great dignity, Katharine retied her scarf.

Clasping Katharine's hand, Suzannah said, "Mr. Jenkins, is there any way we can legally change Marjorie's distribution?"

Harry nodded slowly. "Yes, provided you all agree and the church gets its legacy."

"How can we settle this mess?" asked Suzannah.

"I have a few ideas." Harry was on familiar ground. "The house is valued at two-and-one-half million. There's cash of three million. The wills are conflicting. But the second one, leaving you the house plus a third of the cash, was apparently procured under duress by Frank."

Suzannah bowed her head. "I know, and I want to set things right. But I would like to have the house."

"There are a number of ways to settle this," said Harry. Katharine folded her hands in her lap. Gerry began doodling on his pad of paper.

"But first, I think we should all acknowledge Donnie's role. Had he not been so brave, we would have had a quite different result. Your son, Gerry, got McKeown to confess. Marjorie was very concerned about him. She thought he suffered greatly from your lack of love and attention."

Gerry looked up sharply from his doodling. "What? Jesus. I've spent a ton of money on psychiatrist's and lawyer's bills for that kid."

"That's just it. You pawned him off on others to look out for him."

Gerry tossed down his pen. "Fuck. What was I supposed to do? He's been in trouble since kindergarten."

Harry shrugged. "I know Marjorie wanted to help him any way she could. So we could do this. Suzannah gets the house, less the commission, should she decide to sell. And the three million in cash gets split among you, Gerry, Katharine, and Donnie, in trust."

Gerry punched numbers into his calculator and moments later began to smile. Katharine merely nodded.

A slow smile broke over Suzannah's face. "I agree, Mr. Jenkins. I want to do something with the house."

"I don't think the city would let you turn it into a hostel, Suzannah, if that's what you're thinking," Katharine said quietly.

"I know, but maybe some of the proceeds could be used to help out at Emma's Hostel."

For the first time, Katharine smiled slightly. "Yes. That would be good."

"So what do you think, Gerry?" Harry prodded.

"Done. As long as I control Donnie's trust."

Harry shook his head. "Ask Suzannah and Katharine. They have to approve."

"I think the three of us should control it," said Katharine. "Marjorie wanted Donnie to have some independence."

Gerry's mouth twisted sharply downward. "I suppose you'll want a fee for your services?"

"Of course not." Suzannah spoke sweetly. "But I certainly want some say in Donnie's future." She turned to Harry. "Isn't that the right thing to do, Mr. Jenkins?"

Harry simply nodded. "If we're all agreed," he said, glancing at Gerry, "I'll prepare a draft trust for everyone's review."

Katharine rose unsteadily. "If there's nothing more?"

"By the way," Suzannah said, holding out an envelope to Harry. "I found a few more papers at Marjorie's."

Harry took the envelope, and everyone left.

Prior to the meeting, Harry had prepared a preliminary inventory of the estate assets. It was a tedious but often revealing task.

In his office, he opened the envelope to find a passbook. *Good Lord!* According to the book, Marjorie had an additional five hundred thousand in cash. Quickly, he checked his notes and found that he had no notation of the account, which was located at the Commerce near his office.

He had an appointment with Mudhali, the paper pusher, in half an hour. He could update the passbook at her bank on his way back from the meeting.

Banks are not your friends, he reminded himself as he marched up the steps of the Toronto-Royal. In the past two weeks, Mudhali had called at least every other day, but fortunately Harry had still been able to access all his accounts.

First, he had to get the Chin money; then he would nail the bureaucratic twit. Miss Priverts was in her brass cage.

"I need a bank draft for $175,000 drawn on my trust account, payable to Stephen Barrett in trust." He surveyed her prune-like face for traces of trouble. "Please."

She tapped her computer keys and began the preparation of the draft.

"Then I need another draft for twenty-five thousand from my general account, payable in the same manner."

He held his breath. Pursing her lips, she tapped her keys again. Without comment, she began the preparation of the second draft.

Harry gave a silent sigh. The Chin money could be returned via Stephen later today.

Mr. Mudhali approached. "Mr. Jenkins? A word in my office, please?"

"Indeed! More than a word, I think." Harry gathered up his bank drafts and marched into the assistant manager's office.

Seated, Mudhali began, "We must reach a written agreement, otherwise our lawyers—"

"Let me see the pledge agreement."

"All documentation is in order, sir."

"Please." Harry put on his reading glasses.

Mudhali handed him the requested document.

"What did Mr. Crawford do with all this money?"

The assistant manager rummaged in his file. "On the fifteenth of March, 2000, he required a bank draft payable to cash."

"I see." Harry quickly scanned the pledge agreement, which set out in bold the horrendous sum of five hundred thousand dollars borrowed by Crawford. The only security for the loan was the accounts receivable of Crane, Crawford and Jenkins. At the foot was Crawford's pinched signature.

"You have a copy of the firm partnership agreement in your file?" Harry asked.

Hesitating only a moment, Mudhali said, "Certainly, Mr. Jenkins." He produced the partnership agreement, which Harry set beside the pledge document.

After running his finger down the page, Harry read aloud from the last paragraph. "If this document secures partnership assets, it must be executed by all partners."

Mudhali paled.

Harry picked up the partnership agreement. "This was in your file. You were *on notice* that Crane, Crawford and Jenkins was a partnership." Harry sat back. "My signature is not on that pledge. I was never consulted. My firm is not bound by this agreement."

Mudhali appeared to struggle for breath, but he recovered sufficiently to say, "Nevertheless, the amount remains outstanding. You acknowledged the debt by making a payment."

Harry tossed down the paperwork. "What?" He shoved back his chair. "You might as well have held a gun to my head! That is no acknowledgement." Harry was on his feet. "Listen you miserable paper-pusher. You've blown it now. Head Office will have you counting paper clips once they see you've taken useless security."

Mudhali's face darkened, but he remained silent.

Harry bore down. "You have no sense of right or wrong. No sense of fair or unfair. To you, these are only pieces of paper with no lives or consequences attached."

"Mr. Jenkins, please!" Mudhali held up his hand. "Surely we can work out terms."

Harry began to laugh. *In arrears…in arrears. Three months in jail!* he thought. "If Head Office is so foolish as to pursue this matter, have them contact *my* lawyer." Harry slammed the door, leaving the assistant manager gasping for air.

The bank could never sue on the pledge agreement. Plain as day, his signature was required. Grinning, Harry strode through the hushed concourse beneath the vaulted ceilings and out to the sunshine of Bay Street.

Next stop, the Commerce Bank. Within five minutes, Harry had updated the passbook for Marjorie, given to him by Suzannah.

Indeed, Marjorie's account had been credited with the sum of five hundred thousand dollars by deposit of a bank draft on the fifteenth of March in the year

2000. Of course interest had accrued. It was a substantial sum to be added to the inventory.

Harry stopped on the steps to the Commerce Bank. *March 15, 2000?*

Quickly, he checked his notes from his meeting with Mudhali. Crawford had paid out the loan advance on the same day with a bank draft.

Was it a gift to Marjorie from Richard Crawford, just before he died? By such a convoluted procedure, Richard could have left money to her without naming her in his will. Their affair would remain secret and Marjorie's identity would be protected. Indeed, he was in Marjorie's thrall. If the bank decided to sue Richard's estate, poor Dorothy, his long-suffering widow, would have to pay the debt. Fortunately, the Crawford estate was valued at close to six million.

Harry strolled past the Alton Club back to his office. Smiling, he saw patterns in his life that, in hindsight, seemed to lead inexorably to new beginnings. The violent madness, murder, and fraud had burst open his life in just a few weeks. Crawford was dead, freeing him from his servitude. With Natasha, perhaps the pain of his dead marriage would fade. At last he could step through that shadowy doorway and into the light of a new life. Picking up his pace, he mused that passion and duty had achieved a fine balance, and that perhaps that was the aim of every life.

978-0-595-35820-5
0-595-35820-9

Printed in the United States
38227LVS00002B/22-111